"It's a business deal."

And apparently the conditions and facts and figures were laid out for him on her laptop.

Even when she got all prim and proper on him, Aidan wanted her.

And now that he'd given himself permission to want her, he couldn't seem to stop. If listening to her presentation meant having her in his bed, he would get through this.

But as she went through her slides, he had to interrupt. "Only at night? What about mornings? Or lunchtime? We could use my conference table... The thing is, I don't think we should be too rigid about this. In fact..."

He slipped his arm around her and walked her to the couch. "I think it'll take a lot of pressure off you if we start practicing right away."

D1321703

SHE'S HAVING THE BOSS'S BABY

BY
KATE CARLISLE

All the characters in this book have no existence outside the imagination of the author, and have no relation whatsoever to anyone bearing the same name or names. They are not even distantly inspired by any individual known or unknown to the author, and all the incidents are pure invention.

All Rights Reserved including the right of reproduction in whole or in part in any form. This edition is published by arrangement with Harlequin Enterprises II B.V./S.à.r.l. The text of this publication or any part thereof may not be reproduced or transmitted in any form or by any means, electronic or mechanical, including photocopying, recording, storage in an information retrieval system, or otherwise, without the written permission of the publisher.

This book is sold subject to the condition that it shall not, by way of trade or otherwise, be lent, resold, hired out or otherwise circulated without the prior consent of the publisher in any form of binding or cover other than that in which it is published and without a similar condition including this condition being imposed on the subsequent purchaser.

® and ™ are trademarks owned and used by the trademark owner and/or its licensee. Trademarks marked with ® are registered with the United Kingdom Patent Office and/or the Office for Harmonisation in the Internal Market and in other countries.

Published in Great Britain 2013
by Mills & Boon, an imprint of Harlequin (UK) Limited,
Eton House, 18-24 Paradise Road, Richmond, Surrey TW9 1SR

© Kathleen Beaver 2013

ISBN: 978 0 263 90624 0
ebook ISBN: 978 1 472 01184 8

51-0613

Harlequin (UK) policy is to use papers that are natural, renewable and recyclable products and made from wood grown in sustainable forests. The logging and manufacturing processes conform to the legal environmental regulations of the country of origin.

Printed and bound in Spain
by Blackprint CPI, Barcelona

New York Times bestselling author **Kate Carlisle** was born and raised by the beach in Southern California. After more than twenty years in television production, Kate turned to writing the types of mysteries and romance novels she always loved to read. She still lives by the beach in Southern California with her husband, and when they're not taking long walks in the sand or cooking or reading or painting or taking bookbinding classes or trying to learn a new language, they're traveling the world, visiting family and friends in the strangest places. Kate loves to hear from readers. Visit her website at www.katecarlisle.com.

This book is fondly dedicated
to my smart and talented friend Jurene Hogan,
one of the great romance readers of the world.

One

"What else can go wrong today?"

Aidan Sutherland stared at the latest cryptic email from his foreman on the nearby construction site and swore. Usually, Aidan let stuff like this slide right off him. Despite his power and wealth, he prided himself on his easygoing nature and smooth ability to roll with the punches. It wasn't like him to complain or whine about an unexpected setback.

But this latest problem was number fifty-seven in a whole list of complications and snafus that had cropped up today. And hell, it wasn't even lunchtime. Enough was enough.

He read the foreman's message over again and confirmed that as far as problems went, this one wasn't too earth shattering. Aidan would need to get it taken care of within twenty-four hours though, so he would have to re-prioritize a few agenda items and shift some man power, and the issue would be solved. No sweat.

"So why am I sweating it?" Irritated with himself, he

shoved his chair back from his desk, stood and crossed the wide expanse of his penthouse office suite to the wall of windows. As he stared out at the lavish grounds of the gorgeous Alleria Resort that spread out in all directions, his irritation slowly dissolved and satisfaction rose up in its place.

With a quiet laugh, Aidan thought back to the days when this island paradise had been little more than a pipe dream. As youngsters, he and his twin brother, Logan, had plotted and dreamed of becoming like one of their comic book superheroes. Iron Man, maybe, or Batman, with wealth and power beyond imagination. If they could wangle a superhero talent like X-ray vision, that would be a bonus. But above all, their imaginary scheme involved amassing a vast empire, and for two California kids who were swimming before they could walk, what would better serve as their empire headquarters than a remote tropical island? They would conduct business from a couple of hammocks under a shady coconut palm tree.

Aidan watched as a catamaran set sail from the marina below. He and Logan had pretty much achieved the dream—although their hammock and palm tree headquarters had been traded in for several large suites at the Alleria Resort Hotel. Not bad for two working-class guys who'd spent much of their youth surfing and partying.

For several of those years, the brothers had been lucky enough to sweep most of the surfing competitions they'd taken part in. They'd managed to collect enough prize money to finally fulfill the promise they'd made to their father years before. More than anything else, Dad had wanted them both to go to college.

No one was more surprised than Aidan and Logan when they were accepted to one of the most elite universities on the East Coast. While there, as legend had it, they'd won the deed to their first bar in a fraternity poker game.

Aidan and Logan had also excelled in all their classes, graduated with highest honors, and gone on to collect MBA degrees. But those dry facts had little or no entertainment value, so these days, most business magazine articles featuring the Sutherland brothers chose to highlight their misspent youth by recounting sordid tales of surfing, gambling and partying.

Aidan and his brother didn't really care what the articles claimed. The truth was that they had succeeded beyond their wildest dreams through a capricious combination of business acumen, poker winnings, surfing philosophy, sweat and hard work. Added to all that was some good timing and a hell of a lot of dumb luck, and the result was the present-day empire known as Sutherland Corporation. Now their lavish bars and exclusive resorts could be found in every part of the world, including their very own island, Alleria.

They were living the dream.

The Alleria Resort had become the number-one destination for discerning travelers the world over. It also doubled as the headquarters of Sutherland Corporation. And thanks to the brothers' stewardship, the entire island of Alleria was now a bustling, thriving port of call in the Caribbean.

Aidan returned to his desk and grabbed his coffee mug. While he refilled it from the coffeemaker on the sideboard, he thought about his twin brother. Logan was currently in Europe on his honeymoon with his bride, Grace.

"That's why everything's been going wrong lately," he realized aloud. "Too many weddings."

Once the happy couple returned, things would get back to normal around here, Aidan thought. *Well, not right away,* he amended. Because speaking of weddings, his own father would be taking the plunge soon, too. Aidan shook his head. As if he wasn't already surrounded by enough blissful lovebirds to mess up his mojo for years to come!

He couldn't begrudge Dad and his beloved Sally their nuptials, though. The two had found each other after years of living alone, so Aidan was happy for them. Still, all of his problems had seemed to start around the same time that everyone began to get happy and fall in love.

Dad and Sally had decided to conduct the ceremony right here on Alleria next month, so that was one more item that needed to be coordinated. In the meantime, Aidan was scheduled to fly to California this coming weekend to take care of some legal business that had to be finalized before Dad married Sally Duke.

"Damn." He'd forgotten to get started on those documents for his father. What the hell? It wasn't like Aidan to forget something like that. Was he losing his grip? Hell no, but he *had* lost his secretary. She'd abandoned him to marriage, too. Just when he'd needed her most, his trusted ally had fallen in love and gone off to Jamaica to marry her sweetheart. Why did the woman have to quit the same week Logan left town?

At the risk of repeating himself, what was the deal with all these weddings lately?

All that creeping happiness had begun to close in on him and he was pretty certain it had caused the balance of nature to shift. The end result was that Aidan kept forgetting stuff. It made an odd sort of sense, really. Aidan would never in a million years have anything to do with the state of matrimony himself, and yet here he was, surrounded by weddings. It was downright bizarre. No wonder Aidan had taken his eye off the ball. Everything in his carefully organized world was going up in smoke lately.

He pulled out his smartphone and compared his electronic calendar with the written schedule he kept on his desk, checking to see if anything else had fallen by the wayside lately. Ordinarily, he was on top of every single detail of Sutherland Corporation business, but as he checked his calendar, he noted that since Logan's wedding a week ago, he'd allowed a few things to drift. They wouldn't cause any major problems, but that didn't excuse his forgetfulness.

The Erickson deal, he noted, would have to be handled within the next three weeks. With Logan away on his honeymoon, Aidan decided to hand the project off to Ellie. He'd been doing that a lot lately, he admitted to himself, but only because he was knee deep in other plans and strategy involving the boutique hotel the Duke brothers were about to break ground on a few miles away on the north shore of the island. The Dukes were his cousins and were experts at negotiating with the unions, but they weren't here on the island. Not yet, anyway.

And frankly, Ellie would handle the deal better. While there were no better negotiators on earth than Aidan and Logan, Ellie brought an extra touch of nuance to any discussion. She could handle Erickson, the union bosses and the Dukes with no problem, he thought. Not that he would pile all that on her, but the fact was, if she was in charge, they'd get done. Clearly, with all that was going on, Aidan had to admit he couldn't depend entirely on his own memory right now.

As a rule, Aidan thrived on meticulous attention to detail. And didn't that sound like he walked around with a giant stick up his ass? He didn't. He was cool, calm and laid-back at all times, damn it. An easygoing guy. But he still expected things to run smoothly and he paid his well organized team a lot of money to make sure they always did.

"Knock, knock."

"What?" he demanded, whipping around to glare at whoever was here to aggravate him.

"Ooh, not a good time?"

"Ellie." Aidan relaxed instantly at the sight of Eleanor

Sterling, his senior vice president, standing at his office door. "Come in. Sorry I barked at you."

"Something not going smoothly?"

"Nothing that can't be fixed," he said. "A little mix-up over at the construction site, but we'll work it out. In fact, you're just the person I wanted to talk to about it. But you go first. What's on your mind?"

"I have a list of things to go over with you," she said, holding up the small, sleek computer tablet that was never out of her sight.

"Of course you do," he murmured, chuckling. When had their super-efficient, proactive, forward-thinking senior vice president ever *not* had a list?

Even when his world was tipping crazily out of balance, he could count on Ellie to be exactly who she was. His ruthlessly organized, efficient right-hand man. Woman. Person.

Ellie approached his desk and Aidan's breath got caught somewhere in his throat as he watched her plant herself in the chair opposite him and cross her stunning long legs.

Damn. He turned away to stare at…something else. This had been happening a lot lately and it was one more thing he could blame on all that wedding madness. Or it would be, if it weren't for the fact that he'd been ogling his business associate's legs for a long time now. Every time she came near him lately, he was ready to pounce like a jungle cat. And who could blame him? The woman had world-class legs. And a world-class smile. He was pretty sure she had world-class breasts, as well, but that was none of his business. She had a gorgeous smile and beautiful lips. Clear blue eyes, an adorable nose and lush dark hair that she wore in a straight style that fell like a thick ribbon halfway down her back.

Was this attraction to Ellie one more example of the sneaky universe conspiring to ruin his life? Was there such a thing as orange-blossom poisoning? Had he overdosed on weddings? Absolutely. That's all this was. Too much romance and talk of happy ever after. So of course he'd been noticing Ellie's legs lately. He'd have been blind not to.

There, a perfectly reasonable explanation. He felt better. Except for the knot of need in his stomach and the more *visible* sign of his desire that he fought to suppress before she noticed and ran screaming from his office.

After a long moment, he turned and gave her a nonchalant smile, as if he hadn't been picturing her naked in his bed seconds ago. But hell, a jury of his peers would never blame him for having those thoughts. She was wearing a dress in some cheery, summery color that was sleeveless and short and contoured to fit her well-endowed body perfectly. When had she started dressing so… *Hmm.* Had she always been this sexy and he just hadn't noticed until recently? Damn. Might be time to get his eyes checked, after all.

Whatever, that dress showed off her smooth, lightly tanned arms and her aforementioned awesomely hot legs.

And now that he thought about it, he realized Ellie rarely wore dresses, preferring lightweight tailored suits and what Aidan referred to as "sensible" shoes. But the weather had turned even warmer than usual lately and they did live and work on a tropical island, after all. That might explain those three-inch-high strappy sandals she wore that gave even more definition to her attractively toned legs.

He mentally kicked his ass. Thinking of his senior VP like this was completely unacceptable. The woman brought incredible resourcefulness and negotiating talent to the company. Not sex. Not ever. End of story.

He blamed his wayward thoughts on the fact that he hadn't been out with a woman in… How long had it been? Didn't matter. Ellie was off-limits. He reeled in his urges, sat down at his desk and smiled tightly at Ellie. "So what can I do to you?"

"Excuse me?" she said.

"I mean, do *for* you?" Good grief. "Sorry, I'm a little distracted by that, uh, union issue I mentioned. So what's on your list?"

As she studied the tablet screen, she wriggled in her chair, uncrossed and re-crossed her legs. Aidan was captivated by the movement and wondered if she would mind if he pulled her onto his desk and began to lick every inch of her legs, starting with her ankles and moving up to her—

"Number one on the agenda has to do with the new sports center," Ellie said. "The Paragon contracts are printed and ready to sign."

With his jaw clenched, Aidan forced the sultry image away and shook himself back to attention. Now what was she saying? Oh, yeah. Paragon was the vendor that would be supplying the center with everything from workers' uniforms to gym towels to drinking cups. Aidan and Logan were old surfing buddies with Keith Sands, the Paragon CEO, and knew him well.

"Good," Aidan said. "Let's overnight them to Keith and get that wrapped up."

"Done." She tapped out a message on her screen keyboard, then nibbled on her bottom lip as she studied the screen. Aidan tortured himself by watching her luscious mouth in action and wondered if maybe he needed to take a cold shower.

As he dragged his gaze away, he vowed to find himself a date while visiting California over the weekend. It had been too long since he'd indulged in some good old-fashioned, no-strings-attached sex. That had to be another reason why he was so distracted by Ellie's excellent body, but he had to snap out of it. There was no way he would allow the one-way attraction to grow. Otherwise, he would never shake off this funk. "What's next?"

She pressed the tablet's surface and a new screen appeared. Glancing up, she said, "As you know, the new hotel is on track to break ground in two weeks."

"Right. But there's a holdup with the cement mixer company."

"Yes, I spoke to them," Ellie said. "I think we've worked it out. I'll keep you posted."

"Thanks, I appreciate you taking on that issue. Next agenda item?" Aidan asked.

"Right. This one's a little tricky." She shook her hair back and took a deep breath. "I'm overdue for some time off and I'm sorry for the short notice, but I have to take three weeks off next month, from the second to the twenty-third." She checked her tablet. "I've arranged coverage for all of my assignments so there shouldn't be any problems."

Before Aidan could say a word, Ellie rushed on to the next item on her list. "Now this is good news, but I'll need you to approve it. The hotel's limousine service will upgrade their entire fleet six weeks from now. I've worked out a deal with a company over on St. Bart's to buy the old cars, but we'll need to ship them there by freighter. They're willing to split the freight cost, but I'd rather we be the ones to arrange everything. There's a new Danish shipping company based in Nassau that can do it, but I'll have to let them know fairly soon if we're interested in using them."

"Send me their info and I'll get back to you." He held up his finger to stop her from continuing. "But…let's go back to that last item you mentioned."

"The cement mixer?" she asked, her eyes wide and curious.

He didn't believe that wide-eyed innocent act for a second. "No, Ellie. Your vacation. Three weeks?"

"Yes, but don't worry. I don't leave until next month."

He grabbed his calendar and calculated the dates. "We're

practically at the end of this month. So next month starts next week. You want to leave a week from tomorrow?"

"Yes. Something important just came up. I'm sorry I couldn't give you more notice, but it's urgent that I go."

He frowned at the calendar. "A week from tomorrow?"

"Yes, a week from tomorrow." She said the words slowly, as though she was speaking to a recalcitrant kindergartner.

"That's really short notice."

"I know, Aidan. But I have an important appointment scheduled and the timing is crucial. I have to leave a week from tomorrow."

His eyes widened. "Is something wrong, Ellie? Are you sick?"

"No!" she said at once. "No, I'm fine. But this can't be put off."

"I'm glad it's nothing health-related." He flipped through the week-at-a-glance calendar. "But can't we talk about this? I really need you on the job over the next month or so. You know I'm about to leave for a long weekend. And Logan won't be back for two more weeks. The Erickson deal needs immediate attention, the Duke project needs supervision, and I've got a dozen new secretary applicants I was hoping you'd help me interview. I hate to be hard-nosed about this, but it's really a bad time for you to be gone."

"No, it's not. I've worked out the—"

"Wait," he said, ignoring her as he tapped the calendar page. "The cardboard-box convention is right in the middle of that time period. That's your client. Those guys love you. You can't desert them."

"I'm not. I'm leaving them in good hands. They love our sales staff."

"It's not the same," he said, grasping at excuses. Damn it, he was already without his secretary. How the hell could he keep this place running without Ellie, as well? "You know you have a knack with the conventioneers." He peered at her. What was this sudden vacation all about? Was she planning to meet up with some man? Aidan wasn't sure he liked the idea, not that he had any say in the matter. Of course, that had never stopped him from issuing an opinion. "What's so important that you need to go next week?"

She gazed back at him steadily. "It's personal."

"You can tell me. We're friends."

"You're my boss."

"And your friend."

She smiled. "Trust me, Aidan. You don't want to know."

He folded his hands together on his desk and smiled patiently. "Now that's where you're wrong. What can possibly be so important that you can only give one week's notice and then go off and leave us for three long weeks? We need you here."

"I appreciate that, but I'm entitled to a vacation."

"Of course you are," he said, wondering why he was being so inflexible about this. She was their best employee. Employee? Hell, she was practically a partner in the business. Of course she was entitled to take time off. He just didn't want her to leave right now while things were in flux. It was bad enough he didn't have a secretary. But to lose his right-hand man—er, *woman*—for three weeks? He didn't want to think of the many things that could go wrong. "We have two major construction projects going, there are union issues, my brother is out of the country, I'm going to have to travel, as well. You know we depend on you to keep everything running smoothly."

"But—"

"It's not about whether you *deserve* the time off," he rushed to add. "It's just that, hell, you're always so organized. You plan your vacation time a year in advance. What happened?"

"Something came up," she said primly.

"Damn it, Ellie. What in the world is so important that you'd leave five hundred convention attendees in the lurch?" *Not to mention me,* he didn't say aloud.

She let go an exasperated sigh, then said, "Fine. But don't say I didn't warn you." She bounded out of her chair and paced back and forth in front of his desk. Suddenly she stopped and said in a rush, "I have an appointment with a fertility clinic in Atlanta. The timing is critical because everything depends on my ovulation cycle. Once I arrive in Atlanta, the clinic advised that I'll need two days of complete rest to get over any jet lag my ovaries might suffer. Then it'll take a week to go through their process, and that's followed up with two weeks of, well, rest and waiting."

Aidan's eyes widened. He shook his head. Had his ears plugged up suddenly? He couldn't have heard what he thought he'd just heard. *Ovaries?* Good grief. *Fertility?*

He glared at her. "What in the world are you talking about?"

Wearing a serene smile now, Ellie sat back down in her chair. "I'm going to have a baby."

There. She had finally said it out loud.

Ellie tried to appear calm, tried not to squirm in her chair as Aidan stared sharply at her. Well, it was his own darn fault for pushing the point, she thought. Honestly, she had tried to soft-peddle her vacation plans, tried to avoid explaining all the gory details, but she should've known Aidan Sutherland wouldn't let things slide. He never let things slide.

Yes, she usually planned her vacations a year ahead of time. Yes, she was highly organized, detail oriented, never impulsive, always in control. She didn't do anything without preparing a spreadsheet first. But come on, once in a while a girl had to be spontaneous. That's what she'd heard, anyway. Ellie was pretty sure she'd never been spontaneous in her life. Until now.

She watched Aidan's gaze narrow in on her. He turned his head slightly and leaned forward, almost as though he'd experienced a hearing loss. "Say that again?"

Ellie sighed. She and Aidan had a fabulous working relationship. She thought of him as her best friend at work, even though he was her boss. And even though he was rugged and gregarious, athletic and tanned. And gorgeous. Handsome. Downright sexy. But she was getting off track.

The fact was, she'd liked Aidan from the first day she started her job at Sutherland Corp. The two of them shared a lot of the same interests and as business associates, they'd traveled together on dozens of occasions. Together they had closed numerous deals and even a bar or two when the negotiations turned out to be rougher than they should have been.

It didn't help that she had developed a ridiculous schoolgirl crush on Aidan shortly after she started working with him. It didn't matter though, because she would never do anything so stupid as to act on her feelings. Not only would it destroy their relationship and mark the end of the best job she'd ever had, but it would make her feel like the world's biggest fool. Ellie had never been a fool.

She knew Aidan's question was coming from a decent place inside him, and she had already decided to be completely honest with him if he forced the issue, so she repeated, "I said, I'm going to have a baby."

"Next week?"

"Next week is when the process starts."

"You can't put it off an extra week?"

"No," she said, fighting to maintain her calm. "I'm usually as regular as clockwork so once I get to Atlanta, I've allowed myself a three-day window during which I should start ovula—"

"Stop." He held up his hand. "We're venturing back into the dark realm of too much female information."

"But you keep asking."

"I just want to know why you have to do all this starting next week."

"Because I want to have a baby and I'm not getting any younger." She had no intention of telling him anything more than that.

"But—" He scratched his head, clearly confused. "You're going to a sperm bank."

"I prefer the term fertility clinic. But yes, that's where I'm going."

"But why?"

"Why?" she said, her voice rising as her serenity tottered on the edge of annoyance. "Seriously, Aidan? You want to know why I'm going to a sperm bank— I mean, fertility clinic? I'll go out on a limb here and take a guess that you are aware of what happens in those places."

He huffed impatiently. "Of course. But what I mean is, why don't you just do it the old-fashioned way?"

"Oh," she said slowly. "That."

"Yeah." He folded his arms across his chest. "That."

"Well, it's because… Hmm." What was she supposed to tell him? The truth? Because the truth was that she would have preferred to get pregnant the old-fashioned way. With a man she loved, someone wonderful who wanted to live the rest of his life with her.

Recently there had been one man who'd expressed some interest in her. She had dated him for a few weeks, but as soon as Ellie brought up the subject of children and family, he'd made himself scarce. That was before they'd even had sex so she'd missed out on that, too. She just couldn't get a break.

Even though there were plenty of opportunities to meet

eligible men on the island, none of them ever seemed to want to take the next step. One problem was that most men came to Alleria to party-party-party. They weren't interested in a relationship if it looked like it might last more than a week.

The other problem was that while Ellie knew men thought she was pretty enough, she also knew they found her a little intimidating. And even though she recognized the problem, she didn't know what to do about it. It wasn't that she had an overpowering personality. That would've been an easy fix. No, Ellie's problem was that she was just too smart. She couldn't help it. She seemed to have a photographic memory and she loved learning new things. She retained information and was cheerfully willing to share it with others any time a subject came up. Some people didn't take that well.

And sadly, Ellie didn't have a clue when to keep her mouth shut and let a guy live with the illusion that he was smarter than she was. Men were so odd.

These days, though, Ellie refused to allow that to bother her. Happily, Aidan and his brother appreciated how smart she was and she loved her job because of it. They accepted her and needed her, and that meant a lot more to Ellie than having a man in her life who might cause her to lose too much of herself.

But meanwhile, without a man in her life, there was no one who was willing to make a baby with her.

So after a lot of studying the pros and cons and debating it with herself, she had decided to use artificial insemination to achieve her goal of motherhood.

She was secure in her job and very well compensated. She also had an excellent benefits package, so the idea of raising her child on her own was a reasonable one. She was also lucky to have developed strong friendships with several women on the island, too, and knew they would always be around when she needed them. So she wasn't worried. She and her baby would comprise the perfect little family she had always wanted. Now she just needed some time off to get the job done.

"Ellie, are you going to tell me why you can't just do it the—"

"Yes, yes, the old-fashioned way." She sniffed, straightened her shoulders and held her head high. "I don't think it's any of your business."

"You're probably right." His lips twisted in a sardonic grin. "But you've already given me your ovulation schedule. I mean, why hold back the rest?"

"Oh, for Pete's sake," Ellie said. "Look, we both know that what I do in my free time is nobody's business but my own."

"Of course it is," he said reasonably. "But you have to realize how concerned I am. As I've already said, I'm your friend as well as your employer, and this isn't exactly a vacation you're taking. You're planning to go off to get pregnant. And then what happens? Then you'll come back and work? For how long?"

"Until the baby's born," she said immediately. "At that point I'll take maternity leave for three months and then I'll be back at work."

The resort had an excellent childcare facility so Ellie wasn't worried about finding someone to care for her baby while she worked. That was another benefit of working for the Sutherland brothers.

"Three months." Aidan pushed away from the desk and stood to pace the floor for a full minute. Finally he looked at her. "Okay, I'm not going to think about your being gone for three months. We'll just deal with these upcoming three weeks."

"That might be best," she murmured.

"I can't stand in the way of you going, but what will we do without you for three weeks? It might not sound like a lot of time to you, but we've never gone that long without you before. And right now we're swamped with work and no one else is qualified to fill your shoes."

She smiled because she'd already made a point of finding solutions to those particular problems, thanks to her best friend, Serena, the catering manager.

"Serena and her secretary have agreed to assist the sales force with the convention work. And my secretary will take care of making sure the day-to-day office work gets done. I'll be available by phone if there are any questions."

"Damn, Ellie."

She stood and met him face-to-face. "Look, Aidan. I wouldn't leave if there was a doctor on the island who specialized in fertilization. But there isn't, so I'm going to Atlanta."

"But what if you go through all this and it doesn't…" He seemed to weigh his words and decided not to finish that sentence. Probably smart of him.

She finished the thought for him. "What if the procedure doesn't work?" She'd considered that possibility, too. "I'll try again in a few months."

He gritted his teeth. "Okay, I understand what you want to do and it's not like I have a say in your decision, but I still think you're jumping the gun here. You're so young. What are you? Twenty-eight? Twenty-nine?"

"Thirty."

"That's young," he insisted. "You still have plenty of time to do it the—"

"Yes, yes, the old-fashioned way. You've mentioned it several times already."

"It bears repeating," he said amiably.

She quickly looked down at her tablet to avoid his knowing gaze. Was it getting hot in here? All this conversation about babies and "doing it the old-fashioned way" was stirring up feelings for Aidan that she'd long ago squelched. And not just emotional feelings, but an actual physical attraction to him. And that had to stop right now. "You realize this is absolutely none of your business, right?"

He had the nerve to grin. "Yeah."

She sighed again. "Look, even if I do have plenty of time, I don't have a partner. You know, someone who's interested in providing the necessary equipment to get the job done."

Could she make it any clearer than that?

"Oh. Right." Aidan seemed to ponder that for a moment. "But what about that guy you were dating? Aren't you still seeing him? What's his name?"

"You know very well what his name is," she said drily. "You introduced us, remember?"

"Oh, yeah," he said snidely. "Brad."

"Blake," she said, rolling her eyes. "Blake Farrell."

"Right. What about Blake?"

Self-conscious now, Ellie avoided eye contact. "What about Blake for what?"

Aidan raised one eyebrow, but said nothing.

"Oh, fine," she said, exasperated. She knew exactly what he was referring to. Sex. "If you must know, I'm not seeing Blake anymore."

His mouth opened, then closed. After a pause, he said, "Ah. Sorry it didn't work out."

"You don't sound sorry at all."

"You're right." He grinned wolfishly. "I'm not. He wasn't the guy for you."

"But you introduced me to him."

"You were both standing there," he said with a shrug. "I was just being polite. I never expected you to start dating him. I'm glad you broke up. You can do a lot better than him."

"Now you tell me," she muttered. "After I already asked him to…" She stopped talking, but it was too late.

Aidan's eyes narrowed in on her. "You asked him to be the father of your child?"

"I think this conversation has gone far enough." She grabbed her tablet off the chair and turned to leave.

"Funny, I think it's just getting started." He circled around to meet her face-to-face, effectively preventing her from dashing out of his office. "Ellie, I introduced you to Blake three weeks ago. Are you saying that after three weeks of dating, you asked him to—"

"Yes. Yes, I did." She began pacing again, but couldn't get far with him standing right in front her. "I don't know what I was thinking. But in my defense, we were going out every weekend, having a great time, getting to know each other. So one night at dinner he asked me where I saw myself in five years and I told him."

"You told him what, exactly?"

She wanted to bury herself somewhere. Instead, she drew in a breath and said, "I told him that in five years I saw myself living on Alleria, working for Sutherland Corporation, and taking care of my adorable four-year-old child."

She watched Aidan's eyes widen. His lips quivered. He tried to bite back a grin, but it was useless. He finally began to laugh. "Let me get this straight. You basically told a guy you've been dating for three weeks that you're looking for him to be your baby daddy?"

"Not exactly," she said. But it was no use. His laughter was justified. "Okay, he might've interpreted it that way."

"You think?"

"Stop laughing. What do I know? Blake was the first date I've had in three years."

"Three years?" He looked her up and down. "What's wrong with the guys you know?"

"It's not them, it's me." Oh, dear lord. Could she sound like a bigger loser? She had to get out of there.

But Aidan grabbed her shoulders to keep her there and tilted his head to meet her gaze. "Honey, trust me. It's not you. You're smart, funny, beautiful. Any man would... well..." He faltered, frowning as he let go of her.

She blinked up at him, then frowned, too. "Well, what?"

He scowled as he walked back to his desk. "Just trust me. You're not the problem."

Ellie appreciated his words, but they didn't really help right now. It wasn't much fun admitting that she was a total loser when it came to men. Especially to admit it to Aidan Sutherland, who was not only her boss but also the man she had been crushing on for almost four years.

Not that it meant anything. A crush on a man was healthy, right? Of course it was! Sure, she had a personal hang-up or two, but other than wanting to sleep with her boss, she was fine and dandy. Very put-together, highly organized, successful. She had friends. She wasn't a loser.

She smiled with determination. "I'll say again that I'm sorry I couldn't give you more notice, but I've got everything covered job-wise. I am absolutely certain that things will run smoothly. I just need your blessing to take the time off."

"I won't let you quit your job," he said fiercely. "We need you too much."

She was surprised and delighted by his admission. He had no idea how much his words pleased her, but she was still going through with her plan.

"Aidan, you know me. I love my job. I love Alleria. You and Logan are the best people I've ever worked with. Believe me, I've never been happier and I have no intention of ever leaving voluntarily."

"Good, because I won't let you. You're a vital member of our organization."

"Thank you." She wouldn't say it aloud, but she would be a fool to give up this job. After all this time, with all the raises and bonuses they'd given her, she would never find anything comparable, especially in such a beautiful setting as Alleria.

"I'll never leave," she reiterated.

"But you're going to have a baby," he argued, not quite ready to concede. "That's not a good sign."

"I have every intention of raising my baby here on the island and continuing to work for you and Logan for as long as you'll have me. Okay?"

He scowled, but she knew he was smart enough to know when to give up the fight. Finally he nodded. "Okay."

"Thank you," she said. In a spontaneous gesture, she gave him a tight hug. "I really appreciate your understanding."

"I don't understand anything," he said, but managed a half smile as he walked her to the door. "Call me conventional, but I still believe in the man-woman routine."

Her laugh was lighthearted even if her mind was set. But she decided to humor him anyway. "Fine. You have one week to convince me it's the best way to go."

Not that she had any intention of doing things his way, Ellie thought as she walked back to her office. She'd thought this through down to the last detail, and she wasn't about to change her mind just to satisfy her boss. She'd seen how a messy relationship with a man could turn a woman's life inside out and she wasn't about to let that happen to her. Not ever. Not even for Aidan Sutherland.

Two

Later that evening, Aidan sat in one of the resort's plush beach chairs and stared out at the placid surface of Alleria Bay. He nursed the glass of single malt scotch he'd picked up in the bar earlier before wandering out to the beach to relax and enjoy the quiet evening.

But how could he relax? He'd already been thinking about Ellie in all sorts of inappropriate ways, and then she had come along and added to the problem. True, she'd only been talking about babies. It was Aidan's fault for bringing up sex by suggesting that she do it the traditional way. Now he couldn't get the idea of sex with Ellie out of his head.

But that didn't mean he would act on it. No way. He had to get his mind off his associate and he hoped his upcoming trip to California would help.

Realistically, Ellie wanting a baby was none of his business. But as she'd left his office earlier, she had issued the challenge—joking or not—and Aidan was willing to meet it. He was determined to find her a willing man in a week. The Sutherland twins never backed away from a challenge. But how was he supposed to find a decent guy who would make Ellie happy enough to stay on the island where Aidan needed her? It's not like he could approach one of the guys he knew and ask if they would be willing to impregnate his senior vice president.

That would be weird.

Skimming his feet over the cool sand of the beach, Aidan tried to figure out where he'd lost the argument with Ellie. Not that he'd been given much chance to argue, he thought. Ellie had presented her plan as a fait accompli. She had no intention of backing down, and Aidan had to admit he appreciated that quality in her. She'd made the decision and she was sticking to it.

So why in the world was Aidan making such a big deal over it? The choice to have a baby was Ellie's alone to make. It was her life. If she wanted to have a baby, she should go get pregnant and have a baby.

But then she'd be leaving the island. True, it was only for three weeks, but she'd confessed out loud that if the first time didn't work, she'd be going back again. And again.

Aidan hated to admit it, but things never ran as smoothly when Ellie went away. He would even go so far as to say that things tended to go straight to hell when Ellie was gone. Two years ago, she took five days off and Hurricane Willie struck the island. Last year she was gone for a week and the hotel kitchen staff went on strike.

She was like a barometer for all things Alleria. If Ellie was on the island, life rolled along. When she wasn't, it was more of a crash-and-burn scenario.

Aidan was tempted to fly in a fertility specialist if it meant Ellie would stay on the island. He considered that for a second or two. It was the perfect solution. One that would make everybody happy, right?

So why was he still brooding about it?

Because, Aidan thought as he sipped his scotch, it still meant that Ellie would be using artificial means to have a baby. And that was the one thing Aidan refused to accept. He wasn't ready to examine his feelings too closely, but suffice to say it wasn't *fair* that his beautiful senior vice president was choosing to get pregnant by means of a turkey baster.

"Fair?" he muttered aloud. Fair to whom? To Ellie? Or to the male population at large? After all, she was a beautiful woman. Plenty of men would be thrilled to help her out. Had she given any of them a chance? Hell, no.

Even Blake Farrell. She hadn't given him a chance, not really. After all, they'd only been dating for less than a month. What man in his right mind would agree to accept her obvious baby-daddy ploy so quickly after they'd met?

Aidan scowled. The *right* man would. But Blake Farrell wasn't that guy. Aidan had known Blake Farrell for years. The guy was a player. He ran an air-shipping operation over on Nassau and had recently opened an office in the port of Alleria. He'd bought a small house in town so he was part of the island community now.

But if Aidan had thought for one moment that Ellie would start dating Farrell, Aidan never would've introduced the two. It still rankled him that she'd accepted even one date from him.

Blake wasn't right for Ellie and he definitely was not the appropriate choice to be the father of her child. But who was? Not that Aidan had any say in the matter, but if Ellie needed someone to do the job, there had to be a lot of guys better suited for the job than Blake Farrell.

Frankly, although he didn't want to examine his feelings

on the subject too closely, he had been relieved to hear that there was no current man in Ellie's life.

But now that meant that she was going to have a complete *stranger* father her child. She would be picking some guy's description out of a book—and who was to say the guy was telling the truth about his attributes? Anybody could donate sperm and claim to be a six-foot-five Adonis when in reality he was three feet tall and a troglodyte.

Hadn't she considered that? Scowling to himself, Aidan imagined all kinds of weird possibilities stemming from that damn turkey baster.

"Hell, I should offer to do it myself," he muttered as he sipped his scotch. Abruptly he jerked himself upright in his chair. *Whoa.* He did not just say that. He tossed down a serious amount of scotch to drown out the words.

There was no way he would ever knowingly father a child. He'd made that decision years ago after watching his own father struggle as a single parent. Aidan and Logan's mother had left them when the boys were only seven years old. It had been a defining moment in Aidan's life and while he thoroughly enjoyed the pleasure that women provided, he wasn't about to trust one enough to marry her, let alone have a child with her.

He would never risk a child of his experiencing the abandonment he'd gone through himself. And now he realized that this was a big reason why he wasn't happy that Ellie was planning to go through with the pregnancy on her own. She was walking right into a single parent situation with no idea how difficult her life would become. And she wasn't the only one to consider. Her child would go through life without a dad. That wasn't right.

Had Ellie tried hard enough to find a man to father her child?

But then he remembered the look on her face earlier when she'd said, *It's not them, it's me.*

Hell, of course she'd tried to find a partner, but no one had been smart enough to step forward. She'd been so vulnerable while talking about it, Aidan had almost taken her in his arms and kissed away the pain he'd seen in her eyes. But he hadn't done it, thank God. That would have been a huge mistake.

Not that he wouldn't have enjoyed it, he thought as he stood and walked to the water's edge. That wasn't the point. The point was, it was never going to happen.

Too bad. Because now that he was thinking about topics like trust and women and Ellie, in particular, it occurred to him that there was one woman in the world he did actually trust. Ellie. When it came to business, she was scrupulously honest. She always spoke her mind. And she always had his back in any negotiation they entered. She was almost as good a partner in wheeling and dealing as his brother, Logan, was.

Logan had agreed with Aidan that Ellie would make a good junior partner. Before Logan left on his honeymoon, the brothers had decided to offer Ellie the position. The plan was to wait until Logan got back to the island. They'd never brought in another partner before, but they both agreed that there was nobody better for their organization than Ellie. And if they wanted the company to grow even larger, they needed someone else in the top ranks who had her intelligence, business insight and unwavering principles.

And all that had nothing to do with the fact that she was downright sexy and beautiful. He thought again of those amazing legs of hers, pictured them wrapped around his waist with him buried so far inside her, he could feel it.

The carnal image was so vivid, he almost lost his footing. Damn, his mind was wandering down a perilous path and if he wasn't careful, he'd find himself facedown in the sand.

He recovered quickly and drank down a good slug of scotch. The smooth, liquid heat soothed his throat and snapped him out of his wayward thoughts. His wildly active imagination meant nothing in reality. He liked Ellie, would love to take her to bed, but it wouldn't happen. It couldn't.

How the hell could he risk losing Ellie as a business partner if a romantic thing between them didn't work out? Or worse yet, what if he initiated something and she was so offended she quit?

"She wouldn't just quit," he muttered darkly. "She'd punch you in the nose first and *then* quit. Yeah, that's not gonna happen."

Still, he wanted her to be happy.

But apparently, it was going to take having a baby to accomplish that.

"Hell." He rubbed his face, annoyed with himself. If he was being honest, he would have to admit that if Ellie had approached him and asked him to be the father of her child, he would have had a hard time pushing her away. But he absolutely would've turned her down in the end. Wouldn't he? Of course he would've. There was no way he would say yes to something like that. Even if it was Ellie doing the asking.

"Not that she asked you," he groused, then scowled at his own idiotic statement. It was official: he had lost his mind. Exasperated, he swallowed the rest of the scotch and headed back to his suite before he found himself howling at the moon like the rest of the lunatics in the world.

Ellie yawned, then finished the last of her tea and shut down her computer. She should've gone to bed an hour ago, but since she knew she wouldn't sleep anyway, she had spent more time sifting through the family photos her sister, Brenna, had sent from Atlanta. A picture of Brenna with her darling husband, Brian. One of Brenna and Brian with their two adorable children. Various shots of the kids on their new backyard jungle gym. And the latest one, a blurry ultrasound photo of Brenna's unborn baby.

Doctor's pretty sure it's going to be a boy, Brenna had written in the email. Lilah's so excited to have another brother. No annoying little sister to deal with.

Ellie smiled. She could hear Brenna laughing as she wrote those words, since it was Ellie who'd been the annoying little sister Brenna had dealt with all her life. And thank goodness for that, Ellie thought.

Now Brenna had her own wonderful family and Ellie couldn't wait to see them all again. That was another reason she had chosen the Atlanta clinic. She would get to visit with her sister's happy, loving family again.

Ellie and Brenna hadn't always been this happy. Growing up, their mother had been absent most of the time, even when she was sitting in the same room with them. That was what happened when a woman became so obsessed with a man who wanted nothing to do with her. Rather than give any love or attention to her own children, their mother had kept it all inside, saving it up, just in case their father ever returned. Except he never did. He didn't want anything to do with them. He had moved on, found another woman to marry, a woman who gave birth to children he cared for much more than he had ever cared about his first two daughters.

But Ellie's mother never gave up on him, never stopped loving him or chasing him, never stopped pretending that he would come back one day. She was always ready, always perfectly dressed and coifed in case he showed up at the door. She insisted that the girls be ready, too. And in her own subtle way, their mother never stopped blaming Ellie and Brenna for causing him to leave. That is, when she managed to remember that she had two children who needed her.

One day, when the girls and their mother were enjoying a

rare moment of fun at a local hamburger stand, their mother thought she spied their father walking down the sidewalk. She raced outside to catch him, saw the man cross the street and blindly dashed after him. She was struck and killed by a city bus.

It was one of many lessons that Ellie took with her into adulthood. She would never, ever cling to or chase after a man who didn't love her. Ellie wouldn't do to her own child what her mother had done to Ellie and Brenna.

After all, she didn't want to get hit by a bus.

More than that, she refused to allow her self-esteem to be shattered as her mother's had been. Her mother had made a fool of herself over and over again. She had deluded herself for years and, slowly but surely, the delusions had replaced reality. Ellie would never allow that to happen to her.

She carried her teacup over to the sink and rinsed it out. As the water ran, she thought about the tiny creature in her sister's ultrasound photo, silently waiting to be born into a loving family that couldn't wait to greet their newest little member.

Ellie was so excited for Brenna. The two of them had basically raised themselves after their mother died, staying under the radar so that the county wouldn't send Ellie into foster care. How they'd managed it, they still didn't know. But it meant that they were fiercely loyal to each other. Brenna had taught Ellie so much more about life and real love than she'd ever learned from her mother.

One thing Brenna always wished for herself and Ellie was that someday they would each have their own big, boisterous families to love. She imagined how Christmas mornings would be, with their children staring in awe at all the colorful packages under the tree. It would be a noisy, busy, frenzied moment when they all ripped into their presents and shouted out their joy and excitement.

Ellie smiled at the memory. Now that Brenna's dream had come true, now that she had Brian and a wonderful family of her own, Ellie couldn't be happier. They were her family, too.

Brenna always told Ellie that someday it would happen for her, too. She would meet a man who would love her and want to start a family with her. Ellie had thought she could wait for that day. But five days ago, Blake broke up with her—probably a good thing—and the very next day, her sister announced she was having another baby by way of sending the ultrasound photo.

"You're going to be an auntie again!" the email subject line announced gaily.

Gazing at the fuzzy outline of Brenna's third child, Ellie had realized that *someday* might never come for her. She might always be an auntie, never a mom. That's when she'd impulsively made the decision to do something about it. She would go it alone. And she would do it right away, before she could think about it too much and pick apart all the reasons why she shouldn't do it. She phoned the Atlanta fertility clinic that very minute and made the appointment.

So that was done. Now she just had to deal with one more wrinkle in her plan.

Aidan.

As Ellie recalled Aidan's reaction to her news, her cheeks flushed with heat. *Why not do it the old-fashioned way?* he'd asked her. Would it have shocked him to hear her reply, "Are you offering to do the job?"

Yes, it would've shocked him and probably would've ended her career at Sutherland Corporation. It wasn't often that female employees were fired for sexually harassing the male boss, but there was a first time for everything.

Aidan had promised to try and convince her that the time-honored, man-woman route was the way to go, but she doubted he would bring up the subject again. Especially after she'd made her pitiful confession that she didn't even have a man around to do the job for her, so to speak.

If only Aidan had offered his own services.

"Oh, good grief." She felt herself blushing even worse than before. Was she out of her mind? Aidan was her boss, in case she'd forgotten. There was no end to the list of complications and ramifications of having her own boss be the biological father of her child.

Sadly though, her biggest problem had nothing to do with the fact that Aidan was her boss. It had to do with the fact that she had wanted the man for years. Secretly, of course. She hadn't dwelled on her feelings for him in a long time, and she blamed their discussion about babies and sex for making her think of it now. Except for that conversation, she considered her crush on him mainly shallow and, well, sexual. Nothing wrong with that, right? The man had a great body! He was smart and funny and nice, too. God help her if she ever began to obsess over him, because if her feelings deepened, she would be in big trouble. Hadn't her mother gone through life pining over a man, worshiping him from afar and losing herself in the process?

No, Ellie would never become dependent on a man. She liked Aidan, thought he was sexy, but that was it, thank goodness. There was no way she would ever turn into her mother.

"Hell, no," she muttered defiantly as her hands rolled into fists at the very idea. She tossed her lightweight bathrobe on the bed and climbed under the covers. But as she fluffed her pillow, she wondered what it said about her when, despite the fact that Aidan would never make the offer to get her pregnant, she knew that if he did, she would have a hard time rejecting the offer. No matter how hard she had tried to avoid the attraction she felt for him, a direct proposition would be too tempting to pass up.

"Because you are crazy," she said aloud. But that didn't seem to matter as she continued to reflect on the joys of giving birth to a baby boy whose father was Aidan Sutherland. Her child would grow up to be handsome, rugged, gregarious, smart and athletic, just like his daddy.

She sighed. And even though it would never happen, the thought was so pleasant that she continued to dwell on it as she drifted off to sleep.

Two days later, Aidan held his regular weekly meeting with the resort managers to go over the schedule for the weekend and discuss any problems that might follow them into the next week.

Once the meeting ended, Serena, his catering manager, and Marianne, the head of housekeeping, met at the coffee machine. Aidan waited behind them as the two women filled their mugs and chatted.

"I'll bet she's already packed," Marianne said. She kept her voice low, but she couldn't disguise her excitement. "You know how she is."

"Yes, organized to the teeth," Serena said as she poured a dollop of cream into her cup. "God, I'm going to miss her so much."

"She'll only be gone for three weeks."

"Oh, come on," Serena said quietly. "Once she gets pregnant, do you really think she'll stay?"

"She promised she would."

"But she'll have a baby to take care of."

"Duh," Marianne said. "But she loves it here."

"Of course, who doesn't? But come on, what kind of life will she have trying to raise a child on Alleria?"

"Hello?" Marianne said. "I have two kids and I live here quite nicely, thank you."

Serena slapped her arm lightly. "I know, goofball, but you got yourself a husband first."

Her friend frowned. "True. Hmm."

"If Ellie's determined to have a baby, she'll want a husband eventually and she's sure not going to find one here."

Marianne sighed. "I have to agree with you there. The men who come to Alleria are only looking for short-term action."

Serena gazed at her. "And yet you found Hector here."

"Sure did," Marianne said, winking as she rolled her shoulder seductively. "He came here looking for one hot mama and he found her."

They both giggled and Serena said, "You got lucky and so did Hector. But the last thing most men come here for is a mama, no matter how hot she is."

"I guess you're right," Marianne said. "It breaks my heart."

"Mine, too, but Ellie will soon realize her child needs a father." Serena leaned closer. "Remember I told you about my sister being a single mother? She's struggled for years just to get by. It's not right."

Marianne sighed. "Alleria is no place for a single mother to go looking for a father for her child."

The two women continued to chat as they walked away, never looking back to notice Aidan's stricken look. He gazed at their backs until they disappeared into the hall. Then he sat down and thought about what he'd heard.

Those women were two of Ellie's best friends on the island. If they expected her to leave, how could Aidan expect anything different?

That settled it. He had weighed all the options and there was only one clear way forward. Serena and Marianne were right. Aidan couldn't take the chance that Ellie would realize she'd need to leave the island once she was raising her child on her own. He had to take action. He'd been tossing ideas around for the last three days and it was driving him crazy. But after hearing what those women had said, he knew there was only one solution.

Now he just had to convince Ellie.

"No. No way. Absolutely not," Ellie said as she jumped up from her chair and faced him. "Are you crazy?"

Maybe he was, Aidan thought. When this same thought had occurred to him a few days ago, he'd dismissed it out of hand as a sure sign he was losing his mind. But after he'd overheard that conversation yesterday, he'd reconsidered and now this seemed the most logical solution to his problem. He could give Ellie a baby. They could do it the old-fashioned way. One problem solved.

"More importantly," he continued, ignoring her protests. "I could support the child and you. You wouldn't have to worry about being a single mother. It's the best possible solution to the problem."

"I don't have a problem," she countered.

"Not yet, maybe. But look at what this would mean in the short run. You wouldn't have to travel back and forth and worry about getting jet lag, you know, in your ovaries."

She whipped around. "Seriously, Aidan? Jet lag in my ovaries?"

"Hey, I'm just repeating what you said." He shook his head, knowing he sounded ridiculous. But it was too late to turn back now. "And another thing. On the off chance that the injections don't take the first few times, you wouldn't have to drag yourself back and forth from Atlanta."

She didn't say anything in response, but he could tell she was thinking about that one.

"Plus, you can stay here on the island," he pointed out

reasonably, "as you said you'd prefer to do. Plus, I'm right here to support you through it all."

"Uh-huh," she said softly.

"I did some reading," he continued. "There's often a lot of anxiety attached to this whole process. You need to be careful or you could sabotage yourself. You know, you could make yourself infertile or something."

"First, you're nuts," she said, counting off with her fingers. "And second, you did some reading? That's so sweet."

He shrugged. "I'm your friend. I'm concerned."

"You're my boss. You don't want me to go."

"That's secondary," he insisted so strongly he almost convinced himself. "Your health and well-being are my main concern."

She rolled her eyes. "Right. Look, I appreciate it and everything, but your idea would never work."

He leaned closer. "Why, Ellie?"

She gazed back at him intently. "Because you don't want a child."

"But you do."

"Yes, and I have a perfectly sensible and practical way to make it happen. And it doesn't have anything to do with you."

He drew a breath and changed tactics. "We've known each other a long time, right? We get along great. And hey, we're in the same vicinity. So if you were, you know, ovulating and, you know, the time was right, all you'd have to do is call me and I'd be there for you."

"You make it sound so romantic," she said, patting her heart wryly.

"What? A turkey baster in some clinic is more romantic?" He chuckled. "Besides, this isn't about romance, right? It's about the baby you want. And it's about your child knowing who his father is. Don't you want that for him?"

"Him?"

"Ellie," he said, "just think about it. This makes a lot of sense. I can have our lawyers write up a contract that spells out the terms for child support and whatever else you want it to say."

She blinked at that. After a moment, she said, "I'm not sure I want you obligated to support my child."

He'd never met a woman who didn't want his money, but Ellie wasn't like any other woman he'd ever known. He was still determined to provide support, though, but right now the exact terms didn't matter. What mattered was that she would have the baby she wanted. And she would stay and continue to work for Sutherland, which Aidan wanted. And the deal would be done.

Just to be sure they were on the same page, he said, "I would want a clause that says you and the baby will stay and live on Alleria."

"I always planned to do that."

"But you might change your mind after the baby's born."

She shook her head. "I won't."

"You never know," he argued. "You might want to get married someday."

"I have no intention of getting married," she insisted.

"You never know," he said with a shrug. "And if you changed your mind, how would you meet a man around here? Let's face it, most men who come to Alleria are only looking for short-term action."

She gave him a suspicious look and he wondered if her girlfriends had already mentioned that point to her. Didn't matter. The more points he racked up for his side, the better.

As she sat back down in the chair opposite his desk, she nibbled at her lower lip, clearly nervous. Instantly, his groin strained with arousal and all he knew was that if she kept biting those lush lips of hers, he wouldn't be responsible for his actions.

He was getting more and more fond of this whole idea by the minute.

"I'm pretty sure this is a bad idea," she said.

He adjusted himself before leaning forward and resting his arms on his desk. "It's actually a really good idea, Ellie. Unless…" He frowned at her. "Here I've been assuming all this time that you found me attractive enough to go through with it. Maybe I was wrong."

"Oh, don't be ridiculous," she grumbled. "Of course I find you attractive. You're the most… Oh, never mind. You're just fishing for compliments. I refuse to feed your ego."

"Too late." Aidan couldn't help grinning.

"Look," she said after taking a deep breath and letting it out slowly. "This has nothing to do with whether I think you look like a troll or whatever."

"A troll? Thank you."

"I'm kidding. You're not a troll and you know it." Her smile turned sober. "It's just that I find the whole idea a little awkward, that's all."

"Awkward?"

"Well, yeah, Aidan. To do this, we'd have to be *naked*." She blew out a breath. "We work together. Seeing each other, you know…that's awkward."

Naked. Okay, maybe he was just being a guy here, but the only thing he found awkward about this situation was that she wasn't naked *now*. Still…he sat back and thought about what she'd said for a moment. Basically, she felt awkward and it was all his fault. Hell, if he could kick his own ass, he would do it. "Damn, Ellie. I didn't mean to make you uncomfortable."

Now she looked contrite. "It's okay. I know you didn't set

out to embarrass me or anything. It's not in your nature to be mean. But you have to admit the idea's a little…bizarre."

He took a careful sip of coffee and wondered if his desperation was starting to show. He had overplayed his hand and she was about to turn him down. A woman. Turning him down. Was there an apocalypse about to happen that no one had told him about? Logan would laugh his ass off if he ever found out about this conversation.

"You're right," he said wearily. "The last thing I ever wanted to do was hurt our working relationship. If it's possible, can you please forget I ever said anything?"

"Just give me a minute," she murmured.

"Take all the time you need. In fact, if you'd rather collect your thoughts and meet later…"

But she ignored him as she started to voice her feelings. "It makes a certain kind of sense to stay here on the island and take care of it, I mean, do…*it*…with you." She rushed to add, "Even though it's a terrible idea. Because, you know, it's you and me. We're pals. Or we were. I hope we still are. But more than that, you're my boss and I'm your…you know. Your employee. So that makes it a really bad idea, right?"

Truly desperate now, Aidan played what he hoped was his trump card. "What if you were more than my employee? What if I told you I was planning to make you a partner?"

She didn't react right away and Aidan thought maybe she hadn't heard him. He wasn't going to mention the fact that he and Logan had already decided to offer Ellie the partnership. She deserved it and it was past time they offered it to her. And if a partnership deal would help sway her to accept his other offer, he was willing to add it to the pot. On the other hand, if his other offer was totally offensive to her, the partnership deal might help lighten the insult.

He just wished she would say something one way or the other. It wasn't like her to equivocate so much.

Finally she looked up and squinted at him. "What did you just say?"

He smiled. "I'm offering you an associate partnership in our corporation."

Ellie was pretty sure most of the blood in her head had flowed right out, leaving her brain empty and her ears ringing. She felt dizzy and faint and was still not sure she'd understood him. "Say that again, please."

"Partnership, Ellie," he said. "You heard me. I know you want it."

Of course she wanted it. She had brought up the subject of partnership during her review last December, asking the brothers if they had considered adding a partnership track to incentivize their top senior-level employees. Aidan and Logan had admitted they hadn't yet decided, unsure whether they wanted to include anyone else in their tightly knit two-man operation.

"You—you're offering me a partnership position."

"Yes."

"Why?"

"Because you deserve it. And because I'm determined to do whatever it takes to keep you here working with us."

She would've stayed without the partnership offer, but now she was overwhelmed. First he'd offered his own sperm—and everything that went with it, so to speak. Now he was offering her a partnership deal? Had she won the lottery? What was going on?

"Well, what do you think?" he asked.

"I'm stunned," she admitted. "And a little suspicious of the timing of your offer."

He nodded. "I understand how you might feel that way, but the truth is, Logan and I had already planned to make you the offer once he was back from his honeymoon. I'm just speeding up the process." Standing, he walked over and sat down in the chair next to her. He took hold of her hand, warming her all the way through to her heart. "I know you want to have a baby and I want to help you if you'll let me. It's your choice, absolutely, and no matter what you decide, you'll still be a partner and a friend. I brought up the idea with the best of intentions, no matter how idiotic it sounded to you."

"Oh, Aidan."

"Wait." He held up his hand. "I feel honor bound to add that it wouldn't make me uncomfortable at all to see you naked. In fact, it's pretty much all I've thought about lately."

Her throat went dry. Unless she was delusional, it sounded like Aidan was still interested in helping her conceive naturally. And the more she thought about it, the more she was all for it. Especially with him sitting so close and holding her hand and unconsciously rubbing his thumb along the pulse point at her wrist. Tiny zings of excitement charged through her body with every move of his thumb, driving her crazy in all the best ways.

She knew that accepting his offer could be dangerous to her well-being. But it didn't have to be. She was a strong woman and this was essentially a business proposition, after all. It would be the best possible thing for her baby and a fabulous opportunity for her. She could accept without fear of turning into her mother.

Aidan continued, "The partnership deal is my way of letting you know that no matter what you decide on the baby front, we want you to continue working for Sutherland once you've started your family."

"So it's not some sort of bribe to help me forget your good old-fashioned offer?"

"That depends," he said carefully. "Is it working?"

She laughed. "Yes, it's working. I'm weak. But, Aidan,

you don't have to bribe me to stay. I already told you I have every intention of staying on after the baby's born."

"I'm glad. But the partnership is not a bribe. It's for real." He outlined the particulars of the deal, adding that the lawyers would draft an agreement that would take effect immediately upon signing. It was an associate partnership, the first level of the Sutherland partnership track. She had the opportunity to advance each year until she reached the top level of full capital partnership.

"I'll warn you," Aidan said. "Reaching full partnership could take anywhere from five to ten years. But I want to see you go for it."

Go for it, she repeated silently. But could she say yes to the whole deal? she wondered. It might be smart to back away from having a baby with him. After all, if she did agree, it would mean entering into a deeply personal relationship with Aidan that she wasn't sure she would ever recover from.

Still, part of her wanted to shout, *Yes! Yes!* But she was pretty sure those were her hormones talking. She needed to step back and think this through very carefully. Without Aidan around to tempt her.

She mentally collected herself and said, "I need a few days to think about everything you've offered me."

"Everything?" he repeated.

She bit her lip and nodded. "Yes, everything."

He nodded. "All right. I'm leaving for California tomorrow. Why don't you let me know your decision when I get back on Monday."

She gazed at him solemnly. "I'll have an answer for you then."

Three

"We're cleared for takeoff, Mr. Sutherland."

"Thanks, Leslie," Aidan said, and buckled his seat belt.

The flight attendant walked toward the front of the plane to take her own seat behind the partition that separated the passenger compartment from the crew's quarters. Checking his wristwatch, Aidan realized he had six long hours to kill before they would land in California. He made himself comfortable in the sleek leather chair and stretched his long legs out.

As the powerful Gulfstream engines began to roar and the jet took its place in the middle of the runway, it occurred to Aidan that he should've asked Ellie to come along on the trip. At least he'd have someone to talk to during the long flight. It didn't hurt that she was beautiful to look at, too.

She was also smart. And funny. They always laughed a lot when they traveled together. And if she were here, Aidan wouldn't have to wait four days to make love with her.

But since he was forced to wait, he had nothing but time to consider all the potential problems involved with walking into fatherhood. There were plenty. He had never planned on taking this path, but the bottom line was, this was for Ellie and the child who would know both of his parents.

And it meant he could finally have Ellie naked in his bed.

Since she wasn't there, he opened his briefcase and got to work on several of the projects he'd neglected lately. By the time they were flying over California hours later, he was almost caught up on everything.

He looked up as the flight attendant walked into the passenger area. "Guess it's time to buckle up. I can feel the plane starting to descend."

"Yes," Leslie said. "We should be landing in about fifteen minutes."

"Thanks."

Ellie always spent a few hours each weekend in her office, catching up on business journals and studying the stock market. She enjoyed learning new things. Reading articles about business trends and developments helped expand her mind and broaden her horizons and made her better at her job.

Her girlfriends thought she was crazy. Serena urged her not to read the whole weekend away and told her that if she changed her mind, a few of them were meeting in the bar for cocktails and dinner tonight. Ellie wasn't sure she wanted to go out. She had too much to think about.

But that was the problem. With Aidan's proposition still fresh in her mind, she couldn't concentrate on anything else, especially business. Her brain kept bouncing from one idea to the next to…Aidan.

She finally gave up, pushed the books aside and left the office. As she strolled through the lush coco palm grove to the cozy cottage she called home, located on the edge of the resort grounds, she decided the only way she was going to be able to truly relax was to go swimming.

She slipped on her bathing suit, threw on a short cover-up, grabbed a towel and walked down to the beach. The numerous pools scattered around the resort were beautiful, but they were much too lively for relaxation. Ellie preferred to swim in the calm waters of the bay.

The sun was nearing the horizon, but the air was still warm. She touched the clear water with her toe and found it was the perfect temperature, refreshing without giving her a chill. Dropping the towel on the sand, she walked straight into the bay until the water reached her shoulders. Then she plunged her entire body under the water and swam underwater for as long as her breath lasted. Surfacing, she began to swim with slow, easy strokes that stretched her muscles in all the right places.

Ellie had always loved the water. Once upon a time, she had been an excellent swimmer and had even daydreamed of swimming in the Olympic Games. But then her mother died and swimming became a luxury she couldn't afford.

Ellie and Brenna were the only people besides the mortuary director who had attended their mother's funeral. That was when it hit the two girls that they were completely on their own. Their father had no interest in taking custody of them and their mother had no other living relatives. Ellie was thirteen and scared to death to go into foster care, so sixteen-year-old Brenna decided she would do whatever it took to keep them living together in their mother's small house in the same working-class neighborhood where they'd always lived.

Brenna had an after-school job that brought in a few hundred dollars every month. Their eccentric mother had always kept a large stash of money—almost seven thousand dollars—in a safe place in her closet. They lived frugally, only spending money for food and the barest essentials, and managed to stay under the radar for almost four years, until Ellie's junior year in high school. That's when a school counselor grew suspicious of her living situation and contacted the authorities.

Terrified of what might happen next, the girls packed their mother's car with whatever they could grab and in the middle of the night and drove out of town. They headed south and stopped when they reached the outskirts of Atlanta.

For the next eight months, they lived off the grid, sleeping in their car when they couldn't find an available shelter. Brenna took day jobs cleaning houses and Ellie spent hours in the local library studying for her GED.

They'd survived, Ellie thought as she swam through the balmy water. More than that, they'd thrived, depending on each other and building a bond stronger than most sisters could claim.

A few hundred yards from shore, she stopped, treaded water and stared up at the vivid streaks of orange, pink and purple that filled the sky as the sun sank into the sea.

Looking back at the resort, she still couldn't quite believe that this was her life. She'd come a long way from those days of living in a car. Life hadn't exactly been easy-breezy back then, but she and her sister had stayed together and they had endured.

Soon after Ellie obtained her GED, she turned eighteen and they didn't have to worry about the authorities anymore. They'd rented a small apartment, Ellie had enrolled at the local college and Brenna had started her own housecleaning service.

As she turned and paddled back to shore, Ellie continued to dwell on the strange path her life had taken. She had missed out on so much during those years. Childhood friendships, boys, shopping, cute clothes, the prom, sporting events—all the fun things that normal teenage girls did.

But it couldn't be helped. She and Brenna had realized early on that they couldn't afford to stand out, couldn't afford to have anyone examine their lives too closely.

So there would be no boyfriends, no close girlfriends, no activities that might draw attention. Instead, Ellie had escaped into books, newspapers, magazines, blotting out the hard times while soaking up every morsel of information she could get. And once she got into college, it was as if she was making up for all the time she'd lost in her last year of high school. She'd made some nice girlfriends and even dated once in a while. But more than anything else, she studied constantly, couldn't learn fast enough. Her so-called photographic memory, along with a near fanatical need to succeed, helped her graduate in three years. She had been so captivated by the inner workings of corporations that she had already obtained her MBA when most of her peers were wondering what to wear to the homecoming game.

Now she was happily employed by the Sutherland Corporation, where she was considered brilliant, independent and overachieving—in a good way. She had great friends and she'd dated a few men. She had the means and opportunity to have a child and give that child everything she hadn't had while growing up.

She reached the beach, grabbed her towel and patted it against her wet skin. The sand was still warm on her feet although the sun had set long minutes ago.

"That's enough reminiscing," she muttered aloud as she brushed the water off her arms and legs.

Why had she dredged up all those ancient memories? She rarely thought of the old days anymore. Did they have something to do with Brenna's ultrasound picture? Or were they somehow connected to Aidan's proposition? Were the memories a reminder of how tired she was of always missing out on all the fun?

Because it suddenly dawned on her that if she said yes to Aidan, she wouldn't only be doing it to get herself pregnant. No, she would also be doing it because sex with Aidan would be exciting and *fun*.

And after all these years, Ellie deserved to have some fun. Didn't she?

And speaking of fun, she thought as she grabbed her towel off the sand, her girlfriends would be in the bar at seven o'clock. With a determination she hadn't felt in a while, she wrapped the towel around her waist and walked briskly toward home. If she took a speedy shower and dressed quickly, she could meet the girls in time to buy the first round of drinks.

Aidan never saw the sneak attack coming. In retrospect, he figured that's why they called it a *sneak* attack.

It was two days into his California visit and his cousin Cameron Duke was throwing a pool party in the backyard of his home overlooking Dunsmuir Bay. Aidan lazed on a comfy raft in Cameron's pool, a cold beer perched in the handy bottle holder. The cacophony of kids screaming joyfully, a dog barking, Sally taking orders for sangria, all faded into the background as Aidan tried to remember how long it had been since he'd been able to relax like this. Six months? Longer? Hell, the corporation had been in high gear and he'd been working nonstop for the last year at least.

The sun was warm, the water cool, and as the noise level began to die down, Aidan wished again that he'd brought Ellie with him to California. She would've enjoyed herself and fit right in with this lively crowd. But more than that, he wanted her with him right now, here in the pool, her body wet and slick against his....

Suddenly without warning, the air was filled with screeching banshees as a giant gush of water exploded all around him. Seconds later, more water engulfed him as kids and grownups cannonballed into the pool from every angle.

"Hey!" He scrambled off the raft, grabbing the beer bottle as pool water surged from one end to the other, splashing the deck and creating a mini-tsunami.

"Good save," Brandon shouted above the uproar of the skirmish. "Never waste a perfectly good beer."

Aidan laughed. "My philosophy exactly."

Brandon was the biggest of the three Duke brothers, a former star quarterback in the NFL. Sitting on his broad shoulders was Samantha, his brother Cameron's adorable, curly-haired three-year-old. She laughed and splashed and occasionally smacked the top of Brandon's head like a conga drum.

Abruptly, little hands latched on to Aidan's shoulders. He turned and found Jake, Cameron's five-year-old son, grinning maniacally at him.

"Piggyback ride!" the little boy cried.

"Uh." Aidan looked around to see if there was a parent nearby. The pool was filled with them, but they were all busy with the other kids. Damn. Aidan was on his own.

"Okay, kiddo," Aidan said. "Guess you're stuck with me."

Jake didn't seem to mind. "Go! Go!"

"Okay, okay," Aidan muttered. "Hold on tight," he warned as the boy climbed onto his back. Then Aidan glanced around for somewhere to put the beer bottle he'd saved only moments before, setting it down safely on the flat tile surface that surrounded the pool.

He took off slowly and jogged around the pool, being careful to keep Jake's head above the water line. Looking around, though, he wasn't sure it mattered. All these Duke kids swam like fish, even the youngest ones.

After a few minutes, Aidan glanced back. "Had enough?"

"Nope," Jake said, slapping Aidan's back. "More."

A half hour later, Aidan came to a stop on the shallow-end steps. "I'm worn out, kiddo."

"Okay, you better rest," Jake said. The little boy wrapped his arms around Aidan's neck and hugged him, pressing his cheek to Aidan's. "Thanks, Uncle Aidan." Then he hopped off and swam away.

Aidan swam to the side of the pool and grabbed his beer, refusing to admit how much he had enjoyed the squirmy little kid hanging around his neck.

Three hours later, after Aidan had eaten his body weight in grilled burgers, the best potato salad he'd ever had and Sally's cherry cobbler, he glanced around the spacious patio. The grownups were still gathered at the table talking while the little kids fought mightily to stay awake, but failed miserably.

Five-year-old Jake, the oldest of the kids, had decided to take a trip down the jungle gym slide and had promptly tossed his cookies. Without batting an eye, Cameron rushed him into the house to clean him up.

For some reason, all the efficient family activity reminded Aidan of Ellie and her ability to keep things running smoothly under any circumstance. Of course, everything lately reminded him of the woman waiting for him back home on Alleria. He couldn't wait to go home and get her naked. There wasn't a question in his mind but that she would want the same thing.

A few minutes later, Jake came running outside in fresh pajamas and shocked the hell out of Aidan by climbing onto his lap. Now the little guy was sound asleep in his arms. Talk about a sneak attack. Aidan couldn't quite fathom how all these protective feelings for this scrawny little guy had cropped up.

Was this the kind of emotional stuff that dads went

through? he wondered. Was this what he'd signed on for with Ellie? No, he realized quickly. If Ellie said yes to his offer tomorrow, Aidan would one day become a dad in name only. He would be there for financial support and the occasional family gathering. He rubbed his chest absently, relieved that he wouldn't have to deal with these overwhelming feelings of fear and concern and love and—

"Here you go." Cameron handed him a heavy crystal glass of single malt scotch. "Don't worry about waking up Jake. I swear that kid can sleep through earthquakes and enemy fire."

Cameron sat and both men sipped their drinks in companionable silence, watching the activity around them.

"Time for jammies," Brandon's wife Kelly announced, and scooped tiny Robbie up off the lawn, where he'd been speed crawling, trying to make his escape. The kid put up a halfhearted fuss but after a moment, he laid his head on Kelly's shoulder and closed his eyes.

"This one's zonked out, too," Adam said, and carried T.J. into the house. His wife Trish was already inside taking care of the latest addition to their family, two-month-old Annabelle.

Cameron shook his head. "Never thought the day would come when there'd be more kids than adults at a Duke brothers party."

"The kids are great," Aidan said, and took a sip of scotch.

Cameron laughed. "Spoken like a die-hard bachelor determined never to have any of his own."

"Hey, I meant it," Aidan protested, then shrugged sheepishly. "Is it that obvious?"

"I recognize the code words." Cameron relaxed in his chair. "Kids are great as long as they're someone else's, right?"

Aidan chuckled. He might've been guilty of uttering

those very words on more than one occasion. Oddly enough though, tonight he had liked the feel of Jake, trusting and sound asleep, tucked up against him. Wow. He couldn't believe he'd just had that thought.

"I was never gonna have any of my own, either," Cameron said. "None of us were. Hell, my brothers and I made a sacred pact when we were young. No marriage. No kids. Ever."

Aidan frowned at the familiar sentiment. "So what happened?"

"Julia happened," he said simply. "And Jake. Mom had something to say about it. Come to think of it, my brothers added their two cents' worth, too."

"Sounds like a united front. What'd they all say to change your mind?"

Just then, Julia stood and eased little Jake off of Aidan's lap and into her arms. "I'll take him in to bed."

Cameron jumped up. "Let me do it."

"No, you stay and talk to Aidan," she said, and reached up and kissed him before walking away.

Aidan took another sip of scotch and wondered how quickly he could leave to get home to Ellie.

At fifty thousand feet, Aidan stared out the window at the cloud cover below. He and his father and taken care of their family business so Aidan had left a day early, anxious to get back to the island. So far, he'd spent most of the flight reminiscing about the last few days with his father and Sally and the rest of the Dukes. It was still a little weird to realize that he and his dad and brother were suddenly part of a great big loving family they'd never known until two years ago.

And he wondered what it said about him that he could still feel the imprint of little Jake's slippery wet fingers clinging to his shoulders in the pool. The kid had gotten to him, along with the rest of the brood.

Who'd have guessed that he and Logan would end up with a loud, active extended family after all these years? Growing up, it had been the three of them alone: Aidan, his brother and their dad. But now things were changing. Their family was changing and growing. Was that change another reason why he'd made up his mind so easily about offering to father Ellie's child? He wasn't prepared to answer that just yet.

To divert himself, he stared out the windows. The cloud cover had dissipated and he tried to guess what area of the country they were flying over.

"Looks like Louisiana," he murmured, gazing down at the verdant surface a mile below. Rivulets intertwined like snakes through miles of lush growth and trees, emptying into small lakes and ponds. Bayou, he thought. Definitely Louisiana. That meant he had another two hours in the air before they reached Alleria.

He leaned both arms on the high back of the leather seat and thought of his own unhappy youth. His mother had walked out on the family when he and his brother were seven years old. Both Aidan and Logan always vowed to stay single because women couldn't be trusted. Their mother wasn't the only woman in the world who'd proven that theory true.

And after hearing his cousin Cameron's story about what he'd been through with his own miserable father, it just went to show that there were plenty of men who couldn't be trusted either.

Hell, Aidan knew that. But it hadn't hit so close to home before. Cameron Duke's old man was a son of a bitch.

Aidan realized that he and Logan had really lucked out in that realm. Their father Tom was the best dad any kid could ever have.

But their mother was a mess. Not that she had ever beaten them, or starved or lashed out at them. No, his mother's sins were ones of neglect and abandonment. She just didn't care.

She'd never even taken the trouble to figure out which of them was Aidan and which was Logan. She used to look at one brother or the other and say, "Which one are you?"

That was pathetic, but it wasn't criminal.

So yes, their dad was the best there ever was. But Aidan still had his mother's genes. He'd always worried that he might turn out like his mom and be a terrible parent who only cared about his own selfish needs. But it didn't have to be that way, he realized now. He knew himself, knew he would never be like her. By making his offer to Ellie, he knew her child would be in good hands. Ellie would make a wonderful mother and Aidan would be there to support them both.

Aidan shook away all thoughts of his mother and focused instead on his dad. It had been so good to see him interacting with Sally and all the Dukes, almost as if they'd always been a family. They had welcomed all three Sutherland men unconditionally, but Aidan got a special kick from seeing his dad so happy.

"I have your lunch ready for you, Mr. Sutherland," Leslie said.

"Thanks." Beyond grateful for the distraction, Aidan put aside all those thoughts and sat to wolf down the perfectly cooked pasta and salmon Leslie had prepared. While he ate, he flipped through a business magazine and made some notes. Afterward, he put the finishing touches on some contracts he'd brought with him, then slid his briefcase away for the rest of the flight.

Aidan poured himself a glass of wine and tried to relax. The plane was over the Gulf of Mexico and he couldn't wait to get home. He was getting more and more anxious to see Ellie again and he'd convinced himself that she'd made her decision to take him up on his plan.

He almost laughed when he thought about how he'd planned to find a woman while he was in California. Who

knew his feelings would change so drastically in a week?
Now all he could think about was Ellie. He couldn't wait to
see her again.

He recalled her nervousness about "getting naked" with
him and chuckled, thinking he could hardly wait to calm
her nerves.

Unbidden, an image of little Jake popped into his head.
Weird, wasn't it? Aidan was a man who had never wanted
children and yet he was willing to father a child for his business associate. He squirmed a little uneasily in his seat. Fa-
thering a child and *being* a father were two different things
though, he assured himself. The baby would be his blood
and would have his full support throughout his life. That
didn't mean he would be interacting with it on a daily basis.

And at that thought, another memory of Jake, curled up
and asleep on his lap, zipped through Aidan's mind. He
scowled and pushed it out again. He wasn't interested in
being anyone's dad. But he was most definitely interested in
Ellie and in making sure she had the best for the little family she wanted to create.

Of course, on the off chance that she was still feeling
ambivalent, he would be happy to make the decision for
her. The thought of getting her naked had become a bit of
an obsession with him, so if she needed persuading, he was
the man to do it.

He sat back in his seat and smiled at the different ways
he'd be willing to use to convince Ellie to agree to his offer.

"I've got to go inside," Ellie said, sitting up on her beach
towel and stretching like a sleepy cat. She'd been daydream-
ing for the last hour about Aidan. Oh, who was she kidding?
She'd been thinking about him all weekend, wondering what
it would be like to have sex with him. She would find out
soon enough and the thought made her equally nervous and

thrilled. He would be back tomorrow and she couldn't wait to see him again.

But she had to make sure their arrangement remained strictly business. Yes, she would enjoy herself with Aidan, but she would never allow herself to slide into a state of pure unadulterated passion from which she might never recover. The danger was self-evident; she was, after all, her mother's daughter.

So to maintain the business aspect of the deal, Ellie had spent all day yesterday preparing a computerized list of objectives, rules and contingencies. Once Aidan was back in the office, she would present it to him and explain everything in detail so that they were both on the same page going forward.

She spent a long moment adjusting her eyes to the sun, then stood and began to gather her things.

"Are you sure?" Serena asked, not moving an inch from her beach towel. "It feels so good to lay here and do nothing."

"That's all I've done today," Ellie lamented, as she tossed her sunblock and paperback novel into her small carryall. "I've become a slug."

"I'm so proud of you." Serena sat up and used her hand to block the sun from her eyes. "And I love that new bikini of yours."

"The one you forced me to buy?" Ellie laughed.

"Yes, and you're welcome," Serena said. "It looks fantastic on you."

Ellie felt positively decadent after four hours of doing nothing but swimming and sunning on the small patch of beachfront at the far end of the resort area. Few guests ever ventured down this way so the Alleria employees were welcome to sunbathe here. It was the first time Ellie had ever taken advantage of that perk; the change was thanks to Serena.

Also, thanks to Serena, she'd spent way too much money on a flattering two-piece bathing suit they'd found in one of the resort's fancy shops. That was after Serena had taken one look at Ellie's serviceable one-piece tank suit and been horrified.

"You're a bad influence on me," Ellie said as she reached for her towel and shook the sand off.

"My work here is done." Serena sighed and stood up. "Guess I'd better get going, too. I need to prep a few things for my staff meeting tomorrow morning."

Ellie left Serena at her house and kept walking until she reached her own cottage another few hundred yards away. Her feet were gritty from the sand and her skin was drenched in sunblock, so before going inside, she stopped to use the outdoor shower near the kitchen door.

She tossed her cover-up onto the veranda and stepped under the stream of cool water. She savored the feeling as it splashed against her warm skin, trying to imagine how it would be if Aidan were showering with her. Wonderful, she thought, and slowly ran her hands along her arms and legs and stomach to brush off the sand.

Aidan dropped off his bag and briefcase in his suite, then jogged over to the business offices to find Ellie. She always spent Sunday afternoons at her desk, catching up on business news and any loose ends that needed to be nipped before the work week started.

She wouldn't be expecting him a day early and he figured he'd be catching her off guard. He wondered if he would be able to tell by the look on her face whether or not she was willing to get naked with him—as she put it. Or would they have to discuss things further? Somehow he knew she'd made up her mind. Ellie rarely hesitated when it came to decision making, although, granted, this situation was a unique one.

He strolled past her secretary's desk and went straight to her office door. It was closed so he knocked, then immediately opened it and walked in. "Ellie, I'm back. Did you have a chance to…"

She wasn't at her desk.

Okay, not a big surprise. It was Sunday afternoon, after all. So maybe she was doing laundry or cleaning her house. He crossed the busy lobby and headed outside, taking a shortcut through the main pool area and past the tiki bar. The din of music and laughter faded as he made his way across the property to the residence cottages on the other side of the coco palm garden.

As he neared Ellie's house, he heard a woman singing. One of her neighbors, no doubt. Not a bad voice, he thought, although it sounded a little garbled, like the singer was under water.

None of their guests ever stayed over here in the residence cottages, so it had to be an employee. At least it wasn't Ellie, Aidan knew that much. His prim, proper, straight-laced senior vice president would never…

He stopped in his tracks as he caught sight of the dazzling backside of a woman standing under an outdoor shower, wearing what could charitably be called a string bikini.

His mind shut down as raw primordial need took over. Words formed in his brain, but he couldn't utter them aloud. Sexy. Gorgeous. Body. Want. Now.

Mine.

The woman continued singing, completely oblivious to Aidan's presence. As his mind slowly clicked back into working order, the term *poleaxed* came to mind. He was pretty sure this was what it felt like to be smacked over the head with a two-by-four. He'd never seen anything so stunning in his life.

As the woman rubbed her hands over her skin, Aidan had to bite his tongue to keep from offering to do it for her. Finally she reached for the spigot, cut off the water and turned.

And Aidan felt his chin hit the ground.

Ellie?

Four

Aidan had never seen his senior vice president in a bathing suit before, let alone something like the teasingly skimpy scraps of material she was wearing now. Hard to believe, but the real Ellie was even better than the sexy dream images that had been invading his mind the whole time he was away.

Okay, he thought. *Yeah. He could definitely do this.*

Ellie's eyes were still closed as she wiped water off her face and smoothed her hair back.

Aidan couldn't speak, could only gawk like some teenager at her awe-inspiring breasts. They were barely covered by the jungle-print scraps of material, but they were high and round and perfect for him. Perfect for his hands. Perfect for his mouth.

Her stomach was smooth and touchable, her hips round and shapely and delicious, and her legs…had he already mentioned touchable? What about delicious?

"Ellie?"

Her eyes popped open and she let out a squeal. "Aidan?"

He kind of wished he hadn't said anything as she slung one arm across her breasts. With her other hand, she tried to cover the enchanting apex of her thighs.

"What're you doing here?" she cried. "Oh, no! This is... Oh, just...let me get dressed!"

"Not necessary," he insisted, but she was already running up the steps to her front door. "It's just a bathing suit. I've seen them before."

"Not on me!" She fumbled with her keys and dropped them. "It's unprofessional."

True, Aidan thought. He had to give her that one. Seeing her like this wiped away every image he had of her prim, proper business attire.

"Ellie, stop worrying about it. It's the weekend. You're not at work."

She continued to protest. But suddenly his ears were no longer capable of hearing as she bent over to retrieve her keys, giving him a stunning view of her world-class derriere.

Oh, dear lord. He could die a happy man now.

"You weren't supposed to be home until tomorrow," she said. "I'm...surprised, that's all. Let me take this off. I mean, change into something more suitable."

"Ellie." He snatched the keys from her hand, jammed the proper one into the lock and pushed the door open for her. "We live and work on an island. A *tropical* island. A resort. Everyone wears bathing suits around here—" Though not as well as she did, he added silently. "Quit making such a big deal about this. I don't care."

"I know," she muttered, "but I'm not used to you seeing me—to me being dressed like—to have you show up at my house and—" She blew out a breath and took another one. "Never mind. Well. You're home early."

"Yeah," he said, gazing down at her. "Hi."

"Hi," she whispered.

She was so close, he could almost taste her. Lust had him reaching to pull her closer. As her breasts skimmed his chest, she gulped and pushed away.

"I'm all wet," she said, her voice raspy.

"Again, let me say I don't care," he said.

"I do."

Her voice gave her away and he knew she was affected by the moment. But apparently she was going to fight it. She brushed past him and stepped inside, then waved him in after her.

"You wait here," she said. "I'll just be a minute."

Aidan acceded to her wishes even though he wanted to follow her right into her bedroom and have his way with her, but that would be pushing it. Right?

Frowning, he watched her scurry from the room; then, alone, he took a moment to look around. He'd never been inside Ellie's cottage before, he realized. Restless, he wandered the room, picking out the touches that Ellie had added to make it her own.

Aidan and Logan had chosen the California Craftsman style for these two-bedroom residential cottages. Inside, the designers had added Caribbean flair to the traditional sturdiness with pale painted walls, blond wood floors, ceiling fans, lots of windows and vivid island fabrics on the furniture. Those details gave the rooms more charm and lightness than what was usually found in corporate housing.

But this cottage carried the stamp of Ellie's personality. There were surprising bits and pieces of her personal style everywhere he looked. Colorful pillows were scattered across the couch and chairs. A set of watercolor paintings showed striped umbrellas on the beach and children playing at water's edge. A whimsical bowl of papier-mâché fruit was the centerpiece on the small dining room table. And on every shelf there were framed photographs of friends or relatives, plus knickknacks, seashells, a small bowl of dried leaves and twigs. And books. Lots of books.

"I'm sorry to keep you waiting," she said, rushing back into the room.

"It's not a job interview, Ellie."

"No, of course not." She wore pale linen pants and a thin, sleeveless red blouse. Her hair was still wet but combed and tucked behind her ears. Her feet were bare. She looked almost as delectable right now as she had in her bikini a few minutes ago.

Why hadn't he noticed how sexy and beautiful she was the minute he'd hired her? He'd worked with her for four years and the thought had never crossed his mind until recently. Maybe he needed more than an eye exam. Maybe the doctors should take a look at his brain.

She straightened a magazine on the end table. "So, have you been back long? Would you like something to drink? Did you have a nice weekend with your family?"

She was still nervous. He had to admit he liked it. It was good to know he wasn't the only one affected by that sizzling moment or two they had shared on the front porch. But as tight and uncomfortable as his body was feeling right at the moment, Aidan had to smile. Surely Ellie was the only woman in the world who would expect a man to indulge in small talk so soon after—

After what?

Nothing had happened, really. Nothing like what he wanted to happen anyway.

"Aidan?" She was watching him. "Did you hear me?"

Over the roaring in his blood? Just barely. But he answered her questions anyway.

"I did. I've been home an hour. No, thank you, I don't want a drink. And yes, seeing the family was great," he answered in order of the questions she asked. Casually leaning one shoulder against the heavy bookshelf, he said, "Look, I know I'm home a day early, but I couldn't wait to see you. You know why I'm here, right? I'm hoping you have an answer for me. Do you, Ellie?"

"Um, yes. About that." She fiddled with one of her shirt buttons fretfully, causing him to fixate on her breasts even more than before. She seemed to realize what she was doing because she dropped her hands abruptly and gazed up at him. "I would prefer to discuss it tomorrow in the office."

"You want to discuss it in the office," he repeated slowly as he gave her a cool, assessing look. "Because it's…business?"

"Well, no, but yes." She frowned, annoyed at herself. After taking a deep breath and letting it out slowly, she continued. "Yes, Aidan. It is business. Anything that involves relations between you and me will have an effect on our business dealings. And after all, we'll be signing both a contract and a partnership agreement. Our lives and our jobs are about to become inextricably intertwined, wouldn't you agree?"

Damn, Aidan thought. Even when she got all prim and proper on him, he wanted her. Badly. Now that he'd given himself permission to want her, he couldn't seem to stop.

"Now, you made me a proposition," she continued, "and I would like to negotiate the terms. In that regard, I went ahead and made a list of conditions along with some facts and figures I'd like to go over with you. Tomorrow. In the office."

She'd made a list. Why was he not surprised? But he was impressed and gave her high marks for presenting her case so eloquently. So why did he just want to grab her and kiss her? He would, he vowed. And soon. But right now, it was obvious that Ellie needed to exert some control over the situation, so he was happy to allow it. For now. "Let me first get one thing straight, Ellie. The bottom line is, your answer is yes. You've decided to go ahead with my plan."

"Well, yes. But my conditions—"

"Are on a list," he drawled. "At the office."

"Yes," she said primly. "That's right."

He spied her tablet computer, the one she carried with her at all times, on the side table next to her purse and briefcase. "Do you have a copy of the list on your tablet?"

"Yes, but it's not as effective at making a presentation as my—"

"Let's see it."

"But—"

"Ellie." He pushed away from the bookshelf and approached her. "I don't mind sitting through your *presentation* tomorrow, pie charts, Venn diagrams and all. But I'd like the main issues settled right here, right now."

She scowled, but appeared ready to concede. A good thing since he considered it a very reasonable request.

"Fine." She grabbed her tablet, started it up, then scrolled through several pages to get to her list.

"Wait, let me see that." He turned the tablet so he could view the screen and laughed. "Roman numerals? Bullet points? This isn't a list, it's a business presentation. That's why you wanted to go over it at the office. You created a slide show for me."

Her eyes narrowed and her voice went cold and tight. "I happen to think better with bullet points." She folded her arms tightly across her chest. "Stop laughing."

But she was biting back a smile, so Aidan knew she wasn't too deeply offended. He was just glad she didn't have any clue how badly his body parts were throbbing at the sight of her lush breasts straining against the thin material of her blouse. She might change her attitude.

He ripped his gaze away from her and stared at the

screen. She had divided her list into several main topics: Pre-pregnancy and pregnancy. Post-pregnancy. Baby care and support issues.

Okay, she got points for taking an organized approach to life, but talk about a buzzkill. Time to take back control of this situation. "Send me the pertinent points and I'll have the lawyers draft the agreement we talked about."

"I'll do that," she said. "But that's all about the future. I would like to go over the current issues that concern you and me."

"You and me?" he said, wondering why he'd thought this would be easy. A woman with a sharp, intelligent brain could be a dangerous thing, he reminded himself. "What about you and me? You already said you agreed to my idea."

"Oh, I do agree," she rushed to say. "I thought it all through and I'm very happy to go ahead with the plan. I'm certain that your sperm will be suitable."

"Suitable? Damn, Ellie." He chuckled as he pulled her close to him, but she stopped him again.

"Please, Aidan. You're distracting me and I'd really like you to watch my slide presentation first. It only runs ten minutes and I went to a lot of trouble to make sure everything was covered. I think it'll help clarify our duties and responsibilities to each other."

"Duties and responsibilities?" Aidan shook his head. Leave it to Ellie to explain sex using bullet points.

"Yes," she said. "That's the key to understanding our roles in this project, don't you think?"

"Our *project?*" he said.

"Well, yes. That's how I like to see it. We're collaborating toward achieving a tangible goal and we have guidelines and milestones to meet." She shifted to his side and held up her tablet so they could both get a look at the screen.

"If you'll allow me to go through my slide presentation, all will be explained."

He placed his hands on her shoulders in a sincere gesture. "I admire and respect you, Ellie, but I'm not going to sit through a long slide presentation that explains how to have sex."

"Oh, but this isn't about the *how*. It's more about the *why* and the *when* and the…well, if I can proceed?"

"Fine," he said, gritting his teeth. First time for everything, he told himself. And if it meant having her in his bed, he would force himself to listen. "Let her rip."

"Thank you. Now it's—"

"But I think you're stalling," he said, turning to her. "Believe me, I know my duties and responsibilities. I know how to deliver my extremely healthy sperm the old-fashioned way. And I think we're both in agreement on what we want, right? So I'd say we're ready to get started." He brushed his knuckles slowly down her arm.

She swallowed carefully. "Ready. Oh, yes. Um." She shook her hair back and seemed to regroup. Gripping the tablet again, she said brightly, "That's all covered in item six. Let's just go over the others."

Before he could argue further, she slid her finger across the surface to reveal the first slide. Aidan's eyes were inexorably drawn to the screen. Damned if she hadn't come up with a full-bore bullet point agenda covering his duties and responsibilities, right down to his diet preferences and clothing choices. Some experts thought that the correct choices in both areas were essential toward making his sperm more motile.

The woman's responsibilities were just as eye-opening. There were estrogen hormone levels to be tested and she would have to monitor her temperature. And then there was something called the luteal phase, which caused a little chill to run up his spine. The very word sounded vaguely sinister.

It was all strangely mesmerizing, like a traffic accident on a California freeway. Gruesome and shocking, but he couldn't look away.

The last page was a month-by-month production schedule. Ellie gave him a moment to review it, then said, "I don't have my calendar with me, but luckily, I've already memorized the days."

"Luckily," he muttered, then decided he'd waited long enough. She continued to speak as he leaned in and kissed her neck.

She gasped, then moaned. He moved his lips to her earlobe, then down to her shoulder. After a long moment, she tried to continue. "I'm s-scheduled to start ovulating in the next five to seven d-days, so if you can arrange your schedule, we should have s-sex beginning Friday night and… and…oh, my…continuing through the following Wednesday night, with S-Sunday and Monday being the most optimum days."

He took the tablet and set it down on the table. He'd seen enough. More than enough. Talk about information overload. His eyes were bleeding.

He appreciated that Ellie was ultra-organized, but it was time to lighten things up, even if it meant throwing a wrench or two into her well-ordered plans.

"Only at night?" he wondered, as he urged her closer and ran his hands slowly along her spine, down to her supple bottom. "What about the mornings?"

"Mornings?" she said on a soft sigh. "What do you mean?"

"Some would argue it's the best time of the day for what you have in mind."

"Oh, but—"

"Or lunchtime," he said, leaning back to stare into her eyes. "Sex in the office might be fun, Ellie. We can use my conference table."

"Now you're teasing me."

"You think so?" he said. Her expression was so vulnerable, so earnest, that he wanted to ease her into bed—or onto the dining room table—right here and now. In fact, that was a damn good idea.

"Aidan, I don't think you're listening. This is important."

"I'm listening," he assured her as he slipped his arm around her shoulders and walked her over to the couch, where he urged her to sit down with him. "But for now, let's skip to the bottom line. I'll help you get pregnant and I'll help provide for your child. You'll have a partnership with Sutherland Corp. and stay here on Alleria. We'll have contracts drawn up that specify all the points you've talked about."

"Well, yes, but there's more to discuss."

"The thing is, Ellie, I don't think we should be too rigid about this. After all, we don't want to put too much pressure on you."

"Pressure?" she said, then frowned. "Do you think I'm being rigid? Be honest."

"Of course not," he said, absently skimming his thumb along the soft skin of her arm. "It's smart to cover all the bases."

"Thanks. I think so, too, and I'm glad you agree."

"Good. But as long as we're covering bases, I think waiting until Friday is problematic. It would be better to get started right away."

She considered that little bombshell. "But it won't be any use if the timing isn't right."

"But think about it, Ellie," he said. "You're going to be nervous all the way from now until next Friday night, and that's never a good thing. It'll take a lot of pressure off you if we started practicing right away." Damn, that was a good one, Aidan thought to himself. "That way, next week when the timing is critical, we'll know what we're doing. We'll be ahead of the game."

She stared up at him. "Something tells me you already know what you're doing."

"I do," he said helpfully. "But I'm not the one we're concerned about. You are. And there's something else you might not have considered."

Frowning, she said, "What's that?"

"You probably ought to decide what kind of sex you'd like to have the first time. Plenty of experts say that that's the key to assuring that the entire...*project* goes well."

Her eyes narrowed with doubt. "Why does that matter?"

"It goes a long way toward dispelling the nervousness factor," he explained.

She bit her lip. "I'm afraid I don't have a lot of experience in differentiating the types."

"I do." He turned on the couch to face her so he could see her reactions. "I'll name off a few and you can decide where you'd like to start. There's funny sex, of course. Lots of laughs, no pressure, very relaxing. And there's romantic sex. You know, a little champagne, roses, soft jazz in the background."

"Oh, I like that," she whispered.

"Yeah, that's a crowd pleaser," he said, warming up to his subject. "And then you've got your naughty sex."

She swallowed carefully. "I'm not sure about that one."

"We'll try it out so you can be sure though, right?"

"Um..."

"There are plenty of other choices, too," he continued nonchalantly. "And once you've decided on a type, there are additional factors to consider. Like style, for instance.

Do you want it slow and easy? Fast and hot? Break the glass sex? Swing from the ceiling sex?"

Slowly but surely, the color of her cheeks had turned a deep rose. So he'd managed to excite her a little. He hoped so, hoped she was as turned on by this conversation as he was.

He had to discreetly adjust himself as she licked her lips. "Some of those sound complicated. And dangerous."

"I'll make sure we're perfectly safe." He took her hand in his. "Look, why don't you let me be in charge of those decisions. At least in the beginning."

She let out a sigh of relief. "I would appreciate that."

"And we'll start Tuesday night."

"But that's the day after tomorrow."

"Right," he said. "My place. Eight o'clock."

Alarmed, she stared at him. "But that's too soon."

"I don't think so," he said, smoothing a strand of her hair back behind her ear. "In fact, I think we should get a few preliminaries out of the way right now. After all, practice makes perfect."

And with that, he covered her mouth with his in a kiss that she met with such need and all-consuming heat, he wondered if he would survive until Tuesday.

Aidan was right about one thing, Ellie thought on Tuesday, as she struggled to pay attention to her notes on a new contract. She was going to be nervous until the deed was done. Maybe it really was better that they'd decided to start having sex right away. She would hate to feel so jangled up in knots for another full week.

So, yeah, she thought. Good thing she was having sex tonight. With Aidan. At eight o'clock. Tonight. Oh, mercy.

She had almost thought they'd get the whole thing started the other night when he'd come to her house. The way he had looked at her after her shower had almost turned the cool water on her skin to steam. And the way he'd described all those different types of sex? She knew he'd been goading her, but it had worked. And then he'd kissed her. She'd been so wound up, it was a wonder she hadn't jumped him right then and there, on her couch. In bright daylight.

Naughty sex? She exhaled heavily. She'd heard about naughty sex but had never experienced anything close to it. The two measly sexual encounters she'd had in the past could easily be placed at the farthest opposite end of the spectrum from naughty.

The first time had been a fumbling, blind-leading-the-blind failure. The second time wasn't much better. They were both with Teddy, her history study partner in college.

He had seemed like a nice guy in class, so she'd agreed to go out with him a few times. Their dates were pleasant so, even after his bumbling sexual attempts, she would've continued seeing him if she hadn't overheard him bragging to his friends a few days later. Teddy was so sure she would soon be drowning in the afterglow of his awesome lovemaking that he would be able to induce her to do all his homework from then on.

Seriously? Men could be very weird.

On the other hand, Ellie had no doubt that Aidan was an expert in all things naughty. She pictured his tanned hands sliding up her thighs to explore her deepest depths while his clever mouth rained kisses down her neck, along her breasts, across her stomach and farther down her body....

The contract notes were forgotten as she shoved her chair back from her desk and stood. And breathed. It wouldn't do to faint in her office in the middle of the afternoon. But gosh, she was anxious to get this over with. But, she amended, please don't have it be over too fast. He would make it last for a while, wouldn't he? Aidan would do what he could to make it pleasurable for her. Wouldn't he?

"Of course he will, you knucklehead," she muttered aloud. For heaven's sake, he was so sexy, so masculine, so sure of himself, it wouldn't take much effort at all for him to send her zooming straight to heaven.

Besides, none of the women she'd seen him with over the years had ever looked as though they were disappointed in his company. She frowned at that thought. Aidan had been with dozens of women. How was she going to measure up? Her experience was so small it hardly counted. This could be very embarrassing.

"But you're not in a relationship," she told herself. "This is business. Strictly business."

They were only going through with this *project* so that Ellie could get pregnant. Sending her shivering into ecstasy was not a necessary part of the agenda. Pregnancy was. That was the bottom line. And as a businesswoman, she was all about the bottom line.

But she shivered a little anyway, just thinking about Aidan in bed with her. Touching her. Kissing her. Nibbling her.

"Oh, God." She sucked in more deep breaths to calm herself down. Then, glancing back at her desk, she shook her head.

Aidan had been wrapped up in conference calls all day, so Ellie had honestly thought she would get a lot of work done today. But no. She was useless. The contract would have to wait another day. She was going to go home and pamper herself and get ready for her big night. In bed. With Aidan.

Rolling her eyes at her own foolishness, she grabbed her purse and left the office.

The scene was set for romantic sex.

Aidan glanced around the living room of his penthouse suite and approved of what he saw. He had always been a romantic guy and enjoyed the trappings that went along with it. So he felt confident as he instructed his catering guy where to place the ice bucket and the dessert he'd selected for tonight.

If there was one thing Aidan Sutherland knew how to do, it was set the scene for sex. But this time, he had to admit, he was really enjoying himself, picturing Ellie walking in and seeing all this. Candlelight, champagne on ice, chocolate mousse with whipped cream for dessert, soft, sultry jazz playing low in the background, dozens of roses and star lilies arranged in different vases around the suite.

The doorbell rang and he strolled over to open the door. And couldn't help but smile. Her hair was lifted up off her neck with a few wavy tendrils curling down. He'd never seen her wear her hair like that, but it suited her and made him glad he'd decided to dwell on romance tonight. She wore sexy, strappy sandals and was dressed in a short, colorful sarong-style skirt that wrapped around her waist and a thin turquoise top that accentuated her breasts.

That's how Aidan saw it anyhow. Now that he'd seen her in that bikini, he was pretty sure everything she wore from now on would accentuate her breasts.

"You made it," he said, swinging the door wide to let her in.

She smiled. "Did you think I wouldn't?"

He closed the door behind her. "You looked a little preoccupied in the office today. I wondered if you might be having second thoughts."

No," she said with a firm nod. "This is the plan we agreed on and I'm ready to go through with it."

He pursed his lips in a twisted grin. "There's no firing squad in here, Ellie. You can relax. In fact, I've got just the thing to help us both unwind." He led her over to the dining area, where he popped open the bottle of champagne and poured them both a glass.

"To…success," he said, raising his glass to her.

She laughed and clicked her glass against his. "To success." She took a sip of the bubbly liquid and said, "It's wonderful."

He took a sip and observed her over the rim of his glass. "You look beautiful."

She smiled with pleasure. "Thank you. So do you."

"Thank you," he said with a grin. She was normally so competent and sure of herself, but now her gaze flitted around, clearly indicating she was nervous. She finished the champagne quickly and he filled her glass again.

"Well," she said, after another sip. "Better." As she continued to glance here and there, it seemed to dawn on her that things were a little different. "Oh, you did something."

"Yes." He stood by the table and enjoyed watching her make her discoveries.

"Everything looks so nice. You have candles. Oh, and flowers. So many." She wandered over to the fireplace mantle where the largest vase of roses had been placed. "They're so pretty. Did you do all this for me?"

"You seemed to like the idea of a little romance."

"I do." Her eyes were shining and her mouth was curved in a smile he wanted to taste. "I really do."

"I aim to please," he said easily. "Let's start over here." He crossed the room to meet her halfway. Taking hold of her arm, he led her back to the table.

"Here, try some of this." He took the cover off a silver bowl filled with chocolate mousse and dipped the spoon in. He added a small dollop of whipped cream and raised it to her lips. "Tell me what you think."

"Oh. Oh." Her eyes closed as she savored the taste. Her tongue lapped at a bit of chocolate on her lip. Aidan's stomach muscles twisted in a dark coil of desire and he grew rock hard as he watched her expression turn to one of rapture. "It's heaven."

When she opened her eyes, he put the spoon down. "I'm sorry, Ellie, but there's something we need to take care of right now."

Five

"Oh," she said, blinking as if she were coming awake after a long nap. "About what? Our custody agreement? Aidan, you don't have to worry. I already took care of that. It's been signed and sent back to the lawyers."

"Good, but this has nothing to do with that. This is about…this." He took one more step closer and covered her lips with his in a kiss so tender, so sensual, so much sweeter than any chocolate, he found himself in danger of losing it right there. He clamped on tight to his control because there was no way he was stopping now.

"Just had to get that out of the way," he muttered, running his fingers along the side of her face, his desire to touch her more urgent than the need to breathe.

"Okay," she whispered and swayed a little unsteadily. "Okay. Good. Practice. Like you said. Probably a good idea, really. Makes perfect sense." She licked her lips and stared up at him.

That was enough to push Aidan into going for more. The taste of her lingered on his mouth, like a fine wine that made you thirsty for more.

He pulled her close for another kiss, then changed angles and used his tongue to urge her lips open. She wrapped her arms around his neck and pressed herself against him, her fresh scent surrounding him as her soft curves molded to his hardness. He kept his hold on her gentle while his tongue plunged and wrestled with hers in a sensuous dance that left him on a dangerous edge. He wanted to go deeper, taste more of her sweetness, more of her essence, more of everything.

"More," he murmured, and moved his hand to graze the smooth arc of her breast. His mouth returned to hers, claiming her for his own with another mind-numbing kiss so hot it felt as if he were branding her. Or maybe it was the other way around.

"Yes," she answered, holding on to his waist in an effort to press herself even closer to him. It was a possessive move that he enjoyed way too much. He wanted her even closer, but that wouldn't happen as long as they were both wearing so many clothes.

Taking a step back from her, he grabbed the hem of her top and lifted it up and off in one smooth move. She reached out and did the same with his shirt, tossing it aside.

"Better," she said greedily, and splayed her hands against his bare chest.

He laughed, but the sound emerging from his throat was raw with need. "Almost." He untied the knot at her waist and her skirt slid down her legs to pool on the floor around her feet. He held her arm to steady her as she stepped out of her clothes and slipped off her flirty sandals, ending up in only a lacy pink bra and a tiny matching thong.

"Much better," he managed to say.

As he encouraged her, she seemed to gain more confidence. Now she tentatively hooked her thumbs under the thin straps of her panties and then glanced up at him.

"Yes," he said.

She pulled them down slowly, her gaze fixed on him all the while.

He hadn't thought he could get any more rigid, but he was wrong. In a rush now, he grasped her petite rear with both hands and hoisted her up into his arms. Their mouths met in a frenzy of heat as he walked into the large master suite with her arms clinging to his shoulders.

He knelt on the end of the bed and laid her on the cool linen, then followed her down. With both hands, he brushed her hair back from her face and then ran his palms along her jaw, her throat, her shoulders. When he reached her breasts, he cupped their warm softness and rubbed her pink nipples with his thumbs, causing her to moan with pleasure.

"Beautiful," he whispered and bent down to take her in his mouth, first one breast, then the other, licking, sucking and nibbling as Ellie writhed with delight. Her hands grabbed his shoulders and held him tightly as she moaned her approval.

Sensation soared through him like a heat-seeking missile. His body was hard and aching and he yearned to release himself within her heated depths, but knew it was more important and ultimately more fulfilling to bring her to pleasure first. Mainly because it brought him so much pleasure to touch her like this. Especially her breasts. He couldn't get enough of them.

Truth be told, he'd been thinking about her for two long days and dreaming of this moment for two damn nights. Hell, longer really, if he was being honest. He'd spent most of his time in California dwelling on her. And that was before he'd seen her taking that erotic shower in her bikini.

And now he couldn't get enough of her. And unless he'd missed his mark it was obvious that Ellie felt the same way.

Okay, maybe her true motive was to get the baby she'd always wanted, but she was still enjoying herself.

He wasn't ready to think about her need for a family of her own. Right here and right now was all that mattered. This was real, he thought, as he ran his tongue over her delectable nipples. Sex was real. Ellie's lush body was real. Her staying on the island was real.

Aidan raised his head to look at her and saw her smiling at him. Something twitched in his chest, something warm and unfamiliar that was probably hazardous to his health. He would have to think about that later. Right now, the need to taste her again was overwhelming and he stretched up to meet her mouth with his in a sizzling kiss. As their tongues linked and tangled together, he slid his hand down the length of her body. Her skin was smooth and slightly damp from their exertions and he wanted to savor every inch of it.

He could feel her heart beating in time with his own, could feel her anticipation spike as he moved his hand across her thigh. As he touched her most sensitive skin, she moaned and pressed up against his hand, urging him to touch her everywhere. He strained to control his own needs, but he was on dangerous ground as he entered her warm core and heard her gasp.

"Please, Aidan, please," she said, writhing with pleasure as he stroked her, stoking her heat again and again.

He glanced up at her. "Please what, baby?"

"I want you inside me now," she cried. "Now."

With a feral grin, he moved to his knees to comply with her demand. Spreading her legs, he entered her in one swift move, covering himself to the hilt.

She gasped and clutched his shoulders. "Oh, yes."

"Oh, yeah," he muttered gutturally in response, as he thrust once again to embed himself even more deeply within her tight, lush folds. After a moment, he began to move, slowly at first, deliberately, inexorably, the sweet friction building pressure as he pushed himself into her warmth, then out.

He kissed her again, sweeping in with his tongue to parlay with hers. The provocative movement mirrored their more primal rhythms, pushing him relentlessly to the edge each time, before he was able to reel himself back with what was left of his ragged control.

She gasped with joy, giving him the strength to rally, and with one last burst of power, he plunged again, and again, impaling her with more sensual force than he'd ever been capable of before. As she screamed his name, he thrust inside her one last time, then fell to earth and into her welcoming arms.

Outside, the tropical air was hushed and still. In Aidan's room, Ellie could hear only the sound of their breathing, heavy and tattered, and the soft whirring of the ceiling fan above the bed. Despite her near exhaustion, Ellie was exhilarated. She wanted to burst into song, although most sexual etiquette books would probably frown on that.

She lay on her back and stared up at the ceiling fan, feeling dazed and confused in all the best ways. Who in a million years would've ever believed that she would wind up having incredible, mind-blowing sex with Aidan Sutherland? Not Ellie. Heck, not anyone who knew them. Yet here she was, damp, spent and completely enthralled by what they had just done together.

And before she went spiraling down into a dark place, she quickly told herself that *enthrallment* just meant that she'd had fun. That was all. It didn't mean she would suddenly become obsessed with him, for goodness sake. This was business. Or rather, pre-business.

Tonight was merely a practice run for later when she

would be ovulating, at which time she would hopefully get pregnant. But that didn't mean that what they'd done tonight didn't qualify as amazing and exciting. True, she didn't have a lot of empirical data to compare it to, but she was willing to bet that their lovemaking could match up to anyone else's on the wildest side of the wild scale.

As Aidan turned onto his side and wrapped his arms around her, her heart swelled. He had been so generous, so caring, so thoughtful. So sexy. So forceful and compelling.

She had expected sex with Aidan to be fun. She hadn't expected it to be so deep, so intense, so shattering to her heart and soul. And didn't that spell trouble? Probably so. But she figured as long as she kept the thought tucked in a corner of her mind that this was essentially a business arrangement, she knew she would be able to control her emotions.

"I can tell you're thinking too much," he murmured. "Let's have none of that."

"But it's all good thoughts," she assured him. "I feel good."

"Yes, you do," he said, rolling up onto his elbow and eyeing her as a panther would eye a doe.

Without a word, he dipped his head down and licked her breast, causing her to moan in response. He took her nipple into his mouth and tormented her with his lips, tongue and teeth.

"I have to have you again," he said.

She ran her fingers through his hair, then latched on and pressed him to her breast. "Yes, please," she said.

A while later, she struggled to lift her head off his chest. "Was that naughty sex?"

He chuckled. "Officially speaking, tonight we're featuring romantic sex."

"Romantic sex," she murmured. "I like it. Although I really think I'll like naughty sex, too."

"I'm sure you will," he said, and reached out to nip at her earlobe with his teeth. He licked the tender skin, then moved along her jawline, kissing and nibbling as he went. "Let's be sure to work on that one later in the week."

She shivered. "I'd like that." Experimenting, she reached down and stroked his length, tentatively at first, then with confidence as he grew more rigid in her hand.

"I like that, too," he muttered, gritting his teeth.

"You don't mind?" she whispered.

"I'll mind a lot more if you stop."

"Good," she said as she continued learning every inch of him. She wanted him in every way, wanted to experience more of him, all of him.

And what was wrong with that? she thought. *Want* wasn't the same as *need,* right? Right. She would simply enjoy herself for as long as she was able to. It didn't mean she was obsessed; it meant she was having fun.

Besides, enjoying herself, relaxing, was essential if she was trying to get pregnant. And pregnancy was the ultimate goal. Once she'd achieved that, she would deal with the myriad feelings and worries. For now, she would concentrate on enjoying sex with Aidan.

Stretching up to meet his gaze, she said, "I like the way you feel."

"Feeling's mutual," he was barely able to utter. And then he didn't speak at all.

An hour later, she stirred beside him.

"I should go," she whispered.

"No," he said, surprising them both.

It meant nothing, he reasoned, only that he wanted her in his bed for a while longer. Why not? Their connection was strictly physical. His heart was not engaged, only his libido. That made it okay for her to stay. At least, that's what he told himself because it couldn't be anything more than sex, right? The greatest sex of his life, for sure, but still, it was just sex.

And besides, it was just one night. Everything would go back to normal tomorrow.

"Stay," he urged, ignoring the warmth spreading through his chest, dangerously close to his heart. He wrapped his arms around her and gathered her close so that her curvy backside was pressed against him temptingly. "A few more minutes won't matter."

The next day, Aidan was too busy to leave his office so he didn't run into Ellie at all. He had hoped she would stop by at some point during the day, only because she was his right-hand man...person. They always had business to discuss.

But he didn't buzz her and ask her to come by because, well, he didn't want to seem too eager to see her. Even though, truth be told, he couldn't wait to see her again.

"Great. It's already getting weird," he muttered, scowling at his coffee mug.

He pushed away from the desk and poured himself another cup of coffee. Yeah, it was getting weird, and it was all on him.

He'd originally suggested helping Ellie out so that her child would grow up knowing its father and so he wouldn't have to run his business without her. And yeah, okay, there was that little issue of wanting Ellie in his bed more than just about anything. But now that he'd scratched that itch, so to speak, he should've been over this feeling of constant need for her. Instead, he found himself thinking about her too much, wanting her too much.

So yeah, the weirdness was all coming from him. Idiot.

"It's just sex," he said under his breath. And therein lay

the problem. He hadn't had a good, healthy bout of wild sex in a long time, so naturally, he was still thinking about it. The fact that he'd had that wild sex with *Ellie* wasn't the issue. He would've felt this way about anyone.

Good. Problem solved. He wasn't as big an idiot as he thought he was.

It was no big deal. They were both having a good time. Eventually, Ellie would get her baby. Aidan would achieve his goal of keeping her child from growing up without the support of one of his parents. And Ellie would stay on the island, which meant that the Sutherland Corporation would continue to operate at the same high level of efficiency that Aidan and Logan and their investors had come to expect.

And that meant that all of this wild sex was a win-win for everyone.

Yeah, that was his story and he was sticking to it.

Good. He'd worked it all out, so now he could get back to concentrating on business. He had a load of work to get through today and he was going to stay in the office all night if he had to in order to get it done. He didn't have time to dwell on Ellie's extremely hot body, her shapely thighs or her magnificent breasts, or the startling image of her clever hands wrapped around his—

"Stop that," he berated himself aloud. Taking in a deep, bracing breath, he let it out slowly. "Now get back to work."

Ellie re-read the custody agreement one more time. The lawyers had sent her a fully executed original and since she'd already signed it, she was satisfied with it. It was a done deal. But she still couldn't quite believe Aidan had agreed to go through with it, so she'd decided to read the document again, just to make sure. And oddly enough, just reading the legalities of what Aidan had consented to do for her made Ellie feel even closer to him, somehow. Oh, they were definitely closer now that they were having sex, and that was wonderful. But this agreement made her feel even closer to him on a vital, life-giving level.

They had agreed on many of the essential points she had listed in her slide presentation and most of those items had been integrated into this legal document. But Aidan had fought back persuasively on a few of the others. He simply hadn't been willing to relinquish all his claims to Ellie's future baby.

He wanted to be listed as the father on the child's birth certificate and Ellie was in complete agreement with that. A child should know who her father was, right? Even if that father wanted nothing to do with her.

Ellie rubbed her arms to ward off the chill that that thought brought. Even though her own father had cut off all ties with her and her sister, that didn't mean that Ellie's own child would ever experience that same level of hurt and confusion. No, her child would always know that she was completely loved and wanted by Ellie. They were a complete family, just the two of them. But now Aidan wanted to play a tiny part, too, and she had decided that that was fine. After all, once the baby was here, she didn't expect him to be much more than a friendly visitor in their lives.

But Aidan had surprised her again by requesting a more liberal visitation arrangement than she had originally proposed. Of course, since her original idea was that there be no visitation at all, no connection between her child and Aidan or his family, she supposed she couldn't blame him for asking for a little more leniency on that item.

Still, Ellie had argued with herself on that one. After all, some anonymous sperm donor wouldn't be given those rights, would they? No, of course not. But since it was Aidan and since his family was so lovely, she couldn't find it in her heart to fight him. Besides, they would all be living on

Alleria so it would be pretty hard to avoid having her child run into its father from time to time. Better to be upfront about all of this from the get-go.

But then Aidan had insisted on supporting her and her child monetarily, too. Ellie had tried to turn him down, but he had persisted. She'd pointed out that it was odd for a man who had no interest in children to be so adamant about supporting this child. Aidan had brushed it off as being something any man would do, but Ellie knew he was wrong about that.

Finally, Aidan had included a clause that stated that he intended to rewrite his will to include the child, which, in the privacy of her office, had moved Ellie to tears. She had never expected that level of generosity and support, especially from a man who, let's face it, had only offered to father her child to keep her on the island. That's what she'd originally thought, anyway. Clearly, she was wrong about him in more ways than one.

The following morning, Ellie decided that this must be her week for signing personal legal documents. Soon after she arrived at her office, her assistant dropped a thick, padded envelope on top of her inbox. It was her copy of the Sutherland partnership agreement Aidan had promised her. How he had been able to have the lawyers write it up so quickly was a mystery to her, but she'd read it over carefully, called the lawyer to clarify a few issues, then signed it the next day.

Unable to hold in her excitement, she checked that her secretary wasn't watching, then jumped in the air and clicked her heels with joy. She was now a partner in the Sutherland Corporation! She clutched the document to her heart and tried to hold back the happy tears trying to escape her eyes. It wouldn't do to burst into waterworks in the office, but this was a moment worth savoring. After all, it seemed that so many of her dreams were coming true. A fabulous career advancement, a baby someday soon, and hot sex with her fantasy man.

This called for a celebration. She brushed her hair and added a touch of lip gloss to her lips, then walked down the hall to Aidan's office.

"Are you busy?" she said when he opened the door.

"Always," he said, but since he was smiling and holding the door open, she walked in.

"I wanted to thank you," she said.

"For what?"

She threw her arms up in the air and whirled around. "It's official, I'm a partner! Thank you so much, Aidan. I won't let you down."

He stood there grinning at her, so she hugged him before she could think too much about it.

"It's probably not very businesslike, but I was sitting in my office staring at my signature on the partnership agreement, and realized I just had to share my happiness with someone. I thought of you."

"I'm happy, too, Ellie. And so is Logan. We're both thrilled to have you on board. And we know you won't let us down. You could never do that. You're our right-hand man."

"Woman," she amended.

"Person," he said, and they both laughed. It was an old routine, but she loved it.

They stared at each other in amusement for a long moment. Ellie turned speculative as Aidan's eyes turned a smoldering gray and narrowed in on her. It wasn't the first time she'd felt like she was staring into the eyes of a sexy, too-tempting-for-words predator.

They stayed frozen in place for a few charged seconds, then both of them took one step toward the other and in an instant, his mouth was covering hers in a kiss so incendiary, it was a miracle she didn't burst into flames.

He let her go, sucked in a deep breath, then ripped his jacket off and loosened his tie. As he grabbed at the buttons of his shirt, he dashed to the door, slammed it shut and locked it. "Take off your clothes."

He didn't have to ask her twice. Her shoes, gray linen slacks and pink panties were already strewn on the floor. She was halfway out of her blouse when he grabbed her and hefted her up into his arms. She wrapped her legs around his waist and they kissed again.

"This is going to be fast and hot," he warned her, his rugged body tight with coiled tension.

"Then what are you waiting for?"

He laughed, took a quick glance around and said, "Over there." He rushed her to the wall behind his desk and pressed her back up against the smooth surface.

"Take me," he muttered, holding her steady as she slid down his torso and took his hot, hard arousal inside her so deeply, she cried out.

"Did I hurt you?" he asked immediately.

"No. God, no," she assured him, her eyelids fluttering from the blissful impact. "You just feel so good."

He kissed her hungrily. "So do you."

She began the slow glide up and down, moaning as each thrust touched her more deeply, more thoroughly than anything had ever touched her before.

With her back pressed against the wall, her breasts jutted out at him, teasing him to distraction. He made a quick adjustment in order for his mouth to reach out and feast on her, feeling a hot blast of satisfaction as her nipples tightened in response. He used his tongue to lick and suck them until he had her shuddering in his arms.

He took over for her, grabbing hold of her buttocks and

holding her firmly as he plundered her moist core with hard, slow, thrusts, doubling the gratification for both of them. He moved faster, went deeper, harder, pushing into her with a savage fervor that nearly drove him to the brink of madness. His mind blanked out and pure sensation took over. When Ellie cried out his name, he buried himself inside her with one final thrust and tumbled with her into the sweet void.

Replete with pleasure, unable to move, they stood against the wall hanging on to each other like drunken sailors for several long minutes.

Aidan finally found the strength to carry Ellie across the office to the leather couch, where they sprawled beside each other in full naked splendor. Ellie didn't have the energy to cover herself, but figured Aidan wouldn't mind.

"Now that's a first," he said after a while, still trying to catch his breath.

"I take it that was naughty sex," she whispered, amazed that she was able to speak, let alone string words together to make a full sentence.

"No, that was office sex," he said, then considered his words for a moment. "Which is inherently naughty, I think."

Ellie considered their nakedness and the sight of all their clothing spread across his office carpet. She was still struggling for breath, but now she knew it wasn't just from the activity of moments before. Had a line been crossed here? Her heart was pumping faster and her throat was all tangled up. Too many emotions were zinging through her to allow her to think straight. She'd never felt anything like this before, but there was no way she could say any of that aloud. *Keep it light,* she cautioned herself. "This definitely qualifies as naughty."

He rolled over and kissed her, then reached to fondle her breasts. "Did you like it?"

"I did," she said, trembling from his touch. "I liked it very much."

"Good. Me, too," he said, easing her up and over until she was lying on top of him, bringing him back to life. "So now that we've had naughty office sex, I say we move on to *Congratulations, Partner* sex."

Six

Aidan and Ellie had been sleeping together for a week when Logan and his new bride returned from their honeymoon.

The following day was Logan's first day back at work. He was sitting at Aidan's desk checking the computer while Aidan riffled through the file cabinet on the far wall, when Ellie walked in.

"Welcome back, Logan," Ellie said cheerfully, and rounded the desk to give him a hug before dropping a document on the desk. "I hope you and Grace had a wonderful honeymoon."

"It was fantastic."

"I'm so happy for you," she said, then turned to Aidan. "I'm making that New York phone call in thirty minutes."

"Thank you."

Both men watched her walk out of the office; then Aidan said, "I know we talked about offering Ellie the partnership when you got back, but something came up while you were gone. I made her the offer last week and she accepted."

Logan frowned at Aidan. "Did you notice that Ellie knew it was me sitting here?"

"So?" Aidan said absently as he picked up the document Ellie had delivered.

Logan glanced down at his dark navy business suit, burgundy silk tie and white shirt, then stared across at his brother, who wore the same basic outfit. "I'm sitting at your desk, dressed exactly like you. Anyone in the company would think I *was* you. But Ellie knew it was me."

Aidan gave him a sideways glance. "Ellie's smart. She's been able to tell us apart from day one. No big deal."

Logan stared long and hard at Aidan. "Oh, hell. You're having sex with her! Are you out of your mind?"

Aidan scowled and told himself he never should have let his brother walk into his office. "Where the hell did you get that idea?"

"We're twins, remember?" Logan said. "I can read you like a book. A really *stupid* book with a lousy plotline."

"Get serious." Aidan's gaze slid from his twin's. He never had been able to hide a damn thing from Logan. But damned if he was going to stand here and be lectured. "There's nothing going on. How in the hell did you come up with sex?"

"Easy," Logan said as he pulled two small bottles of sparkling water from the small refrigerator in the credenza along the wall. He popped the tops, handed one to Aidan and walked back to the desk. "And I'm right, too, so stop pretending it's not true."

Aidan took a long gulp of water and tried to figure out why he'd been so anxious for Logan to get home.

His brother wasn't finished ranting. "And what was that about offering Ellie the partnership? Don't you remember we talked about doing it together when I got back from my trip? You couldn't wait?"

"I told you, something came up," Aidan muttered.

"Yeah, I know exactly what came up," Logan said with an evil smirk.

"That's not what I mean," he said, and grabbed a bag of chips from the supplies cupboard to munch on.

A few minutes ago, Aidan had been pleased to see Logan at his office door. He and Grace had been back on the island since the day before, but Aidan hadn't had a chance to talk to Logan until this morning. But right now, Aidan was kind of wishing his brother would take off for another week or two.

This was the problem with being a twin. He couldn't get a damn thing past his brother.

Annoyed with the direction their conversation was heading, Aidan paced back and forth across the office floor. Finally he turned to his brother and explained things in a reasonable tone of voice. "Ellie was making plans to leave the island for a few weeks. I had to do something to stop her."

"So you slept with her?" Logan shook his head. "That was your plan?"

"No. I mean, yes. But that's not why." He scraped his fingers across his scalp in frustration. "It's a long story."

Logan sat in one of the comfortable visitor's chairs and stretched out his long legs. "I've got all day."

Aidan huffed out a breath. "It's complicated."

"Dude, it wasn't complicated until you slept with her."

Irritation spiked. Yeah, he and Logan had always talked together about the women in their lives. But he didn't like Logan talking about Ellie. "Just shut up about that, will you?"

"She's an employee," Logan pointed out. "You're putting the company in a bad position. What if she sues you? Did you consider the possible consequences? You know she could—"

"Stop." Aidan held up his hand. "I'll ignore the fact that

you slept with Grace when she was working here as a cocktail waitress."

He was happy to see his brother frown as that realization sunk into his thick skull.

"She was a fake waitress," Logan mumbled.

"Right. Look, Ellie's a partner now, not an employee. But just in case you're still worried, don't be. She and I signed a contract before we did anything."

Logan jumped up from his chair and gaped at his brother. "What did you say? You signed a contract for sex? What the hell is going on around here?"

"What the hell do you have to be mad about?" Aidan shouted. "This isn't about you."

"If it's about Sutherland, then it's about me, too, you idiot."

"Fine." Aidan scrubbed one hand across his face, took a swig of water and muttered, "The contract wasn't about sex, all right? It's for a baby."

Logan opened his mouth to retort, but no words came out. He took a breath, blew it out and then blinked a few times as if his twin was just a hallucination he was trying to bring into focus. Funny. Aidan had never actually seen Logan speechless. He kind of liked it.

"Well, that shut you up anyway." Aidan handed him the bag of potato chips and continued his pacing.

A full minute later, Logan found his voice again. "I think you'd better sit down and tell me the whole story."

"That went well," Aidan muttered at the end of the day. What with all the interruptions and conference calls and business meetings, his conversation with Logan had stretched out over the entire day, and Logan had just left the office to take Grace to dinner. He'd invited Aidan to join them, but Aidan had declined. He had too much to think about. So instead, he went and grabbed a cheeseburger and fries from the bar, then headed back to his place to watch a football game.

He took a bite of the perfectly prepared burger and savored the flavors, marveling that he still had an appetite after hashing it out with his brother. Aidan had patiently explained everything to Logan. He had defended himself valiantly, making it clear that desperate times called for heroic efforts and that's why Aidan had finally decided to help Ellie get pregnant.

His brother hadn't seen it quite the same way. Far from it, in fact. Not to put too fine a point on it, but Logan had basically laughed his fool ass off.

"Heroic efforts?" he'd said derisively. "Man, you're killing me."

"I mean it," Aidan had insisted. "How else could I guarantee that she'd stay here and work for us? I fell on my sword, man. I made the ultimate sacrifice for the corporation."

He frowned at that, because as swords went, Ellie was a pretty damn good one. And it wasn't as if he'd had to suffer to keep their most valued employee at the resort.

Logan snorted, not an attractive sound. "You *sacrificed* yourself by having sex with Ellie? How the hell is that a sacrifice? She's gorgeous! You like her."

"Wha— Of course I like her," he sputtered. "A lot. She's a good friend. She wants to have a baby and I want that baby to know its father. I wasn't going to let her go off to some sperm bank and then raise a kid all on her own."

Logan chuckled. "Oh man, you've got it bad. Hell, you've been half in love with her ever since she started working here."

Aidan's eyes narrowed on his brother. "What did you just say?"

"Oh, just admit it," Logan said, ignoring Aidan's threatening glare. "Remember when you introduced her to that idiot Blake, then got completely pissed off when they started dating? You're so transparent, it's ridiculous. So now you're finally sleeping with her. It's not such a stretch to predict that you'll fall in love with her. Especially if you have a child together."

Aidan had to shake his head a few times to make sure his ears were really hearing those words. "Okay, you just went off the deep end, bro."

"Say whatever you want in your own defense," Logan drawled. "But I'm telling you, you did all this because you love her."

Ridiculous.

Seriously, it was sad to see how fast Logan's brain had turned to sludge after his wedding.

"Oh, man. Oh, no. Dude, you're pathetic," Aidan had said, hanging his head in sorrow. "Barely one day back from your honeymoon and you're already deluded into thinking the whole world's in love. Birdies singing in the trees, rainbows dancing in the sky, unicorns frolicking in the jungle. Snap out of it, man. You're embarrassing both of us."

Logan held up both hands. "I'm just telling it like I see it."

"I'd get my vision checked if I were you."

Logan had laughed uproariously and shortly after that, he'd taken off to meet Grace.

It was a new low in brotherly accusations, Aidan thought as he took another bite of his fully loaded cheeseburger. He still couldn't believe his own brother had charged him with being in love with Ellie. It was worse than pitiable. It was a sad, sad cliché. Now that Logan had gone and gotten married, he wanted everyone else to be in love. Well, good luck with that.

Aidan shook his head again, feeling nothing but sorry for

Logan. He felt sorry for Grace, too, because his brother was clearly in need of psychiatric care.

On the other hand, he mused, Logan was right about one thing. Ellie was gorgeous. Of course, Logan had no idea just how gorgeous since he wasn't the one who'd seen her in that bikini. A good thing, too, because Aidan would have to kill him if he had.

That had nothing to do with love, by the way, he assured himself. That was just pure male defensive action. No man wanted other guys checking out the woman he was… Aidan frowned. The woman he was currently having sex with. Right. That's all it was.

The image of Ellie in her dripping wet bikini halted his thought process for a few minutes before he managed to get his mind back to the subject at hand. Logan and his wacko thinking.

Yes, his brother was right when he said that Aidan *liked* Ellie. Why wouldn't he? They had worked together closely for four years now, and Ellie traveled with Aidan any time they went to meet with investors. The two of them agreed on almost everything and had a great time together whenever they traveled together. Negotiations were always more fun when Ellie was there with him. Aidan loved watching her come up with all sorts of obscure facts and figures in an instant to impress the investors and their accountants.

Okay, Aidan didn't actually mean that he *loved* watching her do those tricks with numbers. He just meant that he *liked* it. He was *impressed* and *entertained* by her. That's all. He didn't mean *love*, as in *I love you*. He just meant…

"Oh hell, enough already," he muttered, and stuffed a French fry into his mouth. "Chill out. Jeez."

This was all Logan's fault. His brother had wigged out over the whole *love* issue and now Aidan was second-guessing every last word in his head.

Funny how Logan was the big "love expert" these days, considering that both of them had once felt the same way about that useless emotion. Part of their cynicism had come from the complete lack of love their mother had shown them and their father. But their scorn had grown with their life on the surfing circuit, where every woman they'd met had seemed more than willing to pledge her eternal love just to get close to the celebrated twin brothers. Love was a joke.

Hell, his brother had been even more scornful about love than Aidan, considering that the one time Logan had actually convinced himself he was in love, he'd gone and married a woman who had cheated on him to her dying day. She'd put on a good show, but she hadn't known the meaning of love, never mind commitment and faithfulness.

Of course, once Grace had come into Logan's life, he'd changed his mind about all of it. Grace was the real thing, and Aidan couldn't blame his brother for falling in love with her. But did that mean that Aidan had to follow in lockstep? Why would he bother to fall in love with one woman when he could have his choice of so many? It was a no-brainer.

Lately, of course, the only woman he was interested in was Ellie. They were having a good time together and would continue to do so as long as it lasted. Didn't mean he was in love, despite his brother's deranged insistence.

He never should've said anything to Logan. He had a feeling he was going to regret that lapse in judgment for a long time.

"Hell, I *love* this burger," Aidan exclaimed scornfully. Then he popped the last juicy bite into his mouth. "There. See? That's true love for you."

It was early in the morning two days later when Ellie walked to the office and came upon Grace digging in the hard sand around the base of a coco palm tree. The research scientist was dressed for gardening and wore a straw hat with a wide brim to protect her from the strong rays of the sun.

Ellie had become friends with Grace through Serena and Dee, a waitress who worked in the bar. Ellie called out a greeting and Grace waved, then jumped up to give her a hug.

"I haven't seen you in ages," Grace said. "Not since we got back from our honeymoon."

"I don't have to ask if you had a good time," Ellie said. "I can tell just by looking at you."

"It was heavenly," Grace admitted. "But I'll tell you all about it when we girls get together this weekend."

"Can't wait to hear all the details," Ellie said, then glanced around at the trees. "Are you out here hunting for more spores?"

Everyone knew that Grace had come to the island originally to collect the rare Allerian spores for her research. That's when she'd met Logan and they'd fallen in love.

"Yes, this area of the grove is riddled with the little darlings," Grace said, and glanced up at the sky. "Morning's the best time to find them, before the sun gets too hot. I've done all I can do today."

Ellie knew Grace loved her spores, and who could blame her? The Allerian spores had provided the means by which she had discovered several new methods for treating some of the worst diseases known to mankind.

"I'm so glad," Ellie said. "And I heard that your laboratory is almost finished."

"It is." Grace grinned. "Logan added a generous bonus to the deal if the men could get it finished ahead of schedule, so it'll be ready to move in next week. I'm thrilled, as you can imagine, and Logan went out and bought every piece of lab equipment ever created, so I can't wait to get to work."

"That's wonderful," Ellie said. "Your research is so important and it's such an honor to have you here with us."

"Oh, aren't you sweet?" Grace said. She glanced down at the ground where she'd left a basket filled with gloves and lab supplies. "Will you wait while I gather up my stuff? I'll walk with you to the office."

"I'd like that."

A minute later, the two women were headed toward the executive offices at the resort. Grace frowned thoughtfully at her friend. "You look different, Ellie."

"I do?" Ellie said, and laughed. "I'm not sure how to take that. Good different or bad different?"

"Definitely good," Grace assured her. "You look really happy."

"Do I?" Ellie said softly. "I guess that's because I am."

"It must be because of Aidan. Oh!" Grace slapped her hand over her mouth. "That's none of my business."

"I don't mind," Ellie said. "The island is like a small town, isn't it? Everyone knows everyone else's business. But I love it. And I like that I have friends who care about me enough to gossip behind my back."

Grace's eyes widened. "Oh, Ellie, we didn't… I mean, we wouldn't… Oh, dear. I'm embarrassed."

Ellie burst out laughing. "Are you kidding? Don't be. I love it. I didn't have many friends growing up, so now that I do, I love everything that goes along with having friends. Including gossip."

"Oh, but that's just wrong."

"Maybe," Ellie said, "but do you honestly believe we didn't talk about you while you were gone?"

Grace laughed. "I certainly hope you did. And you know, I don't mind at all. As long as nothing too vicious was said."

Ellie patted Grace's arm. "No one could ever say a vicious word about you."

"Same goes for you. I got your back, girlfriend."

They smiled in complete harmony.

"So that's cleared up," Grace said. "Now let's hear all about Aidan. What happened when. And how and why and where. Start at the beginning and don't stop until I've heard all the pertinent details."

Ellie laughed. She was so lucky to have girlfriends after so many years of hiding from people, that now she had no qualms at all about telling Grace everything. She told her about her spur-of-the-moment decision to start a family and the sperm bank and Aidan's offer and how she'd decided to take him up on it.

"I must say I agree with you on that point," Grace said. "A big, handsome man in the flesh beats the heck out of an anonymous turkey baster any day of the week."

"And Aidan is so wonderful," Ellie confided. "I'm seeing a side of him I never knew existed. He's funny and caring and kind and…well, I guess I knew he was all that, but it just seems that the more time I spend with him, the more I care about him."

She didn't add that it worried her, but it did. Her feelings seemed to grow stronger every day and if she wasn't careful, the little crush she'd always had on him could develop into a full-on love that she would never recover from. Just like her mother. It was the stupidest thing Ellie could possibly allow to happen.

And in case she'd forgotten, as soon as she became pregnant, their temporary situation would be over. Aidan wouldn't need to be with her anymore. There would be no reason to see him except during regular business hours. And though she knew it was for the best, that brought a little ache to Ellie's heart.

She'd known going into the deal that Aidan had no intention of going beyond what they'd agreed to do. Once she was pregnant, he would go back to dating the bikini babes who came to the island looking for some short-term action.

Aidan didn't believe in long-term relationships. He'd made that clear from the very beginning.

So right then and there, she renewed her vow to stay strong in the face of those feelings that could destroy her. Still, a tiny wishful part of her was just as determined to keep the dream going for as long as possible and pretend that she and Aidan were more than just temporary lovers.

She suddenly remembered it was Grace she was talking to and quickly added, "Oh, but Logan is wonderful, too, Grace. I just never had as much of a connection with him as I do with Aidan."

"I'm glad to hear it," Grace said with a light laugh. "Otherwise, I would've had to kill you."

At noon a few days later, Ellie walked down the hall to Logan's office, where she would join the brothers for their first private partners' lunch. Ellie was relieved that ever since Logan had returned from his honeymoon, he had welcomed her into the partnership with open arms.

Once they were seated and the catering crew had served their crab salads, Logan held up his glass of sparkling water and toasted her. "Welcome to the penthouse suite, Ellie."

"Yes, welcome," Aidan said. "Of course, since we're on the first floor you can't take that too literally."

It didn't really matter, Ellie thought, glancing around. Logan's office was the mirror image of Aidan's and was essentially a large hotel suite. It was furnished in a casually elegant style with modern furniture arranged to form a comfortable conversation area at one end of the room with a fully functioning office at the other. In between was a conference table and chairs where they were seated for their lunch.

The best part of the room was the view. One entire wall of sliding glass doors opened onto a private terrace. The view beyond the terrace was of the white sand beach and blue water of the bay. Graceful coco palm trees swayed in the breeze.

As the three of them began to eat, Logan led the conversation. "I don't know if Aidan told you, but we've been thinking of making you a partner for months now. Right before I left for my honeymoon, we decided to take care of it as soon as I got back."

"I told her," Aidan admitted to Logan, then flashed Ellie a half smile. "Before he left on his honeymoon, we talked about the fact that he would be gone for three weeks. That can be a long time in this business. It got us thinking that it was time to bring someone in who knows the business as well as we do and who we respect and have complete confidence in."

"That's you, Ellie," Logan said.

"Thank you, Logan," she said. She hadn't thought about it until that moment, but it was no wonder she'd received the partnership agreement so quickly. The lawyers had probably had it written up and waiting for the past few weeks.

"No, thank you," Logan insisted. "We consider you an essential part of the team."

"I consider myself that, too. Thank you both for placing your trust in me. I won't let you down."

"You never have," Aidan said, watching her closely.

She took a deep breath and let it out slowly. "Well, I can only take these compliments for another hour or so, then I think we should get to work."

The men laughingly agreed and soon they were dealing with Logan's agenda for the next six months. First new business was a time-share project they planned to discuss with their investors next month. It would mean a trip to New York and Ellie's mind wandered to an image of her and Aidan spending a romantic weekend in New York City. Walks in Central Park, a romantic dinner at—

"Ellie can handle that right away," Aidan said.

"Good." Logan nodded as he read over his agenda and made notes. "Cross that off the list. What's next?"

"What?" Ellie said, suddenly aware that she'd missed an entire agenda item. "Handle…sure, I can do that. Um, what?" Good grief! Ellie wanted to crawl out of the room. This was so not a good time to turn into a flake. She cleared her throat, tapped her pen on the table surface and tried to sound businesslike. "I apologize. I was trying to calculate what size advance team we'll need to line up for the New York trip." She turned to Aidan. "Exactly what would you like me to handle?"

The look he gave her was provocative enough to make her squirm in her chair. Had she really asked that question out loud? Double entendre, anyone?

"I'd like you to *handle* the Bryson project," Aidan said softly, his subtext unashamedly obvious. To Ellie, at least. She only hoped Logan was too busy taking notes to notice.

Was this tingling, yearning feeling going to crop up every time she was in the same office with Aidan? How would she ever get her work done? Would Logan regret offering her the partnership if he caught her making moon eyes at his brother whenever they sat at the same conference table together? Good grief. She had to straighten up and get back to business. Otherwise, she was doomed.

Twenty minutes later, the lunch meeting ended and Ellie couldn't run out of there fast enough.

Two weeks later on a Saturday morning, Ellie paced barefoot on the cool tile floor of her sunny kitchen, waiting, watching, wondering how five minutes could seem like six hours when one was anticipating that a little pink cross might appear in the window of the pregnancy test stick.

But five minutes passed and there was no cross. Ten minutes later, she checked again. No cross. No nothing.

So she wasn't pregnant.

"Okay," she whispered, tossing the stick into the trash can under the sink. "Just means we'll have to keep trying."

Naturally, a big part of her was disappointed to know there was no tiny person starting to grow inside her. But she tried to be philosophical about it. She would get pregnant when it was meant to happen.

It wasn't like she hadn't been trying hard enough. That wasn't the issue. In fact, the opposite was true. She and Aidan had been almost fanatical in their effort to accomplish their mission by having sex as often as possible over the past few weeks. By now Ellie should've been exhausted and ready to call it quits, but she wasn't crazy. There was no way she was about to stop having sex with Aidan.

At the very thought of Aidan with his broad shoulders, dark blue eyes, windswept hair and long legs stalking across the office to yank her into his strong arms and ravish her, Ellie felt a tingle of excitement zing across her shoulders and down her spine. Another flashing image had him sliding his talented hands along her sensitive skin as his tongue brushed over her breasts, and that tingle burst into a thousand tiny jolts of electricity that zigzagged everywhere throughout her body and caused her knees to turn weak.

"Oh, my," she murmured as she stumbled to sit down at her kitchen table. This would probably be a good time to call Aidan to request that he drop by her house as soon as possible. To work. On their mission. Immediately.

Call her insatiable, but Ellie was having the time of her life. And while the lines might have started to blur between her serious mission to become pregnant and her giddiness over Aidan's stated desire to find new and inventive ways to have sex with her, she certainly appreciated his devotion to her cause. More than that, she appreciated all the thrilling new experiences he'd introduced her to.

She'd never had sex up against a wall before, for instance. Or on a conference room table. Or on the deck of a catamaran in the middle of Alleria Bay. Or on a chaise longue by the pool at midnight.

That tingle was back and her heart was starting to beat a little faster. And in case she started to worry, she reminded herself that she wasn't obsessed with Aidan. She was just having great sex with a gorgeous man. Nothing wrong with that. She wasn't turning into her mother; she was simply enjoying this wonderful time with Aidan.

So she refused to feel sorry for herself for not having accomplished her objective to be pregnant just yet. In fact, she was excited to be able to continue with their sexual encounters. She would just have to remember to ask Aidan to try a little harder the next time.

Seven

Aidan stood at the end of the long bar nursing a scotch as he watched his team of bartenders racing to keep up with the customers. The music was pumped up and so was the boisterous crowd. That's the way Aidan liked it. Friday nights were always a little crazy in the bar since many of the resort guests had just arrived that afternoon for a week of fun. But tonight was especially insane because this was the start of the annual cardboard box convention. And those people were more than ready to party.

Three years ago, Aidan and Logan had discovered a shocking truth. There was no bigger group of wild, raucous party animals than this horde of almost one thousand cardboard box salesmen. Cardboard. Go figure.

The group used to have their convention in different cities every year, but once they found Alleria and met Ellie, that all changed. Now the group refused to go anywhere else. Ellie lavished so much special attention on them that the group was back for the third year in a row.

The box boys, as Aidan and Logan referred to them in private, were one of Ellie's special projects. Attracting new business to the resort had been part of her job description from day one, and bringing the box boy convention to Alleria was one of her first successes.

The group's presence here this week was just one of many reasons why Aidan hadn't wanted her to leave the island when she first announced her plans to go to Atlanta.

Now, as he observed Ellie interacting with a small group of conventioneers gathered at the bar, Aidan was doubly glad he'd convinced her to stay. Glad, because not only could she charm these guys into spending more money on drinks, but also because Aidan could have her in his bed every night.

Not that he was getting used to her being there, he quickly assured himself. He knew it would all end when she became pregnant. But in the meantime, how could he complain about having awesome sex with a beautiful woman like Ellie every night? Hell, he wasn't that big of an idiot, despite what his brother occasionally thought.

In fact, as he watched Ellie work the crowd and as he marveled at what an amazing businesswoman she was, he was tempted to congratulate himself for coming up with the deal that had kept her on the island in the first place.

The truth was, he'd only stopped in to have a drink because he knew that Ellie would be here, taking care of her special guests. Now that he was seeing her surrounded by those men, smiling and talking and joking with them, all he could think about was getting her out of here and taking her somewhere private. It took everything he had to keep from stalking across the floor, sweeping her up into his arms and carrying her off into the night.

Just then, one of the box boys said something that must've

been funny because Ellie threw back her head and laughed. The sweet musical sound set off a shock wave of desire that shot straight to Aidan's gut. And instantly turned him as hard as a brick.

Damn. He gripped his glass carefully as he struggled to maintain an outer calm. He gritted his teeth and mentally talked himself down, but it wasn't easy because he couldn't seem to tear his gaze away from Ellie, who was still smiling and chatting easily with the men. That was just one more reason why she was so perfect for this job. She was friendly and could get along with anyone.

But that wasn't helping his erection disappear.

The music in the club pounded; laughter from the customers at the table seemed harsher, louder. Aidan kept his gaze fixed on Ellie with such intensity that she must have felt it. She turned her head, her gaze caught his and something wild and indefinable jumped into life between them.

He downed the last of his drink, set his empty glass on the bar, nodded to Sam the bartender, and headed straight toward the group of men who were vying for Ellie's attention.

Ellie had felt Aidan's presence within a nanosecond of him walking into the bar twenty minutes ago. Even with her back to the entrance, even surrounded by all these people, she knew he was here. So what did it say about her that she could sense the man's presence from across a large, crowded room?

It worried her, frankly. Would it always be this way? Was it a good thing or a bad thing? Probably bad, if it meant that in a few years, she would be at home feeding her baby and suddenly realize instinctively that Aidan was out on a date with his latest "bikini babe."

Yes, definitely a bad thing, she thought, as she recalled one night when she and her sister had watched their mother wander through the house, wondering and worrying aloud about the man she'd once been married to. What was he doing right now? Was he thinking of her?

Ellie mentally rolled her eyes. There was no way she would turn into that woman!

With a sigh, she tried to ignore all thoughts of Aidan and concentrate on the salesmen who were currently trying to impress her with all their best stories. She didn't mind. They were nice guys, if a bit silly.

A few minutes later, they moved on from stories to jokes, and Ellie had to admit some of them were mildly amusing. Then out of the blue, one of the salesmen—was his name Larry?—told a knock-knock joke that was so funny, she laughed out loud.

"Hey, she liked that one," Larry said, wiggling his eyebrows at his friends.

One of his buddies nudged him with his elbow. "Guess that means the next round of drinks is on you."

She felt Aidan's gaze on her and when she turned her head to meet that look head-on, her entire system jump-started into a frantic rhythm. Her heartbeat thundered in time with the pulsing music. Her stomach did a quick spin and at the very core of her, she went hot and damp.

She swallowed hard when he stalked toward her.

"Good evening, gentlemen," Aidan said jovially. "Hope you don't mind, but I've got to borrow our Ms. Sterling for a few minutes."

She smiled her apologies. There was some good-natured grumbling as Aidan took Ellie's arm and guided her out from the circle of men. He smiled cheerfully the entire time, although Ellie could sense his underlying tension.

"No worries, gentlemen," he said. "You'll see Ellie again tomorrow. Enjoy your evening."

"Aidan, what's wrong?" Ellie asked.

He kept a firm hold on her arm as they walked quickly through the bar and out into the bustling lobby. He paid no attention to the bell captain or the concierge director who both called out his name, just kept walking across the marble floor and into the carpeted hallway that led to his suite.

"You're scaring me, Aidan," she said, hurrying her steps to keep up with his much longer stride. "Is everything all right?"

"Sorry," he muttered. "Everything's fine. I'm just in kind of a hurry."

"Okay," she said, and practically jogged to keep up with him.

They reached his suite and without a word, he swiped his key card, pushed the door open and urged her inside. As soon as the door shut, he tugged her up against his chest and kissed her hard on the lips. The impact was sudden and startling and hot and Ellie couldn't get enough of him. She wrapped her arms around his neck and pulled him even closer to her.

Within seconds, he softened the kiss and she sighed, parting her lips to allow him entrance. Their tongues tangled gently and Ellie felt herself melting against him.

Without a warning, he stepped back, grabbed hold of her light summer dress and whipped it up and over her head, tossing it onto the chair.

Wearing only her bra and panties, Ellie grabbed his shirt and started unbuttoning it with frantic urgency.

"You're overdressed," she groused.

"Let me do it," he said, laughing as he pushed her hands away. After ripping it off his shoulders, he hoisted her into his arms and carried her through the living room and into the bedroom. He tossed her on the bed, knelt above her and unzipped his jeans, releasing his enormous erection.

Ellie shivered as he gripped her bottom, lifted her up

off the mattress and guided her onto his thick length. She groaned in pure delight as he filled her completely.

His mouth devoured hers as they moved together rhythmically and Ellie was so lost in passion, she wondered if she had been created for this moment. As his fervor met hers, they reached the pinnacle together and tumbled into rapture. Her heart was so full, she knew she had never felt so much pleasure, so much love before.

Moments later, he collapsed onto her. After catching his breath, he finally murmured in her ear, "I'm sorry I dragged you out of the bar, but I knew I was going to explode if I couldn't be inside you right away."

"I loved it," she whispered, then cringed. She only hoped her voice sounded casual saying those words. But even if Aidan wasn't spooked by the words, Ellie was. The *L* word was something she never said out loud.

But Aidan was already asleep, so she held him in her arms and they dozed for a while. Sometime in the middle of the night, Aidan woke her up and made love to her slowly. Afterwards, they slept. The next time Ellie awoke, it was morning. The sun was streaming into Aidan's bedroom, but she was alone in his bed.

She sat up, looked around and told herself that she preferred it this way. The sooner she got pregnant and got used to her life without Aidan, the better off she would be.

Hours later, Ellie sat in the bar, chatting with the friendly box boys while Larry, the funny salesman, designed a one-of-a-kind cardboard box for her on his tablet.

When he was finished, he held the screen up so she could see it. "There, just for you. I'm calling it the Ellie. Wait, we can add a design, too."

He tapped his fingers on the sidebar and the box was suddenly filled with a green and red circle pattern surrounded by curlicues.

"Oh, I like that pattern," she said, fascinated by everything he'd done. Who knew the cardboard box guys could be so creative?

"Hi, Ellie."

The deep voice came from behind her. She turned and her eyes widened in surprise at the sight of the tall, good-looking man. "Blake? What're you doing here?"

"Just thought I'd stop in for a drink and I saw you." He glanced around. "Can you take a break and talk?"

"Umm, of course." She turned back to her salesman. "I'm sorry, Larry, but would you excuse me?"

"Sure, Ellie," Larry said, eyeing Blake curiously. "No problem."

She sucked in a bracing breath and tried to mask her distress at the fact that Blake was here unannounced, then gazed up at her ex-boyfriend. "Let's go out to the terrace."

He followed her to a quiet corner of the patio bar and found an empty table. He pulled a chair out for her and as he was sitting, she took the time to study him. He was classically tall, dark and handsome, with dark brown eyes and nearly black hair. Most women would swoon over his movie-star good looks, but Ellie had learned the hard way that looks weren't everything. Not that Blake had hurt her irreparably, but he hadn't turned out to be as nice or as honorable as she'd hoped he would be.

"Would you two like something to drink?"

Ellie looked up and saw Dee, her waitress friend, standing there, looking back and forth from Ellie to Blake.

"Maybe just a glass of water," Ellie said gratefully. "Thanks, Dee."

Blake ordered a beer and Dee was back in less than two

minutes with their orders. "Let me know if you need anything else," she said pointedly.

"I will," Ellie said, smiling up at her friend.

As soon as Dee was out of hearing distance, Blake spoke. "You're looking good, Ellie."

"Thank you. I feel good."

"I wasn't sure if I'd run into you here tonight, but I'm glad I did. I've been doing a lot of thinking. About us. I know I hurt you when I broke up with you, but I was… I don't know, confused, I guess. You shocked me."

"I know, and I'm sorry." She smiled ruefully. "It wasn't fair of me to spring my life story on you."

"I guess I asked for it," he said with a sheepish grin.

She chuckled lightly. "Yes, you did."

He relaxed back in his chair and sipped his beer. "So I hear you're seeing one of the Sutherland brothers. Is it serious?"

Her eyes narrowed. Was that why Blake was here? Was she suddenly more appealing to him now that she was involved with Aidan? And how had he found out about her relationship with Aidan? The island was like a small town, but they had been very discreet, she thought. "We're good friends, that's all."

He surprised her by leaning forward and taking hold of her hand. "If that's true, then I'd like you to consider giving me another chance. I thought we had a good thing going until you laid that bombshell on me."

"Until I told you I wanted to have a child."

"Yeah." He shrugged. "But, hey, if that's what you want, I'm willing to help you out there."

Not if he were the last man on earth, she thought as she pulled her hand away. "That's very kind of you to offer, but I think I'll pass."

"So you are sleeping with Sutherland."

She smiled tightly. "I didn't say that."

He chuckled. "You didn't have to. If you're not interested in getting back with me, then I have to assume you're doing the horizontal bop with him."

The horizontal bop? Was this guy in high school or something? Aidan had been so right about Blake. He was kind of a jerk. She was lucky she'd never had to see this side of him.

Ellie pushed her chair out and stood looking down at him. "Your assumption is wrong, Blake. My refusal to get back together with you has nothing to do with anything but the fact that I'm just not interested. See you around."

Aidan couldn't believe it. He'd seen Ellie leading Blake out to this deserted area of the terrace, so he followed them, remaining back behind a thick, vine-strewn column in order to watch them. It was too bad he couldn't get close enough to hear their conversation.

He refused to question why he even cared except to say that he was worried about Ellie. So that's why he was loitering in the area. Okay, maybe *skulking* would be a more accurate description, but why quibble? He'd never liked Blake for so many reasons and here was another one. The guy was holding Ellie's hand. What the hell? There was no way Ellie could be fooled by his good looks. The guy was a creep.

Maybe she agreed because at that moment, she slipped her hand away from his, then stood and walked away.

But why was she smiling? She shouldn't be smiling after talking to Blake.

Aidan rounded the column and stepped out just as she was about to walk past him. "Hello, there."

She stopped abruptly. "What're you doing out here?"

"Just checking the foliage," he said, brushing his hand along the flowering vine. He nodded toward Blake, who had taken off in the opposite direction. "What did he want?"

Ellie planted both hands on her hips. "Were you spying on me?"

"Maybe. I warned you what he was like. He's a jerk. He's not good enough for you."

"I never said he was."

"You were holding hands with him."

"He grabbed my hand and I pulled it back."

"Not right away."

"Don't be ridiculous," she said. She moved closer, touched his chest and smiled up at him so sweetly that his jaw muscles began to loosen up. "Did you come out here to protect me?"

"I told you he was a jerk," he grumbled. "I came out here to make sure he didn't pull a number on you."

"That was very nice of you, Aidan," she said. "But you and I aren't really a couple, remember? I have to take care of myself. Thank you, though."

"No problem," he murmured, then leaned in and whispered, "And we might not be a real couple, but if Blake had held your hand a second longer, I was going to have to break his arm."

The next day, Ellie spent the day alone, cleaning her house, dusting shelves and scrubbing floors. She did a few loads of laundry and swept her front porch. Afterward, she got caught up on her reading and took a short nap. She realized she needed some rest after so many long nights waking up and making love with Aidan.

Not that she was complaining, she thought, grinning with happiness.

She hadn't seen Blake since the night before and that was fine with her. If she never saw him again, that would be even finer. She just had to wonder why Blake had shown up at all. Why now? Not that it mattered, but still, she hated the thought that she and Aidan might be a source of gossip on the island.

She woke up from her nap as the sun was going down and thought about going over to the hotel bar to grab a quick dinner. But that would mean washing her hair and dressing up, so after weighing her choices, she decided to stay home and relax. She made herself a healthy salad for dinner, then picked up her book and tried to read, but she couldn't get back into the story. She kept picturing Aidan stepping out from behind that column. He'd been watching her and Blake! He'd kept his explanation casual, but Ellie hadn't been fooled. She'd seen a fierce possessiveness in him that she'd never seen before. Did it come merely from the fact that she was his partner? Or was there more going on under the surface?

Did Aidan care about her more than he was willing to admit? The possibility gave her a tiny sliver of hope, but she didn't want to dwell on it too much. After all, a tiny sliver of hope could grow into a big fat obsession, right?

"And now you're starting to obsess about obsession." She sighed. Why couldn't she just be happy with things as they were? She could, by gosh, and right then and there, she resolved to do just that. Be happy. After all, she'd never had this much fun with a man before, never felt as sexy and attractive and radiant as she'd felt lately. She was startled to realize that she had a sensual nature, and it was Aidan who'd helped her see it. Now she wanted to fully embrace that part of her.

She closed up her house, changed into her pajamas and slipped under the sheets. She fell asleep and dreamed the same dream she'd been having for a few weeks now. She dreamed about her baby. But for the first time ever, Aidan was there in her dream, too, smiling as he held their child in his arms.

She moved to join her little family and both Aidan and the baby dissolved into mist, to be replaced by an image of her mother sobbing over the man who got away.

Ellie was jolted awake with tears in her eyes and a deep feeling of loss in her heart.

Eight

He didn't like to admit mistakes, Aidan thought as he jogged along the narrow peninsula of sand that separated the waters of Alleria Bay from the resort's marina. But now he had a feeling he'd made a big one.

The early morning breeze stirred the nearby sailboat riggings, causing them to bump up against the aluminum masts and ping in a sort of odd harmony. Usually Aidan enjoyed hearing the tinny, echoing sound on his early morning runs, but not today. He was too preoccupied with wondering whether he'd miscalculated or not.

He shouldn't have followed Ellie and watched her conversation with Blake. And when she walked away, he should've let her go instead of intercepting her. He should've kept his mouth shut and not said anything about Blake.

What if Aidan's interference drove her back to the other man? He couldn't believe she would go back to Blake, but it should certainly be her decision to make.

The sun hadn't yet risen over the horizon so the beach was nearly deserted except for a few hearty health nuts out for a pre-dawn swim in the bay. Aidan tried to concentrate on the rhythmic pounding of his feet on the soft white sand, tried to match it to the beating of his heart. But it was useless. He couldn't get the image of Ellie and Blake out of his head.

And why the hell had Blake come back *now?* Had he gotten word somehow that Aidan and Ellie were together? Not that they *were* together, not really. But since no one else but Logan knew about their pregnancy pact, it might look that way to outsiders.

"We're not a real couple…" Aidan heard Ellie's voice in his mind again and felt the same sharp stab of something….

He shook his head to push those thoughts out of his mind. Blake. The issue right now was Blake. Was Ellie contemplating getting back together with him? *We're not a real couple.* Damn it. Aidan had no real standing to make demands on her, so how could he insist that she stay away from Blake? Ellie had agreed that Blake was a jerk, but did she mean it? Or had she just said that to placate Aidan?

"Probably just said it to shut you up," he grumbled to himself.

Who could blame her?

She was right. They weren't really together. He had no claim on her. Damn it.

Fine. He'd made a mistake. But if he stepped aside, wouldn't Blake swoop in? Wouldn't that be a bigger mistake? Hell. He had to talk to Ellie again. Apologize. She wasn't pregnant yet, so if she wanted to renew her relationship with Blake, all Aidan could do was step aside. It was the right thing to do, even though Aidan would rather chew on glass than let her go.

Not that it mattered. If Ellie left him for Blake, Aidan

could find another woman in a heartbeat if he wanted to. But that wasn't the point.

"Yeah, what's the point, knucklehead?" he muttered, as he pounded down the beach.

The point was, he liked Ellie. A lot. More than any other woman he'd ever been with, if he was being honest. Not that it meant anything because Aidan had no intention of ever settling down with one woman. Even though his brother had finally met his match with Grace, it wouldn't happen to Aidan. He just wasn't the type to settle down.

Why would he? *Look around you,* he thought. He loved this place, loved the carefree lifestyle. Loved surfing, sailing, wheeling and dealing, beautiful women in bikinis bouncing around everywhere.

Yeah. The more, the merrier. It was way too easy to love 'em and leave 'em when plenty of beautiful women arrived on the island daily and only stayed for a week or two at the most. He called that a win-win.

On the other hand, if he were the type to settle down— which he wasn't—Ellie would be the perfect woman to settle down with.

But since he wasn't that type, he had to give Ellie the space she needed to make her own choices. If she would rather have Blake be the father of her baby, then…fine. Although it grated on Aidan. No, it more than grated. It infuriated him. It made him want to take his fist and shove it right in Blake's face.

He had a feeling that wouldn't make Ellie happy, but his own satisfaction quotient would be through the roof.

Aidan reached the end of the peninsula and stopped to breathe for a minute while enjoying the stunning view of clear blue water as far as the eye could see. He grabbed the small towel he'd tucked into his back pocket and used it to wipe the sweat from his forehead and neck. Then he pivoted in the sand and started the long run back to the hotel.

Hell, if Ellie wanted to go back to Blake, Aidan would have no choice but to let her go. And now that he was thinking about it, he had to admit that from one objective angle, it would be the best of all worlds. Ellie would have a father for her baby, someone she cared about (even though Aidan couldn't figure out why she would care about Blake), and she would stay on the island and raise her kid here and continue to work for Sutherland Corp. That was all Aidan had ever wanted in the first place. It was a win-win-win. Wasn't it?

Of course, there was still the irritating fact that Blake would end up as her baby's father, not Aidan. And that didn't work for him at all. That part was *not* a win. Aidan knew in his gut that he, Aidan, was the one who needed to be Ellie's baby's father. She couldn't trust Blake.

The man had already dumped her once. Who was to say he wouldn't do it again? And this time, he'd be walking out on a kid, much like Aidan's mother had done to him and Logan. No, Blake was absolutely the wrong choice for father material.

And hey, they had an agreement together. A binding legal document. So maybe it would be better if he stuck to the status quo and didn't say a word to Ellie. Why give her a chance to change things when everything was working so well for both of them?

"Hell." He tried to focus on something else, like the clean, briny smell of the fishing boats moored in the marina. The pungent scent reminded him of the first time he and Logan came to the island. They were on a fishing holiday and the bluefish they caught in Alleria Bay were the finest anywhere. They stayed a week longer than they'd planned and when they set sail for home, they were the new owners of the island.

Aidan slowed his pace as he approached the resort. He'd trusted in his luck back then, he reminded himself, and it had turned out well. He'd have to trust to his luck now, too. It wouldn't be easy, but he knew what he had to do. Ellie had to be the one to make the choice. And for Aidan, that meant standing aside to give her the room to do so.

He stopped abruptly at the water's edge. Something he'd refused to dwell on too heavily was the fact that Ellie hadn't gotten pregnant yet. Ellie hadn't brought it up and Aidan had simply figured they would continue having a good time until she announced she was pregnant. But now he wondered if maybe she was blaming him for not getting her pregnant immediately. Maybe she was ready to chuck Aidan and try this with someone new.

"That's ridiculous," he said aloud, immediately brushing that thought aside. Ellie wasn't the type of woman who would do something like that. But even if she was having second thoughts, Aidan refused to believe she would ever do anything so crazy as to choose Blake over him. Yet the fact remained that it was still her choice to make.

As he walked slowly across the white sand toward the terrace, Aidan reached an uncomfortable conclusion. He had started out wanting what was best for Ellie and the baby. Now he had to face the possibility that it might not be *him*.

"You want me to what?"

"I want you to go to Blake if you want to. It's your decision to make."

Ellie stared at him as if he'd just sprouted a second head. Maybe he had. He couldn't quite believe he was saying the words either. But they had to be said.

"It's my decision," she murmured.

"Yes. I shouldn't have followed you outside the other night," Aidan said solemnly. "It wasn't my place to interfere. Blake has offered you a choice and you need to do what's right for you."

Ellie searched his face for so long, he was about to start squirming. This wasn't easy for him, but it was the right thing to do.

Finally she said, "But you and I have an agreement."

"That's true," he said. "But you're running the show here, Ellie. I shouldn't have watched you and Blake when you were talking—it's just that that guy really bugs me and—never mind. Not the point. It was wrong of me to intrude. And if Blake cares about you…"

"You said he was a liar and a jerk," she reminded him. "Did you change your mind about him?"

"No, I didn't change my mind about him," Aidan said, resisting the urge to scowl. "I still don't like him. But this isn't about me. Look, I'm just afraid I might've pushed you into something you weren't ready for. So if you want to reconsider Blake, or any other guy, I need to give you the space to make a measured decision. It's your choice to make."

"I don't know what to say," she murmured, looking pensive.

He wanted to take her in his arms and kiss away every last ounce of doubt she'd ever had about herself. But he stayed on track and bit out the next words. "You have every right to go back to Blake if that's what you want."

"What do you want, Aidan?"

His jaw clenched and he pressed his lips together tightly, then forced himself to say the words. "I want you to do whatever will make you happy. You deserve to be happy, Ellie. And you deserve to make your own decision without me influencing you. More importantly, your baby deserves a father of your choosing."

And, damn it, she should choose him! But Aidan couldn't say that out loud.

She nodded slowly. "So you're saying you'd be fine if I decided that Blake or some other man would be a better choice to be the father of my child."

Hell, no! Was she going to make him say it out loud? Aidan wasn't sure he could. Finally he uttered the only thing left to say. "If that's what you want to do."

Ellie couldn't believe they were having this conversation. Her heart felt as if it were breaking in a thousand little bits. Did he really want her to choose Blake, or did he think he was being noble, offering her a choice? She had to remember that in the beginning, all Aidan had really wanted was to keep her on the island. If she went back to Blake, that goal would be achieved. As Aidan would say, it was a win-win.

Of course, there was no win for Ellie because apparently Aidan would be perfectly happy to see her go, and yet she would never return to Blake. She wasn't about to admit that to Aidan, though. Not now, with him so unwilling to take a stand either way.

Her head was spinning in confusion and pain. Could he really just let her go? She pressed a fist to her heart. Why did it have to hurt so much? She had tried so hard to avoid those pitfalls into which her mother had descended and now she herself was spiraling down into her own personal hell.

Right now there was only one thing she knew for sure. She needed to get away and think this through. She needed to stay away from Aidan and sadly, she couldn't do that if they were having sex together.

"What's going on, Ellie?" he said, a note of concern in his voice. "What are you thinking?"

She took a deep breath and gazed up at him. "I need some time to think, Aidan. I admit you've confused me. I need to stay away from you for a little while, just until I can put things into perspective."

His eyes narrowed on her. "Exactly what does that mean, Ellie?"

"It means we won't be having sex for a while."

"What?" he said. "Why the hell not?"

He looked so outraged that she squeezed his hand to comfort him. "I'm so sorry. I know our arrangement is strictly business, so maybe this is unfair of me to say. But I have to be honest with you. It's upsetting to hear that you don't have a problem with my going back to Blake. I thought we were having so much fun together, but now I see…well, I'm not sure of anything right now. Please just give me a little time to figure out what my next move will be."

"What if you find out you're pregnant?" Aidan said.

"Oh." She had to blink back a sudden wash of tears. She hadn't even taken that possibility into consideration. She took a few more deep breaths, then said, "I hadn't even thought about that. But if I find out I'm pregnant, there'll be no need to wonder who the father should be."

Ellie folded another crisp cloth napkin and added it to the pile. Ever since she was a young girl, whenever she needed to think about something important, she liked to do it while ironing. It was a mindless yet productive activity so she was able to accomplish something while doing almost nothing but allowing words and images to zip around in her head.

There was no way in the world she would ever start dating Blake again. Didn't Aidan know that? Of course he did. He was just feeling guilty about trying to influence her feelings about Blake.

But what annoyed the holy heck out of her wasn't the fact that Aidan had come to offer her a choice to go back to Blake or not. No, it was the fact that he didn't care one way or another what she chose to do! That's what bothered her most.

It hurt, frankly. She was bewildered and uncertain and just a little panicky about what to do next.

The smartest thing to do would be to avoid Aidan for the next two weeks, until she found out if she was pregnant or not. It wouldn't be easy because every time she saw him, all she wanted to do was kiss him and jump into bed with him. And that would be wrong. Although she couldn't quite remember why.

But at least she had told him the truth. At least he knew that he had upset her. The truth was important, she thought. But while she was telling Aidan the truth, maybe it was time for her to face the truth about herself. She was her mother's daughter. Was she turning into that woman? Ellie hated to think so, but she did seem to be wrapping herself up in Aidan's world more and more. And if that continued, she would eventually lose herself. And that frightened her more than anything else.

She stared at the stack of twenty neatly ironed napkins and the three smoothly folded tablecloths beside them. She wasn't nearly finished thinking about her problem and glanced around for something more to iron. Would it be too silly to iron her dish towels?

"Oh, no, you're not obsessed much," she muttered, and quickly put the iron and ironing board away.

He never should've said a damn word.

Knowing he'd upset Ellie was like having a drill pierce a hole through his gut. Over and over again. Her words played constantly in his head until he thought he would go crazy. He still couldn't believe that she'd apologized for being unfair to *him*. She'd tried to comfort him, for God's sake.

He thought he'd been doing the right thing for Ellie, but he was wrong. All he'd really wanted was for her to choose him over Blake. He'd wanted to hear her say the words. Like his own ego needed so much massaging? What the hell was wrong with him?

"Damn it," he muttered, as he slammed the tennis ball across the net. She was so sweet, he obviously didn't deserve her. But screw that. Even if she was too good for him, the bottom line was she was stuck with him. And let's face it, if she was too good for Aidan, then she was way too good for Blake. And that settled it. She wasn't going back to that worthless guy again. Not as long as Aidan had breath left in his body.

"Heads up, bro," Logan called from the other side of the net after the tennis ball whizzed right past Aidan's ear. "You're completely out of it today."

That was pretty much true, Aidan thought. The fact that he hadn't found Ellie in his bed that morning, for the first time in weeks, had rendered him almost useless today. He was going to have to do something about it, and soon. But he wasn't about to admit any of that to Logan.

"I can still beat you with one hand tied behind my back," he yelled. "Serve another one."

It was day seven without sex.

Aidan saw Ellie every day in the office, where she was the epitome of professionalism. She worked as hard as she ever had and was cordial and helpful at all times to Aidan and everyone else in the company.

It was driving Aidan insane. He had reached the end of his rope. Telling Ellie she was free to go back to Blake was surely the worst idea he had ever come up with.

Last night he'd actually gone into the bar to find a woman, any woman, to have no-strings-attached sex. He'd seen a few attractive women he knew would be willing to go for it, but every time he approached one of them, he changed his mind. They weren't that appealing, after all.

"What the hell is wrong with you?"

Aidan looked up and saw his brother standing in the doorway of his office. "Buzz off."

Logan ignored that and walked over to his desk. "Your temporary secretary is threatening to quit and Sarah from the mail room is in tears. What is your problem?"

"She forgot to sort my mail," Aidan griped.

Logan leaned closer. "I'm sorry, but I don't think I heard you right."

Aidan refused to repeat the idiotic complaint he'd just uttered. Instead, he grumbled, "You heard me."

"You're right, I did. And I'm wondering something."

"What?" Aidan glared up at him.

"Who the hell died and made you King?" Logan shouted in his face. "Sort your own damn mail!"

That's exactly what he was doing, but he wasn't about to admit it to Logan. "Thanks for your advice. Now you can leave."

"Not until you tell me what bug crawled up your ass and died." Logan began to pace back and forth in front of his desk. "You've been acting like a jackass for days now and everyone in the hotel is fed up with you. So pull yourself together. Either take a damn vacation, or get a hobby, or go get laid, but do something. Work it out, for God's sake."

"I can't get laid," Aidan muttered.

Logan stopped in his tracks. "Excuse me?"

"I said, get out of my office."

"No," Logan said slowly. "I think you said you can't get laid."

"Never mind what I said. I'm busy. Get out."

Logan grinned. "Is there a medical issue I should be concerned about?"

Aidan stood and pointed to the door. "Get. Out."

But Logan wasn't going anywhere and he had the nerve to laugh. "Oh, wait a minute. I know what this is about."

"You don't know jack, man."

"Yeah, this is about Ellie."

"It has nothing to do with Ellie."

"Really?" Logan thought for a second. "But when Grace talked to her, she said… Well, you probably don't care. Okay, I'll be going."

"Wait. What did Grace say? What did Ellie tell her?"

"Sorry. Gotta go."

"You're not going anywhere."

Logan snorted with laughter. "Oh, this is rich. You're in love with her."

"Get out."

"Okay, I'm going." He snickered and headed for the door. When he got there, he stopped and turned. "But do us all a favor and just admit it to yourself."

"There's not a damn thing I need to admit to anyone."

Logan held up his hands in surrender. "Fine, be miserable. Just stop taking it out on the staff."

Logan closed the door. Aidan sagged back in his chair and wondered what horrible sin he'd committed in a previous lifetime that had cursed him to be born a twin.

The following night, Aidan prepared to work later than usual on the contracts for another new restaurant in Tierra del Alleria, the island's only town. Tierra, as the locals called it, was a Victorian-era port town that overlooked a picturesque harbor that had grown in the last five years from a lazy fishing village to a hub for wealthy yacht owners, sports fishermen and the occasional small cruise ship. People came to experience the stunning views, laid-back charm, fabulous weather and world-class restaurants that lined the beach and pier.

The new restaurant owners planned to take advantage of the growing trend in gourmet artisanal vegetarian fare. Aidan figured the menu items would appeal especially to visiting celebrities and the wealthy wives of all those cigar-smoking yacht owners.

Thinking about the town reminded him of the dinner he'd shared there a few weeks ago with Ellie. They had snuck away from the hotel for the evening to wander and shop along the quaint waterfront. It was the most normal evening he'd spent in years, he thought. They had stopped for dinner at one of Aidan's favorite restaurants, a French bistro with phenomenal food and an excellent wine list. They were seated at the most prized table with a stunning view overlooking the scenic harbor and the sea of blue water that stretched on forever.

Ellie had ordered a rich cassoulet and Aidan the steak frites. The meat was tender and rare, the French fries deep fried to perfection. There was béarnaise sauce that Ellie had practically swooned over and each time she dipped a fry in the sauce and bit into it, Aidan felt himself grow more taut. They had rushed back home and made love for hours.

Damn it, where had that thought come from?

Aidan dragged himself back to the work before him, forcing himself to read through the various contracts for the new restaurant until he realized that one of the subcontractors' agreements was missing. He flipped through the file, but it wasn't there. Without much thought he buzzed Ellie, knowing she would be able to track it down for him.

A few minutes later, she walked into his office and his eyes drank in the sight of her. She wore a fire-engine-red dress with a short matching jacket and he wondered what the hell she was doing getting all dressed up like that.

As she approached the desk, he caught the scent of something irresistible. Was she wearing a new perfume? For some reason, that thought irritated him almost as much as the alluring blend of vanilla and citrus blossoms did.

He meant to thank her for bringing the contract by, but somehow the words came out differently. "What the hell did you say to Grace?"

She stopped and stared at him. "I beg your pardon?"

"You heard me," he said as he stood up and rounded the desk. "I don't want you talking to Grace without clearing it with me first."

"Really?" she said, tilting her head at him. "Is that some kind of new partnership rule? I'm not allowed to have a conversation with my girlfriends?"

That wasn't what he meant, was it? He scowled. "Not if it's about... Never mind. I just don't want you to—"

Her eyes narrowed and she stepped closer. "You don't want me to what?"

"Look, Ellie," he said, trying to sound reasonable. "It's none of my business if you and Blake..."

"What about me and Blake?" she said, her tone challenging.

He gritted his teeth and changed the subject. "Never mind. Just give me the file and go home."

"I'll give you the damn file." She slammed it down on his desk.

"Temper," he chided.

She pursed her lips and got right up in his face. "But who says I'm going home?"

A red haze of fury filled his vision at the thought of her going off to Blake's house.

"You're not going anywhere," he said, his voice low and threatening.

"Oh? And who's going to stop me?"

"Me." He grabbed her by her jacket lapels and yanked her against him and his mouth covered hers in an act of overt possession. She returned the favor with equal passion, her hips writhing against his already rock-hard erection as her lips searched his in a needy quest for more.

It was wonderful, Ellie thought, her mind drifting in a fog of sensual pleasure. Aidan was wild. Dangerous. Better than ever before. Or maybe it only seemed that way because it had been a lifetime since he'd kissed her.

Not that it meant anything. It was just sex. Wild, hot, fabulous sex, but still. It didn't mean anything more than that to Aidan. Or to her, she reminded herself. So even if he thought he could make demands on her, he still had no intention of ever settling down with one woman.

Ellie had been trying for seven long days to resist him, but she couldn't do it anymore. She knew she'd been obsessing over him, but she couldn't help herself. The good news was that she had finally recognized what her mom must have been going through all those years ago. It wasn't easy, but in her heart, Ellie had finally forgiven her. That was a big step.

And as for Ellie, she simply didn't want to deny her true self anymore. She resolved here and now to just enjoy what she and Aidan had for as long as she could. She was tired of obsessing about obsession. If fun was all Aidan was offering, then fun is what she wanted to have.

He grabbed her hair and pulled gently, wrenching their lips apart. "I mean it, Ellie. You're not going to see Blake."

She smiled. "Of course I'm not."

"Ever again," he warned.

"I already told him a week ago."

"Good. Come here," he muttered and kissed her again.

Two weeks later, the Duke cousins arrived on the island for the wedding of Tom Sutherland and Sally Duke.

Aidan and Logan greeted everyone as they climbed out of the limousine.

He gave Sally a hug. She stared up at him and pressed her hands to his cheeks. "Oh Aidan, I'm so happy you're my family."

The words struck him like a punch to the solar plexus.

"I'm happy, too," he managed, before Sally turned to Logan. Surreptitiously he blinked back a few drops of moisture that sprang to his eyes. Where the hell had that come from?

"Oh, look who's here," Sally cried, and rushed across the porte cochere.

Aidan turned in time to see her greet Ellie with a big hug and kisses on both cheeks. He frowned. How did those two know each other?

Logan elbowed him just then and chuckled. "Check it out. You are so dead."

Aidan was suddenly reminded of Sally's reputation as a matchmaker and was instantly suspicious. "How do they know each other?"

Logan shrugged. "They must've met on Sally's last trip here. Don't worry about it. I'm sure it's all friendly and harmless."

"Dude," Aidan said quietly. "On her last trip here, you accused her of being a witch."

"A *good* witch," Logan reminded him under his breath.

"Right, but still."

The last time Sally had visited Alleria, she'd spent a long time talking to Grace. Their cousin Brandon Duke had caught up with Aidan and advised him to warn his brother Logan that Sally liked to play matchmaker—and she played for keeps. She had uncanny luck in that area and the three Duke brothers were living proof. All three confirmed bachelors were now happily married with babies and the whole deal.

"You thought I was crazy for being concerned," Aidan said. "Remember?"

"Yeah, and I was right," Logan said. "You were crazy."

"I was just looking out for your best interests. And what good did it do? Look at you now. Happily married." His tone it was tinged with pity.

"True," Logan said cheerfully. "And now it looks like Sally and Ellie are new best friends. Hmm. Coincidence? I think not."

"Damn," Aidan muttered as he watched the two women chattering up a storm. "I'm gonna have to watch their every move now."

"Why bother?" Logan said, chuckling. "Just give in to the inevitable."

Aidan scowled. "You're doing it again."

"Doing what?"

"Wanting everyone else to get married just because you were dumb enough to get shackled."

"Yeah, that's me." Logan scratched his head. "What was I thinking? I like Ellie. Why would I want her to be stuck with you?"

"Very funny," Aidan said derisively.

"Dude, you just refuse to accept the fact that you're in love with Ellie."

"Oh, great," Aidan said. "One more delusional statement from the newly married man."

Logan slapped his back. "I'm gonna love watching you fall, bro."

Tom Sutherland and Sally Duke were married two days later surrounded by their closest friends and family. The setting was a secluded lagoon and waterfall nestled in the foothills of the rain forest with Alleria Bay as a backdrop.

Ellie was honored to be invited and was thrilled for Sally and Tom, who seemed so happy to have found each other after many years of living on their own. It was amazing to

Ellie that Sally, a widow who had spent so many years trying to track down her late husband's missing brother, Tom, had finally found him.

With a soft sigh, Ellie thought that nobody deserved her very own "happy ever after" more than Sally Duke.

"Everything is so beautiful," Grace whispered. "Thanks for helping with the decorations."

"There wasn't much to do," Ellie said. "This setting is perfect just as it is."

"It's my favorite spot on the island," Grace said shyly.

Ellie smiled. Her friend had confessed to finding the hidden lagoon while spore hunting one day and had returned to enjoy it many times with Logan.

Ellie wished she could return here someday with Aidan. It had to be the most romantic spot she'd ever seen. That thought reminded her of Aidan and she glanced over at the handsome twin brothers standing by their father's side.

As the ceremony began, Ellie paid special attention to the vows the couple spoke. The words were so simple, yet filled with so much emotion and love that Ellie was almost overwhelmed by everything she was feeling. As Grace passed her a tissue, Ellie chocked it up to the simple fact that this was a wedding, after all. She'd choked up during her sister's wedding, too. And Logan and Grace's nuptials had been lovely, as well.

To keep herself from dissolving into tears, she stared straight at Aidan, knowing his presence would help to ground her. He looked so incredibly handsome standing with Logan and Tom, surrounded by all that natural beauty.

At that moment, Aidan turned and winked at her. Ellie smiled at him. And realized it didn't matter that someday he might be the father of her child. Didn't matter that they'd signed a legal agreement. Didn't matter that she seemed to have succumbed completely to being her mother's daughter when it came to obsessing over one man. Didn't matter that she'd never expected to fall in love and marry a man. The plain fact was that she loved Aidan Sutherland with all her heart and wanted to be with him for the rest of her life. Even if she was never lucky enough to have a baby, she would always want to be with Aidan.

And that was impossible.

All of a sudden, she couldn't breathe. She stood abruptly and stumbled to the aisle. Grace grabbed her hand and Ellie mumbled an apology as she left the ceremony. She made her way along the flower-petal-strewn path and staggered down the hill until she reached a bend in the trail. There she was able to sag against the trunk of a coco palm tree out of sight of the others.

"Oh, God. Oh, God." In a panic, she struggled to get enough breath into her lungs so she wouldn't pass out. Because she was suddenly struck by the immensity of her feelings. She was truly and irrevocably in love with the man.

Yes, yes, fine, she had always been attracted to Aidan. She'd always cared about him. But this was so much bigger than what she had felt before. Her heart ached with the enormity of it all. Did it show on her face? How could it not? There was no way she could return to the ceremony now.

"You fool," she whispered. She'd known all along that Aidan would never settle down with one woman. He clearly had some aversion to commitment that would never allow him to give himself to Ellie alone. Just look at the endless line of bikini-clad women he'd dated over the years. So now what?

"Ellie?"

She whirled around and saw Grace tiptoeing toward her. "Are you all right?"

Ellie gulped back tears. "You should go back to the ceremony, Grace. Logan will miss you."

"Logan's fine. I'm more worried about you."

Ellie shook her head, but didn't say anything.

"Oh, what's wrong, sweetie?"

"I can't talk about it," she whispered.

Grace sighed and took hold of Ellie's hand. "Weddings can be treacherous events, can't they? So unfair to us sensitive types."

"It's true," Ellie whispered.

Absently, Grace pushed an errant strand of Ellie's hair behind her ear. "Are you sure you don't want to talk about it?"

Ellie nodded.

"Is it Aidan?"

Ellie's eyes widened, but she clamped her mouth shut for fear that if she spoke one word, her eyes would let loose a flood of epic proportions.

"I know you love him," Grace said gently.

"Oh, God," she moaned. "You can tell?"

"Of course, sweetie," Grace said, nodding. "It's obvious to me how you feel, but apparently not to him. Men can be such dolts."

Ellie giggled. She wasn't prone to giggling, but she couldn't help it around Grace, who was such a brilliant scientist, but whose words were completely down to earth.

"Especially Sutherland men," Grace added. "They can be a real bummer to a girl's self-assurance. But who can blame us for falling for them? Let's face it, they're hot."

Ellie sighed. "I'll say."

"I'm just impressed that you were smart enough to recognize the signs for yourself." Grace shook her head in dismay. "I was totally clueless."

"But you're a genius," Ellie protested.

"Some genius," Grace scoffed, then smiled wickedly. "But I'm getting smarter every day."

"Then you must see how useless my feelings for Aidan are. He has no intention of ever settling down."

"No, of course he doesn't," Grace said seriously. "Never. Not Aidan. No way."

"You're not helping."

Grace laughed lightly. "Ellie, Aidan would have to be a complete fool not to fall in love with you. And my husband's twin brother is no fool."

Ellie smiled. "I appreciate you saying that, even if it's complete nonsense."

Grace laughed and rubbed her arm. "You look like you're feeling a little better. Can I coax you to come back to the wedding?"

"I guess so," Ellie said. "But will you promise not to tell anyone how stupid I was?"

"You're far from stupid, but if it makes you feel better, I promise. Now let's get back before the Sutherland men miss us too much."

Nine

She caught the bridal bouquet.

Aidan was standing on the sidelines drinking a beer with his brother and their Duke cousins as the ladies all gathered on the dance floor behind Sally. Without any warning, Sally heaved that big bundle of pink and white flowers and ribbons over her head, directly into the hands of Ellie, who had the good grace to look terrified by her good luck.

Sally turned and when she saw who'd caught the bouquet, she laughed. Clapping her hands happily, she called out, "I was aiming right for you, Ellie."

"What the hell?" Aidan muttered to no one in particular.

Earlier, during the hors d'oeuvres and champagne portion of the party, Aidan had caught Sally and Ellie deep in conversation again. He'd had a moment of concern but wouldn't have thought much more about it, except that Cameron had walked up at that exact moment.

"Listen, Aidan," Cameron had said, nudging his chin toward Sally and Ellie. "I've heard that you and Ellie have something going on, so I have to warn you. My mother has these weird special powers. You know that, right?"

"I've heard stories," Aidan said, not willing to agree and sound completely deranged.

Cameron shrugged. "Well, everything you've heard is true. So unless you and Ellie are planning to take your own trip down the aisle one of these days, I'd go over and nip that conversation in the bud."

Aidan frowned as Sally and Ellie laughed quietly together over something. Then he noticed that another few yards beyond the two women, his brother, Logan, stood with Adam and Brandon Duke. The three men were staring straight at him. When Aidan scowled, they all began to laugh uproariously.

He turned to Cameron, who had obviously been goaded into giving him grief. "Okay. Thanks for the warning, man, but I think I can handle it from here."

"Really?" Cameron said, raising one eyebrow. "Are you feeling lucky?"

So that had happened, and Aidan had quickly brushed it off as a practical joke played on him by his moronic twin. But then Sally had deliberately thrown her bridal bouquet straight at Ellie, who hadn't even lined up with the other ladies to catch it. What was that all about? Wasn't there some bizarre old omen that the woman catching the bridal bouquet would be the next to get married? He was going to have to look that up. Fast.

"Nice catch, champ," Logan said to Ellie, who laughed and grabbed him in a big hug.

The Dukes' wives all gathered around Ellie to congratulate her.

"Guess you're next," Trish teased.

Aidan felt a hard lump of something cold and near-panic-like settle in the pit of his stomach.

"I don't think so," Ellie said, but she blushed as she held the bouquet up to breathe in the floral scent. "I wasn't even trying to catch it."

"Then it's doubly meant to be," said Kelly, Brandon's wife.

Aidan frowned.

"Doesn't she look beautiful holding those flowers?" Sally said fondly.

Aidan jolted, then looked down, a little disturbed to see Sally standing next to him and staring directly up at him. He'd been so distracted by the flower toss that he'd let her sneak through his defenses.

He debated whether to call her out right then and there. Because really, this little matchmaking act of hers was beyond obvious, at least to anyone paying attention. Unfortunately, Ellie seemed to be the only one who wasn't paying attention.

A little desperate now, he glanced around. What about the Duke brothers? Was there no solidarity among males anymore? Where were his cousins and twin brother when he needed them? Instead of coming to his aid, they were all standing back enjoying the show. What the hell?

They'd all been innocent victims of Sally's relentless attempts to get them all married off. And she'd succeeded! Aidan was the last line of defense. The least they all could do was rally to his side when he needed them most. They were all brothers now. They needed to band together. But no. Looked like they were all anxious to see the last of them fall.

"Aidan, dear, are you all right?" Sally said with a concerned pat on his arm.

"Huh? What? Oh yeah, Sally. Fine," Aidan said, feeling like a cornered rat.

"Well, then?"

He had to mentally retrace their conversation. "Oh, yeah. Absolutely right. That was nice of you. Ellie looks great with the flowers."

"Yes, she does," the older woman said softly, tucking her arm through his. "Such a beautiful girl. You're so lucky to have her."

"As a business partner? That's for darn sure." That was all he was willing to say. Lucky? Damn straight he was lucky. He had thought he'd lost her to Blake, but now that he had her back, he wanted her for however long it lasted.

He followed Sally's gaze across the room and found Ellie. Sally was absolutely right. Ellie looked flat-out gorgeous today, flowers or no. She was wearing her hair up on top of her head in that sexy style he'd grown to like so much, if only because he couldn't wait to pull the pins out one by one and watch as each of her thick strands of hair draped gently across her shoulders. The pink roses she held in her hands looked perfect against her soft skin and rosy lips.

Still, Sally was up to no good.

The orchestra members came back from their break and began to play a slow, romantic love song. Several couples walked out onto the dance floor and began to sway to the melody.

"Oh, the music has started back up," Sally declared, and patted Aidan's arm once more. "I want to see all my sons dancing."

He had no argument with her there. Turning to her, he smiled and held out his hand. "May I have this dance, Mom?"

She let out a little gasp and Aidan had the distinct pleasure of watching her eyes well up with tears.

Two days later, the Dukes left the island and Ellie missed them horribly for an entire day. She loved having all those wonderful women around. They had included her in everything and it had turned into a sorority party. Or at least, it seemed like every sorority party Ellie had ever heard of or seen in the movies, since she'd never been involved in a sorority herself. The night before the wedding, Sally, Trish, Julia, Kelly, Grace, Ellie and Sally's two best friends, Beatrice and Marjorie, had stayed up late gossiping and laughing and sharing secrets and plans for the future.

"You'll come visit us in California," Sally had said, just before they'd all piled into two limousines to take them to the island's airport. She had gripped Ellie's hands and then hugged her so tightly that Ellie had felt tears prickling her eyes.

It wasn't an exaggeration for Ellie to feel that, for a few days, Sally Duke had been the mother she'd never had. She was warm and kind, older and wiser, a woman who loved unconditionally and would always be there for her children, no matter what. During their conversations, Sally had made her laugh and think and wonder and dream. Ellie hoped she could be that same sort of mother to her child someday, and she tucked Sally's California invitation away in a special place in her heart.

And now that things on the island had calmed down a bit, Ellie decided to follow Sally's advice. The older woman had made it sound so easy. Just tell him how you feel, Sally had said. Honesty was always the best way to go.

So with a deep, bracing breath, Ellie called up Aidan and invited him to her cottage that night for dinner. Tonight she would tell Aidan she loved him. Excited and more than a little bit nervous, she left the office early to set the scene for the most romantic evening ever.

Aidan set the phone down carefully and stared out the window.

"What's wrong?" Logan said, sitting across the desk from

him. "Who was that? You look like you just received a warning from the grave."

"Close enough," Aidan said numbly as his eyes narrowed in thought. "That was Ellie. She's invited me to her place for dinner tonight."

"Jeez, man, I thought something terrible happened."

"Maybe it did." His mind was racing, trying to stay a step or two ahead of the gorgeous woman who was taking up way too many of his thoughts lately. "Who knows what she has in mind?"

"Aw hell, you're right. This is despicable." Logan smirked. "A dinner invitation? Man, that's low. How could she do this to you? I hope you told her to take a hike."

Aidan made a rude gesture. "Go ahead and mock me, but this isn't funny. Ellie spent the last four days conspiring with Sally Duke at every opportunity. Now all of a sudden she wants to make dinner for me?"

"Oh man, that's sneaky," Logan said. "Yeah, you're right to be terrified—"

"Who says I'm terrified?"

"You should be. She could slip some aphrodisiac into the mix and turn you into her love slave."

Aidan tried not to dwell on the sudden image of Ellie carrying a satin whip and wearing a little black mask. And nothing else.

He gulped in air and pushed his chair back. "I'm finished talking to you."

Logan laughed. "You can't really be paranoid about this, can you? It's just dinner. And probably wild sex afterwards. Is that a problem?"

He frowned. "Maybe not."

"We've all been giving Sally too much credit," Logan said sensibly. "All we're really talking about is dinner and sex. End of story."

"It's not the end of the story." Aidan glared at his brother. "Are you blind? We have empirical evidence of Sally's power."

Logan was laughing so hard, he had to rest his elbows on his knees. "Oh man, I want to hear this."

Aidan held up his fingers and ticked off the evidence. "One, Sally talked to Grace. Two, you're now married to Grace. And *that's* the end of the story."

"My God," Logan said, feigning shock and dismay. "You're right."

"Thank you."

Logan grinned. "So what are you going to do about it?"

"I already told her I'd come for dinner."

"Call and cancel," Logan said easily.

Aidan frowned. "I don't want to do that. It would hurt her feelings."

"What do you care?" Logan asked. "You could be dodging a bullet here if she's truly plotting to get you to marry her."

"I know." Aidan thought about it and then sighed. "No, she's going to a lot of trouble to make a nice dinner. That's all this is. She doesn't want to get married. Hell, at first she was going to have a baby through a sperm bank so there's no way she's interested in getting married. It's ridiculous to worry about it."

"Then why are you worried about it?"

"I'm not," Aidan insisted. "We have an agreement. We even signed a *contract*. There's nothing else going on, so why am I letting Sally and all of you guys get to me? That ends here and now."

"Does it?"

Aidan blew out a breath of frustration. "I don't know."

Logan shot him a look of profound pity, then said, "Tell you what, bro. If it'll make you feel any better, I'm willing to work the Switch for you."

Aidan's eyebrows shot up at Logan's suggestion and he weighed the possibilities and drawbacks for a moment. The Switch was an old twin trick they'd used a few times in the past. As recently as a few months ago, they had pulled the Switch on Grace, but she had seen through the ruse within seconds and had laughed when Aidan tried to insist he was his brother.

As far as Aidan was concerned, that was as close to a declaration of love as you could get. After all, their own mother had never been able to tell the twins apart. Since then, they'd met no woman who could differentiate one twin from the other. Until Grace. That's when Aidan had realized that she was the perfect woman for his brother.

"Wait," Aidan said. "This won't work. She can already tell the difference between us. Remember that day in the office? You were sitting at my desk, but she knew it was you."

"That could've been a fluke," Logan said logically.

"I guess so."

The only thing Aidan knew for sure was that if he didn't take Logan up on his plan to do the Switch, his brother would issue a final decree to put up or shut up. So ultimately, Aidan's choice was a simple one.

"Fine," he said finally. "Let's do it."

"Cool," Logan said with a grin, as he rubbed his hands together. "Just don't tell Gracie. Now. What time is dinner?"

Ellie had just finished lighting the row of twinkling votive candles on the mantle when her doorbell rang. Thousands of butterflies in her stomach fluttered to life and she commanded them to calm down, but they just ignored her. Rubbing her tummy, she had to accept that she would always have this tingly fluttering reaction whenever Aidan came around.

She opened the door and smiled at him. "Hi."

"Hi." He extended a small bunch of pink and purple flowers toward her. "These are for you."

"Oh, how beautiful. Thank you." She took them and waved him inside. "Come in."

"Thanks."

Ellie started to ask Logan what he was doing here, but something made her hesitate. Aidan couldn't be sick or Logan would've said something right away. So what was wrong here? Maybe Aidan was on his way and Grace was planning to join them, too. That would be fun. Ellie had made enough pasta for ten people. But finally she decided to wait and hear what Logan had to say before she asked any questions.

"You look beautiful, Ellie," Logan murmured.

"Thank you. You look nice, too. Would you mind opening the champagne?" She pointed to the coffee table, where she had laid out a platter of appetizers, a bucket of champagne and two flutes.

"I'll be glad to," Logan said. He went through the motions, popped the cork off, filled the glasses, and handed her one. "What shall we drink to?"

Ellie smiled as she realized Logan wasn't going to say a word. They were teasing her! She wondered if Aidan was hiding out on the veranda, waiting to burst the door open and shout *surprise*.

"Let's drink to surprises," she said, and clicked her glass against his.

"To surprises." He took a sip, then set his glass down on the table. "Come here." He reached for Ellie and took her into his embrace. "Mmm, this feels good."

Ellie tried to sigh, but it was no use. She began to giggle. Her shoulders shook until she finally managed to push away from him—and laughed out loud.

"What is it, Ellie? What's wrong, honey?" He rubbed her back. "Please don't cry."

"Cry?" It took her a few more seconds before she could speak again. "I'm not crying."

"Then what are you doing?"

"That was my question," she said, shaking her head as her laughter subsided. "Logan, what're you doing here?"

"Logan?" he said indignantly. "I'm not Logan. I'm Aidan."

She rested her fists on her hips and shook her head. "Logan, does Grace know what you're up to?"

"Why would Grace care?" he said, trying to look out-raged. "And stop calling me Logan."

"All right, fine. I'll stop." And suddenly she grabbed hold of his shirt and pulled him up against her. Staring into his eyes, she said, "Kiss me, please."

He gulped and said, "How about some more champagne, first?"

She let him go and smacked him on the arm. "Not before you tell me what's going on. Or would you rather I call Grace and ask her?"

"Damn it, Ellie," he said, shoving his hands in his pockets. "How the hell did you know it was me?"

"Is that some kind of joke? You guys may be twins, but it's easy to tell you apart."

"No, it isn't," he groused.

"Yes, it is," she argued. "I could tell you two apart from the first day I met you."

"How?" he demanded.

She was taken aback and reached for her champagne glass. After taking a sip, she said, "I'm not sure what to tell you. There are so many ways the two of you are different."

"No," Logan insisted. "There aren't."

Ellie chuckled. "Well, it's certainly true that both of you are incredibly handsome men."

"Yes, that's a given."

She laughed out loud. "Oh, Logan. What more is there to say?"

"Give it a shot," he said with an appealing grin.

This was the Logan she knew from the office, the man with whom she'd always enjoyed joking and sparring intellectually. Still, how could she possibly explain all the subtle differences she'd seen from the start between him and his brother?

She stared at Logan now and tried to pretend she was looking at Aidan. But it was impossible. They were virtually identical, from their haircuts down to their shoe size. They were both tall, both handsome, with the same shade of dark blond hair and dark blue eyes. But Aidan was more approachable, more touchable, more…lovable.

Although Grace would probably disagree with her, Ellie thought to herself.

"When Aidan smiles," she said finally, "his mouth curves up ever so slightly higher than yours."

"It does?"

"Yes, definitely," Ellie said with an emphatic nod. "And his eyes twinkle a bit more. Those are two differences I've noticed."

"Really?" Logan raised one eyebrow. "Did you ever consider the fact that his smile was a little brighter because of the way he feels about you?"

She paused to consider that. "No."

"Well, think about it."

As much as she wanted to, she brushed that improbable theory away instead and continued. "Aidan's wit is a bit sharper than yours."

"Sharper? Wait." He held up his hand. "I know you're not trying to say he's smarter than me."

"No," she said with a laugh. "But his sense of irony seems,

I don't know, more highly developed than yours." The fact was that Aidan made her smile, made her giggle and laugh, made her want to be a better person, made her want to spend her life with him. But she wasn't about to mention all that to his brother.

"So you're saying he makes you laugh?"

"Yes, that's it."

Logan smiled. "Again, this is your fault."

"My fault? How is it my fault?"

He shrugged. "You two travel so much together that you've developed an incredibly tight friendship. And that's totally cool. But it means that Aidan only shows his ironic side—and by *ironic,* I mean sarcastic and mocking—with the people he feels closest to. Like me. And you."

"But you and I travel together, too."

"Yes, but not as often."

"And you're also my friend, right?"

"I like to think so. But you and I don't seem to have the same sizzling chemistry between us that you have with my brother."

She felt herself beginning to blush. "Thank goodness, or Grace would take out a contract on me."

He chuckled softly, but it faded as a thought occurred to him. "Ellie, why aren't you attracted to me?"

She smiled. "You almost sound offended."

"I am," he said with mock sulkiness. "I'm just as cute as Aidan."

She laughed and patted his cheek. "Yes, you are. And Grace is a lucky woman."

"That's for sure," he said, grinning.

"And she's probably wondering where you are," Ellie added lightly.

"She knows I'm having dinner with you."

"Alone?"

His lips twisted. "Not exactly."

She checked her wristwatch. "If you hurry, you can still get back and have dinner together."

He gazed at her intently, as if to assure himself that she would be all right.

"I'll be fine," she promised, smiling confidently.

After a moment, he seemed to understand that she would be. "Okay, maybe I'll take off."

Her smile faded. Apparently, Aidan didn't plan on showing up tonight. She supposed she should've been flattered that the two men had gone to all this trouble to trick or tease her, but there was one question she wanted an answer to. She hated to ask, but she needed to know.

"Logan, can you tell me something before you go?" she said as she walked him to the door.

"Sure."

"Where is Aidan tonight? Is he out on a date with another woman?"

He whipped around. "What? Hell, no. Why would you think something like that?"

She bit her lip anxiously. "I just can't think of another explanation of why you'd show up instead of him. Maybe he met someone or…maybe he just got busy doing something else." She despised the helpless tone in her voice and shook herself out of it. "Oh, never mind. Forget I said anything. Have a good evening and say hello to Grace for me."

"Ellie, wait." He gripped her arm. "This was stupid. It was my idea. It's something we've done a few times before in the past and I thought it would be funny, but it's not."

"But Aidan went along with it."

He shrugged apologetically. "I didn't give him much choice."

"Why?"

"Look, Aidan cares about you a lot. And it scares him to death. When you called to invite him for dinner, he…"

She nodded slowly as she realized what he was inferring. "He thinks I'm pushing him into something."

"Yeah, and no matter what he says, he wants to go there. So do me a favor, okay?"

"What's that?"

Logan's smile was conspiratorial. "Keep pushing."

Ten

"She's in love with you."

"That's ridiculous," Aidan said, although the words caused a tug in his chest. With a sigh, he muted the basketball game he was watching. "Why are you even here? You should be having dinner with Ellie right now."

Logan grimaced. "Dude, she knew it was me the minute she opened the door. There wasn't much to say after that, so I made my excuses and left."

"You left her alone?" Somehow that bothered Aidan, knowing Ellie was all alone.

"Not the point," Logan snapped. "But yes, I left her alone. She wasn't in much of a mood for entertaining once she realized I wasn't you—and *you* weren't coming. She was hurt, and I don't feel real good about that. But my point is that she knew I wasn't you within seconds. The only other woman who's ever been able to tell us apart that quickly was Grace."

"I don't like where this is heading," Aidan groused.

"You're descending into Married Guy Hell again, aren't you?"

Frustrated, Logan paced back and forth in front of the television. He stopped abruptly and wagged his finger at Aidan. "Do you remember pulling the Switch on Grace? It wasn't that long ago."

"Sure," Aidan said casually, but began to frown as he remembered exactly what had happened. It had been his idea to pull the Switch on Grace because he had believed she was using Logan to further her career. And within seconds of the moment they met on the beach, Grace had recognized that he was Aidan and not Logan.

That was the first time Aidan had ever met a woman who could distinguish so easily between the two of them. And Aidan had realized after talking to her for those few minutes, that Grace was in love with his brother.

Funny how the world had now turned upside down and Logan and he had changed places.

It didn't matter. Logan might believe it, but it couldn't be true. Ellie didn't love him. She only wanted a baby, not a long-term relationship. Right? Nothing had changed, had it?

He cast a glance at Logan, who was still blocking the basketball game with his pacing. Aidan decided to strike a reasonable tone. "Ellie's known us a lot longer than Grace had, so it's natural that she would be able to differentiate between us."

"Not that fast. Besides, she said she's been able to tell us apart since the first day we all met in New York. We have different ways of smiling or something."

Aidan frowned thoughtfully. She'd always been able to tell them apart? "Get off it."

"Seriously, she described your smile. And your eyes." Logan accompanied his words with a gagging sound.

"Shut up," Aidan said mildly.

Logan held his hands up. "It's all true, bro. I was frankly sickened by the whole conversation, but this is what I do for you."

Aidan snorted a laugh, but he quickly sobered. "So you left her alone."

"Yeah, and now I'm gonna leave you alone and go home to my wife."

Ellie latched the front door and turned off the porch light. While she was disappointed and hurt that Aidan hadn't shown up for dinner, she also felt an odd surge of hope after talking to Logan. Maybe he was right and all Aidan needed was another push or two—or three—and he would fall neatly into her arms.

Ellie knew life couldn't be that simple, but after spending the last few days talking with Sally Duke, she had begun to realize that telling the truth was the most important thing she could do for herself.

And tonight, after talking to Logan and then, once he left, musing over their conversation and tying it in with Sally's words, Ellie experienced an amazing moment of insight. It had to do with her mother, of all things.

Ellie realized that it wasn't her mother's *obsession* that had destroyed her; it was the lies she'd told herself. Her mom had repeated the same lies over and over again, so often that she began to believe them. Her mother had spent her life lying to herself and that was her ultimate downfall.

As Ellie brushed her hair and removed her makeup, she was more determined than ever that if she wanted to be free of her mother's legacy once and for all, she had to tell Aidan the truth. Whether he wanted to hear it or not.

He'd hurt her. He didn't need his brother to tell him that. He knew Ellie. Now he stood at her door and wondered if she would even let him into her house. Would she listen to him? Hell, he didn't even know what to say to her besides begging her forgiveness.

Logan had said that Ellie loved him. That she'd always been able to tell them apart. So was Aidan coming to see her to hear her say those words?

Aidan shoved the panicky feelings to the back of his mind and knocked on her door. And waited.

When Ellie didn't come to the door immediately, he began to fear that she really wouldn't let him in. Well, she was going to have to let him inside because she loved him, damn it.

Finally she showed up, opening the door in her pajamas and bathrobe.

"Aidan, what are you doing here?"

"You invited me for dinner," he said in a rush.

"I did," she said calmly. "But when you didn't show up, I packaged it up and stuck it in the freezer." She seemed to debate whether to let him inside or not, but after a moment she opened the door wide. "Come in, Aidan."

Once inside, he pulled her into his arms and held her, stroking her hair and mumbling apologies. "I'm sorry. God, I'm an idiot."

She rubbed his back in reassuring strokes, comforting him more than he deserved.

Finally, he held her by the shoulders to meet her gaze. "My brother and I sometimes forget that we're not twelve years old. I apologize for playing that trick on you and for ruining the meal you prepared. I'd like to make it up to you by taking you to dinner tomorrow night."

She took a deep breath and said, "Dinner would be nice, thank you."

"What else can I do to prove how sorry I am?"

"Oh, Aidan, I know you're sorry," she said softly.

He kissed her tenderly. "I'd like to stay with you tonight."

"Why, Aidan?"

"Why?" He stared at her, stunned. "Because, you know, we're together. You like me. And I like you. And we…you know."

"You like me?"

"Of course I do, damn it." He scraped his hands through his hair in frustration because he knew he wasn't getting his point across. "You know that."

She took a deep, slow breath, then reached up and framed his face with her hands. "What I know is that I love you, Aidan. I know those words aren't what you want to hear, but it's how I feel. And after talking to Logan earlier, I realized that it was time for me to be completely honest with you. So if you still want to be with me after hearing that, then you're welcome to stay."

His gaze didn't quite meet hers as he wrapped his arms around her and buried his face in her hair. "I'd like to stay."

He hadn't returned the words and Ellie didn't expect him to. He'd apologized again for switching places with Logan and she had forgiven him again with a smile.

But she couldn't deny that her heart ached. She would live with the pain for now because she had no choice. But she had told him the truth and that helped. The simple fact was that she wanted to be with Aidan for as long as it lasted.

Logan had advised her to keep pushing Aidan, but she was hesitant to follow his counsel. After all, she could only push the man for so long with no results before her self-confidence crumbled. If that happened, she would lose everything.

So over the next two weeks, Ellie buried herself in her work. Call it self-preservation, but she avoided all but the most cursory business conversations with Aidan, even at night. They continued to spend their nights together and it was wonderful as always, but where they used to chat about anything under the sun, now Ellie did everything she could to keep the subjects centered on business, on the office, on work in general. Nothing personal. She had to do that. To protect herself more than anything else.

Ellie had already confessed her love. Aidan knew how she felt so there was really no point in saying so over and over again. Besides, if she did, if she allowed herself to indulge in loving him openly, she would get caught up in pretending that they might actually have a life together and forget that the only thing they had between them was a thin, legal document. They didn't have love. Didn't have a future. All they had was a rather elusive goal to get her pregnant. Once they achieved that, Ellie had no doubt that Aidan would begin to make excuses to stay away from her. Eventually she wouldn't see him at all except at work or when he and his family wanted to visit with their baby.

And if that wasn't the most depressing thing in the world, she had also begun to notice that Aidan seemed perfectly willing to give her all the space she wanted, thus confirming in her mind that she was indeed losing him. But that was impossible, she chided herself. How could she lose him when she'd never really had him to begin with?

Aidan brought the small fishing boat to a stop in a secluded bay on the other side of the island from the resort. As he set up the deck chairs and grabbed the fishing poles, Logan pulled two bottles of beer from the ice chest, popped them open and handed one to his brother.

Aidan took a long slug, then set the beer bottle into the built-in drink holder on the arm of his chair. He baited his hook, then cast it into the water.

"Perfect day," he said, relaxing in his deck chair.

"Yeah, beautiful." Logan joined him and readied his fishing rod. "I love this spot."

"Yeah, me too."

"Best decision we ever made was to buy this island."

"I'm with you there."

They continued to fish in blessed silence for three and a half minutes or so, until Aidan blurted, "She's driving me crazy."

Logan laughed out loud. "I should've taken bets on how long you could last without bringing up the subject of Ellie."

"It's not funny," Aidan grumbled. "She won't stop working."

"I'll just mention this in case it hasn't crossed your mind," Logan said. "But Ellie is our partner now. When she works hard, we make money. See how that works out? It's a good thing. A win-win."

"I'm clear on the concept," Aidan said drily. "I'm just a little worried about her, that's all. Lately she's completely obsessed with work. Eats, sleeps and breathes it. It's all she talks about. Even when I try to change the subject to something else she's interested in, like books or movies, she winds the conversation right back to the office."

"Must make for some stimulating pillow talk."

"Shut up."

"Wait. Are you two still…you know?" Logan made a tangled gesture with his fingers.

"Shut up," Aidan repeated more forcefully.

"Is that a no?"

"No, it's not," Aidan said. "We're doing just fine in that department, thank you for your interest."

"Just trying to get the full picture."

Aidan scowled. "But even at night lately, Ellie doesn't say much unless it's work related."

"Might be a defense mechanism," Logan said as he adjusted the rim of his ball cap to better shield his eyes from the sun.

"What the hell's that supposed to mean?"

Logan's line tugged and he moved quickly to test it. "False alarm," he muttered, sitting back in his chair. "Okay, so you've got to look at this whole situation from her point of view. It's not like you've vowed eternal love to her, so she's starting to face facts. You're only sticking around to get her pregnant. Once that happens, you're gone. So even though she's in love with you, she doesn't see a future with you." He shrugged. "And so she's starting to pull back emotionally."

Aidan scowled at him. "Thank you, Dr. Freud."

"Hey, you asked. And please, you don't have to be a psychiatrist to see it. Just not blind…like some people."

"I'm not blind. I'm…focused."

"On all the wrong things."

"This is your fault," Aidan blurted.

"How do you figure that?" Logan sounded outraged.

Aidan eyed him suspiciously. "Now that I think about it, she started changing right after you pulled the Switch."

"Don't go blaming this on me," Logan said, laughing as he took another sip of beer. "If you'll recall, you began pulling away from her at Dad's wedding. That's when you started getting paranoid because of Sally."

"No, I didn't." But as he thought back, Aidan realized he'd forgotten how much he'd mistrusted his new mom. He would have to call her one of these days and tell her he was sorry about that.

He reeled in his line and re-baited his hook, then tossed it back into the water. And thought about Ellie.

She loved him.

She'd told him right to his face and he hadn't said a word back. But what could he say? He was crazy about her, but that was hardly love. Now that he thought about it, he wasn't even sure what love was. He just knew he wanted to be with Ellie all the time. Was that love? Hell, he was going to go crazy over that stupid question, and his brother wasn't helping.

"You're not helping," Aidan muttered aloud.

"You talking to me?"

"Never mind."

"I'm worried about you, bro," Logan said, but he was grinning like an idiot and didn't look worried at all.

Aidan shook his head in disgust. He grabbed his beer bottle and downed the rest of it. He would never truly understand women or love or anything related to those two subjects and it was useless to start trying now.

Suddenly a hefty fish yanked at his line and he pulled back and began to reel it in. He and his brother grinned at each other.

Fishing, he thought as he fought with the line. He understood fishing. Trying to figure anything else out only led to madness.

Two days later, Ellie stared in astonishment as a little pink cross appeared in the screen of the testing stick.

"Oh, my," she whispered. No wonder she'd been so ridiculously emotional lately. Was it any surprise that she'd been behaving like a nutcase, drowning herself in work until she couldn't see straight? She'd been a maniac for weeks now. And no wonder.

"I'm pregnant!" she exclaimed. She rose from the chair and twirled around her kitchen. She could feel her heart thumping wildly in her chest. "Wait 'til I tell Aidan. He's going to be so…"

She stopped, inhaled and exhaled a few times to catch her breath, and wondered. Aidan was going to be…what? Thrilled? Blissful? Indifferent?

"Thrilled, definitely," she said firmly, and danced around again. But her steps faltered immediately. She was going to be a mother, so now wasn't the time to dwell on foolish dreams of a family that included Aidan. Yes, he had insisted on supporting her and the baby. He'd written it into the contract. But that didn't mean he would be falling in love, moving in and starting a life together.

But that wasn't fair, she told herself. Of course Aidan would be thrilled about the baby. He was a good man and he cared about her a lot, she knew he did. He just didn't love her.

Or maybe he did love her, as Logan seemed to have indicated the night he came to her house. He seemed to believe that Aidan simply wasn't willing or able to say the words or act on his feelings. And that was fine, she thought resolutely, trying to convince herself of the lie.

"So much for telling the truth," she muttered, then quickly shook away the words. This wasn't the time to be thinking unhappy thoughts. She was pregnant and happy about it. This is what she'd wanted for so long; a man had never been a part of the equation.

But oh, now she wanted a man to be a part of her life. One man in particular. She couldn't imagine living without Aidan's warm arms around her and his ruggedly beautiful body snuggled up to hers. The thought of his skin rubbing up against hers, his amazing hands, and mouth and… Hmm.

There was a time when Ellie would've been embarrassed by her sexy thoughts, but not anymore. She had discovered the sensual side of herself, thanks to Aidan. And she wasn't ready to deny that part of her life, even with a child on the way. In fact, she was anxious to explore that side of herself even more now, and she wanted to do it with Aidan.

She wrapped her arms around her stomach and said a little prayer of thanks and hope that she and the little life growing inside her would be healthy and together they would make a happy little family some day soon.

But more than anything else, she hoped that Aidan would open his eyes and realize that this was right where he belonged.

With resolve, she left her house and crossed the coco palm grove to find Aidan and share the news. As she rounded the terrace, she saw Aidan walking toward a table of guests. Her heart gave a little jolt at the sight of him looking so handsome in a crisp white shirt tucked into beige linen trousers. So simple, yet so swoon-worthy, she thought with a smile.

She raised her arm to wave at him, but just then, one of the women jumped up from the table and wrapped her arms around his neck. Her curvaceous bikini-clad bottom barely covered her butt as she wiggled against him.

Ellie could hear the woman's shrieks of excitement all the way across the expansive terrace.

"Squeee! Aidan! Squeee!"

Those probably weren't her exact words, but it was something along those lines. The three women seated at the table chattered loud enough for Ellie to hear that the woman hugging Aidan had been here before and had been telling them about the hot guy who owned the resort.

Well, she was right about that. He was hot.

Ellie's vision blurred. Had Squeee Woman been with Aidan before? Had she been one of his bikini babes?

Without another clear thought, Ellie spun around and headed back to her cottage.

She felt faintly nauseated and it had nothing to do with being pregnant. No, this feeling had everything to do with her being dumb enough to fall in love with a man who had only been trying to finagle a way to keep her working on the island and give her child two caring parents instead of just one. To accomplish that, he had offered her a baby and the partnership she had always wanted.

As she walked through the palm grove, she conceded that she should be grateful. After all, Aidan had lived up to his part of their bargain. She couldn't fault him for that. Ellie had the partnership she had always wanted, and more importantly, she would soon have the baby she'd always dreamed of. Their bargain had been met. Now Aidan could return to his carefree, commitment-free lifestyle.

The only question in Ellie's mind now was, how could she continue to live here and work with Aidan, knowing she was in love with him and knowing he didn't love her back?

She had really thought she could do it, but just now, seeing that woman throw herself at Aidan, had changed her mind in an instant. She simply couldn't imagine herself caring for a newborn baby while Aidan went back to flirting with the bikini babes. That woman snuggling up to him just now had brought that painful fact into clear focus.

But that didn't mean she would run off like a coward with her tail between her legs. Ellie wasn't that person. There was no way she would quit her beloved job. She had signed a partnership contract. She was a full junior partner in Sutherland Corporation. She was a damned fine businesswoman and she would never walk away from that. And she refused to give up her wonderful life and all her good friends on the island. She loved it here. So no, leaving was absolutely not an option.

Besides, Ellie would never deny her child a fulfilling relationship with its father, even if Aidan refused to have anything to do with the baby—which he wouldn't do, she hastened to add. He wasn't that kind of man. Even though he had vowed never to get married, he was too good a person to turn his back on any child he'd fathered.

So she was in a quandary. There was no question about whether she would stay on the island or not. She was staying. But she could no longer live here at the resort, not with Aidan so close yet so unavailable. And that was another painful realization, because she loved her little cottage on the resort grounds. She wondered absently if she would be able to find a small house on the south shore. Or maybe something closer to town. It was only a short drive away.

"Oh, God." It was all too confusing to sort out right away. And it was downright heartbreaking, if she was being honest.

What she needed to do right now was go somewhere, get away and think. Somewhere quiet. Somewhere off the island so she wouldn't be tempted to run to Aidan and beg him to take her in his arms, touch her, love her. Which she would never do, for goodness sake.

Don't even think about doing something so beyond idiotic, she scolded herself. She would never try and cling to a man who didn't love her. That was exactly what her mother had done and look where it had gotten her. Ellie would never do to her own child what her mother had done to Ellie and Brenna.

With resolve, she ran into her house and pulled her overnight bag down from the closet. She tossed several casual outfits into it, added some underwear and toiletries, a few books and a pair of pajamas. She zipped the bag shut and went out to the kitchen to make four quick phone calls.

After that, she sent Aidan a quick text message to let him know she had to leave the island for a few days. An emergency, she said. But this time, she would be gone before he could do anything about it.

She grabbed her bag and locked up her house, then headed for the hotel. She detoured through the kitchen to avoid seeing Aidan with his guests on the terrace. Serena stood at a counter writing notes, but looked up from her clipboard to greet her. "Hey, you. Don't forget girls' night next Thursday."

"I won't," Ellie assured her. As she crossed the lobby,

the assistant concierge said hello and two of the bartenders shouted her name. She smiled and waved to all of them but kept walking toward the hotel entry to meet the limo driver she'd called.

She called out a greeting to Marianne as they passed each other. That's when Ellie slowed her pace a little as she realized that here was one more thing to cheer about. Ellie was no longer the overachieving, anchorless girl she'd been as a teenager . She had a home here on Alleria, and she had a life, and friends, and she was a normal, healthy woman with a heart filled to the brim with love to share with the right man. And she deserved that man to love her back equally. And soon she would have a baby, and her child deserved all of those things, too.

And she was no longer willing to settle for less.

"Ellie!"

Ellie turned and saw Grace jogging toward her, just as her limousine pulled up.

"Hi, I saw you from the lobby and I…" Grace noticed her suitcase. "Are you going somewhere?"

The driver stepped out of the car and took her bag.

"I'm going to visit my sister for a couple of days."

Grace gave her a hug. "I'll miss you."

Ellie felt her throat close up.

Grace frowned. "Is everything all right?"

"Yes. No. Yes. Oh, God." Ellie burst into tears.

"Oh, honey." Grace pulled her into her arms and hugged her. "What did Aidan do to hurt you?"

"Aidan? No. Nothing. He's happy. I'm fine." Ellie hiccupped and quickly dried her tears. "This is silly," she muttered and straightened her shoulders in an attempt to be an adult about things. "Good heavens, I'll only be gone for a few days, but saying goodbye always chokes me up a little. Like weddings. Pay no attention to me."

"They do that to me, too," Grace said, nodding in sympathy.

Ellie knew she hadn't tricked Grace, but her friend was sweet to give her a pass.

"Please call me if you want to talk," Grace added. "And hurry back. You know everyone here loves you, Ellie."

"I do." She sniffed, in danger of spilling more tears but determined not to. "Thank you, Grace. I'm so lucky to have you for my friend."

"I'm the lucky one, Ellie. I need all the friends I can get." She squeezed Ellie's arm. "And so does Aidan. Believe me, he needs you more than you'll ever know."

"We'll see," she said, and pasted a cheery smile on her face. She had a feeling she looked demented, but smiling was the only thing she could think to do to stop the onslaught of more wretched tears. "I'd better go now. I have to make my plane."

"Bye, Ellie," Grace said softly. "See you soon."

"What do you mean, she's gone? Where the hell is she?"

"I'm sorry, Mr. Sutherland," Ellie's efficient secretary said. "All she said was that she had to leave the island for a few days."

Aidan stormed out of Ellie's office suite and returned to his own. Where the hell had she disappeared to? What "emergency" did she have to run off to?

He'd seen her dashing away from the terrace over an hour ago and would've gone after her, but he'd been waylaid by some returning guests who'd insisted on talking his ear off.

Not that he would ever complain about the resort's guests since they provided a portion of the hefty income that kept Sutherland Corporation in business. But frankly, he'd had his fill of all those overly made-up, bikini-clad socialites whose only job was to spend money jetting from one destination point to the next, according to the season.

And another thing. He didn't understand any woman who piled on makeup and perfume just to sit and sweat by a pool in the tropics, but that was a question for another day.

He knew Ellie had seen him on the terrace, but she hadn't stopped and waited for him. He'd figured she was in a hurry to get somewhere and he would find her later. The minute he'd seen her on the terrace, he'd concocted a plan to whisk her away to the rain forest for a sultry afternoon of lovemaking under the waterfall. He missed having her in his arms.

But when he'd gotten back to his office, he'd found her text message saying she was leaving the island. That's what he got for forgetting his phone in the office. That was another thing he blamed entirely on Ellie. He'd been so discombobulated by her behavior lately that he was forgetting to tie his own shoelaces. Yesterday, he'd almost missed their weekly conference call with the New York investors. Logan had been forced to send out a search party for him.

"Not important right now," he muttered. He needed to figure out where Ellie had gone and go after her. He tried calling her cell phone, but she didn't answer. Where in hell had she gone?

"I hope you're happy."

He turned and saw Grace standing at his doorway. "Why? What do you know?"

"I just know that Ellie is the best thing that ever happened to you and you're going to lose her."

"No, I'm not," he said a bit desperately. "You know where she's gone. Tell me so I can go after her."

"Why?"

Aidan stared at her, wondering if Grace was losing her grip on reality.

"What do you mean, why? Because I need her here, that's why."

"Yes, but why do you need her?" Grace folded her arms over her chest, tipped her head to one side and narrowed her gaze on him. "Did she forget to sign an important contract? Did she neglect to make a phone call to a new client?"

Logan walked up and stood behind Grace. Aidan glared at his brother, but Logan just smiled and wrapped his arm around Grace.

"I don't have time for this," Aidan said. He checked his phone for the tenth time in two minutes, but there were no new messages from Ellie.

With an abrupt huff of frustration, Grace stomped her foot. "Aidan, why do you want to go after Ellie?"

"Yeah, bro," Logan drawled. "There's nothing too pressing going on right now. Let her take a few days off."

"No. I need her here."

"Why?" Logan asked.

He needed her. Wasn't that enough? "Okay, both of you, get out."

Grace shook her head. "You're such a knucklehead."

Aidan raised an eyebrow at that, then glanced at his brother. "Does she call you names like that?"

"Not so much anymore," he said.

"Great. So it's just me."

Logan walked over to the bar and poured two shots of scotch. He handed one to Aidan, who scowled, but took the glass and downed it.

"Thanks, I needed that," Aidan said. "Now you can go."

"I don't think so," Grace said.

"Nope, we're just getting started." Logan sat down in the visitor's chair and pulled Grace onto his lap.

"This should be good," Aidan muttered, and had no choice but to sit back down at his desk.

"I don't care if you're too stupid to admit you're in love with the woman," Logan said. "What I do care about is that we might've just lost the best business partner we'll ever have because you're too boneheaded to admit it."

"Something happened to make Ellie leave," Grace said. "What did you do?"

"I didn't do anything. I was on my way to take her up to the lagoon for the day."

"Oh, that's so romantic," Grace said, and smiled at Logan. But then she turned and frowned at Aidan. "So why did she run off?"

Aidan thought about seeing Ellie across the terrace. She'd looked right at him, then turned and left. Why? Then it hit him.

"Damn it," he muttered. "There were some guests flirting with me. It didn't mean anything, but that's the moment Ellie…"

"But Ellie's not the jealous type," Logan said. "It must've been something you said."

"She's not the jealous type, but she does have a gentle heart," Grace said. "And she's pretty certain you're not willing to give her yours. Seeing you with those women might've brought that hard lesson home to her."

Aidan brushed his hand through his hair in frustration. Grace's words made sense, even if he hated hearing them.

"Why are you keeping Ellie at arm's length?" Logan asked quietly. "Why won't you just admit that you love her as much as she loves you? You can trust her, Aidan. She won't hurt you."

Aidan sneered at his brother. "Look who's Mr. Relationship Expert."

Logan laughed. "Turnabout is fair play, dude. Remember a while back when you played the expert?"

Aidan nodded. "Yeah, back when you played the idiot."

Logan chuckled. Gazing at his wife, he stroked her hair. "Yeah. That was me."

Unable to watch the two lovebirds any longer, Aidan got up and poured himself another shot of scotch. He stared at the glass, then glanced out the window at the incredible view of palm trees swaying along the white sand beach with the azure waters of Alleria Bay in the distance. It was one more symbol of what they'd strived to accomplish throughout their lives. This piece of land should've meant everything to him. But right now, it didn't mean much because Ellie wasn't here with him. Was that the real reason why he'd tried to keep her on the island in the first place? Damn. It had nothing to do with keeping the business going. It had to do with keeping Ellie near him. Everything was better when she was by his side. In business, in pleasure, on the island, flying off to New York. Everything worked when Ellie was with him.

God, she'd only been gone an hour or so and he missed her. Where was she? He needed her here. On the island. With him. This island, this symbol of accomplishment, meant nothing if he couldn't share it with the one person he'd grown to love more than anything else in the world.

"So what's your plan, man?" Logan asked him.

Aidan gritted his teeth, knowing there was only one thing to do. He drained the shot glass and slammed it down on the counter, then turned and faced his brother and Grace. "My plan is to grovel as much as it takes to get her back."

"But why, Aidan?" Grace asked softly.

Aidan smiled as he realized that Ellie had asked him the same question that night he and Logan had pulled the Switch. He had rushed to her house to see her and had wanted to spend the night with her and all she had said was, *Why?*

He turned to his brother and Grace. "Because I love her."

"Good answer," Logan said. "Just might work."

* * *

Ellie had just settled on the couch and was about ready to doze off when the doorbell rang. For a moment, her shoulders tightened at the thought of Aidan coming for her. But he didn't even know where she was! It was just one more example of her crazy obsession with the man.

Besides, it was mid-morning in Atlanta, not Alleria. Aidan was a thousand miles away. Brenna had rushed out to the market while the kids were in preschool. Her husband, Brian, was at work. And Ellie was already tired, so she decided to ignore the doorbell.

When the doorbell rang again, Ellie grumbled. It was probably someone Brenna knew, so she really should answer the door. When it rang yet again, it was clear that the person wasn't going to go away.

"Hold your horses," she muttered as she stood and walked to the door. She pulled it open and blinked, not quite trusting her eyesight. Had she conjured him up by magic? Did he have to look so wonderful that he made her mouth water? She wanted him so badly, she could feel her knees weakening.

"Aidan."

Without waiting for an invitation, he walked right into the house, shoved the door closed, pulled her into his arms and kissed her.

She savored his presence, the brush of his clothing against hers, his scent, the taste of him on her lips, and wished the moment would last forever. But it couldn't, of course.

"I know you're in love with me, Ellie," he said immediately after the kiss ended. "I'm taking you home."

"I'm in love with you?" she said. "Is that all you came here to tell me? Go home, Aidan."

"Don't deny it," he said. "You love me."

She stomped away from him, then whipped around. "Why would I deny it? I've already told you I'm in love with you.

It's no big revelation. But if you think I'm going to drop everything and go back with you to Alleria, you're wrong."

"We need you, Ellie."

"We?" she said, a little too loudly.

He sighed heavily. "All right. I need you. Okay? I can't seem to do anything without you."

"Oh, right, you need me," she said in a withering tone. "You don't look too happy about it."

"I'm happy," he said loudly.

"Just admit it, Aidan. You'll say any outlandish thing you can think of to get me to come back to work."

"I don't care if you come back to work," he retorted. "You can quit your job for all I care. I just want you to come back to me. I need you in my life."

"But you have so many other women who want you." Oh, no, she thought. Why did she say that? She sounded like a jealous harpy.

And he knew it. Which was why he was grinning broadly now. "I knew you saw me on the terrace. Why didn't you rescue me from that horrible woman? She ambushed me."

"Oh, please," she muttered. "You poor baby."

"It's true," he said, biting back a smile. "Besides, I was on my way to find you so we could sneak off to the waterfall and make love all afternoon."

She almost sighed at the thought of them lazing away the day in the rain forest. She wanted him so much, it was killing her.

"But you ran away," he said, brooding. "I couldn't find you anywhere. Why?"

She wanted to tell him why, wanted to throw herself into his arms and beg him to love her. Instead, she asked, "What are you doing here, Aidan?"

He gazed at her musingly. "I was an idiot not to realize

years ago how amazing you are. I've wanted you all this time."

She blinked. "What? Why didn't you say something?"

"Did you hear the part about my being an idiot?"

She blurted out a laugh. "It's my favorite thing you've said so far."

"It's true, Ellie. I've been so stupid. It took your leaving to make me realize how much time I've lost, but I'll make it up to you, I promise." He held her shoulders and gazed into her eyes. "I love you, Ellie. I love everything about you."

"Y-you love me?"

"I do. I even love your slide presentations and your sensible pantsuits and the way you shove your pencil behind your ear when you're concentrating on your notes."

"Oh, good grief, Aidan," she said, covering her face with both hands. "I sound like a schoolmarm."

"I love schoolmarms," he said, pulling her hands away and kissing them, one finger at a time. "And pantsuits." After a moment, he met her gaze again. "But if it's not too sexist, can I admit I prefer your little bikini most of all?"

"Of course you do," she said drily.

"I cannot tell a lie." He smiled, and one corner of his mouth curved even higher than the other, just as Ellie had explained to Logan. His grin widened and his eyes twinkled and she fell in love with him all over again.

"Oh, Aidan," she whispered.

He smoothed her hair back from her face. "Please come home. I promise you're the only bikini babe I've ever loved. Please, Ellie. I miss you in my bed, but most of all, I miss you in my life."

She took a breath and let it out. "I miss you, too."

"Come home, then," he said, squeezing her hands in a sensual plea. "Come home and start a family with me. We can tear up the custody agreement because I want a big family with lots of babies. I promise they'll always know how much I love them and their beautiful mother. Please come back to the island, back to our home. Marry me and love me always, Ellie."

How could she say anything but yes? "I love you so much, Aidan. Of course I'll come home with you and marry you."

"Thank you," he whispered. He kissed her again and she could feel the promise in his touch.

When he opened his eyes and gazed at her again, she smiled shyly. "I'm glad to hear you say you want babies, because I'm pregnant, Aidan."

His eyes widened and he gazed down at her. "Oh, my God. Is it true?"

She took his hand and pressed it lightly against her stomach. "Do you mind?"

"Mind?" he said, and then laughed. "No. I think I'm speechless. But very, very happy." And he kissed her again.

Ellie couldn't believe her heart could be so filled with love without bursting.

When she opened her eyes, Aidan was staring intently at her. "I can't wait to get home," he murmured. "I want to make love with you all night long. And I still intend to take a day very soon and go up to the waterfall where I plan to explore every beautiful inch of you."

Ellie shivered with need. That tingling feeling she always felt around him was back and she couldn't wait to show him how much she loved him. Every day for the rest of their lives together. With a smile, she took hold of his hand. "Take me home, Aidan. Take me back to Alleria where we both belong."

Epilogue

Three years later

"Twins?" Logan exclaimed. "Are you kidding?"

Ellie rubbed the slight bump of her tummy, then smiled up at Aidan as his hand covered hers.

"That's what the doctor says," Aidan explained to his brother as they relaxed under the pergola overlooking the secluded cove. They were surrounded by their large, extended family and Aidan couldn't help smiling as he watched his two-year-old son, Bobby, stretch to plant his sandy feet in his older cousin Jake's footsteps.

There were kids everywhere. The Duke and Sutherland families had established a new tradition of spending the holidays together at the charming boutique hotel the Duke brothers had built on the northern coast of Alleria. The hotel had been built into the side of a cliff and overlooked one of Alleria's beautiful views. Flowering vines cascaded down the hillside and the pristine white sand beach was dotted with colorful umbrellas. Sailboats bobbed in the azure waters beyond the breakwater.

Logan and Grace were here with their eighteen-month-old twin girls, Rosie and Lily, and the three Duke cousins had brought their entire brood. As far as Aidan was concerned, there was nothing better than Christmas in the tropics, and he was looking forward to a rollicking Christmas dinner with the whole gang later that afternoon.

His dad and Sally had made the trip, too, of course. Sally had made it a habit to keep in close touch with Aidan and Logan and considered them to be her boys along with her three Duke sons.

Aidan watched Sally laugh at something one of her grandchildren said. He rubbed at the twinge in his chest as he recalled the exact moment when he had realized that Sally had become the mother of his heart.

"Twins run in the family," his dad, Tom, said, smiling fondly at Ellie.

"They must," Logan said with a laugh.

First there had been Aidan and Logan, then Logan and Grace gave birth to twin daughters, and now Ellie was pregnant with twins.

Sally touched Tom's knee. "Are there more twins we don't know about?"

"Oh, yeah," Tom said. "My father was a twin, too. But his brother, my uncle Ransom, was lost at sea during World War II."

"That's so sad," Grace said, keeping an eagle eye on little Rosie and Lily as they dug in the sand with their colorful plastic shovels.

"Yeah." Tom sipped his beer. "My dad never accepted it though. He always had a feeling that his brother was still alive somewhere. You know, that twin radar of his wouldn't let him give up on his brother."

"So you could have an uncle living somewhere?" Sally said, her eyes wide. "Have you ever tried to find him?"

"No," Tom said, then started to laugh. "But something tells me I've just given you a new project to dig your teeth into."

"Yes, you have," Sally said with a big smile. "And I can't wait."

Aidan chuckled. If anyone could do it, Sally could. She had been a widow for many years and had spent part of that time trying to track down her late husband's brother, Tom, otherwise known as Aidan and Logan's dad. When Sally finally found him, the two had fallen in love, so who better than Sally to search for a lost uncle?

"You have to admit she's good at finding people," Logan said.

Aidan met Ellie's soft gaze and he felt the familiar jolt of happiness he always got when he looked at his beautiful wife. "She helped me find you."

"I think we found each other," Ellie whispered.

No thanks to his own stubbornness, Aidan thought silently as he gripped her hand in his. Thank goodness he'd come to his senses in time.

Now as he stretched his legs out on the chaise longue he shared with his wife, he considered himself the luckiest man on the planet. Ellie enriched his life in so many ways and he tried each day to show her how much love and happiness he held in his heart for her. They were perfect partners in every way possible and had given each other exactly what Ellie had always wanted and what Aidan had finally discovered he wanted just as badly. A family of their own.

* * * * *

"Sorry I'm late."

Something about that deep voice made the hair on the back of her neck shiver. She'd definitely heard it before. But where…

The breath she had just inhaled backed up in her lungs. Oh no, it *couldn't* be.

She glanced up at him out of the corner of her eye as he approached the table…and swiftly looked away, heart pounding. He had the same smoldering black eyes, the solid, square jaw, the full lips that had kissed her senseless. But it couldn't be him. Could it? Her mind must be playing tricks on her.

She had a strict rule of never sleeping with a coworker. Especially one she would be working with directly. And definitely not one whose work she would be putting under the microscope.

"Rob," Demitrio said. "This is Caroline Taylor. Caroline, this is my son, Rob, our director of marketing."

She had no choice but to look up, to meet his eyes…

CAROSELLI'S
BABY CHASE

BY
MICHELLE CELMER

All the characters in this book have no existence outside the imagination of the author, and have no relation whatsoever to anyone bearing the same name or names. They are not even distantly inspired by any individual known or unknown to the author, and all the incidents are pure invention.

All Rights Reserved including the right of reproduction in whole or in part in any form. This edition is published by arrangement with Harlequin Enterprises II B.V./S.à.r.l. The text of this publication or any part thereof may not be reproduced or transmitted in any form or by any means, electronic or mechanical, including photocopying, recording, storage in an information retrieval system, or otherwise, without the written permission of the publisher.

This book is sold subject to the condition that it shall not, by way of trade or otherwise, be lent, resold, hired out or otherwise circulated without the prior consent of the publisher in any form of binding or cover other than that in which it is published and without a similar condition including this condition being imposed on the subsequent purchaser.

® and ™ are trademarks owned and used by the trademark owner and/or its licensee. Trademarks marked with ® are registered with the United Kingdom Patent Office and/or the Office for Harmonisation in the Internal Market and in other countries.

Published in Great Britain 2013
by Mills & Boon, an imprint of Harlequin (UK) Limited,
Eton House, 18-24 Paradise Road, Richmond, Surrey TW9 1SR

© Michelle Celmer 2013

ISBN: 978 0 263 90624 0
ebook ISBN: 978 1 472 01185 5

51-0613

Harlequin (UK) policy is to use papers that are natural, renewable and recyclable products and made from wood grown in sustainable forests. The logging and manufacturing processes conform to the legal environmental regulations of the country of origin.

Printed and bound in Spain
by Blackprint CPI, Barcelona

Michelle Celmer is a bestselling author of more than thirty books. When she's not writing, she likes to spend time with her husband, kids, grandchildren and a menagerie of animals.

Michelle loves to hear from readers. Visit her website, www.michellecelmer.com, like her on Facebook or write her at PO Box 300, Clawson, MI 48017, USA.

In memory of my nephew Devon,
who in seventeen years touched more lives
than most people manage in a lifetime

Prologue

Once a year since her death, on the day of her birth, December thirtieth, Giuseppe Caroselli honored Angelica, his wife of sixty-eight years and mother of his three sons, by making her favorite cake, raspberry walnut torte with dark chocolate frosting.

Caroselli chocolate, of course.

In less than an hour his family would be there to celebrate with him. To pass photos and share memories. On his request, his grandsons Rob and Tony had arrived early. They each sat on a barstool at the kitchen island, watching him carefully measure the ingredients and mix them together, the way they had when they were boys.

From birth, his three grandsons—Robert, Anthony Jr. and Nicholas—had been groomed to someday take over Caroselli Chocolate, the business Giuseppe had built from the ground up, after emigrating from Italy.

What he hadn't counted on was their being so resistant

to carrying on the Caroselli name. And if they didn't set-tle down and have sons of their own, the Carosellis would be no more. At least Nicholas now had the marriage part taken care of.

"As I'm sure you already know, Nicholas has forfeited his portion of the thirty-million dollars."

"He told us," Tony said, a perpetual frown on his face. So serious, that one. He needed to learn to take life in stride. Have fun.

"That means fifteen million each to you boys if you marry and produce a male heir," he told them.

"That's a lot of money," Rob said. He was the most driven of the three, the one who would no doubt take his father Demitrio's place as CEO one day. If Demitrio would only put aside his doubts and trust his son.

"It is a lot of money," Giuseppe agreed. Money that he had no intention of actually giving them. What sort of man would he be if he singled out only two of his seven grand-children? And as he had suspected, Nick was so happy to be married, so content with his life, he had turned down his share.

One down, two to go.

And Giuseppe didn't doubt that like their cousin, in the end, Tony and Rob would make the right decision and do him proud.

In fact, he was counting on it.

One

As he watched his date leave the hotel bar wrapped around another man, Robert Caroselli wanted to feel angry or put out, or even mildly annoyed, but he couldn't work up the steam. He hadn't wanted to come to this party, but he'd let Olivia, a woman he'd been seeing casually, talk him into it last minute.

"I don't really feel like celebrating," he'd told her when she called him around nine. He had already turned off the television and was planning to crawl into bed and with any luck sleep away the next three months or so. It was that or face daily the fact that his family, the owners of Caroselli Chocolate, had lost complete faith in him as a marketing director.

Yes, sales for the last quarter were down, but they were in a recession for Christ's sake. Hiring Caroline Taylor, a so-called marketing genius from Los Angeles, was not only an insult, but also total overkill as far as he was concerned. But against the entire family, his objections carried little weight.

On top of that he had the added pressure of finding a wife. A woman to give him a male heir. By thirty-one most of his cousins, and the majority of his college buddies, were already married. It wasn't as if he'd made a conscious decision to stay single. His dedication to the family business had kept him too busy to settle down. He couldn't deny that ten-million dollars had been a tempting incentive, but fifteen million? That was difficult to pass up. Especially when it meant that if he didn't get his cut, his cousin Tony would walk away with the entire thirty million. He would never hear the end of it.

But if he was going to find a woman to be his wife and bear his children, it wouldn't be in a bar. And it definitely wouldn't be Olivia. Which was why he'd planned to stay home.

"You *can't* stay home alone on New Year's Eve!" Olivia had said. "Who will you kiss? You can't start the New Year without a kiss at midnight. It's…un-American!"

She hadn't seemed too concerned with whom he would kiss when she walked out the door with someone else. Not that he blamed her for bailing on him. He hadn't exactly been the life of the party. When they arrived around ten, he scoped out a counter-height table with two vacant barstools near the back corner, claimed it and hadn't moved since. Now he was on his—he counted the empty glasses in front of him—third Scotch and feeling a hell of a lot more relaxed than when he got there.

Alcohol flowed freely at every Caroselli family function—hell, his family would use any excuse to get together, drink and gossip—but Rob rarely indulged. He never much cared for the out-of-control feeling that came with intoxication. Tonight was a rare exception.

From his table he had a decent view of the entire bar, which was crammed above capacity with people, who, from his vantage point, undulated like the waves off the shore of Lake Michigan. Or maybe that was the liquor playing tricks with his vision.

"Excuse me!"

At the sudden shout, Rob jerked to attention. He blinked, then blinked again, positive he was imagining the angel who stood beside his table. A halo of pale blond hair hung in loose curls that nearly brushed her narrow waist, and framed a heart-shaped face that glowed with youth and good health. His gaze slipped lower and he realized that this particular angel had a body made for sin. She couldn't have been more than a few inches over five-feet tall, but she packed one hell of a figure into her skinny jeans and clingy blue sweater. A complete contrast to the wholesome beauty of her face.

"Is this seat taken?" she shouted over the music. "And just to be clear, I am *not* hitting on you. I've been on my feet all day and there isn't a single other free seat in this entire place."

He gestured to the chair across from his. "Help yourself."

"Thank you." She slid onto the stool, sighing with pleasure as her feet left the floor. "You're a lifesaver."

"No problem."

She offered him one fine-boned hand with short, neatly filed nails. "Carrie—"

Her last name was drowned out by the blare of a noise-maker. She shook his hand, her grip surprisingly firm for someone so petite and delicate-looking.

"Hi, Carrie, I'm Rob."

"Nice to meet you, Ron," she said.

He opened his mouth to correct her, but she flashed him

a smile so easy and sweet, so disarming, she could call him anything she wanted and it wouldn't have mattered to him. "Can I buy you a drink?"

She cocked her head to one side and smiled. "Are *you* hitting on *me*?"

He had never been the type to flirt, but he heard himself saying, "Would it be a problem if I was?"

She leaned forward to study him and his gaze was naturally drawn to the deep cleft at the front of her low-cut sweater. "I guess that just depends."

"On what?"

"Why a man like you would be sitting here alone at eleven-fifteen on New Year's Eve."

"A man like me?"

She rolled her eyes. "Don't even try to pretend that you don't know how hot you are. You should have women crawling all over you."

"I'm alone because my date left with someone else."

She blinked. "Was she blind or just stupid?"

He laughed. "Bored, I think. I'm not in a mood to celebrate."

Although the night was definitely looking up.

"You must have a girlfriend," she said.

He shook his head.

"Wife?"

He held up his ringless left hand.

She paused, then asked, "Gay?"

He laughed again. "Straight as an arrow."

"Hmm," she said, looking puzzled. "Are you a jerk?"

She sure didn't pull any punches. He liked a woman who was direct and to the point. "I'd like to believe I'm not, but I suppose everyone has their moments."

She nodded thoughtfully. "Honesty...I like that. My answer is yes. You can buy me a drink."

"What would you like?"

She nodded to his glass. "Whatever you're having."

He looked around, but the waitresses in the vicinity were overwhelmed with customers, so he figured it would be quicker to go right to the source. "Be right back," he said, heading for the bar.

It took several minutes to navigate through the crowd, and another five or ten before the bartender served him. As he walked back to the table, he half expected Carrie to be gone. He was pleasantly surprised to find her sitting there waiting for him, and suddenly grateful that he wouldn't have to watch the ball drop alone. He might even get a New Year's kiss out of it. Or maybe that would be pushing his luck. Maybe just a quick one, or if she wasn't into kissing a total stranger, a peck on the cheek even.

"Here you go." He set her drink in front of her and reclaimed his chair.

"That took so long, I started to think you left," she said.

"And I wasn't sure if you would still be here when I got back."

"I'm not blind or stupid," she said with a grin, and he felt a tug of attraction so intense, he nearly reached across the table for her hand.

"Do you live in the area?" she asked, sipping her drink.

"Lincoln Park."

"Is that far from here?"

"Not too far. I take it you're not from Chicago."

"West Coast born and bred. I'm here for work. I'm staying in the hotel. That's how I wound up in this particular bar."

"You must have someone back home."

"Not for a while."

"Are the men there blind or just stupid?"

She smiled, and he felt that tug again, only this time

it was lower, and it wasn't her hand he wanted to touch. That New Year's kiss was sounding even more appealing. He would have to call Olivia tomorrow and thank her for dragging him out.

"A lot of men feel threatened by a strong, successful woman," she said.

Rob had quite a few strong, successful women in his family, and compared to them, Carrie looked anything but threatening. His first instinct, when she had approached his table, was to pick her up and hug her.

"I also have the tendency to gravitate toward men who are bad for me," she said.

"Bad for you how?"

"I like jerks. It's my way of sabotaging the relationship before it even begins." She sipped her drink. "I have intimacy issues."

"If you know that, then why don't you date someone different?"

"Knowing what the problem is doesn't necessarily make it any easier to fix."

Well, she had the honesty thing down to a science. The women he met typically played up their good qualities, not their faults. Which he couldn't deny was, in an odd way, a refreshing change of pace. A sort of "this is me, take it or leave it" philosophy.

"When was your last serious relationship?" he asked.

"I've never really had one."

"Really? What are you? Twenty-four? Twenty-five?"

Carrie laughed. "Aren't you good for my ego. I'm twenty-eight."

"I've never met a woman past the age of eighteen who hasn't been in at least one serious relationship."

"Which you clearly find fascinating," she said, looking amused.

"I do." In more ways than just that. She was like the perfect woman. Sexy, desirable, with a decent sense of humor and completely uninterested in a relationship. Had he hit the jackpot or what?

"How about you?" Carrie asked. "Ever been in a serious relationship?"

"Engaged, but that was a long time ago. Back in college."

"What happened?"

"You could say that we wanted different things."

"What did you want?"

He shrugged. "Marriage, kids, the usual stuff."

"What did she want?"

"My roommate, Evan."

She winced. "Ouch."

"Better I found out what she was like before we were married than after. At that point I decided to focus on my career."

"So you're married to your job?"

"More or less."

"It's not unusual for me to work fourteen-hour days, so I totally get that."

She would be the first woman who ever did. And he found himself wishing she were staying in Chicago longer than a few days. She was someone he wouldn't mind getting to know better.

After talking for a few minutes more, and some serious flirting, they had both drained their glasses, so he hailed a waitress for two more drinks. There was more talking, more flirting—but mostly flirting—then Carrie had a third drink, and by then it was nearly midnight. At one minute till, the music stopped, and everyone focused on the big-screen television over the bar to watch the ball drop.

"So," Carrie said, "because neither of us has anyone to kiss…"

"I was told that it's un-American to start the New Year off without a kiss," he said.

"I guess that doesn't leave us much choice, then."

With a grin, he held out his hand and she took it. She slid down off the stool, and didn't show a bit of resistance as he tugged her closer. He should have been watching the ball drop, but he couldn't seem to peel his eyes away from her face. Standing this close he would have expected to see at least an imperfection or two, but her skin was flawless, her eyes such a clear gray they appeared bottomless. His eyes dropped to her mouth, to lips that looked full and soft and kissable.

Only an hour ago he had been dreading the arrival of the New Year, now he could hardly wait for those last thirty seconds to pass. Then it was twenty seconds, and when it reached ten, everyone in the bar started to count. Except for him and Carrie. Their eyes locked, and they stood so close now that her warm breath feathered against his lips. They waited in anticipation. Five…four…three…two…

Unable to wait another second, he slanted his mouth over hers and the cheers and hoots, the shrill of noisemakers and the chorus of "Auld Lang Syne" being sung—it all faded into the background. Her lips parted under his. He heard her sigh as he sank his fingers through the silky ribbons of her hair, felt her melt against him when he pulled her closer. The softness of her lips, the sweet taste of her mouth, were more intoxicating than any drink. And he wanted her, knew he had to have her, even if it was for only one night.

He wasn't sure how long they stood there kissing, their arms wrapped around one another, but when he finally broke the kiss, they were both breathless and Carrie's cheeks were rosy and hot.

"At the risk of sounding too forward," she said, "would you like to come up to my room?"

Of course he wanted to. "Are you sure that's what you want?"

That must have been the right answer, because she smiled and took his hand. "I am now. I figure, why not start the year with a *bang?*"

He grinned, squeezed her hand and said, "Let's go."

Two

Start the year off with a bang indeed, Carrie thought as the cab inched along in bumper-to-bumper traffic through the slushy streets of Chicago. Two days later and her neck still ached, there was a bruise on her shin where she had banged it on the headboard, and she had angry-looking rug burns on her knees, but it had been *so* worth it. She hadn't been *banged* so well, or so many times in a row, in years. The man was insatiable, and gave as good as he got. Better even. And as she had imagined, he looked just as good out of his clothes as he did in them. She would even go so far as to say that it was the single most satisfying, fun and adventurous sexual experience of her life. Then he had to go and ruin it by skulking off in the middle of the night without even saying goodbye.

He hadn't left his phone number, which she could have looked up if she had caught his last name. But all evidence pointed to his not wanting to be found. For all she knew,

Ron wasn't even his real name, and he had been sitting there alone looking for someone just like her, someone to *bang* in the New Year with. Maybe all he'd really wanted was cheap sex.

Oh, well. At least it had been really *good* cheap sex. And in her own defense, she'd hit the minibar in her room before she had even ventured downstairs and had been more than a little drunk. It was possible that he wasn't even as good-looking as she thought. Or that great of a lover.

She wasn't sure if that should make her feel better or worse.

She had been in Chicago barely forty-eight hours, and already she'd invited a strange man up to her room, had sex and had gotten dumped. That had to be some kind of world record.

But Ron—if that was really his name—wasn't totally to blame. She did have the tendency to come on a little strong, and sometimes men took it the wrong way. Under normal circumstances she was outspoken. Get her a little tipsy and she had the tendency to say things she probably shouldn't. According to her stepfather, her sassy mouth had been her biggest problem. And his cure for that had always been a solid crack across said mouth with the back of his hand.

She didn't recall everything she and Ron had discussed that night, but she seemed to remember some of it being very personal in nature.

"This is it," the cab driver said as the car rolled to a stop outside Caroselli Chocolate headquarters. As soon as the contracts were signed, and a timetable set, she would look for an apartment or condo to lease. There was nothing she hated more than living out of suitcases for extended periods of time.

She paid him, grabbed her briefcase, climbed out of the cab and walked to the revolving front door, the damp cold seeping through her coat, the heels of her pumps clicking against the slushy pavement. She pushed her way inside, into a lobby of glass, stainless steel and marble, and walked to the guard station, the alluring scent of chocolate drawing her gaze to the gift shop at the other end of the lobby.

"Caroline Taylor. I'm here for a meeting," she told the guard.

"Good morning, Ms. Taylor. They're expecting you." He handed her a name badge that said "Guest," which she clipped to the lapel of her suit jacket. "Take the elevator behind me up to the third floor and see the receptionist."

"Thank you." She walked to the elevator, back straight, head high. There was no lack of security cameras, and it was critical to make a good impression the second she walked in the door. Despite her reputation, and her impeccable record for getting the job done, some people, men of a certain era in particular, sometimes doubted her abilities. And this being a family business, she had no doubt that she would be working with several generations of Carosellis.

As she rode up to the third floor she shrugged out of her overcoat and draped it over her arm. When the doors slid open she stepped out of the elevator into another reception area. A young woman whose nameplate announced her as Sheila Price was seated behind a large desk, and beside her stood an attractive, older gentleman in a very expensive, exquisitely tailored suit. Considering his age, and the air of authority he exuded, she was guessing he was one of the three Caroselli brothers, the sons of Giuseppe who now ran the company.

She walked to the desk, nervous energy propelling her steps. She hadn't planned to expand her business outside the West Coast area for another year or two, but Caroselli Chocolate was the largest and most prestigious company to approach her thus far, and when they called, it was too good an opportunity to pass up. Of course, if she botched it up, it would decimate her reputation and probably destroy her career.

But that wasn't going to happen.

"Welcome, Ms. Taylor," the man said, stepping forward to greet her. "I'm Demitrio Caroselli."

"It's a pleasure," she said, shaking his hand, a little surprised that the CEO himself was there to greet her.

"Can I take your coat?" Sheila asked.

"Yes, thank you," she said, handing it over.

"Everyone is waiting for us in the conference room," Demitrio said, gesturing down a long hallway lined with offices. "It's this way."

Being a private contractor, Carrie answered to no one, and being in such high demand, she walked into every meeting knowing she had the upper hand. That didn't mean she wasn't slightly nervous. But she seriously doubted they would have shelled out the expense of a first-class plane ticket and a five-star hotel if they weren't seriously planning to sign the contract.

"Do you prefer Caroline or Ms. Taylor?" he asked.

"Caroline or Carrie," she told him.

"We appreciate your coming to see us on such short notice," he said. "And so close to the holidays."

"I'm happy to be here." The assignment back in L.A. that she was supposed to have started this week had been cancelled when the company went under last month; otherwise she wouldn't have been available until much later this year.

"Is this your first visit to Chicago?"

"It is. From what I've seen it's a beautiful city. The snow will take some getting used to, though." The hall was silent and most of the offices they passed were dark. "Is it always this quiet?"

"We're not technically back from the holiday break until next Monday," he said. "The holiday season is a very busy time for us so we give everyone the first week of the year off."

At the end of the hall he opened a door marked "Conference Room" and Carrie held her breath as they stepped inside. In front of a bank of windows that spanned the entire length of the room stood a strikingly beautiful young woman who looked more suited to a fashion runway than a company boardroom. On one side of a marble-topped table long enough to seat a dozen-plus people sat two dashing older men and opposite them, two younger men, who frankly buried the needle on the totally hot-and-sexy scale.

Well, *damn,* the Caroselli family sure did grow them tall dark and sexy.

She assumed one of them was Robert Caroselli, the man whose department she was there to analyze and pick apart. In her experience, that didn't typically go over very well, and resulted in a certain degree of opposition. Especially when the person in charge was a man.

"Caroline," Demitrio said, "these are my brothers Leo, our CFO, and Tony, our COO."

The two older men rose to shake her hand. Tony was shorter and stockier in build. Leo was the tallest of the three and very fit for a man his age. Despite their physical differences, there was no mistaking the fact that they were related.

"Nice to meet you, gentlemen."

"And this is my niece, Elana. She heads up our accounting division."

Elana sauntered over to shake Carrie's hand. Her firm grip was all business, her smile cool and sophisticated, but her dark eyes were warm and friendly. Carrie was fairly adept at reading people, and if she had to guess, she would say that Elana was incredibly intelligent, though underestimated at times because of her beauty.

"On this side we have my nephew, Nick," Demitrio said. "He's the genius behind our new projects."

Nick, the one on the left, rose to shake her hand. He was charmingly attractive in a slightly rumpled I'm-sexy-and-rich-therefore-I-can-wear-a-wrinkled-shirt sort of way. The twinkle in his dark eyes, and slightly lopsided grin as he shook her hand said he was a flirt, while the wedding band on his left hand said he was very likely a harmless one.

"And last but not least," Demitrio said, while Carrie braced herself, "this is Tony Jr., director of overseas production and sales."

What about Robert?

Tony Jr. stood so tall that even in three-inch heels Carrie had to crane her neck to meet his eyes. His professional nod and distracted smile said that he had something other than the business at hand on his mind.

"Please have a seat," Demitrio said, gesturing to the empty chair beside Nick. "We're waiting for one more, then we can get started."

She'd barely settled in her seat when behind her she heard the door open, and a deep voice say, "Sorry I'm late. My secretary isn't back today, so I had to pick these reports up on my way in."

Something about that voice made the hair on the back of her neck shiver to attention. She'd definitely heard it before. But where…

The breath she had just inhaled backed up in her lungs. Oh no, it *couldn't* be.

She glanced up at him out of the corner of her eye as he approached the table, his attention on the pile of folders he carried, and when she focused on his face…

She swiftly looked away, heart pounding. He had the

same smoldering black eyes, the solid, square jaw, the full lips that had kissed her senseless. At first glance the resemblance was uncanny. But it couldn't be him. Could it?

He mumbled an "excuse me" as he laid a folder in front of her. On his right hand was a college ring identical to the one she had seen the other night, and as the scent of his aftershave drifted her way, the wave of familiarity was so strong that her heart skipped a beat.

She stared at the folder cover, unable to focus. Hell, she could barely *breathe*.

It's not him, she assured herself. *It just looks like him, and smells like him, and* sounds *like him…and wears the same ring as him.* But it *had* to be a coincidence, her mind playing tricks on her.

She had a strict rule of never sleeping with a coworker. Especially one she would be working with directly. And definitely not one whose work she would be putting under the microscope. She'd made that mistake once before, on her first high-profile job with a previous client. Previous because the affair had ended in disaster, the aftermath ugly.

It wasn't necessary for the entire team to like her, but maintaining their respect was crucial. When she recalled the things she and Ron had said to one another, the things she let him do…the sheer mortification made her want to curl inside her own skin and hide, or slide down out of her chair under the table.

As he rounded the table she kept her eyes on the folder, pretending to read, afraid to lift her head. Maybe if it was Ron, he wouldn't recognize her. They had both been pretty drunk.

"Rob," Demitrio said, "this is Caroline Taylor. Caroline, this is my son Rob, our director of marketing."

She had no choice but to look up, to meet his eyes, and when she did, her head spun and her heart sank.

Unless "Rob" had an identical twin, he was in fact Ron, her New Year's bang.

Rob blinked, then blinked again. In the conservative suit that hid her pinup model figure, with her granny hairstyle, he almost didn't recognize Carrie. But the slightly too-large clear gray eyes were a dead giveaway.

She sat frozen, watching him expectantly, and his first thought was that this had to be some sort of prank. Were Nick and Tony screwing with him? He'd bragged to them about the blonde beauty he'd spent the night with. Which his cousins knew was completely out of character for him. He didn't do drunken one-night stands. Typically, he didn't do drunken *anything*.

Was this some twisted practical joke? Had they gone to the hotel to look for her, maybe paid her to pose as Caroline Taylor to mess with Rob's head?

He looked from Nick to Tony, waiting for someone to say something, for everyone at the table to burst out laughing. And when they didn't, when they all watched him, looking increasingly puzzled by his lack of a response, he began to get a *very* bad feeling.

"Rob?" his dad said, brow creased with concern. "Is everything all right?"

"Fine," he said, a bit too enthusiastically, and forcing a smile that felt molded from plastic, he told Ms. Taylor, "It's a pleasure to meet you."

Not.

When he'd slipped out of her bed, he'd had no intention of ever seeing her again. Talk about dumb freaking luck.

Caroline nodded in his general direction, her head held a little too high, her shoulders too square and her back too straight, as if she'd been cut out of cardboard and propped up in the chair. She was clearly no happier to see him than he was to see her.

"Well, why don't we get started," his dad said, and everyone opened their folders. Rob tried to concentrate as they went over the contracts, and discussed Ms. Taylor's credentials and her projected time line, but he found his mind—and his eyes—wandering to the woman across the table. She downplayed her looks for work, he assumed in an attempt to gain respect from men who might otherwise objectify her or see her as too pretty to be smart. But he knew what she was hiding under that shapeless suit. The siren's figure and satin-soft skin. He knew the way her hair looked cascading down her bare back in silky ribbons, pale and buttery against her milky complexion, and how it brushed his chest as she straddled him. Even though parts of that night were a bit fuzzy, he knew he could never erase from his mind the image of her lying beneath him, wrapped in his arms, her breathy moans as he—

"Rob?" his dad said.

Rob jerked to attention. "Yeah, sorry."

"It seems we've covered everything."

Already?

"Why don't you take Caroline on a tour of the building while the rest of us have a short discussion. I'll call you when we're ready."

They had covered everything, and he hadn't heard a word of it. Now they would make the final decision, and they were going to do it without him. He'd been clear from day one that he considered her presence there a waste of time and money, and he had never once swayed from that opinion. Still it was a slap in the face to be excluded, not just for him, but for the entire marketing staff that he represented.

Or maybe, getting her alone for a few minutes wasn't such a bad idea. And meeting her wasn't "dumb luck" after all. Maybe a little time alone would give him the opportunity to make her see reason. See that she didn't belong here. Then she would no longer be his problem.

With a smile—a genuine one this time—he rose from his seat and said, "If you'll follow me, Ms. Taylor."

She stood, spine straight, shoulders back, flashing the others a confident smile, as if she already knew she had it in the bag. "I look forward to your decision."

Rob held the door for her, then followed her out, closing it firmly behind him. He turned to her and said in a low voice, "I think we need to talk."

Her eyes shooting daggers, her voice dripping with venom, she said, "Oh, you think so...*Ron?*"

He gestured down the hall. "My office is this way."

They walked there in silence, but he could feel her anger reverberating against the walls like an operatic vibrato.

His secretary's chair was unoccupied as they walked past, and when they were in his office he shut the door. He turned to face her and thought, *Here we go.* "I can see that you're upset."

"Upset," she said, her voice rising an octave. "Not only did you *lie* about your name, but did you have to skulk away in the middle of the night?"

If that's all she was mad about, he considered himself lucky. "First off, I did not lie to you about my name. I said it was Rob. You called me Ron and I saw no point in correcting you."

"I can't believe you didn't make the connection. Carrie Taylor, Caroline Taylor? You didn't at least suspect we might be one in the same person?"

"It was loud in the bar. I didn't even hear your last name. And we never discussed what we do for a living, so how was I supposed to guess who you were? I've met a lot of people named Carrie. You don't have a monopoly on the name."

"And as for skulking off in the middle of the night?"

"It was not the middle of the night. It was early morning and I didn't want to wake you. You were so drunk I'm not sure I could have if I tried. And I did not skulk. I got dressed and left, end of story."

"First off, I wasn't *that* drunk. And didn't it occur to you to at least leave a note?"

"Why would I? We agreed it would never be more than one night. It was over."

She rolled her eyes. "You know *nothing* about women do you? You could have said goodbye, told me that you had a good time."

"I assumed, in our case, actions spoke louder than words."

She didn't seem to have a snarky reply for that one. She couldn't deny it had been damned good for her, too.

"What I don't understand is why we're in here," Rob told her, "when you should be in the conference room telling them you can't work here."

Her brows rose. "Why would I do that?"

"Well, first, despite what my family believes, your services are not required or desired by anyone on my staff. And considering the circumstances, I don't think your presence here would be appropriate."

"What circumstances are those?"

Was she kidding? "The ones we've been discussing

since we stepped in here. It's unlikely either of us could be objective in light of what happened the other night."

"I don't know about you, but now that I know what a macho jerk you are, it isn't going to be an issue for me. In fact, I think I'm going to enjoy it."

He had been accused of being inattentive, arrogant and at times insufferable, but macho jerk was a new one. "Are you sure about that?"

"Absolutely."

"You can remain completely objective?"

"Yep."

Rob was not the type of man to behave rashly. He never made a move before he'd had time to completely think through a situation, weigh the pros and cons. So maybe it was pride that propelled him forward, or the satisfaction of proving her wrong, or just compromised judgment that motivated him to take her by the arms, pull her to him and crush his mouth down on hers.

Carrie made an indignant sound and pushed at his chest. She resisted for all of three seconds, then her fingers curled into the lapels of his jacket and her lips parted beneath his.

Having made his point, he should have let go. Instead he wrapped his arms around her, pulled her closer. It had been just like this on New Year's, his brain shutting down the second he kissed her, his body reacting on pure instinct, a carnal need to overpower and dominate. One that he'd never felt with a woman before her. Because despite her claim, he was not a macho jerk. Of all his cousins and uncles, he was probably the least chauvinistic man in the family. Her gender had no bearing whatsoever on his professional opinion.

Carrie slid her hands up his chest, tunneled them through his hair, taking two fistfuls and jerking his head back so she could kiss—*ow*—make that *bite* his neck.

Growling, he backed her against his office door, cringing as her head hit the surface with a *thunk,* cushioned only by the ugly bun in her hair, but it only seemed to fuel her desire.

"I want you right here, against this door," she said, her eyes locking on his as she slid her hand between their bodies, gripping his erection through his slacks.

Sucking in a breath, he grabbed the hem of her skirt and shoved his hand underneath, sliding it up her leg, and—damn—she was wearing a garter. He had just reached the top of her bare inner thigh, his fingers brushing the crotch of her panties, when his cell phone started to ring.

Damn it. Talk about lousy timing.

Carrie grumbled unhappily as he pulled his hand from under her skirt and backed away from the hand that had been busy unzipping his fly. "Yeah," he answered.

"We're ready for you," his father said.

"Be right there." He hung up without saying goodbye, so his dad wouldn't hear his labored breathing, and told Carrie, "They're ready for you."

She nodded, her cheeks rosy, pupils dilated. "I just need a minute to catch my breath."

He shoved his phone back in his pocket and zipped his pants. "Now do you see what I mean?"

"That you have pitiful lack of self-control?" Carrie said, straightening her jacket and smoothing the wrinkles from a skirt six inches too long for her height. "I definitely noticed that."

"I didn't see you trying to stop me."

She looked up at him, her lipstick kissed away, a stubborn tilt to her chin. "You enjoy being right, don't you?"

"Not always." Not this time. They had chemistry, but

that was about it. With fifteen million dollars riding on his choice, she was the exact opposite of what he was looking for in a woman. Not only did he consider her the enemy, but she'd said herself that she had intimacy issues, and she had never been in a serious relationship. Rob needed a woman with baby fever, someone to marry and pop out a male heir. She wasn't it, and having her around to tempt him would only make a difficult situation that much more tense.

"So, have I made my point?" he asked Carrie.

"You certainly have," she said. "We should get back to the conference room."

They walked side by side down the corridor, an uncomfortable silence building a wedge between them. There was nothing left to say. It had been fun, and now it was over. She would go back to California, and he and his team would work out a plan to beef up sales. And hopefully, sooner rather than later, he would find a woman to give him a son, and everyone would be happy.

The conference room was silent as they stepped inside. Carrie took her seat, and Rob returned to his.

"Sorry to make you wait," his dad told her.

"I completely understand," she said.

Rob waited for her to break the bad news, but she just sat there.

"After going over the final numbers," his uncle Leo said, "we're pleased to tell you that we agree to your terms and we would like you to start first thing next Monday morning."

Rob waited for the big letdown, wondered how everyone would take her turning down their offer.

"I don't come cheap," she said, then looked directly at Rob. "But I don't disappoint."

She may as well have drawn her sword and challenged him to a duel. And clearly she had only been humoring him. She had never intended to turn down the assignment.

If that was really the way she wanted to play this, fine. *You want a fight, sweetheart? Well, now you've got one.*

Three

After the contracts were signed, everyone filed out of the conference room, shaking Carrie's hand, congratulating her and welcoming her to the company. Rob watched, gathering the binders—a task typically left for an assistant—growing increasingly impatient as Elana stopped to admire Carrie's briefcase of all things, and they launched into a conversation about women's purses and accessories. When he'd run out of ways to stall, he flat-out asked Elana, "Could I have a minute with Ms. Taylor?"

Flashing him a knowing look and a wry smile, Elana said, "Sure, Robby. See you Monday, Carrie."

Elana knew that there was no faster way to irritate him than to address him by his childhood nickname. The first half of it anyway. It had been years since anyone dare uttered the phrase that had been the bane of his existence from kindergarten to his first year of college.

She left, closing the door behind her, and Rob turned to Carrie, who was sliding papers into her briefcase.

"Well?" he said.

She closed the case and smiled up at him. "Something wrong…*Robby?*"

That was it—Elana was dead meat. "Why did you lie to me?"

She smiled, the picture of innocence. "When did I lie to you?"

"We agreed that in light of what happened, working together would be a bad idea."

"No, *you* said working together would be bad, and I commented on how you enjoy being right. I never said you *were* right."

"So you were just screwing with me?"

She propped her hands on the conference table, leaning in. "Not unlike the way *you* were screwing with *me*."

She definitely had him there. And he had best be going, before he told her what he really thought of her. "I'll see you Monday."

She smiled brightly. "Sure thing, Robby. Oh, and by the way, the first step will be analyzing your marketing data. I'll need a few things from you."

Gathering his patience, he said, "All right."

"I'll need all the data you have for the past twenty years."

He blinked. "*Twenty* years?"

"That's right."

He wondered if she really needed to go that far back, or if she was trying to make his life a living hell. Probably the latter, and could he blame her if she was? But that, she should realize, was a two-way street.

"It could take some time to compile everything. We've

been in the process of digitizing our older files. Some of it might still be in hard copy."

"That's fine. Just have it on my desk Monday morning."

"If you hadn't noticed, there's no one here. Everyone is on holiday vacation until Monday."

"Well," she said, the sweet smile not wavering a fraction. "Who better to do it than the director himself. Which reminds me, I'll need you available, and at my disposal at all times in case I have any questions."

Gritting his teeth, he nodded, then turned and walked to the door.

"Hey, Robby?"

Jaw tense, he turned back to her.

"I'm not the enemy. This will be as productive or as difficult as you make it. I think you'll find that I can be very pleasant to work with."

"So I noticed," he said, his eyes raking over her. "Will we be meeting for a quickie in my office daily, or just once or twice a week?" He didn't even like her, but his libido didn't seem to notice or care. It was telling him to rip that shapeless, ugly suit from her body, to pluck the pins from her granny hairstyle so he could watch her silky blond curls cascade down her shoulders.

She sighed and shook her head, as if she felt sorry for him. "Robby, is that the best you can do? You think I haven't heard worse? During the course of my career I've been called sweetie and sugar and pumpkin. I've been groped and fondled, objectified and demoralized. I've seen it all, and in the end I always get the job done, and I manage to do it with dignity."

She slung her case strap over her shoulder and said, "We can do this the easy way or the hard way. If you think you'd like to take me on, by all means give it your best shot. But

I should warn you, I always get what I want, and I'm not above fighting dirty."

He should have anticipated that. No one got as far as she had in the business world without being tough as nails. And shame on him for underestimating her.

She walked out, the heels of her shoes clicking as she marched down the hall. He had no plan to demoralize or objectify her, or to call her condescending names. And the only physical contact they might have would be totally at her discretion. He had every intention of treating her with the utmost respect, because he didn't doubt that she had earned it. His cooperation, however, was another matter altogether.

Rob walked to his office and sat down at his computer to send his staff and his secretary an email dictating what Carrie would need—one they would see Monday when they returned to work. He refused to make his people work a weekend they had been promised as vacation.

There was a knock on his door, and he looked up to see Tony and Nick standing there.

"Hey." He motioned them in, and Nick shut the door.

"So what was that all about?" Tony asked him.

"Yeah," Nick said, "what the heck did you say to her when you two left the conference room?"

"You probably wouldn't believe me if I told you." Rob could barely believe it himself. "Do you think my dad noticed?"

"Dude, *everyone* noticed," Nick said. "You looked as if either you wanted to kill each other, or tear each other's clothes off."

It was a little bit of both. "Remember the woman I told you about? The blonde from the bar?"

Tony nodded. "What about her?"

Nick being Nick, he was way ahead of Tony. He started to laugh. "No way. No one's luck could be *that* bad."

"Apparently it can."

Tony looked from Nick to Rob, and then he laughed. "Are you saying that Caroline Taylor is Carrie from the bar?"

He glared at them both. "I'm glad you find this so amusing."

"More ironic than amusing," Tony said.

"Yeah," Nick agreed. "But still funny as hell."

If it were happening to anyone but him, Rob probably would have thought so, too.

"So what are you going to do?" Tony asked.

"What can I do? I already asked her to leave, said it would be a conflict of interest for her to stay, and you can see how well that went."

"Did you see how much we're paying her?" Tony said. "Can you blame her for not walking away?"

"Well, I'm going to make sure that she earns every penny."

Tony shook his head, like he thought that was a bad idea. "You know that if you screw with her, your dad will be pissed."

"Not if he doesn't find out."

"You don't think she'll rat you out?" Nick asked.

"Only if she wants the entire family to know how she and I first met. If it gets around that she picks up men in bars for one-night stands, her credibility will be in the toilet. Every potential future client will believe that a bedroom romp is included in the contract."

"You don't think that's a little harsh?" Nick said.

If she could play dirty, so could he. "I'm not the one who declared war in front of the entire family. And you can damn well bet she plans to discredit me and my team every opportunity she gets."

"Are you sure? She comes off as smart and savvy but not vindictive."

If Nick had just heard her in the conference room, he might feel differently. And if she could be ruthless, so could Rob. She was on his turf now, and she would play by his rules.

"Nick and I are getting a late breakfast at the diner," Tony said. "Are you going to hang around and work, or do you want to come?"

He thought of all the work Carrie expected him to complete before Monday and smiled. "Breakfast sounds good."

He was getting ready to stand when his office phone rang. It was his sister Megan. "Give me fifteen minutes and I'll meet you by the elevator."

"We'll get our coats," Tony said.

"Hey, Meggie," he said. "What's up?"

"I just heard from the real estate agent," she said, her voice squeaky with excitement. "They accepted my offer! The apartment is mine!"

"Congratulations," Rob said. His younger sister had spent the past nine months looking for exactly the right place, and had been outbid on the first two. "And you're sure it's within your budget?"

"That's my other good news! You know Rose Goldwyn?"

Rob had met her briefly at work, then a few times at family gatherings. She was a recent hire. The daughter of the woman who had been *Nonno's* secretary for the better part of his career.

Rose seemed nice enough, but there was something about her, something just a little…off. "What about her?" Rob said.

"She's going to be my roommate."

"But you hardly know her."

"Actually we've been talking a lot lately. We have a lot in common."

"Isn't she like twenty years older than you?"

"What difference does that make?"

"I don't know, Meg. Something about her…"

"What?"

"I don't trust her."

"Robby, I'm twenty-five" was her plucky response. "It's not your job to protect me anymore."

It would always be his job to protect her. She was an infant when his parents adopted her, and although he was six years older, they had always been close. He'd set her classmates straight when they made fun of her for looking "different" than the rest of her family. "Do me a favor and at least have legal do a background check on her. Just in case."

Her sigh of exasperation meant she was giving in. "Fine, if it makes you happy."

"It does." From the hallway he heard a door slam, then after a two- or three-second pause, raised voices. One of them definitely belonged to their father.

What the hell?

"Meggie, I have to go. I'll call you later."

"Love you, Robby!"

"Love you, too, Megs."

He got up and walked past his secretary's desk into the hall. At one end, near the conference room stood his dad and his uncle Tony, and his dad looked furious.

"I was never given a choice," his dad was saying, to which his uncle Tony answered, "You gave that up when you left her."

Whatever that meant, his dad's face flushed deep red

and he gave his brother a firm, two-handed shove that sent him stumbling backward several feet into the conference room door.

Rob had seen his dad and uncles argue, and at times it could get heated, but he had never seen them come to blows. Uncle Tony was stocky and muscular, but Demitrio, Rob's dad, was taller, younger and trained by the military to fight. That apparently wasn't going to stop Uncle Tony because he looked as if he were about to lunge.

From behind him, Rob heard his cousin Tony yell, "What the hell is going on?" and turned to see Nick and him running down the hall toward the older men. Rob followed them.

Both older men, red-faced and out of breath, jaws and fists clenched, stopped and turned to him.

"What the hell, Dad?" Tony said. "What is with the two of you lately?"

Demitrio turned to Tony Sr. "Why don't you tell him, Tony."

"I'd like to know, too," Rob said. The last time Uncle Tony had been to their house, Rob showed up to find his mom in tears. He wanted to know why.

"Boys, this is between me and my brother," Tony Sr. said. "There's no need to be concerned—"

"Dad!" Tony said. "You were two seconds from beating the crap out of each other."

"It wouldn't be the first time I beat the crap out of him," Demitrio said, glaring at his brother.

"When you were kids maybe," Rob said, "but you're in your *sixties*. You could have a heart attack."

"Did I miss the fun?"

Rob turned to see Leo, Nick's dad, walking toward them.

"They're fighting," Tony said, as if he still couldn't believe it. "*Physically* fighting."

"It's nothing to worry about, boys," Leo said, laughing heartily. "You wouldn't believe how many times I had to get between these two when we were kids. It's that middle-child curse, I guess." He stepped strategically between his brothers and gave each of them a slap on the back. "Come on, gentlemen, let's go in my office and settle this." He turned to Rob and his cousins. "You boys can head on out. I've got this."

Reluctantly the three cousins walked to the elevator.

"So what do you think that was about?" Tony asked him.

"I don't know," Rob said. "But it's been building for a while now. Things have been tense for a couple of months."

"Don't forget, Tony's mom was arguing with your dad at Thanksgiving," Nick told Rob. Sarah, Tony's mom, used to date Rob's dad before he joined the army. The fact that Tony Sr. married her shortly after he left had been a minor source of friction among the three of them over the years. Certainly, it was nothing they would come to blows over now, unless the dynamics of those relationships had changed....

"Tony, you don't think that your mom and my dad..."

"Honestly, Rob, I don't know what to think anymore. But things have seemed off with my parents, as well. I went to a New Year's party with them and they seemed...I don't know, out of sync, if that makes sense. They're typically very physically affectionate with each other, and I barely saw them touch."

"Maybe my dad can help them figure it out," Nick said.

"Is your dad still sleeping with your mom?" Rob asked him.

Nick made a face. "Yeah. It's bad enough knowing about it, but to actually see them...you know..." He shuddered involuntarily. "Talk about scarring a person for life."

"That'll teach you to barge into your mom's house without knocking," Tony told him.

"I think it's pretty cool that after being divorced for so long, they reconnected," Rob said.

"They do seem happy," Tony told Nick. "Maybe I shouldn't mention this, but they were at the New Year's party, too. They couldn't keep their hands off each other, and they disappeared long before the ball dropped."

"Regardless," Nick said, "I'll never get how two people who despised each other, and had a messy and uncivilized divorce that scarred all three of their children, could suddenly change their minds and hop in the sack."

"I'm sure that if they'd had a choice, they would have preferred to be happy the first time around," Tony said.

Nick shrugged. "Yeah, I guess. So long as I don't have to see my dad's bare ass again, they can be 'happy' all they want."

"So, breakfast?" Tony said.

They said goodbye to Sheila as they passed the reception desk, then rode the elevator down to the lobby. Dennis, the security guard, nodded as they walked past.

"Who are you betting on in the playoffs?" Nick asked him, walking backward to the door.

"Steelers-Lions," Dennis said. "And the Lions will take it."

"No way! The Lions haven't won a championship since what, the fifties?"

"Fifty-seven," Dennis said. "But this is the year."

Nick laughed. "Dream on. I say Steelers-Chargers, and the Steelers will take the championship."

Dennis grinned and shook his head. "Keep dreaming, boss."

Nick laughed as they walked out the door into the bitter wind. Parking was a bitch downtown, so they pulled up their collars and walked the three blocks to the restaurant. The pavement was slick, so it was slow-going, and by the time they got to the diner it was already filling up with the lunch crowd. Every seat was taken and there was a line of people ahead of them.

"Feel like waiting?" Tony asked.

Rob shrugged. "Could be a while."

"I say we wait," Nick said. "It's too damn cold to go back out there."

"Hey, Caroselli!" someone called. Rob followed the voice, cursing under his breath when he realized whom it belonged to.

Four

"Is that Carrie?" Nick asked.

"That's her," Rob said. She sat alone in a booth near the back, and she was waving them over. She was still wearing the ugly suit, but she'd lost the shapeless jacket. She'd let her hair down so it fell in soft waves over the shoulder of a rose-colored shirt made of some sort of stretchy nylon that clung to her curves.

Tony's mouth dropped open. "Holy hell. No wonder you picked her up. Look at her."

"Yeah," Nick said. "Her body is…wow."

Yes, it was, and as much as he didn't want to, Rob couldn't help but look. Just as he couldn't help it the other night either. In her clothes she was smokin' hot, but out of them she was a goddess. A work of art.

But that was where the attraction ended.

"Looks like she wants to share her table," Nick said.

"I'd rather wait for a table," Rob told him. She had ruined enough of his day.

"Stop being a baby and go," Tony said, giving him a shove from behind. "You're going to have to get used to being around her."

But not outside of a work scenario, Rob thought, grumbling to himself all the way to her booth. And while he could have turned and walked out, he refused to show defeat, to let her win. To drive him from a restaurant he'd eaten in weekly for the past ten years.

She smiled up at them as they approached. "Hello, gentlemen. I saw you walk up and thought rather than wait, you might like to share. I stood in line about twenty minutes myself."

"We'd love to join you," Nick said, flashing her his "Charming Nick" smile. He and Tony slid into the empty side of the booth, leaving Rob no choice but to slide in beside Carrie, which earned each of them a malevolent look.

The booths weren't exactly spacious, and with her briefcase on the seat next to the window, there was no hope of putting any real space between them. She was so close he could feel her body heat, and every time either of them moved, their shoulders or arms bumped.

This day was going from bad to worse.

He refused to acknowledge the scent of her perfume, or shampoo, or whatever it was that had driven him mad the other night, or the lusty urges he was feeling as her leg brushed against his. The desire to run his hand up the inside of her thigh again, until he reached the garter holding up her stockings, had him shifting restlessly in his seat.

"Are we a little antsy?" Carrie asked him, but thankfully, before he had to come up with a viable excuse, the waitress appeared.

"Hey, boys," she said, stopping at the table with a pot

of coffee and four beat-up plastic cups of iced water. What the place lacked in class, it made up for in good food and quality service. "What can I getcha?"

Without even looking at the menu, they all ordered their usual breakfast, and after reviewing the menu, Carrie ordered the special, which was a lot of food for a woman her size.

"I take it you gentlemen come here often," Carrie said, reaching across the table for a coffee creamer, her shoulder bumping against Rob's.

"Best greasy spoon in the greater Chicago area," Tony said. "How did you stumble across it?"

"On my way out I asked Dennis where I could get a decent breakfast." She added a packet of artificial sweetener to her cup. "He told me to come here."

If Dennis wasn't such an exemplary employee, Rob might have considered that grounds for termination.

"So what do you think of Chicago?" Nick asked her.

"It's very cold. And windy."

"They call it the Windy City for a reason," Tony said.

"I'll bet you can't wait to get back to the West Coast," Rob said, and she shot him a sideways glance, as if to say, *Don't you wish*.

"I think I'll like it here," she said. "Though probably more when it warms up a little."

"Do you know where you'll be staying?" Nick asked.

"Not yet. I'm hoping to find a rental. I don't suppose you know a good local agent?"

"My brother-in-law David is in real estate law," Tony said, pulling out his phone. "He could probably give you the name of someone reliable."

He found the number in his address book, and she entered it into her phone.

"I miss the days when we used to write things on paper," Nick said.

"Have you got a piece of paper?" Rob asked, and grinning, Nick held up his napkin. "Pen?"

Nick felt his pockets, then frowned and said, "I used to carry one all the time."

"I would be lost without my phone," Carrie said. "My whole life is in this thing. Of course I keep it all backed up on my laptop, which I also could not live without."

"So what kind of place are you looking for?" Nick asked.

"A two-bedroom apartment or condo, preferably furnished, in a building with a fitness room and a pool, or close to a pool. I like to swim every morning."

"I think I may know just the place," Nick said. "My wife, Terri, has a condo that she's been thinking of putting on the market, but it would probably mean taking a loss. She had entertained the idea of renting it out, but she's heard so many horror stories about bad tenants that she's been hesitant. It has pretty much everything you would need, and there's a fitness center with a pool a couple of blocks away. And it's not too far from work."

It also wasn't too far from Rob's loft, which didn't exactly thrill him.

"It sounds perfect," Carrie said. "I can pay her the full three months up front."

"I'll talk to her today and give you a call."

"Sounds great," she said, exchanging numbers with him, which irritated Rob even more. It was bad enough that she would be around for three months. Did she have to pretend to be so nice to everyone? Which she was clearly only doing to make Rob look like the bad guy.

"So, on the rare occasions that I might have a free day," Carrie said, "what attractions would you gentlemen recommend? There are so many things to do in the city, I wouldn't even know where to begin."

His cousins tossed around suggestions like the planetarium and the aquarium and the Museum of Contemporary Art.

"How about you?" she asked Rob. "What would you suggest?"

"The Museum of Science and Industry."

"Really," she said, looking thoughtful. "For some reason I imagined your preferring someplace a little less... academic. Like a sports museum."

"And you assumed that because, why? You know me so well?"

She looked amused, as if this was some big joke to her.

The waitress dropped their food off at the table and when Rob looked at Carrie's plate, he could feel his arteries tighten. The special consisted of three eggs, four sausage links, hash browns, white toast and a stack of pancakes six inches high. A heart attack on a plate, his fitness instructor would call it. Which was why Rob had ordered his usual egg white vegetarian omelet, lean ham, tomato slices and dry whole wheat toast, of which he would allow himself half a slice. Unlike some people at the table, his goal was to live past his fortieth birthday.

"Do the three of you live in the city?" she asked them, and when her leg bumped his, he wrote it off as accidental, until he felt the brush of one shoeless foot slide against his ankle.

Was she coming onto him?

He shot her a sideways glance, but she was looking at Nick, chewing and nodding thoughtfully as she listened to him describe where each of them lived in relation to Caroselli Chocolate.

Okay, maybe it had been an accident. But what about

the way she just happened to get syrup on her fingers, and instead of wiping them with a napkin, sucked it slowly from each digit, one at a time. Which of course reminded him of her sucking on something else.

He grabbed his iced water and guzzled half the glass.

"Not hungry?" Carrie asked, looking over at his untouched food. He'd been so busy obsessing over her that he hadn't even thought about his breakfast.

"Letting it cool," he told her, forking up a large bite and shoveling it in, burning the hell out of his tongue in the process.

"So I'm under the impression you three aren't just cousins, but good friends," Carrie said.

"What makes you think that?" Tony asked.

"I'm very intuitive about things like that."

"Not so much when we were younger," Nick said. "Mostly because of the age difference, but our family is very close-knit, so we saw each other constantly. But, yeah, we're all pretty close now."

"So, then I guess Robby told you that we had sex on New Year's Eve."

Rob dropped his fork halfway to his mouth, Nick choked on his eggs and Tony nearly sprayed the table with a mouthful of coffee.

"What makes you think I would do that?" Rob said, even though that was exactly what he had done.

She smiled serenely. "As I said, I'm intuitive about that sort of thing."

"He may have mentioned it," Tony said, shrugging apologetically to Rob.

"I hope he also mentioned that we didn't know who the other was until this morning."

"That was fairly obvious," Nick said. "And you really don't have to explain."

"I prefer to get things out in the open. I wouldn't want anyone getting the wrong impression."

"Of course not," Tony said.

"Carrie," Rob started, and she held a hand up to shush him.

"I'm not angry," she said. "Men like to talk about their conquests, I get that. Hell, I called my friend Alice first thing the next morning. It's not as if we ever expected to see each other again. I'd just appreciate if it didn't go any further than this table."

"No one will hear it from me," Tony said.

"Me neither," Nick piped in, looking amused. "What you two do in your free time is no one else's business."

Was she doing this here, now, only so that she would have witnesses? So that if he promised not to say anything, then did, it would make him look like an even bigger jerk than he already might be.

She was good at this. But so was he.

"While we're being so honest, should we tell them what happened in my office this morning?"

Tony shot him a look. "Really not necessary."

"You mean what didn't happen," she said and told Nick and Tony with regret, "We ran out of time."

Both men looked to Rob, waiting for his reply, because obviously he hadn't gotten the response he'd hoped for by putting her on the spot. Did nothing rattle her?

"And it won't be happening again," he said, establishing that he was the one to end it, not her.

"And of course I understand why," she said. "I've learned from experience that it's a terrible idea to engage in a physical relationship with a coworker, especially a subordinate."

Subordinate? She was the subordinate, the temporary

consultant. Did she honestly see herself as ranking higher than him?

"I'd like your opinion on something," Carrie said, leaning forward to address Nick and Tony. "Say you have a one-night stand with a woman. You both know that it's never going to be more than one night. Now, it's the wee hours of the morning, she's asleep and you decide to go. Do you wake her and say goodbye, or maybe leave a note? Or do you just leave without a word?"

Nick glanced over at Rob. "I might get my ass kicked for saying this, but I would definitely wake her and say goodbye."

Carrie turned to Tony. "And you?"

"I would at least leave a note."

Carrie looked over at Rob and gave him a "so there" look.

"Boy, would you look at the time," Nick said, glancing at his wrist when, ironically enough, he wasn't wearing a watch. "Tony, we've got the thing we need to get to."

For an instant Tony looked confused, then he said, "Oh yeah, right, that *thing*. Of course. We wouldn't want to be late for that."

Nick grabbed the check that the waitress had left on the table.

"Here, let me give you cash for mine," Carrie said, reaching into her bag.

"Oh no, this one is on me," Nick said as he and Tony slid out of the booth.

"Thank you," she said. "I'll buy next time."

If there ever was a *next time,* they could count Rob out.

"You two enjoy the rest of your breakfast," Tony told them. As if Rob had any appetite left.

As soon as they were gone he switched to the empty side of the booth, which was actually worse than sitting beside Carrie. The deep cleft of cleavage at the low-cut collar of her top drew his gaze like a moth to a flame. The dull light leaking through the open blinds gave her pale gray eyes an almost-translucent quality.

"Well, that was fun," Carrie said.

"Amused yourself, did you?"

She smiled, sliding her empty plate to the edge of the table as the busboy cleared the dirty dishes and utensils. She sure could put away the food. She had stopped just shy of licking her plate clean.

"Tony and Nick seem like really nice guys," Carrie said. "I take it Tony isn't married."

"No, he isn't."

"Single?"

"Why? Are you interested?"

She cocked her head slightly. "Why? Are you jealous?"

"He just came out of a relationship, and the last thing he needs is someone like you messing with his head."

"Is that what I'm doing?" she asked, resting her elbow on the table and propping her chin in her hand. Then he felt a shoeless foot sliding up his left calf.

Damn her.

When she'd made it up to his knee, and clearly had no intention of stopping, he grabbed her stocking foot and removed it from his leg with a warning look, thankful for his long wool coat to hide anything that had *sprung up*. "You're taking cheap shots."

"Am I?"

"You don't really believe that I'm your subordinate."

The head cocked again. "When did I say that?"

"Just a minute ago. You said it was especially bad to get involved with a subordinate."

"So, from that you assumed I meant you? Had you considered that I was talking *to* you *about* me? Or that maybe

I was speaking in general terms, and not about anyone specific."

Actually no, he hadn't considered that.

"Are you always so hyperdefensive?" she asked.

"Never." Only when he was with her.

"Like I said, this will be as easy or as hard as you decide to make it." Her brow lifted slightly, but by the time he recognized the devilish look on her face, it was too late. He sucked in a surprised breath when he felt her still shoeless foot slide into his lap. "Hard, it is," she said with a smile.

"Would you stop that," he hissed, shoving her foot away from his crotch, hoping no one sitting nearby noticed. Did the woman have no shame? And why could he not think of anything but getting her back to her hotel room, out of her clothes and into bed? "Is this your idea of acting like a professional?"

"I'm simply trying to illustrate a point."

"What point? You're certifiable?"

"That when it comes to our relationship, work or otherwise, you do not always call the shots. Because, Robby, you have some *serious* control issues."

"*I* have control issues? This from the woman who can't keep her foot out of my crotch?"

She just smiled, as if she found the entire situation thoroughly amusing. "I'm going to go. I'll see you bright and early Monday."

"Unfortunately, yes, you will."

She pulled on her suit jacket and coat, and he watched her as she grabbed her bag, slid out of the booth and walked to the door. She stepped outside, her loose hair flying wildly in the brisk wind. She hailed a cab, and only after she climbed inside could he drag his gaze away from the window.

Unpredictable. That's what she was. And while he was

nowhere close to the control freak she'd painted him to be, he did prefer a modicum of consistency.

And if today's behavior was a preview of what he had to look forward to, maintaining control of the situation was his only option.

Five

Carrie sat at the hotel bar, having a celebratory margarita, which at 12:04 p.m. was completely acceptable, even though her internal clock still thought it was two hours earlier.

Even though there had been a few kinks in the process, all in all, she considered this morning's meeting a success. And though she had the tendency—in her stepfather's opinion—to be "mouthy," she felt that under the circumstances, she'd been impressively diplomatic. If she'd left out the part where they attacked each other in Rob's office.

The memory made her cringe. But she had regrouped, damn it, then gone back into that conference room and kicked some major Caroselli ass.

She'd found that in business, her impulsive nature could either be an asset or a liability, with very little gray area. This assignment could be a raging success, or a knock-down, drag-out disaster. So far so good, but honestly, it could still go either way. She had broken the cardinal rule of not sleeping with a coworker. And even though she had done it unknowingly, that didn't make the situation any less complicated.

As much as she hated to admit it, that stunt she'd pulled in the diner could have easily backfired. If he hadn't pulled her foot from his crotch, if he'd instead smiled and suggested they go back to her hotel room, she probably would have dragged him there by his tie. And though the cab ride there would have given them both time to come to their senses, the damage would have been done, and the ball would be in his court now.

Fortunately, the next serve was hers, and she was going for the point.

She licked salt off the rim of her glass and took a sip of her margarita, letting the tangy combination of sweet and salty roll around on her tongue. She glanced over at the businessman three barstools away, who she suspected had been working up the nerve to talk to her.

"Buy you a drink?" he said the instant they made eye contact.

Not only was he twice her age with thinning hair and a belly that sagged over his belt, but he also wore a chunky gold wedding band on his left hand.

Seriously? Did she really look that desperate?

She shook her head and gave him her not-in-this-lifetime look.

Her phone rang and, happy for the interruption, she dug around in her briefcase to find it, smiling when she saw her best friend Alice's number on the screen.

"So how did the meeting go?" Alice asked, and Carrie could picture her stretched out on the sofa in the trendy SoHo loft she shared with her sister, her glossy black hair smooth and sleek and tucked behind her ears. She never sat on a piece of furniture so much as draped herself across it.

At five feet eleven inches, and no more than one hundred and twenty pounds soaking wet, to say that Alice was wispy was an understatement. Hence her very lucrative career as a runway model. In college, where they'd been thrown together by chance as roommates, they had been like Mutt and Jeff. Two women could not have been more different in looks or personality, but with their similar backgrounds involving alcoholic parents, they had instantly bonded and despite living on completely opposite ends of the country, had remained the best of friends. Alice was her only *real* friend.

Normally Alice would be calling her from Milan or Paris or some other fashionably hip location, but a healing broken foot would be keeping her off the runway until the fall.

"They signed the contracts," Carrie told her. "So I'm in Chicago for the next three months."

"That's fabulous!"

"They didn't haggle over money either, which you know I hate. As far as business goes, the meeting itself couldn't have gone more smoothly."

"But?"

"What makes you think there's a but?"

"Gut feeling. I'm right, aren't I?"

She sighed. "I broke my cardinal rule. But it was an accident."

"I must be thinking of a different cardinal rule, because I fail to see how it's possible to *accidentally* sleep with someone."

"Nope, that's the rule. And I'm living proof that it is possible."

"Oh, I can't wait to hear this," Alice said, and Carrie

could just picture her catlike grin, the spark of amusement in her violet eyes—colored contacts of course, although she would deny it if asked.

"It's a little hard to believe," Carrie told her.

"Honey," she said with a laugh, "coming from you, I'd believe just about anything."

"That guy I told you about—Ron."

"Mr. Steamy Sex from the bar?"

"Yeah, well, apparently I heard him wrong. His name was actually *Rob*."

"Oh. And that's a problem because?"

"His name is Rob *Caroselli*. And he's the director of marketing at Caroselli Chocolate."

Alice was a tough person to shock, so her gasp was almost worth the mess Carrie was in.

Okay, maybe not, but it was at least a slight consolation.

Carrie told her the whole story, from the minute Rob walked into the conference room until lunch when she had her foot in his lap.

"Well, you were right about one thing," Alice said. "If anyone but you had told me that story, I doubt I would have believed them. But as impulsive as you are—"

"I'm not *that* impulsive," she argued, signaling the bartender for another drink.

"Your first night in a new city you picked up a total stranger in a bar and invited him back to your room."

Carrie cringed. "Yeah, there was that."

"Not that I'm saying you could have or should have anticipated this happening. That part was just dumb luck. Really, really bad dumb luck."

"But on the bright side, I think that now I've got him right where I want him."

"Until you wind up in bed with him again," Alice said.

"I can't sleep with him again."

"You mean you *shouldn't* sleep with him. Yet you almost went for it in his office this morning. Correct?"

"A moment of weakness. I was still getting over the shock of seeing him again."

"And in the diner?"

"I was making a point."

"And did you make your point?"

"I sure did." Below the waist anyway. "Why do I get the feeling I'm going to regret telling you any of this?"

"Because you know that if I think you're acting like an irresponsible moron, I'm going to tell you."

"And you think I am?"

"I think that you might be backsliding a little. Just remind yourself, you are no longer that lonely little girl who pulls fire alarms and stays out past curfew to get attention. You are a strong, mature woman who is in control of her own destiny."

"I know." But that little girl was still in there, and occasionally she persuaded the confident, mature woman to do some not-so-mature things. "The weird part is that I don't even like him very much. But then I get close to him and I just want to rip his clothes off and touch him all over."

"Probably not a good idea. You know, Rex and I used to have chemistry like that."

Alice's boyfriend, Rex, was an up-and-coming fashion designer whose rising star seemed to be keeping him out of the country more than he was in it lately. And even when he was in town, she didn't seem truly happy.

"When will he be back in New York?" Carrie asked.

"Two weeks. This time he promised."

He had promised her lots of things, and so far he hadn't exactly come through. Alice was beautiful and sophisticated and smart, but had miserably low self-esteem. Because of that, she let the men in her life walk all over her.

All types of men clamored for her attention, yet she always picked the aloof, distant ones whose attention she had to beg for. A fact she was quite aware of. But as Carrie had told Rob, a person could recognize the problem and still not know how to fix it.

"How's the foot healing?" Carrie asked her.

"Slowly. The physical therapy is helping. My doctor assured me that I'll be back on my feet before the shows next fall. It's crazy how you can be walking down the sidewalk, minding your own business, then *pow,* out of nowhere everything changes."

The *pow* in that scenario being the bike messenger who knocked her off the curb into the path of a moving taxi. She was lucky to be alive.

"And speaking of therapy," Alice said, "I have an appointment in an hour, so I should let you go. But I want you to make me a promise. If you get even the slightest urge to jump Mr. Steamy Sex again, I want you to call me immediately so I can talk some sense into you. Anytime, day or night."

"Okay."

"You promise?"

She sighed.

"Carrie?"

"Okay, okay, I promise," she said, hoping it wasn't one of those promises that came back to bite her in the butt.

Two days later Carrie hopped in a cab to meet Nick's wife, Terri, at the condo she hoped would be her new temporary home.

She was pleasantly surprised when the cab pulled up in front of a row of attached, newish-looking, charming brick homes with two-car garages. So far so good.

The homes were still decorated for the holidays. All but

the one the driver stopped at. Which wasn't so unusual considering no one was living there. Still, it looked so forlorn and neglected. But thankfully very well-maintained. At least on the outside.

She paid the driver, realizing that if she didn't want to blow her entire earnings on cab fare, it might be more cost effective to lease a car while she was there. She didn't exactly relish the thought of taking public transportation in the dead of winter either.

She climbed out of the cab and paused on the sidewalk to look up and down the street. All the residences were well-maintained, and a large group of children of various ages played in the snow several doors down, which led her to assume the neighborhood was family-oriented and safe.

She headed up the walk and as she stepped up onto the porch, the front door opened and a woman appeared to greet her.

"Hi. Caroline?"

"Carrie," she said, shaking her hand.

"I'm Terri. Come on in." Like her husband, Terri was tall and dark. She was also very attractive in an athletic, tomboyish way, and not at all the sort of woman she would have pictured Nick with. "Drop your coat anywhere and I'll give you a tour."

Carrie's first impression, as she stepped inside and shrugged out of her coat, was *beige*. Beige walls, beige carpet, beige leather furniture. Even the lamps were beige. And the air smelled like pine cleaner.

"As you can see, I left almost everything here when I moved into Nick's place," she said. "It's nothing fancy."

Carrie draped her coat over the back of the sofa beside Terri's and set her purse on top. "It's nice."

"According to Nick, to say I have the decorating sense of a brick is an insult to bricks."

"I'm no decorating genius either. I paid someone to do my place in Los Angeles. This is simple. Elegant."

"It's boring," Terri said. "And if you don't like it, don't be afraid to say so. You won't hurt my feelings."

She wasn't looking for anything fancy. Just something functional and low-maintenance that wouldn't break the bank. "So far so good."

Terri looked surprised. "You want to see more?"

"Absolutely." She could hate the rest of the condo and she would probably rent it anyway rather than hurt Terri's feelings.

Carrie had a way of reading people, and her first impression of Terri was that she had a tough outer shell but was soft and vulnerable on the inside.

The master suite had slightly more color. A queen-size bed with a pale rose duvet, a chest of drawers in a warm honey pine and a roomy walk-in closet that led to a very clean—and yes, beige—en suite bathroom that smelled of bleach and glass cleaner. The only color was pale pink towels and a pink bath mat. The countertops and walls were bare.

"There are towels, sheets…everything you'll need in the linen closet. I just changed the sheets on the bed and scrubbed the bathroom." Terri smiled sheepishly. "I'm slightly fanatical about keeping things clean and tidy."

"Linen closet?" Carrie asked, gesturing to a pair of louvered doors.

"Laundry." She pulled the doors open to show Carrie a stacked washer and dryer.

"Nice." She didn't miss the days before she had money, when she had to haul her dirty laundry down three flights of stairs and either sit in a dingy little laundry room down below the building in the parking structure, or drive two miles to the nearest Laundromat.

The second bedroom was set up as an office, with a desk, bookcase, file cabinet and printer stand. Again, nothing fancy, but very functional, and the window overlooked a postage-stamp-sized backyard.

"This is perfect," she told Terri.

"This room, you mean?"

"No, the whole place. It's exactly what I need."

"You really think so?"

"I do. Can I see the kitchen?"

"Of course. Right this way."

The kitchen, which was—surprise—also on the pale side, was as clean and organized as the rest of the house, and separated by a wall from the living space. She preferred a more open concept, but how much time would she be spending there really?

"I don't cook, so it's not very impressive," Terri said. "Just your basic pots and pans, dishes and utensils."

"I don't cook very often either," Carrie told her. "I like to, but I never have the time. I typically work eighty-hour weeks."

"I used to be like that, too, but my ob-gyn thinks all the stress is screwing with my cycle, and we're trying to get pregnant. So, I cut my hours way back. Used to be, when you opened the freezer it was full of frozen dinners. Thank goodness for husbands who love to cook. Although I've gained about ten pounds since the wedding."

"How long have you been married?"

"Less than two months."

"Oh, so you're still newlyweds."

"Technically. But we've been best friends since we were nine years old. And I don't want to be one of those moms in her fifties carting her kids to grade school, or pushing seventy when they graduate high school. For a process that's supposed to be so natural, you would not believe how complicated it can be."

It wasn't something Carrie had ever thought about. She didn't know much about pregnancy, or even babies. She just assumed that when you were ready, you had sex at the right time and *poof,* you got pregnant. That was the way it seemed to work for her college friends who had gotten married and started families. Hell, there were even a handful of girls in high school who seemed to have no problems getting themselves knocked up. A few of them multiple times.

"So what do you think of the condo?" Terri asked. "Again, I won't be insulted if you don't like it, or if you'd like to look at other places before making a decision."

"I think," Carrie said with a smile, "I'll take it."

Six

"You're sure?" Terri asked.

Carrie laughed. "Yes, I'm very sure. Did you bring a lease agreement?"

"It's in my coat. I'll get it."

They took a seat at the kitchen table and went over the paperwork. When it came to filling in the price of rent, Terri looked over at her. "So we're talking rent plus utilities, including cable TV and internet."

"Name your price," Carrie told her, and she offered up a sum that seemed awfully low for all of that, especially in the heart of a major city. "Are you sure you don't want more? I don't expect any sort of special treatment. I want to pay what's fair."

"Nick and I talked about it. We're not looking to make a profit, just cover expenses."

"You're positive?"

She nodded. "That's the way things are done in the

Caroselli family. They're a very generous bunch. They suck people into the fold."

"Is a personal check okay?"

"If it bounces, I'll know where to find you," Terri joked.

Carrie wrote the check out for three months' worth of rent, tore it from the book and handed it to Terri, feeling guilty to be paying such a low sum.

"Are you sure you want to pay all three months up front?"

"It's just easier for me that way. One less thing I have to worry about remembering." She slid her checkbook back into her bag. "So when you said that the Carosellis *suck* people in, what exactly did you mean by that?"

She must have looked apprehensive because Terri chuckled and said, "Don't worry, it's nothing creepy or weird. Take me, for example. When I moved to Chicago, I was nine. I had just lost my parents and I was living with an aunt who wasn't exactly thrilled to play Mommy to some bratty kid she had never met before. I guess you could say that I was a lost soul. Then I became friends with Nick, and I met his family, and it was like they adopted me. Nick likes to joke that if his mom had to choose between the two of us, she would pick me."

"That's really nice," Carrie said. "Everyone should have family."

"Do you have a big family?"

"I have a few cousins, and a couple of aunts and uncles spread out across the southwest, but I haven't seen them in years. Mostly it's just me and my mom."

"You're close?" she asked, and when Carrie didn't answer right away, Terri said, "I'm sorry, it's really none of my business. The Carosellis are also very nosy, and I guess it rubbed off on me."

"It's okay. It's just that my relationship with my mom

is a little…complicated. We don't really see each other very often. I work a lot and she spends most of her time in a bottle."

Terri nodded. "Ah, I see."

"There's a lot of resentment from my end, and apathy from hers. I have the typical characteristics of a child with an alcoholic parent." She paused and said, "Was that too much information?"

"No, not at all. I didn't even know there were typical characteristics. Which ones do you have, if you don't mind my asking?"

"I'm super-responsible and I take myself way too seriously. Your basic overachiever. When I'm trying to have fun, I feel as if I should be doing something more constructive. But due to a lack of self-esteem, I feel that nothing I do is good enough. I also have trust issues, so I have trouble forming intimate relationships. And telling you all of this is probably just some unconscious way of mine to push you away before I'm able to form any sort of friendship or bond."

"Wow, that's intense," Terri said.

"Yeah, those psych courses I took in college were a real eye-opener. Up until then, under the circumstances, I figured I was fairly well-adjusted. Psychology was actually my major for a while, until it dawned on me that no one as screwed up as I was had any right to be counseling anyone else. That's an enormous responsibility and there was no way I could trust myself to be completely impartial. So I switched my major to marketing. I'm still using what I learned about psychology, without the possibility of screwing with someone's head." She paused and said, "Well, not in a bad way at least. I just encourage them to buy stuff."

"It seems as though you aren't so screwed up that you

didn't realize you're screwed up." Terri frowned. "Does that make sense?"

"It does, actually."

"Hey, do you have plans for tomorrow night?"

Her first thought was of Rob, which was wrong in so many ways. "Nope. I don't really know anyone in the city."

"Nick and I are having some friends over and I'd really like you to come."

"Really? After everything I just told you?"

"Oh, don't worry. You'll fit right in."

Carrie wasn't quite sure how to take that, then decided it was probably meant as a compliment. "In that case, I'd love to."

"It's at seven," she said, writing down the address. "Do you have a way to get there?"

"I can take a cab."

"Or I could ask Rob to swing by and pick you up. It's on his way."

"Oh, I think it would be better if I took a cab."

"If you're worried about getting home safe, Rob isn't much of a drinker. Come to think of it, I don't recall ever seeing him drunk."

"The night I met him he drank a lot," Carrie said, not even realizing what she was saying until the words left her mouth. Everyone was supposed to think their first meeting was in the conference room.

"Yeah, I heard," Terri said.

She blinked. "You did?"

"Word of advice, if you don't want me to know something, don't tell Nick. We're one of those couples who actually tell each other everything."

"Good to know." Carrie recalled the way she had announced to the entire table at the diner about her and Rob's affair, *and* what happened in Rob's office, meaning Terri probably knew about that, too.

Way to go, genius. What had Alice said about her impulsive tendencies? She really needed to think things through before she opened her mouth. She wondered how many others in the Caroselli family knew.

"Did he happen to tell anyone else?" she asked Terri.

"I doubt it. And I don't think Tony would tell anyone either."

She hoped not. She didn't want people to get the impression she slept around, because nothing could be further from the truth.

"For the record, that's not typical behavior for me," she told Terri.

"And for what's it worth, it's not typical behavior for him either," Terri said. "You must have made quite an impression on him. Personally, I think you two make an adorable couple."

"Oh, but we aren't. A couple, I mean. I make it a rule not to date people I work with. If I'd had even the slightest clue as to who he was when I met him in that bar—"

"Carrie, I understand. Believe me. Maybe it was just… fate."

If it was, fate had played a very cruel trick on both of them. "We couldn't be more wrong for each other. In more ways than I can even count."

"Six months ago, if you had told me I would be married to Nick and trying to have a baby, I would have thought you were nuts. Yet here we are."

"So what happened? What changed?"

"That is a very long story, and I promise to tell you about it when you come to the party tomorrow."

"I hardly know you and you're already blackmailing me?"

Terri smiled wryly. "It's the Caroselli way."

"I'll definitely be there, but I'll find my own ride."

"Well, I should go," Terri said. "If there's anything you need, or if you have a question, just give me or Nick a call."

"It was really nice talking to you," Carrie told her.

"I think so, too," Terri said, looking a little embarrassed. She struck Carrie as the type who probably had more male than female friends. While Carrie had very few of either.

"And thanks for the advice," Carrie said.

"Anytime." Terri pulled on her coat, then fished a set of keys from her pocket and handed them to Carrie. "Those open the front and garage door."

"Thanks. See you tomorrow."

When she was gone, Carrie started to explore the kitchen cabinets, feeling a little like a snoop. But she was sure that Terri would have removed anything of a personal nature before she rented out the condo.

She opened the refrigerator and smiled. On the shelf sat an unopened half gallon of low-fat milk, a dozen organic eggs and a loaf of organic nine-grain bread. One shelf down was a bottle of very expensive champagne.

Terri had gone above and beyond to make her feel welcome, and Carrie hoped they would have time to get to know one another better.

Carrie returned to the hotel to collect her things, then took a cab back to the condo, doing her best to memorize the street names so she could find her way around when she had a car. It had begun to snow, so rather than have the driver track it through the living room and potentially ruin the carpet, she had him leave the bags in the garage.

She opened the door to total darkness, cursing herself for not remembering to leave a light on. She felt around on the inside wall for a light switch. She found it and as she was flipping it upward, she felt a cold hand settle on top of hers.

She shrieked and yanked her hand back, the bright light temporarily blinding her. She blinked hard and when she opened her eyes again, no one was there. She peeked around the corner, but the only thing there was a door. Probably to the basement.

She took a slow, deep breath to calm her pounding heart. It was just her imagination. No one was there. She'd clearly been watching too many episodes of *Ghost Hunter*.

She turned to grab her bags, nearly colliding with the very large person standing there. She shrieked again, then realized that it was only Rob.

"You scared me half to death!" she said.

He wore a long black wool coat and black leather gloves...and an amused grin. Fat flakes of snow dotted his dark hair and he'd left snowy footprints on the garage floor. "A little jumpy?"

"What do you want?"

"What made you scream?"

"*You* did!"

"No, the first time."

"Nothing. I was imagining things."

"Imagining what?"

She shook her head. "*Nothing*. It wasn't real."

He narrowed his eyes. "What wasn't real?"

She blew out an exasperated breath. "If you must know, when I reached around for the light switch, I could swear somebody put their hand over mine, but when I turned on the light, no one was there."

"It must have been the lady in the basement."

She blinked. "The *who?*"

"We call her the lady in the basement. Not everyone senses her. Terri and Nick never did, but a lot of other people have. Sometimes she touches people, some people hear her walking up and down the stairs. Some hear her crying. I smell her perfume."

She couldn't tell if he was being serious or just messing with her. "Really?"

"I can smell it from the instant I step in the garage door until I step into the kitchen. Maybe three feet. Then it's gone. I've felt her brush against me, and once I felt a hand on my shoulder."

"No way." She leaned into the doorway and sniffed, but all she smelled was pine cleaner and bleach.

"You have to actually step inside," Rob said. "Or it doesn't work."

She eyed him skeptically. Had she honestly just rented a house with a dead lady living in the basement? And wasn't that sort of thing supposed to be disclosed before the lease was signed? Or was Rob just full of it?

Of course he was.

"You're lying," she said.

"I'm dead serious. Try it if you don't believe me."

It was walk in this door or walk around to the front door, which would make her look even more ridiculous than she probably did now. So basically she was damned if she did and damned if she didn't.

Promising herself that no matter what happened she would not react, she lifted her foot and stepped up over the threshold, then followed with the opposite foot, and the second it touched the floor—

A hand clamped down over her shoulder, and even though deep down she knew it was Rob, a startled screech ripped from her throat.

Heart pounding, she spun around and gave him a hard shove. "You're an *ass*."

"And you are *way* too gullible," he said, laughing and shaking his head. "I can't believe you fell for that."

"I didn't think it was possible, but I like you even less than I did before."

"It was worth it to see the look on your face."

She stomped into the house and switched on the kitchen light, expecting him to follow. And he did, hauling two of her bags inside with him.

"What are you doing?"

"Where do you want them?" he asked.

She was about to tell him she would do it herself, then thought, what the heck. He might as well get used to following directions from her. "They all go in the bedroom."

He had clearly been there before, because he seemed to know where all the light switches and the bedrooms were located.

She shrugged out of her coat, wondering if she might find a box of tea bags somewhere.

On his second trip through to the bedroom, Rob asked, "Are you sure you packed enough stuff? These things weigh a ton."

"You try packing three months' worth of stuff," she called after him as he disappeared down the hall. "That's a long time to be away from home."

Two of the smaller bags had nothing in them but shoes. One was filled with casual clothes, though she realized now that much of it was too light for the cold weather. She would have to do some clothes shopping, and soon. The rest was work clothes, some of which were also inappropriate for the season. Living in a warmer climate, it was difficult to imagine how cold Midwestern winters could be.

"What are you doing here anyway?" she asked on his final trip back to the garage. "And how did you even know where I was?"

He walked back in with the last two bags. "I talked to Nick."

Of course he would know, because Terri told Nick everything. Not that it was some big secret. She just didn't want Rob thinking it was okay to come by and hassle her whenever he felt like it.

This time she followed him into the bedroom. He set her bags down with the others by the closet, then turned to her.

"Which doesn't explain why you're here," she said, folding her arms, giving him her stern look.

"To give you this." He tugged his gloves off, pulled a flash drive out of his inside coat pocket and handed it to her.

"What is it?"

"The financial reports you asked Elana for."

"Oh. She could have given them to me Monday."

He shrugged. "I figured you would probably want to get an early start on this."

Actually, no, she planned to start Monday, when her contract started. But it was interesting that Rob chose to bring it when he didn't have to.

"Thanks," she said, and crossed the room to set it on the nightstand. But when she turned back around, Rob was no longer standing by the closet. He was in front of the bedroom door, blocking her only exit from the room. And he was wearing that *look*.

All the parts of her that had been craving his touch shivered to attention. What on earth had possessed her to follow him in here? If there was a single worst place for them to be together, it was a bedroom.

Rolling her eyes in response to the visual overture, she walked over to her bags and grabbed one that was filled with shoes. She went into the closet with it, found a good place to put them, then bent at the waist to unzip the bag—

and not just because she was trying to make her butt look good either. One by one she pulled the shoes out, pairing them together on the floor.

She heard him in the bedroom, just outside the closet, the hiss of his arms through the satin lining of his coat sleeves. Okay, so he was taking his coat off. That didn't mean he would try anything. He had been the one to proclaim that it was over the other morning. What was he going to do? Break his own rules? Although it would be fun to turn the tables again and turn him down.

She could do that. Right? All she had to do was call Alice and she would talk her out of it.

Before she could make up her mind, she felt his hands slide around her hips, his fingers gripping as he rubbed his crotch across her behind. He was already noticeably turned on, and she wasn't faring much better.

"Really," she said, looking back at him. "This is so… cliché."

"You're one to talk." He slid his fingers under the hem of her sweater, brushing them across her bare skin. "Besides, you didn't seem to mind it like this the other night."

No, she hadn't, had she? And it was very cliché of him to remind her.

Where the hell was her phone? She needed to call Alice pronto.

As she straightened up, he slid his hands around to her belly, pulling her back against him. Oh, that was nice. But not half as nice as when his hands slid up to cup her breasts a second after.

She sighed and let her head drop back against his chest. "I distinctly recall your telling me that this was not going to happen again. And you were right."

"Well, I changed my mind."

"You can't do that."

"I just did." He tucked her hair to one side, kissed the back of her neck, the heat from his body melting her brain.

"We're coworkers," she reminded him.

"Technically we're not. Not yet. Your contract doesn't officially begin until Monday."

He made a valid point. And because they had already slept together, the pre-working-relationship part was already a lost cause. Right?

So what was the big deal if they did it one more time? If she held it up beside the "big picture," it was a tiny, tiny thing. Barely a blip. And why bother Alice when this was clearly going to be the last time?

His hands were under her sweater now, his hot palms scorching a path across her skin. He nibbled the side of her neck, then sucked hard.

A guy hadn't given her a hickey since she was fifteen, but it was unbelievably erotic to think that he was marking her, branding her as his.

She turned to face him, sliding her arms around his neck. "Okay, but just this one time, and that's it."

"Agreed. Unless we have to do it again tomorrow, because it's only Saturday. Then of course there's Sunday…"

"But not after Monday."

"Definitely." He lifted her right off her feet and carried her to the bed. There was no better way to make a house feel like a home than to have really awesome sex in it.

Seven

Rob tossed her not so gently onto the mattress and pulled his shirt up over his head.

She pulled her shirt off, too, then her bra. "For the record, I still don't like you."

"I know," he said, red-hot lust in his eyes as he unfastened his pants. "Take off your jeans."

She unfastened them and shoved them down, and his dropped to the floor. His pants *and* his underwear.

"This is just sex," she told him, as he tugged her panties down her legs. "We're not friends."

"Definitely not." He knelt at the end of the mattress and began to kiss his way up her legs, pushing them apart as he worked his way higher, and when he reached the apex of her thighs, he kissed her there, then took her into his mouth.

She had forgotten that he had such a talented tongue. But as good as it was, she wanted him inside her when she came, and he must have been thinking the same thing. He moved over her, settled between her open thighs, his weight pressing her into the mattress in the most appealing way.

He took her hands in his and pinned them over her head. "Tell me you want me."

"This was your idea," she said. "So clearly you're the one who wants *me*."

He lowered his head to lick her nipple, then suck it into his mouth. *Hard*. She gasped and pushed up against his grip.

"Tell me you want me," he said, and the devilish look in his eyes said he would take whatever measures necessary to make her cooperate…like slide his erection against her, teasing her with the tip, until she was restless and needy.

"Fine, I want you," she said, shifting underneath him.

His deadpan expression said that wasn't exactly what he'd had in mind. But there was something else, an undercurrent of emotion that made her wonder if he actually *needed* to hear it.

She looked into his eyes and said, "I want you."

With a swift and not-so-gentle thrust that stole her breath, he was inside of her. Then he pulled back and thrust again and pleasure rippled through her like a shock wave. A few more of those and it would be all over for her. She held her breath, anticipating the next thrust, but instead Rob stopped, cursing under his breath.

"Something wrong?" she asked him.

He looked down at her. "Are you using any kind of birth control?"

She shook her head.

"At present, neither am I, so before it's too late…"

She shoved him off her. "Yes, definitely. Please."

Thank goodness he'd noticed in time. She couldn't even imagine what a disaster it would have been if he hadn't. She was at the worst possible time in her cycle to be taking chances.

If there was a world speed record for rolling on a condom, she was sure he broke it. But this time, as he lowered himself over her, he took things a bit slower. Fast, slow, she didn't care, so long as he was touching her.

"You're so beautiful," he said, his eyes searching her face, as if he were trying to memorize her down to the tiniest detail. Hot friction burned at her core, mounting with every slow, steady thrust. She could feel the pleasure coiling tight, the pressure building. She was going to tell him that they needed to slow down, but it was already too late. Her body, her entire being was sucked under into a whirlpool of pleasure. Rob growled and tensed as he came.

And as good as it felt, she was almost sorry that it was over, that it hadn't lasted longer. Of course, if this was anything like that night in the hotel, they weren't anywhere near finished.

Carrie woke the next morning and sat up in bed, disoriented by the unfamiliar room. Then she remembered that she was living in the condo now. In Chicago.

And last night…

She looked over at the empty spot beside her and sighed. The son of a bitch had sneaked out on her again. She looked around for a note, but once again, he hadn't bothered to leave one.

It figured.

In a huff, she tugged on her robe and trudged sleepily to the kitchen to make a pot of coffee. There was a handwritten note stuck to the refrigerator door with a magnet:

*Sorry, had to work. I had a great time last night.
Left at 7, no skulking involved. Wanna not be friends
again tonight after the party?*

It was silly, but the fact that he'd listened, and really
heard her, that he remembered to leave a note this time,
and especially one so sweet and funny, made her dislike
him a little less. And that scared her. What they were
doing now was simple and impartial. It didn't mean anything, which made it very, very safe. But what if they really started to like each other?

Oh, what was she worried about? The next time she saw
him he would say something rude or chauvinistic and she
would be back to hating him.

Carrie showered and dressed, and was standing in the
kitchen getting ready to call a cab to take her to the nearest mall when she heard a creaking sound, as if someone
had opened the inside garage door. Expecting to see Rob,
or even Terri, she stepped around the corner, but there
was no one there and the door was still shut and locked
from last night.

What the—

That was when she looked over at the basement door
and realized it was open. But it had been closed and latched
when they came in last night. She recalled feeling the hand
over hers and her heart skipped a beat. It was possible that
Rob had opened it this morning before he left. But why?

The more likely and logical explanation was that the
door wasn't latched all the way and had drifted open.

She grabbed the doorknob and pulled it closed, making sure that it really latched this time. Feeling better, she
called the cab and left to go shopping. She found herself
some nice casual things, and most of them from the clear-
ance rack.

She forgot all about the basement door until she was in the kitchen fixing herself a cup of hot tea later that evening, and she had the sudden, eerie sensation that someone was watching her.

She knew she was just imagining things, but feeling the tiniest bit apprehensive anyway, she edged her way over and peered around the edge of the wall…sighing with relief when she found the door firmly latched.

Of course it was still closed, and the hand she'd felt had just been her imagination. She felt silly for believing it could be anything else.

The kettle whistled, and she shut off the burner. She poured water into her cup, and was about to take a sip when she heard it. The distinct creak of a door.

No way. She had to be imagining it.

She forced herself to walk over and peek around the wall.

"I'll be damned," she said into the silence. The basement door was open again.

Rob knocked on Carrie's front door at ten minutes to seven.

She opened the door a crack and peeked out, blinking with surprise. "What are you doing here?"

"Picking you up for the party."

She narrowed her eyes at him. "I'm confused."

"The party at Nick and Terri's. You are going, aren't you?"

"Yes, but I told Terri I would find my own ride."

"Well, I didn't talk to Terri."

"Oh. So why are you here?"

"To save you cab fare. Because it was on my way. To be nice." He shrugged and said, "Pick one."

"To get laid."

"That would work, too." He stamped his feet to keep the blood from freezing in his veins. "Whatever it takes for you to let me inside before my feet freeze to the porch."

She hesitated. "We are not friends."

"I'm well aware of that."

She finally moved back to let him in. He stepped inside and she shut the door. When he saw what she was wearing, he nearly swallowed his own tongue. In a figure-hugging denim miniskirt, knee-high spike-heeled boots and a clingy pink sweater, she clearly had no qualms about showing off her figure. "Wow. You look nice."

"You don't think it's too much?"

Even if it was, he would pay her to keep wearing it. Each time he thought he'd seen her at her sexiest, she managed to outdo herself.

"If we drive there together, people are going to get the idea that we're a couple," she said.

He shrugged. "Does it really matter what anyone thinks?"

"It's different for you. You're a man. If you score with a woman at work, you're a stud. If I do that, I'm a slut."

"Really. Was there a particular woman at work that you're interested in?"

She rolled her eyes. "You know what I mean."

"We could just tell people the truth, and say that I picked you up because it was on my way. Or, if it makes you feel better, you can go in first, and I can come in a few minutes later."

"That could work," she said. "And even if people suspect we're together, they'll eventually get the idea that we don't like each other. At all."

"Exactly. Get your coat."

She hesitated. "Before we go, I have to ask you something."

"Okay."

"You have to promise not to make fun of me."

Oh, this should be good. "All right. I promise."

"When you told me that thing about the lady in the basement, you really were kidding, right?"

"Of course I was kidding. Why? Did you feel the hand again?"

"No, I did not."

"But something happened, didn't it?"

"At first I thought it was a fluke…"

"What?"

"The basement door has been sort of…opening by itself."

He cast her a disbelieving look.

"I'm dead serious. I close it, then check it a little while later, and it's open like an inch or two."

"You probably aren't latching it all the way."

"No, I most definitely did latch it."

"If you did, it wouldn't have opened."

She propped her hands on her hips, glaring at him. "Are you honestly suggesting that I am incapable of latching a door?"

It was more plausible than the door opening by itself. "Let's take a look at it," he said. She followed him through the kitchen, her heels clicking on the tile floor. The basement door was open about an inch.

"See?" she said. "I closed and latched it less than fifteen minutes ago."

She was letting her imagination get the best of her. He pulled it closed and made sure that it was latched securely. He tried to open it without turning the knob and it wouldn't budge. There was no way that door would open without someone physically turning the handle. "Okay," he said, watching the knob. "Let's see it open."

"It doesn't work that way. I sat and watched it for like fifteen minutes and it didn't move, so I walked away. Five minutes later it was open again."

"Then let's go in the other room."

"I have to finish getting ready."

He looked her up and down. "You look ready to me."

That earned him another eye roll. "If you want to drive me, you'll have to wait."

It wasn't that he wanted to drive her. It just seemed rude not to. And if it increased his chances of getting her naked again tonight, why the hell not?

Knowing how long women could take getting ready, he shrugged out of his coat and made himself comfortable on the sofa. After a moment or two, curiosity got the best of him. He pushed himself up from the sofa and quietly sneaked through the kitchen to look around the corner. The basement door was as he'd left it. He tried the knob and it was securely latched.

As he suspected, there were no supernatural forces at work here. She had probably been in a rush and hadn't latched it, or maybe she really didn't know how to properly latch a door.

He went and sat back down on the sofa to wait for her, checking the door two more times with the same results. It was still closed tight.

Carrie reemerged several minutes later, pulling on her coat. If she'd done anything different to her appearance, he couldn't tell. Maybe she was one of those women who just didn't feel the night was complete unless she made a man wait for fifteen or twenty minutes.

"So, did you check the door?" she asked him.

"Three times. It didn't budge."

Looking discouraged, she said, "I *swear* it opened by itself."

He shrugged. "I don't know what to say. If it had mysteriously opened I would have told you."

"I *did* close it all the way."

"Okay."

"But you don't believe me."

"I didn't say that."

"You didn't have to." Exasperated, she looked over at the clock and said, "We had better go."

She grabbed her clutch from the coffee table. "I want to go out the garage door so I can grab the opener. If we're going to 'not be friends' after the party tonight, I want you to put your car in the garage."

"Why?"

She shot him a look.

Clearly she didn't want anyone to know he was there. Like he would argue over such an inconsequential detail when sex was involved. "Fine. Paint it camouflage for all I care."

He grabbed his coat and was tugging it on as they walked through the kitchen to the garage door, and she stopped so abruptly that he actually ran into her.

"Rob, that's really not funny," she said, looking at the basement door. Someone or something must have been making a point because the door wasn't open an inch or two this time. It was open all the way.

Eight

"It opens by itself?" Terri looked as skeptical as Rob had when Carrie told him about the basement door. They stood in Terri and Nick's kitchen with several of their friends, including Tony's sister Elana, and a guy named Mark who was making no secret of the fact that he found Carrie attractive. He was cute in an average way. Average height, average weight, naturally blond hair that was thinning a bit on top. And though he went a little gung ho with the aftershave, he seemed very nice, if not slightly forward in his intentions. But when he stood close to her, the air didn't crackle with energy, and her heart didn't beat faster, and when he touched her arm, her skin didn't shiver with awareness. In other words, he was no Rob.

She had already formed a gentle rejection in case Mark asked her out. Which seemed inevitable at this point.

"I take it that never happened when you lived there," Carrie said.

Terri shrugged. "If it did I never noticed. Far as I remember, the door was always closed. I hardly ever go down there. I mostly just use it for storage."

"Storage of what?" Elana asked. "Human remains?"

Terri shot her a withering look. "Old furniture."

Lisa, who worked in Nick's department at Caroselli Chocolate, asked, "Haunted furniture?"

"Not that I know of. But some of it is pretty old. Things my aunt had in her attic when she died. Stuff that has been in the family for a couple hundred years. I doubt I'll ever use any of it, but it seemed wrong to sell it."

Carrie glanced over to the living room where Tony, Rob and a very attractive Asian woman Carrie hadn't yet been introduced to stood by the sofa talking. The woman had come to the party late, and whoever she was, Rob seemed utterly enthralled by what she was saying, hanging on her every word.

Abruptly, as if he'd sensed her eyes on him, Rob looked over at Carrie and caught her staring. The corner of his mouth tilted into a wry smile.

Even though they had arrived together, they hadn't said more than ten words to each other in the two hours they had been there. A few times when he'd walked past, his arm had brushed hers, and once, when they reached into the chips bowl at the same time, their fingers touched. He'd given her his "look" and all she'd been able to think about since then was how they would go back to her place and "not be friends" all night long.

As far as she had seen, Rob had been nursing the same drink since they arrived, confirming what Terri had told her about his not being much of a drinker. Carrie on the other hand was on her fourth glass of wine. Each time she drained her glass, Mark would automatically refill it.

She was beginning to think that he was trying to get her drunk. He seemed a bit tipsy himself.

"Anything else weird happen?" Terri asked her.

"There was one other thing. I was in the garage and reached inside to feel around for the light switch, and I felt a hand settle on top of mine. A very cold hand."

"Eew," Elana said with a shudder, rubbing her arms. "That just gave me goose bumps."

"Me, too," Terri said. "I definitely never experienced anything like that, and if I had, I think I probably would have moved. In fact, if you want to look for a different place, I totally understand."

"The idea that someone or something is there is a little creepy," Carrie admitted. "But I don't get a negative vibe. I don't feel threatened at all. Or even scared."

"Have you been down in the basement?" Mark asked.

"I don't know if I'm that brave," she said.

He slipped an arm around her shoulder, grinned down at her and said, "I'll protect you."

The strong scent of liquor on his breath actually burned her eyes. She waited for him to remove his arm, but he left it there. It didn't feel *awful* exactly. Just a little…awkward. And not sexually stimulating in the least. Which had her automatically looking over at Rob, who was leaning in somewhat close to the Asian woman. He laughed at something she said, then slipped an arm around her shoulder.

Carrie tried to ignore an annoying little jab of jealousy. Whom he did or didn't hook up with at a party was none of her business. Although at the rate things were going, she might be taking a cab home and spending the night alone. Which was fine. He hadn't promised that they would spend the night together. In fact, it was probably better if they didn't.

And if that was true, why did she feel so crummy?

"We should call a medium," Elana said.

"As opposed to a small or a large," Mark joked, but no one laughed.

Elana rolled her eyes. "Like the one on that cable show who talks to the dead."

"I've seen that show," Terri said. "But isn't she in New York?"

"Long Island," Elana said. "I wonder if there's a reputable one in Chicago?"

"Or maybe you need an exorcist," Mark joked, the weight of his arm making her shoulder ache. It seemed that now he was leaning on her more for support, to stay upright.

"Whatever it is, I don't think it's evil," Carrie said, shifting away, only to have him lean more heavily on her. She glanced over at Rob. He laughed at something the Asian woman said, then kissed her cheek.

Yep, she was definitely on her own tonight. She tried not to let herself feel too disappointed. It would have ended Sunday anyway.

"We should have a séance," Elana suggested. "Do they still sell Ouija boards? I used to have one when I was a kid. Until *Nonna* found it and freaked out. She was very superstitious."

"Did you ever actually talk to the spirits with it?" Lisa asked.

"We used to pretend we did to scare each other, but I'm pretty sure everyone was moving the little plastic thing on their own."

"Whatever it is down there, maybe disturbing it would be a bad idea," Terri said.

And because she was the one who lived there, Carrie added, "I agree. I have no problem sharing, as long as it stays in the basement. I'll stay out of its way if it stays out of mine."

She had that feeling of being watched, but when she turned to look at Rob, his attention was on his companion. All this talk of ghosts and the supernatural was making her paranoid.

The weight of Mark leaning on her shoulder was not only uncomfortable, but it was also starting to grate on her nerves, and his cloying aftershave was giving her a headache. At the risk of him falling over, she swiftly ducked from under his arm. He teetered, then caught his balance on the edge of the counter.

"Bathroom?" she asked Terri. She didn't have to go, but she needed a minute or two of fresh air.

"Down the hall on the left," Terri told her, "and if that one is busy, there's one in my office and another in the master bedroom, through the closet." She lowered her voice and said, "If Mark is annoying you, just tell him to back off. He's a decent guy when he's not drinking. Unfortunately, that isn't very often."

In that case, Carrie was less worried about hurting his feelings. The last thing she needed or wanted was another alcoholic in her life, complicating things. "Thanks, I will."

As she headed down the hall, her phone started to ring. She checked the display and saw that it was Alice. Again. Out of guilt she had been avoiding her calls. She would talk to her next week, when she could honestly say that she wasn't sleeping with Rob. It was just too difficult to explain.

The first bathroom was occupied, so she tried the door on the right at the end of the hall and found herself in the master bedroom. Feeling a little weird being in someone else's bedroom, she crossed the room and walked through the closet to the bathroom. She stepped inside and was about to close the door, when someone on the other side pushed it open. She felt a sudden stab of alarm, thinking it was probably Mark. But it was Rob who stepped inside.

"You startled me," Carrie said, a hand pressed over her cleavage, in the exact spot he wanted to bury his face.

"Were you expecting Mark?" Rob asked, closing and locking the door behind him. "You two were looking awfully cozy."

She folded her arms and stuck out her chin. "Jealous?"

"Not at all, because we both know he's not half the man that I am."

"Maybe I think he is," she said, but her eyes betrayed her, just as they had in the kitchen, when Mark was hanging all over her. He could tell that she was as annoyed as he had been.

"No, you don't. That's why you couldn't keep your eyes off me."

"What are you doing in here anyway? Shouldn't you be out talking to your girlfriend?"

He paused for a second, then said, "Don't worry, she'll be along in a minute. All three of us disappearing at the same time would be way too obvious."

All *three* of them? She blinked, then glanced at the door. "That had better be a joke."

"What's the matter?" he said, walking toward her, grinning when she backed away from him. "You don't like to share?"

"You're not funny, you know."

"My 'girlfriend' is Megan."

"Okay."

"Megan Caroselli. My sister."

She blinked again, looking confused, then said, "Oh."

"My *adopted* sister."

She nodded and said, "Okay," as if it suddenly made sense.

He stepped closer, backing her against the countertop. "I like that you were jealous, though."

"I was not jealous," she said, jutting that chin out again.

He wasn't buying the tough act. "You want me," he said.

She rolled her eyes. "Could you be more arrogant?"

He grinned, reaching up to cup her cheek in his palm, swiping his thumb across her lower lip. All he'd been able to think about since he showed up at her place was getting her out of her clothes and back into bed. Staying away from her all evening, pretending he wasn't lusting after her, had been torture. And apparently he hadn't done a very good job of hiding his feelings where Nick was concerned.

Nick had cornered him about an hour ago and said, "Why don't you go over and talk to her?"

"Who?" Rob asked.

"You know damn well who. You two can't keep your eyes off each other."

He didn't see any point in lying to his cousin. "She doesn't want people to think we're involved."

"Anyone with eyes and half a brain is going to eventually notice that you two are lusting after each other. Hell, the temperature in the room rises a good ten degrees when you get within five feet of each other."

Rob honestly hadn't realized it was so obvious, and had been diligent about not going near her or even looking at her for the past hour or so—which had been a lot more difficult than he would have anticipated. Especially when Mark started to put the moves on her. But it seemed as though the more Rob ignored her, the more he lusted for her. When she finally brushed Mark off, Rob had been about ten seconds from punching him in the nose. And though he hadn't actually planned to follow Carrie to the bathroom, his feet had carried him there.

"We can't do this here," Carrie said, yet when he leaned in and kissed the side of her neck, she put up zero resistance. "Someone will hear us."

"We'll be quiet," he said, nuzzling her ear, breathing in the scent of her perfume. "You smell good."

"Rob, stop."

He should have cared who heard, but he didn't. He turned her so she was facing the mirror, watched her over her shoulder. "Say that like you mean it and I will."

"I mean it," she said, but he could tell that she didn't. She just didn't want to admit it. Didn't want to let down her guard and surrender herself to the desire that was eating them both alive.

He reached around to cup her breasts, squeezing the firm mounds. She moaned and her eyes rolled closed. Her hands fisted stubbornly rather than touch him, but they didn't push him away either. He couldn't be in the same room with her for very long without putting his own hands all over her. Which could be a major problem come Monday when they were forced to work together.

He pulled her against him, grinding his erection against her backside, and when she still wouldn't give in, he shoved his hands up under her sweater. He freed her from the lace cups of her bra, and as he palmed her bare breasts, she lost it. She moaned and slid her hands up, hooking them around his neck, pulling his head down for a hot and hungry kiss. He yanked the hem of her miniskirt up her thighs, growling when he saw her bare bottom and realized she wasn't wearing panties.

"I didn't have a clean pair," she said, which they both knew was a lie.

"Sure you didn't." He slipped a hand between her

thighs, watching her in the mirror as he stroked, as her cheeks flushed a deep crimson. "Still want me to stop?"

She clearly had lost the will to fight, grinding her ass against the front of his jeans. "Make it fast, before someone realizes we both disappeared."

He unfastened his pants, pulled out the condom he'd put in his pocket and rolled it on. He bent her over the vanity, grabbed her hips and slammed into her. She cried out and bucked her head back, bracing her hands on the vanity edge, meeting him thrust for thrust. Never before had he been so rough with a woman. In his mind women were soft, delicate creatures who required the utmost sensitivity. But with Carrie…he didn't even know how to put it into words. He wanted to dominate her and…*take* her. Make her scream in ecstasy, surrender her body and her mind to him. Her soul. And the more she resisted, the more determined he was to break her.

Their difference in height was making his calves cramp up and throwing off his concentration. He turned Carrie around to face him, lifted her up off her feet and pinned her against the wall next to the shower. Her legs clamped around his hips, nails dug into his shoulders as he thrust inside of her. She murmured encouragement, words like "harder" and "faster," and a few others that he would never use in mixed company. She let him know exactly what she wanted, and how she wanted it. And he couldn't stop now if his life depended on it. Some repressed, primal need had taken over, was driving him past the boundaries of decency. He wanted to put his hands all over her, make her writhe and scream and beg him for more. He'd been with his share of women, yet until that night in her hotel room, he'd had no idea that sex could be so intensely erotic. That he could not just want a woman, but *need* her. In a way that was so primal even he didn't understand it. For a man who thrived on staying in control, being trapped under the spell of a woman, especially one as independent as Carrie, was a place he had never imagined himself. And as hard as he tried he couldn't seem to fight it.

Hell, he wasn't even sure that he *wanted* to anymore.

When he had reached the absolute limit of his control, as sweet release pulled tight in his groin, Carrie smothered a moan against his shoulder and shuddered in his arms, her body clamping around him like a vise, milking him into ecstasy. His orgasm was so intense and draining, his legs so shaky afterward, he had to set her down for fear of dropping her on the hard tile floor.

They were both sweaty and breathless, and crimson blotches stained Carrie's cheeks.

"What is the matter with us?" Carrie said in a harsh whisper, tugging her skirt back down. "We just had sex in your cousin's *bathroom*."

"I know," he said, cleaning up before he zipped himself back into his pants.

Carrie adjusted her bra, tugging the cups back into place. "And you don't see anything wrong with that?"

"I'm just as baffled by this as you are," he said, tucking his shirt in.

"So what are we going to do about it?" she demanded, finger-combing her hair, smoothing away the just-had-sex look.

"Well, right now, I'm going to walk back out to the living room. After a minute or two you'll follow me. You'll tell me you aren't feeling well, and ask me if I'll drive you home. I'll roll my eyes and act indignant, then we'll leave and go to your place. And when we get there we're going to do this again, only this time we can make as much noise as we'd like."

She paused to consider that for several seconds, and

must have determined that it was a good plan, because she gave him a not-so-gentle shove toward the door and said, "What are you waiting for? Get out there."

Nine

The most intense sexual experience of Carrie's life was officially over.

Or so she and Rob had established this morning before he went home to get ready for work. And now, as she walked from the cab to the Caroselli building, after spending nearly twenty-four hours together in bed with him, they had to make everyone believe that they were nothing more than coworkers. At first she didn't think it would be a problem, because she didn't even like him— which she couldn't deny was what had made him so appealing. As a rule she didn't date nice guys. In fact, she avoided them like the plague. She dated jerks. Men who treated her like crap.

Rob seemed to have so much "creep" potential, but then everything had changed. Not only could they burn up the sheets together, but she was beginning to suspect that he was a genuinely nice guy. Under normal circumstances she just wouldn't see him again. If he called or texted, she would ignore him until he got the hint and gave up. That wouldn't be so easy with Rob. Not when she had to interact with him daily, five days a week or more, for the next three months.

He'd even offered to pick her up and drive her to work, because it was on his way, and she'd had to gently remind him that they couldn't be seen together outside of the office. She'd taken a cab instead, and planned, during her first free moment, to arrange for a rental or short-term lease. And because she was a novice at driving in the snow, preferably something four-wheel drive and built like a tank.

Dennis nodded and smiled as she walked past him to the elevator and pushed the button for the third floor. Feeling just the tiniest bit apprehensive she rode up. When she entered the reception area, Sheila greeted her with a smile and said, "Rob would like to see you first thing."

"Thanks," she said, returning the smile. Did Rob not realize that until he gave her a place to work, she had nowhere to go but his office?

She walked down the hall and stepped inside his outer office, where a stern-looking secretary sat. She glanced up from her computer, gave Carrie a quick once-over and seemed to determine that she didn't like her—or so her sour expression would imply. "Go on in, he's expecting you."

Definite tension with this one, which undoubtedly meant that she was loyal to her boss, the one whose work Carrie was here to criticize.

"Thank you, Ms...." Even though the woman's nameplate was in plain sight on her desk, it didn't hurt to break the ice.

"*Mrs.* White," she said, icicles dripping off each word.

Ignoring her frosty introduction, Carrie smiled. "It's

a pleasure to meet you, Mrs. White. I'm Caroline Taylor, but everyone calls me Carrie."

"Ms. Taylor," she said with a curt nod.

This one would be a tough egg to crack, but Carrie would do it. She had a way of putting people at ease, winning them over. Look how well it had worked on Rob.

A little *too* well.

Only as she approached his office door was Carrie hit with a sudden and intense wave of apprehension. Which was silly given their history. Or maybe what she was really feeling was exhilaration. She could barely go five minutes without thinking of him, without recalling the way he touched her, how he looked tangled in the sheets, ripples of muscles under smooth, sweat-soaked skin.

But it was over now and she would just have to learn to rein in her wandering thoughts.

Steeling herself, she knocked sharply on the door, then let herself in, melting when she saw Rob sitting there, tapping away at his keyboard, a steaming cup of coffee beside him on his desk.

"You asked to see me?" she said, catching the subtle scent of his aftershave, wishing she could run her hand over his smooth, freshly shaved cheek. Even though she couldn't deny that the rasp of the dark, wiry stubble he'd woken up with this morning had been a turn-on.

Without looking up, he nodded and said, "Be with you in just one second...."

She stood waiting while he typed a bit more, manipulated the mouse for several seconds, frowned, then started typing again. All she could see was the back of the computer monitor, so she had no clue what he might be working on. Or if it even was work. For all she knew he could have been updating his status on Facebook, or corresponding with his online sweetheart. Even though he swore he didn't have a girlfriend. Maybe this would be easier if he did.

While she waited she gazed around his office, which she hadn't really taken the time to notice the last time she was there. In her own defense, it was tough to concentrate on the decor when Rob's hand was up her skirt.

The room was neat, with an unmistakable masculine feel, but not so macho that she had the urge to stuff a wad of chewing tobacco in her cheek. The dark mahogany furniture gave the space a rich, professional feel, but a collection of family photos hanging on the wall and various live plants created a casual atmosphere.

When Rob finally seemed satisfied with what he'd typed, he pushed the keyboard tray in, rose to his feet and greeted her with a very professional "Good morning."

"Sorry I wasn't here sooner. The cab was late picking me up." She waited for him to say something about how, if she'd accepted a ride from him, she wouldn't be late.

He didn't. He just shrugged and said, "No problem."

"What's on the agenda this morning?" she asked, eager to get to work, to keep her mind busy on other things.

"We have a meeting in the conference room in five minutes." He eyed the coat draped over her arm and the briefcase slung over her shoulder. "Why don't I show you to your office first."

He led her down the hall toward the conference room, the scent of his aftershave intoxicating, the casual confidence in his movements mesmerizing. She imagined that once they were in her office he would close the door and pull her into his arms. He would kiss her and tell her that he couldn't keep his hands off her, that he couldn't live without her and that he would die if he couldn't have her again.

When they reached the end of the hall, he hung a left

and gestured to the first office on the right-hand side. "Here it is."

Not only did he not pull her into his arms, but he also didn't even step into the room with her. He waited in the hall while she looked around.

"Will it suffice?" he asked.

It was about half the size of Rob's office and generically outfitted with a desk, bookcase and metal file cabinet. The walls were white and bare, and the carpet an office-gray Berber. Nothing special but functional. "It'll do just fine."

"Great. While you settle in I'll be in the conference room."

He started to turn and before she knew what she was doing, she heard herself say, "Rob, wait."

He turned back to her. "Yes?"

Okay, now what? She wanted to say something, she just didn't know what, or if she even should.

He was standing there, waiting patiently for her to continue, so she blurted out, "I'll need a few things, like Wi-Fi passwords, and I'll need access to a printer."

"We'll discuss all of that in the conference room." He paused, then said, "Anything else?"

Yes, there was something else, she just didn't know how to put it into words. Not without making herself look clingy and pathetic. She forced a smile and shook her head. "No, nothing."

"Then I'll see you down there."

Feeling disappointed for no good reason, she hung her coat on a hook behind the door and stowed her purse in the bottom drawer of her desk. She would need everything in her briefcase for the meeting, so she held on to it.

She had never before questioned her ability to do her job, but as she walked down the hall alone to the conference room, nerves jabbed away at her confidence. Maybe it was the complicated nature of her relationship with Rob that was getting in the way. Yes, they had ended their sexual relationship, but there were still feelings there. It would take time for them to go away completely. And maybe it was a little late to consider this, but what if the past few days hadn't been about sexual attraction as much as his using her to learn her weaknesses? Maybe he would use that information against her to discredit her in front of the people in his department.

Maybe all the while that she had been gushing over what a nice guy he was, it had been an act to lull her into a false sense of security.

A possibility she probably should have considered before she surrendered to him body and soul.

She stopped just outside the conference room door, suddenly convinced she had made a horrible mistake. That by letting her emotions get the best of her, she was about to walk into her worst nightmare. It was imperative that no matter what, she not let anyone see the pain that such a betrayal would cause her.

Taking a deep breath, she stepped into the conference room, head held high, shoulders squared. Rob and three other people sat around the conference table. Her first surprise was that he wasn't sitting at the head of the table, where she would have expected him to be. Her second was that she was greeted with smiles and not scowls when Rob said, "Everyone, this is Caroline Taylor. Over the next three months I expect you to give her your full cooperation."

Huh?

Full cooperation? He wasn't going to give her a hard time? Make her feel unwelcome as he had last week? He was actually going to be nice about this? And why did it suddenly make him about a million times *more* appealing.

Now she was thinking that it would be better if he'd been a jerk. But it was still early. He still had time to knock off some rude or scathing comments. Hell, he had three whole months to prove what a creep he really was. Maybe she had just seen him on his best behavior.

He introduced his team—Alexandra "call me Al" Lujack, Will Cooper and Grant Kelley. They each looked to be in their mid to late twenties and couldn't have been more than a few years out of college.

"Have a seat," Rob said, gesturing to the head of the table, surrendering his authority to her. Crap, he was even nicer than she thought.

She chose the chair beside Al instead and pulled what she needed from her case. "First, I'd like to say that I'm very happy to be here, and I'm looking forward to working with all of you. I want everyone to know it's not my intention to come in and take over the department or diminish anyone's authority. I believe that teamwork is the only way to accomplish goals, and that means I like to hear ideas from everyone. The first six to eight weeks we'll spend analyzing the data, longer if we have to, then we'll discuss our findings, and together outline a viable plan. Does that work for everyone?"

Looking skeptical, Grant asked, "Will it really take that long?"

"It will if we're thorough, and bear in mind we'll be going back twenty years."

There were looks of surprise all around.

"Why so far?" Al asked. "Wouldn't data that old be irrelevant?"

"Not at all. There are many factors we need to consider, and I don't want to risk missing a thing. This will explain my methods." She passed around the folders she had created, outlining all the data they would need and why.

Several minutes passed as they reviewed the material, and Grant said, "As deep as you're digging, compiling data that old could be tricky."

"I have complete faith in everyone."

"As do I," Rob added, going to bat for her once again.

They spent the rest of the day in the conference room, calling in for lunch. She hadn't exactly been sure what kind of leader Rob would be, but from what she could tell so far, he was firm but fair, and it was obvious that his employees respected him. And while they may not have trusted her, they definitely trusted him. And he seemed to, if not trust her, be giving her the benefit of the doubt.

The meeting broke up at six, and everyone went home, or so Carrie assumed. She planned to work only another hour or so, then head home, but when she checked the time later, it was nearly eight-thirty.

"Planning on staying all night?"

Startled, she looked up to find Rob leaning in her office doorway, jacket off, tie loosened, looking too darn yummy for his own good. The dark shadow of stubble across his jaw gave him that I'm-too-sexy-for-my-suit look.

There probably wasn't anyone left in the building....

Carrie, don't even go there.

"I thought everyone had left for the night," Carrie said, and Rob struggled to keep his gaze above her neck, and not on the pillows of cleavage pushing against the form-fitting nylon top she wore under the suit jacket that was now hanging on the back of her chair. Her suit was another story altogether. Unlike last week's shapeless, unflattering garment, this one had a fitted jacket with a tapered waist, and a hip-hugging skirt that reached only midthigh. Her hair was up, but this time it looked looser and sexier somehow. Or maybe it was the same and he was seeing her differently now.

She managed to look both professional and sexy as hell.

It had been torture, not to mention distracting, but he'd managed to keep his hands and eyes off her all day. Well, maybe not his eyes, not completely, but he was careful not to be too obvious.

"I'm here until eight or nine most nights," Rob told her.

"No wonder you don't have a girlfriend," she said, closing her laptop.

That was part of the reason. A fairly large part, actually. "I'm heading home and I thought you might like a ride. No one is here to see us in my car together. Unless that's not the real reason you turned down a ride this morning."

"Of course it's the reason," she said, looking indignant. "What other reason would there be?"

He shrugged. That was the million-dollar question.

She had insisted that they end their affair, that it was the only way to keep a civilized work environment, and claimed she would have no problem with pesky residual feelings. Because while she admitted that they were incredibly good in bed together, she still didn't "like" him. But when he'd asked how she could sleep with someone whom she didn't even like, she'd admitted that she didn't actually dislike him either. He had the feeling that she liked him more than she was letting on.

He could honestly say that he had never met anyone quite like her. And because they had such an intense sexual attraction, and neither was looking for any kind of commitment that extended past the bedroom door, he didn't see the harm in continuing to fool around the full three months that she was here, or at least until they grew tired of each other. But he was honoring her wishes and keeping his distance. For the most part.

"If there is no other reason, then you have no reason to say no to a ride home," he said, and he could see that he had her.

"I guess that would be okay, as long as it's just a ride."

He shrugged. "What else would it be?"

She gave him that look, like he knew damn well.

If someone would be making a move tonight, or any other night, she could rest easy that it wouldn't be him. When he was through with her, she would be begging for it.

"In that case, I'll meet you by the elevator in ten minutes."

"Make it fifteen," he said, just to be difficult. Even he had to have a little fun.

"Fine, fifteen," she agreed, looking exasperated.

Rob went back to his office and finished up a few things, and about twenty minutes later walked to the elevator. She was already standing there waiting, but to her credit she didn't point out that he was late, though he could tell that she wanted to. She had no idea just how easy it would be to ruffle her feathers.

They rode the elevator to the garage, and as the doors opened they stepped off into a wall of icy-cold air.

She shivered under her heavy coat. "I don't think I'll ever get used to this cold."

"Try wearing a hat," he said. "And invest in a well-insulated pair of boots."

"I might just try that," she said, hurrying along beside him to his car. Which was hard to miss being the only one in the lot.

"What happened to the Mercedes?" she asked, as they approached his Escalade.

"They were calling for snow today. This handles better."

When they buckled in with the engine running and the seats warming, she told him, "I wanted to say thank you. For today."

"No problem." He pulled the SUV around to the parking garage entrance and lowered his window to swipe his key card and open the security gate. As he pulled onto the street, he asked her, "Out of curiosity, what did I do today?"

"You showed acceptance when I walked into the conference room, and displayed confidence in me. In doing so, the team will be that much more likely to work well together. It was a nice thing to do."

"I didn't do it to be nice," he said. Mostly he just did it to get laid. He wouldn't seal the deal again by making her life hell.

"Whether you meant it or not, you were."

"I'm still not convinced that just isn't a big waste of time and money. Your methods—"

"Have never failed me before. Just ask my previous clients."

"However," he continued, "you're here, and you're obviously not leaving until the job is done, so there's no good reason not to cooperate." And after going over her plan today, he was slightly less skeptical than he'd been before. Not to mention that now that he really knew her, he couldn't work up the will to disrespect her in front of his team. It just didn't seem right.

"To be honest, it's a bit annoying," she said.

"What's annoying?"

"Your niceness."

"I could act like an ass if it would make you happy."

"That's the thing, I don't think you know how to not be nice."

"And that's annoying?"

"A bit."

There was no doubt about it, Carrie was in a class all by herself.

Ten

Rob glanced over at Carrie, wearing a look that suggested she was just slightly left of center. Or maybe a little more than slightly.

"So, you prefer men who aren't nice?" he said.

"I didn't say that. I just said your niceness is annoying. It's probably that I'm not used to it. I date a lot of jerks."

"And you do this, why?"

She shrugged. "I just do. They're the kind of man I naturally attract. It's an inherited trait. With the exception of my biological father, my mom had lousy taste in men, and so did her mom."

"Why do you think that is?"

"I'm sure the drinking hasn't helped. Although my grandma has been sober since I was little."

"And your mom?"

"She drinks every day. My real dad was killed in the Gulf War, which was when my mom started really drinking. As much as I love her, she was always very fragile. When she lost my dad, she just couldn't handle it. We ended up moving in with my grandma because my mom couldn't pull herself together. She would go to the bar after dinner, stay out until closing, sleep until I got home from school, then after dinner it was back to the bar. It was like that until she met my stepfather, Ben. He was older than her, with an ex-wife and two grown kids in Arizona."

"And he was a jerk?" Rob asked.

"At first he was a godsend. He took care of my mom, and he paid attention to me. He took me to movies and out for ice cream and he would help me with my schoolwork. They were together for only a month when we moved in with him. That was when things started to change."

"I'm assuming for the worse."

"He was an alcoholic, too, but a functioning one. He only drank after work and on the weekends, but when he did drink, he drank a lot. And he was a mean drunk. I learned just how mean the first time I mouthed off to him."

"What did he do?"

"Cracked me across the mouth."

Rob glanced over at her. "He *hit* you?"

"It was backhanded, and only hard enough so that it stung. But as I'm sure you've noticed, I'm not the kind of person who keeps her opinions to herself, so it happened a lot."

"Didn't your mom stop him?"

"She tried once, but he got so mad that she never said anything again."

"Did he hit her, too?"

"There was no need. She did whatever he asked, never argued. I guess in that respect she was the perfect wife."

His grip seemed to tighten on the steering wheel. "Did you tell your grandmother?"

"No way. She was so relieved when Ben came along. She was sick a lot of the time and she didn't have the energy or the patience to take care of my mom. She thought Ben was an angel sent down from heaven. I knew that if I told her what he was really like she would worry. I figured I could handle him on my own. And I did for the most part. My mouth did get me in trouble with my teachers occasionally, but I was an excellent student. It was my ticket out."

"So you stayed there until you graduated?"

"Not quite. When I was sixteen he and I got into a huge fight. I came home three hours past curfew on a school night and he met me at the door."

His brow furrowed, as if he were expecting something unpleasant. "And?"

"Words were exchanged, my mouth got away from me as usual, and I won't deny that I said some pretty horrible things. Nothing that wasn't true, though. He came unglued. He slapped me that time, his full palm against my cheek. It rattled my brain and split my lip and left a bruise the shape of his hand on my face.

"I told him I was going to call the police. He knew he'd crossed the line, so he jumped in his car and took off. He was gone all night. The police showed up around 6:00 a.m. to let us know that he'd been in an accident. He hit a tree and died instantly. There was an open booze bottle in the car, so they assumed it was a DUI, but after the autopsy they discovered that he'd had a heart attack. And he had advanced cirrhosis. He would have been dead in a couple of years anyway."

"How did your mom take it?"

"Surprisingly well. The half-million-dollar insurance payout helped. Plus he had another fifty thousand in investments. She sold the house, bought a condo close to the beach. As far as I know, she's happy."

He shot her another glance. "As far as you know?"

"As you can imagine, there's a fair amount of resentment there on my part, and me being me, I have a tough time putting a filter on it, so when we do talk she walks away from it feeling guilty, which just makes her drink more. Which makes me feel bad. We're both better off if we don't talk often, and when we do, we keep the conversations short. It's not an ideal situation, but it works for us."

"I couldn't imagine not talking to at least one of my parents every day," Rob said, stopping at a red light. "But I guess that comes with being a part of a family business."

"How long have you worked for Caroselli Chocolate?"

"Since birth practically. But I wasn't officially hired until I was thirteen and I started working part-time in one of the stores. When I graduated from college I moved to the main office."

"What did you do then?"

"I started out in the mail room, then worked my way up to the marketing department."

That surprised her. "You had a marketing degree and they started you in the *mail room?*"

"Everyone in the family pays their dues. There's no special treatment and it's very competitive. That includes salary. I could leave the company and go to a marketing firm and almost double my salary. I make most of my money in profit sharing."

"Is there anyone in your family who doesn't work for Caroselli Chocolate?"

Rob pulled down her street. "Tony's sister Christine is mostly a stay-at-home mom. Same thing with Nick's sister Jessica, but they both help out in the stores when they're short-staffed, or around the chocolate holidays."

"Christmas, Thanksgiving, Halloween, Easter and Valentine's Day," she said.

"Very good."

She smiled smugly. "I do my homework. You would be stunned by how much I know about the chocolate industry."

Rob swung the SUV into the driveway, and right away Carrie noticed that something was off. It took several seconds to realize what it was.

"The light is on in the living room."

Rob peered through the windshield to the front of the condo. "So it is. Do you keep it on a timer?"

"No. And it wasn't on when I left this morning."

"Are you sure?"

"Of course I'm sure." First she couldn't close a door, now she was incapable of remembering if she left a light on? Or was she reading way too much into every little thing he said, trying to make him into a bad guy even if he really wasn't? And if so, what did that mean?

Nothing very good, she was pretty sure about that.

She pulled the garage door opener out of her purse. "I planned to go in through the garage, so I left the kitchen light on."

"Maybe the ghost turned it on," he said, and she shot him a scathing look. He shrugged. "Or maybe not."

"I know you think you're funny, but you're not."

Opening doors was one thing, but lights that turned themselves on? It was more likely a burglar than anything supernatural…which was even worse now that she thought about it.

She hit the button for the garage door opener, thinking that whoever it was, if they heard it, would come flying out the front door.

No one did. Still, she was uneasy about just waltzing inside. What if someone was in there waiting for her? Someone too stupid to shut off the light that would alert her to his presence. Just because he was stupid didn't mean he wasn't dangerous.

"You look worried," Rob said.

"Wouldn't you be?"

"Not if I had a poltergeist living in my basement."

She didn't justify that one with a verbal response, but her eye roll said it all.

"You want me to come inside with you just in case?"

She hesitated. The last thing she wanted was Rob, with his sexy stubble, smoldering eyes and ripped muscles, coming into her house and oozing sex appeal all over the place. Sure, he'd been a perfect gentleman all day, but what if he suddenly decided that the platonic arrangement wasn't working for him and he made a move on her?

And suppose there was a deranged psycho in her house waiting to chop her into little pieces and feed her to his pet python? Or make a coat out of her flesh? Which was worse? Death and mutilation or really good sex she shouldn't be having?

Wow, that was a tough one.

"Would you mind?" she asked. "Just in case."

"If I minded I wouldn't have asked. Although if there really was someone in there, hearing the garage door opening probably would have scared them off."

"I'm not sure that's a chance I'm willing to take."

"Let's go." He shut off the engine and they both got out. "Let me go in first," he said as they walked through the garage. To do otherwise would sort of defeat the purpose of asking him in, but she followed close behind him, stopping just shy of clinging to the back of his black wool coat. So close that when he stopped just before the door, she nearly ran into him.

"Key?" he said, holding out his hand.

"Oh, right." She dug through her purse and pulled it out.

She grabbed her phone, too, just in case she had to make a quick call to 9-1-1.

He unlocked the door and pushed it open. The kitchen light was on, just as she had left it, and of course the basement door was open. She followed Rob inside, closing it as she walked past. For all the good it would do. The next time she walked back here it would probably be open again.

As they stepped into the kitchen, the first thing she noticed was the open, half-empty bottle of wine on the counter.

"Did you leave that there?" he asked.

"Why yes, I always have a glass of wine with my breakfast."

He was the one giving the look this time.

"When I left this morning it was in the refrigerator."

He pulled off one leather glove and touched the bottle. "It's still cold."

Who would break into her house and drink a glass of wine?

"I don't suppose you've started smoking," he said.

"No, why?"

He pointed to the kitchen table, where a pack of cigarettes and an old, beat-up silver Zippo lighter lay. She hadn't seen that particular lighter in something like eight years. She gave a sigh of relief to know that they weren't in any imminent danger. At least he wasn't. But Carrie had the feeling she was in for the lecture of her life.

"Alice!" Carrie shouted. "Get in here."

Alice?

Rob looked over at Carrie. Who the hell was Alice?

Before he could ask, a woman appeared in the kitchen doorway. She was nearly as tall as Rob and thin to the point of being gaunt. Silky, pin-straight, jet-black hair framed a face that was as long and thin as the rest of her. She was more striking than beautiful, the kind of woman who would stand out in a crowd.

Dynamic.

"Rob, this is my best friend, Alice," Carrie said. He recalled her mentioning a friend of that name when they were at the diner. He didn't realize that she lived in Chicago.

"Rob?" Alice said, looking him up and down, her crimson lips curling into a slightly lopsided, wry smile. "As in Rob Caroselli, aka Mr. New Year's Eve?"

"The one and only," he said, noticing, as she stepped over to offer him a delicate yet long-fingered hand to shake, she seemed to be walking with a slight limp. She wore black leggings and a long black tunic top. Even her shoes, well-worn ballet flats, were black.

"What are you doing here?" Carrie asked her.

"I haven't been able to reach you in days and assumed you were up to something, which—" she looked pointedly at Rob "—clearly you are."

"He just gave me a ride home. I haven't had a chance to lease a car yet."

Skepticism narrowed Alice's eyes, which were slightly turned up in the corners and an unearthly shade of violet. "Does he always walk you inside?"

"We thought someone had broken in! And by the way, how *did* you get in?"

"How long have we known each other?" Alice said. "You always keep a spare near the front door. It was just a matter of finding it."

Rob looked at Carrie. "You keep a spare key by the *front door?*"

She shook her head and said, "Not now, please."

Alice folded her long, skinny arms under her nearly nonexistent breasts. "You *promised.*"

Promised what? Rob wondered.

"I see you're smoking again," Carrie shot back.

Nice deflection.

"I got *dumped,*" Alice said. "What's your excuse?"

Whatever Alice was referring to, it would seem that Carrie had no excuse. Or she couldn't think of one just then.

"That's what I thought," Alice said. "You clearly need supervision."

"It's over," Carrie said, then looked up at Rob. "Tell her it's over."

He looked from one woman to the other, and though he had a pretty good idea of what she meant, he said, "I decline to answer on the grounds that it might incriminate me."

"Did Rex really dump you?" Carrie asked her.

Alice tossed her satiny black hair. "I guess I should have seen it coming. He was never home. And when he was, he was never really there. When I told him that my runway career is officially over, he must have figured the gravy train was drying up for good."

"What do you mean it's over?" Carrie asked, setting her purse and briefcase on the kitchen table. "I thought you just needed time to heal."

"I may have been overly optimistic when I told you that. They said there was a slight chance I wouldn't get full mobility back. But the physical therapy isn't helping and my doctor thinks I might need *another* surgery."

"Oh, honey," Carrie said, shrugging out of her coat. "I'm so sorry."

"I can still do face, or some catalog work, as long as I'm not on my feet for too long or I get a cankle on the left side."

Carrie turned to Rob. "Alice is a very successful runway model."

"Was," Alice said.

"How long will you be staying?" Carrie asked her.

"I guess it just depends on how long you want me around."

"Stay as long as you like. I can easily turn the office into a bedroom."

"You don't have to do that. I'm perfectly comfortable on the couch. It will be like we're in college again," Alice said, trying to sound cheerful, but her smile looked stiff and forced. Then she looked Rob up and down and added, "Are we going to do the hair band again?"

Rob blinked. "*Do* the hair band?"

"When we were roommates in college we had a system," Carrie explained. "If one of us brought a guy home, we would loop a hair band around the door."

"Oh, like a band for your hair," he said. "That makes more sense."

"Than what?"

He shook his head. "Never mind."

Even if there were any '80s hair bands left, those guys would be ancient by now.

"There won't be a need for the hair band because as I said, it's over." Carrie turned to him. "Would you please tell her that it's over?"

"So you brought guys back to your room a lot in college?"

Carrie rolled her eyes. "Ugh! You're no help."

"I don't know," Alice said, looking him up and down again. "Now that I see him, maybe you should sleep with him again. You could do a lot worse."

"True," Carrie said, giving him the same critical once-over in a way that made him feel a lot like a slab of meat. "But he's kind of…well…*nice*."

Alice's horrified look said she had the same distorted ideas about men that Carrie did. "Never mind."

"On that note, I'm going to go…I don't know…mistreat a kitten or something," he said. "Alice, it was a pleasure to meet you. Carrie, I'll see you at work tomorrow."

"Thanks for coming in with me," she said, walking him to the garage. He recalled specifically that she had closed the basement door on the way in, yet it stood open again.

"It was no problem. Are you sure I can't pick you up on my way in tomorrow?"

"I'm good, thanks."

He wanted to kiss her goodbye, but he didn't. Even though he was pretty sure she wouldn't object. But she was going to come to him this time. And when she was ready, she would. He just had to be patient.

He did know one thing for sure as he got in his car and headed for home: having someone like Alice around was going to be very interesting.

Eleven

On her way down to the break room for coffee, Carrie had to pass Rob's office, and though she had promised herself she wasn't going to go out of her way to see him unless it was completely necessary, it seemed rude not to stop in and thank him for walking her into her condo last night.

So instead of going straight down the hall, she hung a sharp right and stepped into the outer office where Mrs. White sat. Only it wasn't Mrs. White sitting there today. This woman was much younger—in her mid to late forties—and very beautiful. She wore her pale blond hair shoulder-length and pulled back from her face. She was sitting down, but Carrie could see by the long, slender legs encased in cream-colored wool pants that she was tall. *Elegant* was the first word that came to mind.

Maybe Mrs. White was out sick and she was a temp from another department.

"I'm looking for Rob," Carrie told her.

"That makes two of us," the woman said, in a husky voice with a slightly watered-down French accent. "Shall we fight over him?"

Carrie blinked. Fight over… Was she joking? Who did she think Carrie was?

The desk phone rang and Carrie waited for her to answer, but she ignored it. Probably not a temp.

"I just needed to talk to him for a second," Carrie said. "I can come back."

"You're Caroline Taylor?" the woman said.

"That's right." *And who are you?* she wanted to say. She was stunningly beautiful. For all Carrie knew, Rob had a thing for older women.

"I've heard so much about you. From Robby and his father. You're here to save the company?"

"I'm certainly going to try." Unsure of what else to say, she told the woman, "When you see Rob, can you tell him…you know, never mind. It wasn't important."

"I was only teasing you. He is with his father. He should be back any minute." She gestured to the chair opposite the desk. "Sit, wait with me."

Before she could decide to stay or leave, Rob walked in.

He looked from the blonde woman to Carrie and said, "Oh, hi. I see you two have met."

"Well, we didn't actually—"

"Is your father ready?" the woman asked him.

"He said to give him a few more minutes."

"Always a few more minutes," she said with a sigh, telling Carrie, "Husbands, they *always* make you wait."

Husbands? If Demitrio was her husband, that meant she had to be Rob's mother. Carrie never imagined that a woman so fair could give birth to such a dark child. Rob clearly favored his father's side of the family.

"I'm sorry, did you need something?" Rob asked Carrie.

"No."

Then why are you here? his look said.

"I just wanted to talk to you for a second. It's nothing that can't wait." In fact, she never should have come to his office in the first place.

"You two talk," Rob's mother said. "I think I will go see if I can pull Robby's father away from his work."

She stood, and Carrie was right. She was tall—barely an inch shorter than her son. It seemed to be about the only family resemblance Carrie could see. And she must have been older than Carrie thought, unless she'd had Rob when she was twelve.

"It was nice to meet you," she said, shaking Carrie's hand. Then she kissed Rob's cheek and sauntered out.

At the risk of sounding like a dope, Carrie said, "Am I correct in assuming that was your mother?"

"She didn't tell you who she was?"

"She just asked me if I wanted to fight over you."

He smiled and shook his head. "She has a bizarre sense of humor."

Carrie had a sudden, terrifying thought. If Rob's mom knew who Carrie was, did she also know what they'd done? "She doesn't know, right?"

"Know what?"

Duh. She lowered her voice to a loud whisper, just in case someone happened to be in the hall. "About New Year's. About you and me."

He looked at her funny. "You honestly think I tell my mom about my sexual conquests?"

"I don't know—hey, wait. A sexual *conquest?* Is that what I was?"

"You know what I mean, and *no,* I didn't tell her anything," he said, looking offended.

"Sorry. I just thought the French were more open about that kind of thing."

Rob sat on the edge of his desk. "She's not from France. She's from Quebec."

"Six of one, half a dozen of the other."

"Whatever. Point is, no, I didn't tell her. I *never* tell her. As far as I know, she thinks I'm still a virgin."

As if. "I'm sure she knows you're not."

He rubbed his hand across the stubble on his cheek. "Did we ever determine why you came to my office? Because I specifically recall your saying that when we're at work we should pretend not to like each other. Did you change your mind? Did you want to *not like me* in here for a while?"

Oh, so tempting…

"It was something work-related," she told him. "But I've completely forgotten what."

He grinned. "I think you just missed me."

"As if," she said, hating that he was right. From now on, no visits to his office unless it really was work-related.

"Well, when you remember what it was, you know where to find me. Or anything else you might need me for."

"Thanks," she said, and oh, did she wish she could take him up on that.

Rob sat at the conference table three days later with Will and Al, waiting for Carrie and Grant so they could discuss the data they had been compiling, thinking about what Carrie and Alice had said about nice guys. He wasn't sure why he found the idea so annoying, but it continued to nag at him.

"Would you two say I'm a nice guy?" he asked Will and Al.

"Sure," Will said.

"Eh." Al shrugged. "You're okay."

He shot her a look.

She grinned and said, "I'm kidding. Of course you're a nice guy."

"Under what circumstances would you consider that a bad thing?"

Looking confused, Al asked, "Why would that ever be a bad thing?"

"That's what I was wondering," Rob said. "Why would a woman prefer to date a jerk over a nice guy?"

"Does this have something to do with Carrie?" Will asked.

Rob blinked. "Why would you think that?"

"Because of your affair."

"Will!" Al said, giving him a shove.

When Rob got over the shock of his statement, which took a good thirty seconds, he said, "Did Nick or Tony say something to you?"

"They didn't have to," Al said apologetically.

"Yeah," Will agreed, "it's kind of obvious."

No way Rob was that transparent. "Obvious how? We hardly say two words to each other."

"Exactly," Will told him.

"I think what Will is trying to say is that you and Carrie try too hard to act like you *don't* like each other. But when you look at each other…"

"What?" Rob demanded.

"*Major* heat."

Before Rob could confirm or deny their suspicions, Grant rushed in, still wearing his coat. "Sorry I'm late. Traffic was hell this morning."

"It's okay," Al said. "Carrie isn't here yet either."

"Actually she walked in right after me, so she should be along any minute." Grant shrugged out of his coat and hung it on the back of his chair. "She probably stopped in her office."

"We were just talking about Rob and Carrie's affair," Will told him, which earned him another shove from his coworker.

"What about it?" Grant asked, taking a seat.

In response to Rob's blink of surprise, Will said, "Like Al told you, *heat*."

If it was so obvious to them, what about everyone else?

"Good morning!" Carrie said, gliding through the door, her usual cheerful self, and everyone went dead silent.

She set her coffee and a folder down on the conference table and took a seat. Then noticing the lack of conversation, she looked around and asked, "Is something wrong?"

No one seemed to know what to say. Including Rob.

So of course he blurted out the absolute worst thing he could under the circumstances. "Apparently everyone here thinks we're having an affair."

Carrie blinked. "Excuse me?"

"It's not just us, Rob," Al said apologetically. "Pretty much everyone thinks so."

"Why would people think that?" Carrie said, sounding equal parts offended and nervous.

"I'm pretty sure you didn't give yourself that hickey on the back of your neck," Will said.

"Will!" Al said, glaring at him.

Carrie slapped a hand over her neck and cut her eyes to Rob, and her look clearly said, *Oh no, you didn't.*

Oh yes, he had. Their last night together. At the time he had no idea that she wore her hair up for work every day, or he would have branded her somewhere slightly less obvious. He hadn't even realized that anyone else had noticed.

"I must have burned myself with the curling iron," Carrie said, using the same lame excuse his sister Megan had in high school, and Rob could see that no one was buying it.

"Even if it weren't for that, Rob's attitude adjustment made it pretty obvious," Will said.

"Attitude adjustment?" Carrie asked him.

"It's no secret that he didn't think your services were required," Will said. "Then suddenly he was all gung ho to have you here. Everyone just put two and two together."

Carrie went stone-still, and a red blush stained her cheeks. Rob knew exactly what Will was getting at. So did Al. She shoved him hard and shot him a look that said, *Are you kidding me?*

Will just shrugged, as if he didn't have a clue what he'd said wrong.

Al rolled her eyes in disgust. "My *brainless* coworker here did not mean to imply that you were trying to win Rob over by sleeping with him," Al said. "Right, Will?"

The color drained from Will's face and he actually looked as if he might be sick. "Oh…God…Carrie, no, that was not what I meant. Not at all."

"Don't worry about it," Carrie told him, but Rob could see that her feelings were hurt, and even worse, her pride had taken a huge hit.

He had been hoping that by getting their suspicions out in the open, he could have made light of the situation. Even passed it off as a joke. He should have kept his damn mouth shut.

"We haven't seen Rob this happy in a long time," Grant said, joining the painful conversation, which Rob had to admit took courage. "We simply assumed, because your presence here was the only thing different in his life, it probably had something to do with you. I sincerely apologize if we were out of line."

"Then let me say, for the record, Rob and I are *not* having an affair." Carrie sounded calm, but there was an undercurrent of anger in her voice that had Rob worrying that she might blow. That or dissolve into tears, which would probably be worse.

"People, could you give us a few minutes," Rob said.

"Absolutely," Al said, and they practically ran from the conference room. Not that Rob could blame them.

He got up and closed the door behind them, and when he turned back to the table, Carrie was on her feet and standing by the window, her gaze on the street below.

"Well," she said, "that was unbelievably humiliating."

"I am so sorry. I shouldn't have said anything."

"No, I'm glad you did. It's always good to know when people are laughing at you behind your back."

"That's not what they were doing."

"Now do you see?" She turned to him, anger leaking into her voice. "Do you understand why I didn't want anyone to know about us?"

"I honestly don't think Will meant it like that. He has the tendency to put his foot in his mouth." In fact, he was the one who had started this stupid conversation.

"Maybe he didn't mean it that time, but you know they all thought it at some point. That's the way it is in business for a successful woman. No one believes you got there on your own merit."

"You are extremely good at what you do, and everyone knows it. They told me that you and I have obvious chemistry, and that's basically how they knew about us."

"Terrific," she said.

"They're right."

"I know they are. And we can't do a damn thing about it."

"I know." If he really cared about her feelings, cared about *her,* he would back off. Which was exactly what he planned to do. Which sucked, because he honestly believed they could have had something really good, if Carrie could just let her guard down. Even if it was only temporary. Or hell, she could have wound up being the mother of his fifteen-million-dollar heir. Even if it had been a possibility, it would never happen now.

"We could still be friends," he said.

"No, we can't, because people will always wonder if it's more than that."

He shrugged. "So what? Does it really matter that much what other people think?"

"To me it does. I know that probably seems silly to you, but I can't help it. I'm a people pleaser. It's in my genetic makeup. I wouldn't expect someone like you to understand."

"Someone like me?"

"You're rich and handsome and successful. And nice. And fantastic in bed. You're the closest thing to a perfect man that I've ever met. Do you have any idea how intimidating that is? And how inferior it makes me feel?"

"That's ridiculous."

"Yes, it is. And I know that, but it's still how I feel."

"No," he said, taking out his wallet. "What I mean is, it's ridiculous to think of me as perfect. I'm not. Not even close."

He pulled out the small stack of photos that he always carried with him, the ones he looked at every time he was tempted to put something unhealthy in his mouth or skip his morning workout. It was a reminder of just how far he'd come, and how much he didn't want to go back to being that unhealthy, pathetic person.

"Here," he said, handing the pictures to her. "This kid is far from perfect."

As she looked through them, Carrie's eyes grew wide

and her mouth forming a perfect O. "Oh, my gosh, is this *you?*"

"Roly Poly Robby. That's what they used to call me."

"You were so…"

"Fat?"

"I was going to say chubby."

"No, for the better part of my childhood, until I started college, I fluctuated between being twenty-five and fifty pounds overweight. I was *fat.*"

"Slow metabolism?"

He laughed. "No, I liked food. I still do. But back then I didn't have much in the way of self-control, and no interest whatsoever in exercising. I was the uncoordinated, unpopular fat kid who got picked on in grade school, and chosen last in gym class. In middle school I learned I could make the other kids laugh with me instead by telling self-deprecating jokes about my weight, which didn't make me any less miserable. But I convinced my friends and my family that I was confident and happy looking the way I did. I pretended not to mind that girls I liked dated my buddies, when with me they were only interested in being *friends.*"

"But you did mind."

"What teenage boy doesn't?"

"Did you ever try to lose the weight?"

"I don't think there was a time when I *wasn't* trying to lose it. There was always some new diet fad to try. I would do okay for a few weeks, drop ten or fifteen pounds, but I always fell back into my old habits and gained it back. I loathed myself for being so weak. It took me a long time to figure out that diets don't work. That I was just setting myself up to fail, and losing the weight meant completely changing my lifestyle. Becoming healthy."

"And look at you. Your body is…amazing. That must make you proud."

"Sure it does. But the work doesn't end when you reach your goal weight. There isn't a day that I don't struggle with it. The pathetic little fat kid is still in there."

"The exterior doesn't change who you are on the inside. That's what matters."

"Tell me honestly, if we had met in high school with me looking the way I did, would you have been the least bit interested in dating me?"

"I told you, I only date jerks. But if I did choose to judge someone based on their looks or their weight, that's my problem, not theirs. And I apologize for judging you, and calling you perfect before I knew the whole story."

"I've been called worse."

"You do realize what a great guy you are, right? And I'm not just talking looks or physique. You're the entire package. Take it from someone who has met her share of creeps. And I would be the luckiest woman in the world to be with you."

"Yet you're not going to be with me."

"The truth is, you deserve better. I would eventually screw it up. I always do. I would hurt you, and I don't want to see that happen."

For a woman so well put together, who seemed to know just what she wanted, her lack of confidence was astonishing. And the last thing he wanted was to be responsible for making her feel even worse than she already did.

"I'll see to it that everyone is set straight about our relationship," he told her. "I don't foresee anyone hassling you about it, but if anyone does, I'll take care of it."

She shook her head. "That will only make matters worse. If there's a problem, I can deal with it myself."

"Whatever you want. Should we call the others back

in so we can get this progress report started? My dad and Uncle Tony would like to see something from us by end of day and I don't want to rock the boat right now."

"This is probably none of my business," she said, "but I sense a definite rift between your dad and your uncle Tony."

"There's always been a bit of animosity between my uncles and my dad, but in the past couple of months…I don't know. Something is up. My dad keeps saying that nothing is wrong, but it's obvious that he and my uncle Tony are at odds."

"Why is there animosity, if you don't mind my asking? I mean, dysfunctional family relationships are kind of my specialty."

"When my dad was a kid, he was the black sheep of the family. The brilliant-but-bored type. He was constantly getting into trouble in school, and then later with the law. My *nonno*—"

"*Nonno?*"

"It's Italian for grandfather."

"Giuseppe?"

He nodded. "He came here from Italy, and he brought with him a lot of old world traditional values. My dad rebelled against them all, and even worse, he wanted nothing to do with the family business. Finally *Nonno* got fed up. When my dad was twenty-five he was arrested after a bar fight and *Nonno* gave him a choice—sit in jail or join the army. He chose the army."

"Tough love."

"The toughest. Though it was a toss-up as to who was tougher, him or *Nonna*."

"Your grandmother?"

He nodded.

"It obviously did your dad some good."

"Definitely. He went to college and graduated top of his class. After that he came to work for Caroselli Chocolate and shot up the ranks. When *Nonno* retired he made my dad CEO, which both his brothers resented. Plus there's always been some added tension between my dad and Tony."

"Why is that?"

"When my dad went into the army, Tony married his girlfriend, Sarah."

"Yikes."

"Yeah. You can't say that my family history isn't colorful."

"I've learned that most are. But as close as your family is, I'm sure everything will work out."

He hoped she was right. Or everything *Nonno* worked for could crumble around them.

Twelve

Carrie loved what she did for a living. As long as she'd been a consultant, there had hardly been a morning when she woke dreading the workday, even though in the past there had been individuals she dreaded working with.

Usually it was the challenge of saving the company that thrilled her. The act of solving the puzzle. But the past couple of weeks she had begun to realize that this time it was more than that. This time it was the people working for the company that she cared about. It really was like a big family, and hard as she had tried to keep her distance, they had sucked her right in.

As coworkers she and Rob got along exceptionally well together. Their management styles were similar, and what differences they did have seemed to complement each other rather than clash. It was as if he could anticipate her next move before she even made it, and they were so in sync that they'd even begun finishing each other's sentences. If ever she had to choose her favorite assignment, hands down this was it. Yet she was torn between loving it, and the fear of getting *too* close.

When Carrie wasn't working, most of her free time was spent with Alice—who wasn't nearly as blasé about her breakup with Rex or her career change as she'd let on. But there were times when she found herself wishing she could be with Rob. Sometimes at work they would stand close to one another and she would get that soul-deep longing to touch him, or he would look at her a certain way and her knees would go weak. She missed the intimacy of their physical relationship—and not just the sex. She missed the way they would lie in bed, side by side, fingers entwined, and just talk. Usually about nothing in particular.

He could be intense at times, and was passionate in his convictions, but his dry wit appealed to her snarky sense of humor. He didn't take crap from her or anyone else, and when someone gave him a hard time he didn't hesitate to call them out on it. He had integrity, and radiated a confidence that was infectious. With a few simple words of praise he could make a person feel as if they were something really special, because while he wasn't a negative boss, he only handed out compliments where they were earned. Which seemed to make his employees strive to please him. Hell, even she felt a little nervous about possibly letting him down, when as a rule she never let herself become emotionally invested in a client. And she typically never formed attachments. But so far, nothing about this job was what she would call typical.

She even began to think that Rob being a nice guy wasn't such a bad thing after all and if there was a man out there who could ever put up with her, he might have actually been it. Which of course scared the living hell out of her. Alice had once accused Carrie of being afraid to be happy, and Carrie was beginning to wonder if maybe she was right. Maybe she was worried that with happiness came the possibility of losing that happiness. It was so much easier to have low expectations, and hurt less when the inevitable letdown came.

Alice used to be her number one supporter when it came to Carrie's hang-ups, but lately she seemed to be defecting to the other side.

"You're an idiot," she said after Carrie hung up from a work-related phone call to Rob that had turned into a two-hour-long conversation that had absolutely nothing to do with marketing reports.

Carrie looked up from the work spread out on the bed. "We've been friends for over ten years and you're just now noticing this?"

"Do you honestly not see how good you two are together? How much he cares about you? And I mean *really* cares. You just talked for two hours. I was lucky if I could get Rex to talk for ten minutes."

"He deserves better than someone like me."

"Isn't that up to him to decide?"

Alice wasn't in any position to be passing judgment. She excelled at snagging emotionally unavailable men. Which always landed her where she was right now. Miserable and alone with shattered self-esteem.

"We're coworkers," Carrie said. "I don't date coworkers."

"You told me yourself how well you guys work together, so that lame excuse is not going to cut it anymore."

"I live in Los Angeles, he lives in Chicago. Talk about a long-distance relationship."

"Other than your mom, who you barely even talk to, what do you really have in Los Angeles that you couldn't have here?"

The answer should have come immediately, and it surprised Carrie to realize that she had no answer. What did she have in Los Angeles, other than work, which frankly she could do anywhere? Her best friend lived all the way across the country, and she worked so much she didn't have time to make other friends. Or at least, that was what she liked to tell herself.

"I'm tired of sleeping on the couch," Alice said out of the blue.

"I told you before that I could turn the office into a bedroom."

"You're not tired of me yet?"

"Of course not. I was sort of hoping that you would stay here with me until I go back to L.A."

"In that case I should probably order some bedroom furniture."

"Renting it would be a lot cheaper."

She sighed. "As much as I love to shop, you're probably right. Until I decide what to do with my life, I should probably watch my spending."

"I'll call Terri tomorrow and make sure it's okay."

"I'll look online for a furniture rental place."

Carrie called Terri from work the next afternoon.

"Of course you can turn the office into a bedroom," Terri said. "Just stick what's in there down in the basement."

"Perfect! Thanks, Terri."

"And by the way, I was going to call you. We're having a get-together next weekend. We would love it if you would come."

And she would love to be there, which was exactly why she shouldn't go. She was letting herself get too close. This was just supposed to be a business trip. "My friend Alice is visiting and I would feel bad leaving her alone."

"Bring her with you."

Terri was making it very hard to say no gracefully. "The thing is, she just got out of a relationship and I'm not sure if she's ready to put herself back out there just yet. But I will ask."

"I hope we see you."

Carrie wished she could.

A few minutes after she hung up with Terri, Alice called. "Did you talk to Terri?"

"She said it's fine, and we can move the furniture that's in there down to the basement."

"I already picked out the furniture. I thought I would have them deliver it Monday. We can move the office furniture tomorrow. Unless you're planning to work again this weekend."

"I think I've earned a Saturday off," she said. It was hard to believe that today would mark the end of her fourth week in Chicago, and her third at Caroselli Chocolate. And they still had so much work to do.

After they hung up Carrie immersed herself in work until Rob appeared in her doorway later. With his sleeves rolled to his elbows and his tie loosened, he looked too yummy for words. She longed to undress him, and run her tongue over every conceivable inch of his delicious body.

"Tony and I are packing it in and going out for a burger," he said. "Care to join us?"

She looked at the clock, surprised that it was already after seven. "I can't."

He folded his arms. "You're not still worried that people will think we're a couple, are you?"

"No, not anymore." Everyone seemed fairly clear on that concept now. Though it wouldn't take much to get the rumor mill spinning again. If there was one thing the Carosellis loved more than chocolate, it was gossip. "I'm taking the weekend off, so I want to finish this report before I go. It's going to be at least another hour or two."

"You sure? Dinner is on me."

"Maybe next time."

He shrugged. "Okay, see you tomorrow."

"See ya."

He was already long gone when it occurred to her that she wouldn't be there tomorrow, so she in fact would not see him. Which was probably a really good thing. She was very careful to stay safely behind the border she had set for herself. Yet every now and then she caught her toes inching past the line. That was when she knew she had to back off, recapture her perspective.

She worked until nine, and was gathering her things when she swore she heard the sound of footsteps out in the hall. It was rare that anyone worked past six on Friday, and for a split second she wondered if Rob had come back.

She got up from her desk and peeked out of her office, just in time to see someone turn the corner at the end of the hall, where it dead-ended at Demitrio's office. Someone too small to be Rob or any other man.

Had his secretary come back for something maybe?

She walked quietly down the hall and peeked around the corner. Whoever it was, she was messing with the door to the outer office.

What have we here? she wondered. A little interoffice espionage?

"Excuse me," she said and the woman in question squealed with surprise, dropping whatever was in her hand. As it clinked against the granite floor, Carrie realized that it was a large silver paper clip that had been straightened out.

Was she *picking* the lock?

The woman spun around and Carrie recognized her immediately. "Rose?"

"Carrie," she said, slapping a hand over her heart. "You scared me. I thought everyone had left."

Carrie only knew Rose from the break room, and though she found her to be a bit odd, she'd never had a problem with her. But something was definitely going on. "What are you doing?"

Her cheeks blushed bright red as she bent down to grab the paper clip. "I realize how this looks," she said nervously, "but it's not what you think."

"You're picking the lock on the CEO's office door."

"Demitrio's secretary has a binder full of old reports for me that need to be digitized. She left early, but said it would be on the corner of her desk. I lost track of time, and by the time I came down to get it, Demitrio had left and locked up. I tried to reach her, and when I couldn't, I panicked. I thought maybe I could pick the lock."

She looked sincere, so why did Carrie get the feeling she was lying through her teeth. "Would you like me to call Rob? Maybe he has a key to his father's office."

"Oh, wait! My phone is ringing. Excuse me."

Carrie didn't hear a phone ring, but supposed Rose could have had it set on silent.

She scurried several feet away before answering it. "Hello," she said. "Oh, thank goodness you got my messages...are you sure it can wait?" She paused, then said, "Okay, see you Monday." She turned to Carrie, shoving the phone back in her pocket. "It's okay. She said I can do it Monday."

Carrie found it awfully convenient that she called at that exact moment. A little *too* convenient. Not only that, but

Mary, Demitrio's secretary, was a talker. They'd never had a conversation that lasted less than ten minutes.

"Would you mind if we keep this between us?" Rose said, her cheeks crimson. "I would be mortified if anyone knew what I did."

"Sure," Carrie said, fully intending to tell Rob the entire story the next time she saw him.

At noon the next day, when she and Alice were supposed to be moving furniture to the basement, Carrie found her draped on the couch half-asleep instead.

"Are you ready?" Carrie asked her.

"Ready for what?"

"To move the office furniture."

Alice blinked. "With my healing ankle? I couldn't possibly."

"Then why did you tell me you would?"

"I never said *I* would do it personally."

Did she think Carrie would be able to do it alone? "I need help."

"Don't worry." She sat up, stretching like a cat. "I called for reinforcements."

"Reinforcements?" Who did she even know in Chicago? Or had she hired professional movers?

As if on cue, the doorbell rang. Alice put her foot down, wincing as she tried to push herself up from the couch. "Be a dear and get that for me, would you?"

Be a dear?

She walked to the door wondering why Alice was acting so odd. She pulled it open, surprised to find Rob standing there. Tony was behind him.

"We're here," Rob said.

Thanks, Captain Obvious. "I see that. *Why* are you here?"

Confused, the two men looked at each other, then Rob turned back to her. "Alice called. She said you needed help moving furniture."

"Oh, did she?" Carrie turned to give her friend the evil eye, but the sofa was empty. She'd set Carrie up, now she was going to bail on her? How many times had Carrie specifically said that she didn't want to see Rob outside the office?

"Come on in," she said, letting the men inside. She couldn't leave them out in the cold while she murdered Alice. Besides, she really did need their help. They might even lend a hand disposing of Alice's body.

Under his wool coat Rob looked like something out of a handyman fantasy in faded, threadbare blue jeans, a flannel shirt with the sleeves rolled up and well-worn work boots. The kind of ensemble that would be fun to tear off him with her bare hands. Which was exactly what she wanted to do.

Yep, Alice was dead meat.

Wearing black jeans, a black long-sleeved T-shirt and sneakers, Tony wasn't looking too shabby either.

"If you two will excuse me a minute, I need to have a word with my roommate."

"You want us to get started?" Rob asked.

"Nope," she called over her shoulder as she headed down the hall. "I'll be right back."

Her bedroom door was closed, and when she tried to turn the knob, it was locked. She had locked Carrie out of her own bedroom?

"Alice!" she hissed. "Open the door."

"I have a terrible migraine," Alice said weakly. "You'll have to manage without me."

"Migraine, my ass," she mumbled as she walked back to the living room, where Rob and Tony were still waiting.

"Everything all right?" Rob asked.

"Fine. Alice is…resting in my room."

Rob's brow rose. *"Resting?"*

The last thing she wanted was for Rob to realize that this was a setup. He might actually believe that Carrie had something to do with it.

Carrie lowered her voice and said, "Actually, she's hiding. She's taking the breakup pretty hard. And the career stuff."

"Tony is a recent dumpee, too," Rob told Carrie.

"Dude, really?" Tony said, looking irritated. "Tell the whole world, why don't you."

Rob grinned, and Carrie wondered if that had been payback for past fat jokes.

"Alice said you're clearing out the office," Rob said.

"We're making it a bedroom." They followed her down the hall. "So this is it," she said as they stepped into the spare room. "It all has to go. Terri said to put everything in the basement."

"The haunted basement?" Tony said.

She couldn't believe that a big burly guy like him could possibly be afraid of a door-opening spirit. "Whatever or whoever it is down there, it's harmless," Carrie assured him.

Both men took an end of the desk, carried it out of the room and down the hall.

"Where in the basement do you want it?" Rob asked her.

"Oh, anywhere there's room," she said.

"Nowhere specific?"

She shrugged. "Just any old place is fine."

Rob stopped just shy of the basement door, wearing a wry smile. "You've never been down there, have you?"

"Why would you assume that?"

Tony looked down the stairs, then back at her. "Have you?"

"Yes," she said indignantly, then paused and added, "Sort of."

"Sort of, how?" Rob asked.

She'd once made it about halfway down the stairs, but the creak of the door moving behind her had propelled her back up. She'd moved so swiftly, in fact, that she could swear her feet never touched the stairs. "Even if there is something down there, it's not as if it can hurt us."

"Then you won't mind going first," Rob said, gesturing her down.

Unwilling to admit just how nervous she was at the prospect of going down there, she raised her chin a notch, met his challenging gaze and said, "Of course I'll go first."

"We'll be right behind you," Rob said.

She switched on the light and peered down. Worst-case scenario, she might see or hear something unusual. And because whatever kept opening the door seemed inclined to stay in the basement, she had nothing to worry about. Plus she had two strapping men to protect her.

Yet she was still edgy.

She started down, forcing her feet forward, growing colder as she descended, unsure if it was due to a lack of heat or the presence of something unworldly. She was hesitant to hold the rail, lest she might feel that disembodied hand settle over hers again. Her heart was pounding double time when she reached the last step and her foot hit the concrete floor.

She realized, with no small degree of relief, that the only things down there she could see were boxes and old furniture. *Extremely* old furniture and lots of it. Pieces that she was guessing were from the late nineteenth century. It must have been worth a small fortune.

"I guess we should put the stuff from the office off to

the side over there," she said, gesturing to the only relatively vacant area.

They set down the desk and Rob asked, "Are you coming back up with us?"

"I think I'll stay down here," she said, curiosity outweighing her fear.

"Okay, we'll be right back."

She wove her way through the maze of different pieces, checking them out. Some were plain and functional, others ornately embellished and fragile-looking. She knew next to nothing about antique furniture, but the variety of grains and colors said the pieces were built from several different types of wood. Whoever owned all of this must have been a collector.

There were several dining room and bedroom sets, and a fair share of living room pieces. She ran her hand across the surface of a beautifully carved sideboard, expecting to find a layer of dust but either the air in the condo was unprecedentedly clean, or Terri sneaked in while she was at work and dusted everything.

"Find your ghost?" Rob asked as he and Tony appeared with a large file cabinet.

"Not exactly. But doesn't it seem unusually clean down here? There isn't a spot of dust on this furniture."

"Terri is a little fanatical about keeping things clean," Rob reminded her.

Yes, but a basement? Besides, she hadn't been there in a month.

"We just have to grab the bookcase and we'll be done," he said.

"Okay," she answered distractedly, entertaining a third possibility, but it was a little creepy to contemplate that not only was the ghost fanatical about keeping doors open, but it was a clean freak as well. Could a ghost have OCD?

Carrie heard a soft creaking sound, and she could swear the very faint wail of a baby crying.

No way. It must have been something Alice was watching upstairs, and the sound was leaking down through the floorboards.

And what if it wasn't?

"Do you guys hear that?" she said, turning to where Rob had been standing. But apparently they had already gone back up the stairs for the next load.

She listened hard and the sound seemed to be coming from the far end of the basement, where the bedroom pieces were stored. Coincidentally, right under the bedrooms.

Screwing up all of her courage, she made her way through the furniture, following the sound, and the closer she got, the less it sounded as if it were coming from upstairs. She finally made it to the end of the basement, in the darkest corner and found, stored behind a wide chest of drawers that was desperately in need of refinishing, a child's cradle that looked hand-carved. As her eyes adjusted to the low light, and she got a better look at it, the hair on her arms and back of her neck shivered to standing and her heart skipped a beat.

The cradle was rocking.

She blinked, then blinked again, sure that her eyes were playing tricks on her. But it really was rocking. Not only that, but the crying was louder now, as if it were right in front of her. Loud wailing that wasn't really loud at all. It was all around her, but almost as if she were hearing it on the inside of her head. She stood there mesmerized watching it move back and forth, back and forth, and as she did she felt herself reaching out to touch it…then a hand slammed down on her shoulder and a blood-curdling scream ripped from her throat.

Thirteen

"It's just me!" Rob said as Carrie whipped around, losing her balance and falling against the bureau she'd been looking behind.

"Are you trying to give me a heart attack?" she shrieked, giving him a shove.

"I'm sorry," he said, holding his hands up to ward off another attack. "I called your name three times and you didn't answer me. I came back here to see what you were looking at but I tripped on a table leg."

From behind them he heard the thud of footsteps on the stairs, and turned to see Tony descending two steps at a time. Following him by only a few seconds was Alice, who once again was dressed all in black.

"What the hell happened?" Tony and Alice said at the same time, then turned to each other in surprise, as if they had completely missed one another on the stairs.

"Nothing," Rob said. "I just surprised her."

"Surprised me? You scared the crap out of me."

"I told you, I tripped."

"Did you see it?" she demanded.

"See what?"

"The cradle. It was rocking. And I could swear I heard a baby crying."

Uh-oh. Had he scared her so thoroughly that she had lost touch with reality? "What cradle?"

"Back there." She pointed to the spot behind the bureau she'd been staring at when he fell into her.

He peered behind it, and though the light was dim he could definitely see the outline of something small and low to the floor, wedged between the bureau and the wall.

"Is it still rocking?" she asked.

As far as he could tell it wasn't moving. "Let me see if I can…" He leaned over the bureau, his stomach resting on the top, reaching…

He grabbed the side of the cradle and pulled it up off the floor. It was light, and looked to him to be almost small enough to be a child's toy rather than a functional piece of furniture, but as he held it up to the light he could see that it was handmade and very old.

Her concerns suddenly gone, Carrie started making her way back to where Tony and Alice stood, gesturing him to follow. "Bring it over here!"

He had never known Carrie to be anything but level-headed and rational, but she was neither right now.

He held the cradle up over his head and carried it through the maze of furniture. When he reached the other side, where the three of them stood waiting for him, he set it on the cold concrete floor. It was simple but functional, and looked surprisingly well-kept considering its age, but probably not very safe by modern standards.

"Watch it!" Carrie said excitedly. "I swear it was rocking all by itself. And I heard a baby crying."

"A *human* baby?" Rob asked, which Carrie's exasperated look would suggest was a stupid question.

"Of course a human baby," she said. "Didn't anyone else hear it?"

Rob shook his head, and they both turned to Tony and Alice, who were ignoring them and busy giving each other the once-over. Rob realized that they hadn't been introduced yet. "Tony, this is Carrie's friend Alice, from New York. Alice, this is my cousin Tony."

"A pleasure," Alice said, shaking Tony's hand, a catlike grin curling her lips.

"The pleasure is all mine," Tony said, and they looked utterly enthralled by one another.

"How about a drink?" Alice said, her eyes never leaving Tony's.

"I'd love one," Tony said, gesturing to the stairs. "After you."

As they disappeared up the stairs, Carrie turned to Rob and said, "What the heck just happened?"

Rob shrugged. "I guess they liked what they saw."

"In that case, maybe it's a good thing that you made me scream." She looked down at the cradle, which as far as Rob could see, wasn't moving at all. Sounding defeated, she said, "It's not going to do it for you."

"It might."

They stood in silence and watched it for several minutes, but nothing happened.

"I swear it was moving," she told him.

"I believe you. If doors can open by themselves, why would a self-rocking cradle be such a stretch of the imagination?"

"Either that, or I'm losing my mind."

"It *was* a little weird that you wouldn't answer me. At first I thought you were upset about something. And then I thought maybe you were getting sick."

"Eew," she said, nose wrinkling.

"But as I got closer, it seemed as if you were in a trance or something."

"I guess I sort of felt like I was. And when you fell against me, I think I was reaching down to touch it. But I wasn't doing it consciously. Does that make sense?"

"Not really."

"I could see my arm moving, but I didn't feel as if I was controlling it."

"Are you saying that you were possessed?"

She shrugged. "Maybe I was. I sure didn't feel like myself."

If she were anyone else, he would think she was either nuts or looking to get attention, but that wasn't Carrie. She was one of the most down-to-earth, sane people he'd ever met, despite all her hang-ups. A genuine straight shooter. She looked so damn adorable in her skinny jeans and a UCLA sweatshirt, her hair pulled back in a ponytail that bounced when she walked. And he wanted her just as much as he had in the hotel bar that night. He'd racked his brain trying to come up with a way to make her see that she was wrong. He didn't deserve better than her, because there was no one better. Not that he'd ever met. The problem was making her believe that.

"I guess we should get back upstairs," she said.

"You want me to bring the cradle up?"

She looked at all the furniture piled there, then at the forlorn little cradle on the floor. He thought of the children who might have slept in it and actually felt guilty for leaving it down there. It looked so small and lonely.

Small and lonely? Where the hell had that come from? Now *he* was acting possessed.

"Bring it up," she said. "I'll clean it up. Maybe someone can get some use out of it."

He lifted the cradle off the floor, and as he did, he could swear he felt a rush of cold air brush past him. Clearly he was imagining things.

He followed Carrie up the stairs, holding the cradle, and when they stepped through the door, she pushed it closed behind him.

Just before he heard the knob latch, from the basement below, he could swear he heard the sound of not a baby, but a woman crying.

"They bailed on us." Carrie held up the note she found stuck to the refrigerator and showed it to Rob.

Went for a drink. Back later.

"I guess Tony forgot that we came here together in his car," Rob said.

Carrie wasn't thrilled by the idea of being stuck with Rob, and even though it was a setup, she couldn't muster the will to be upset with Alice. She'd been cooped up in the house for three weeks. It would do her good to get out and socialize. She needed this. And maybe she and Tony would hit it off. Alice could certainly benefit from meeting a nice guy for a change. Not that Carrie knew Tony all that well. But if he was anything like the rest of his family, she had nothing to worry about.

She had the sudden vision of her and Alice both settling down in Chicago, and a double wedding with Carrie and Rob and Alice and Tony tying the knot.

A double wedding? Seriously? Where the heck had that come from?

She shook away the ridiculous notion.

"I'm sure they won't be too long," she said. At least she hoped they wouldn't.

"Where do you want the cradle?" Rob said, and she realized he was still holding it.

"The living room, I guess, until I figure out what I'm going to do with it. It just didn't seem right to keep it in the basement."

"I know what you mean," he said, carrying it into the living room for her.

"You do?"

He set it down by the couch, then sat down. "Weirdly enough, yes."

The fact that she'd felt that way was weird, but his feeling it, too? That was downright creepy. Maybe, instead of cleaning it up, she should hire an exorcist.

She sat in the chair. "Do you like old furniture?"

"Not particularly."

Neither did she. She didn't dislike it, but her preference was a more modern look. But the cradle, there was just something about it....

"Maybe that's why the door kept opening," Rob said. "Maybe whatever is down there wanted you to find it and bring it up. Maybe that's why it touched you that first night."

She narrowed her eyes at him. "Are you serious or just making fun of me?"

"I heard it, too," he said.

"The baby crying?"

"Just before you closed the basement door. But it didn't sound like a baby. It was a woman."

The hair on the back of her neck rose. "Wow, that's really creepy."

"I have to admit that it is."

"Speaking of creepy," Carrie said, "something happened at work last night that I thought I should mention."

"Don't tell me doors are opening by themselves there, too," he said, with a grin so adorable she wanted to eat him up.

"This is about a door that wouldn't open, actually."

She told him how she had caught Rose trying to break into his father's office, and how his secretary conveniently called at the last second.

"You think she was lying?" Rob asked her.

"I'm usually pretty good at reading people, and I definitely had that feeling. But that doesn't mean I'm right. I just thought I should tell you."

"I'm glad you did. Just between us, there's something about her that bothers me."

"Me, too! She's so quiet—not that quiet people are bad—but it always seems as if she's up to no good or hiding something. Do you know what I mean?"

"I do. She and my sister have become pretty good friends. Megan bought an apartment and Rose is going to be moving in the end of this month."

"You're worried?"

"Yeah. Her mom worked at Caroselli Chocolate for years as *Nonno's* secretary, so when she showed up looking for a job, my uncle Leo felt obligated to hire her."

"In what position?"

"At first, just general office stuff, but then she offered to digitize all our old records, and that's been her job description ever since."

"So she has access to a lot of company information."

"You think she's a spy?"

She shrugged. "It does happen."

"I think I'll do some digging. See what I can come up with." He looked at his watch. "If Tony ever comes back."

It was obvious that he didn't feel like hanging around. She didn't know if she should feel relieved or disappointed. "I can drive you home."

"You wouldn't mind?"

"Consider it my thanks for moving the furniture." It beat having him stuck there until God knew when, driving her crazy. "I'll get my coat."

It was snowing lightly as she backed out of the garage. She still wasn't crazy about driving in the snow, but it wasn't half as bad as she'd expected, and the compact SUV she'd leased totally kicked ass.

"Are we supposed to get much snow?" she asked Rob.

"They said something about six inches tonight."

"So," she said, glancing over at him, "average?"

He laughed and shook his head. "That's what I hear."

She could really go for six inches tonight. Or in Rob's case, seven or eight.

What? No! Did she really just think that? She had to get her mind out of the gutter and stop flirting with him. This is why she didn't like to see him outside of work. She forgot how to behave. And being in such a confined space with him, the scent of his aftershave was doing funny things to her head.

It was making her fantasize about things. Bad things, like what he would do if she took her hand off the steering wheel and laid it on his knee, maybe slid it up his inner thigh…

Don't even think about it.

This is why it was such a bad idea to see each other socially. She had no self-control.

"Make a left here," Rob said. "My building is two blocks down."

They couldn't have gone more than half a mile from

her place. "I knew you were close, but I didn't realize it was this close."

"If it wasn't so cold, I would have just walked."

The area was an eclectic blend of old restored and new buildings. Rob's was a converted warehouse. "Beautiful building," she said. "What floor are you on?"

"I have the penthouse."

"Sounds nice."

"It's open concept. Very modern. Want to come up and see it?"

Hell no. "Um…sure."

What? No, you don't!

If she got him alone in his place, she wasn't sure if she could be responsible for her actions. In fact, she knew she couldn't.

"Do you have a roommate?" she asked.

"No, why?"

She shrugged. "Just curious."

She needed to come up with an excuse as to why she couldn't go inside. But as he pointed out a parking space just a little ways down the street, the car seemed to drive itself there.

This was a *really* bad idea. But that didn't stop her from getting out of the car and walking with him to the building. It was as if she was having an out-of-body experience, watching the scene from above but not really participating.

The lobby was clean and modern and even better, toasty warm.

"How long have you lived here?" she asked while they waited for the elevator, hoping that idle conversation would keep her from doing something crazy like throwing herself at him. She'd actually had sex in an elevator before. It wasn't all it was cracked up to be. But with Rob, there was no such thing as bad sex. Or even mediocre sex.

They stepped off the elevator into a hallway with just two doors. He pointed to the one on the right. "This is me."

He unlocked the door and gestured her through, and as she stepped inside, what she saw took her breath away.

When he said open concept he hadn't been kidding. The apartment was one big open space with a gourmet kitchen, a dining space and a cozy living area. A mix of steel and wood beams crisscrossed above their heads, and a winding iron staircase led to a loft-style bedroom. Tall windows that looked original to the building lined one entire side of the unit.

"This is beautiful!" she said.

"Take off your coat."

"Oh…I can't stay."

He shrugged out of his coat and hung it on a hook beside the door. "You in a hurry to be somewhere?"

"Well…no, but—"

"So stay a few minutes." He held his hand out for her coat. "You don't have to worry, I'm not going to put the moves on you."

As if she needed encouragement from him. If anyone was going to be putting moves on, it probably would be her. Knowing that, she slipped off her coat anyway and he hung it beside his own.

"I'll give you the grand tour."

He showed her around, pointing out all the unique, special touches, but she was having trouble concentrating. Her eyes kept wandering to his ass, which looked exceptionally nice in jeans. He had his usual afternoon stubble and she longed to feel the roughness of it against her palms and her lips…maybe her thighs. She kept her hands wedged in the pockets of her jeans so she wouldn't be tempted to use them, and as they climbed the winding stairs to his bedroom, she couldn't help thinking that she was making a huge mistake.

"The bedroom is my favorite room."

She didn't ask why. She didn't want to know, but as they walked to the window, it was obvious.

The view from downstairs was nice, but from up here, it was breathtaking. She could see the entire neighborhood, and in the distance, the skyline of downtown.

"It's amazing," she said, aware that he was standing just a few inches behind her. So close she could feel his body heat and smell his aftershave—or maybe that was just how the room naturally smelled. On an oversize chair beside her lay the clothes that Rob had worn to work yesterday—yes, she paid attention—and she had to fight the urge to pick up his shirt and hold it to her nose, breathe in the scent of his skin on the fabric.

Maybe when he wasn't looking...

"I can lie in bed and watch the fireworks at Navy Pier."

"Nice," she said. She could think of other things they could do in bed, too. They could make their own fireworks.

"Is everything okay?" he said. "You're awfully quiet."

She shrugged. "Not much to say, I guess."

"You always have something to say."

He was right. She didn't like quiet. She was always filling the empty space with conversation. Today was different. Today she was terrified that she would say something she shouldn't, which might encourage him to do something *he* shouldn't. Something she would find it impossible to say no to.

She turned to him, looked up into his dark, bottomless eyes. The longing that she saw there, the unmasked *need,* made her knees go weak.

She never should have turned around.

"I want you," she said, regretting the words the instant they left her lips.

He nodded. "I know."

"But I can't. I can't want you."

"I know that, too."

Did he have to be so damn agreeable?

"The thing is, you're a lot bigger than me," she said. "If you were to grab me and throw me down on the bed, there wouldn't be much I could do to stop you."

"So you have someone else to blame later?" He took a step back. "Not a chance."

She blinked in surprise. He was turning her down?

"This isn't a game," he said. "Not to me, anyway. Not anymore."

"I know that."

"Then you need to make up your mind. Either you want me or you don't."

"I do, but—"

"No buts," he said. "Either we're together or we aren't."

"What about work?"

"Work is work. We keep it professional. It's no one's business what we do outside the office."

No, but they sure liked to make it their business.

"You can't tell anyone. Not even Nick and Tony." She paused and said, "Well, I guess it would be okay to tell them. If they ask. I would never expect you to lie to them. But no one else."

"So I should forget about that announcement I was going to run in the Sunday paper?"

She smiled. He *always* made her smile. He made her... happy. Why would she deprive herself of that? What reason did she have to say no?

Because you like him, dummy. Too much. In her entire life she had never met anyone she would have even considered seeing long term, yet here she was doing crazy things like imagining double weddings. This was a totally new experience for her. It was exciting and terrifying. What if she got too attached? What would she do when it was over? Did she really want to put herself through that?

But what if this time was different? What if there wasn't a letdown? What if there really was someone for everyone, and Rob was her someone? Wouldn't it be worth it to at least find out? To at least give him a chance?

She thought about what Alice said, about what Carrie had to go back to in Los Angeles, and she was right. When Carrie wasn't working, her life was barren and lonely. Here she at least had people who genuinely seemed to care about her.

"I want you," she said.

He looked skeptical. "But?"

She shook her head. "No buts. Not this time."

"You're sure?"

"Very sure." She slid her arms around his neck, rose up on her toes and kissed him.

Fourteen

"Is he in there?" Carrie asked, poking her head into Mrs. White's office.

"He already went down to the conference room," she said, her tone considerably less chilly than it had been eight weeks ago.

No matter how impersonal or cold the older woman was, from day one Carrie had greeted her with a smile and treated her with respect. It had taken a while to realize that she wasn't really a bitch, just very focused and private. And one hell of a good secretary. She liked to come in and do her job and she didn't like to be interrupted, which Carrie could certainly relate to. And she was fiercely loyal to Rob. He told Carrie that when he was a kid she worked in one of the stores and was a totally different person. He said she would always slip him an extra piece of his favorite candy when he came in with his mother to visit. Even if his mother said no more—which was usually the case.

Then Mrs. White's only son was killed in an accident, and she hadn't been the same since.

So Carrie and she would never be pals, or even friends, but their working relationship was now amicable.

"Did he get my report?" she asked Mrs. White.

"He did. He took it with him."

She shouldn't be nervous, but she was. After compiling all the data, Carrie had worked up a rough plan of what she thought was a viable solution to Caroselli Chocolate's sales drop. Now she would present it to the rest of the team and hoped they agreed she was on the right track and were willing to implement a plan. She was especially nervous about what Rob would think. For the past five weeks, since they began officially secretly "dating," they had managed to keep their private and professional relationships separate. But if he thought her idea was total crap, her pride was going to take a hit. And her feelings would probably be hurt.

"You'll do fine," Mrs. White said.

"Huh?" Carrie blinked, sure she'd heard her wrong.

"You're smart and the entire team respects you. You'll do fine."

Mrs. White was giving her a pep talk?

Coming from her, that actually made Carrie feel much better. "I have a lot riding on this."

"Well, no matter what happens in there, it won't change the way Rob feels about you."

Carrie opened her mouth to deny that they had anything but a professional relationship, then realized, by Mrs. White's wry smile, it would be a waste of time. Instead she sighed and said, "I hope not."

"I've known Rob almost his entire life. I've never seen him like this before."

"Like what?"

"Happy. Focused on something other than work."

"Mrs. White," she started, wanting to say something nice to the woman, but she shooed Carrie away.

"Go. He's waiting."

Carrie walked down the hall to the conference room. Mrs. White wasn't the only one who noticed a change in Rob. Tony, whom Carrie saw quite often now that he was dating Alice, had said basically the same thing.

"He's a different person when he's with you," he'd told Carrie, and she could only assume he meant that it was a good thing. It seemed to Carrie that Rob was happy, but with no frame of reference it was hard to know exactly how happy he really was now compared to before her arrival. She couldn't really ask anyone else, because no one else knew about them, so she was constantly second-guessing herself. Believing that things with her and Rob were so good, they were *too* good, and even if they ever did start to talk long term—which they hadn't—the relationship was bound to fail.

Maybe Alice was right. Maybe she *was* afraid to be happy. The question was, how did she stop being afraid? How did she learn to trust her own feelings, when deep down they were telling her that he was the one?

She stopped in front of the conference room door, took a deep breath, squared her shoulders and walked in. She'd expected the entire team to be there, but it was just Rob.

"Hey," she said. "Where is everyone?"

Her report was on the desk in front of him. "I wanted to talk, just the two of us first."

Uh-oh. That couldn't be good.

He gestured to the chair across the table from him. "Have a seat."

"You think it's crap, don't you?" she said, sliding into

a chair, feeling a bit like she was facing a one-man firing squad.

"On the contrary," he said. "I think it's brilliant."

She blinked. "Really?"

"And I'll show you why." From under her report he pulled a second report and slid it across the table to her. It was dated almost six months ago.

"What is this?" she asked.

"The report we put together before they made the decision to hire you. Take a look."

She flipped it open, noticing immediately how similar it was to hers—which wasn't too unexpected—but when she got to the proposed solution, her jaw dropped. "Oh, crap."

Rob laughed. "Yeah."

"Why didn't you show me this before?"

"Because you're the marketing genius."

She wasn't the only one. Rob and his team had drawn the same conclusions that she had, and with a few slight variations, the outline of his proposed plan was identical to hers. "Did you show them this?"

"They shot it down," he said. "Told me it was too radical. That we should stick to tradition."

It was radical because that was what the company needed to divert a potential disaster. Tradition was nice in theory, but to survive in the current economy, one had to change with the times.

No wonder Rob had been so resistant to hiring her. He'd come up with a plan himself that he knew was exactly what the company needed, but they hadn't trusted his judgment.

"They were wrong," she said.

"I know."

So they had just paid a tremendous fee to have her tell them what they had already been told. She could just imagine how well that was going to go over. What it would do to her reputation.

She dropped her head in her hands. "Oh, my God, I am so screwed."

"Why? You did exactly what they asked you to do. It's not your fault if they're too stubborn to listen to their own people."

"What are we going to do?"

"Work up a very detailed plan to present to them. Maybe this time they will listen."

"And if they don't? If they reject it again?"

He shrugged. "I'll resign."

She blinked. "You would really do that?"

"They're my family, and I love them, but that only goes so far. This is business. Family or not, how long would you stay on a sinking ship before you decided to jump?"

He was right. "So we'll give them the report and hope for the best."

The conference room door opened and Carrie expected to see Al, Will and Grant, but it was Nick who walked in.

"Sorry to interrupt. Have you got a minute?"

"Sure," Rob said. "What's up?"

"The news is going to spread fast, so I wanted to be the one to tell you."

"Tell me what?" Rob asked.

"Terri is pregnant."

At first Rob looked surprised, then he laughed and said, "Congratulations!"

He got up and walked around the table to shake Nick's hand, then gave him one of those man-hug things.

"I know how badly you guys wanted this," Rob said.

"We've actually known for about a month, but Terri wanted to wait to make sure everything was okay. You can't even imagine how tough that was."

"And is it?" Rob asked. "All okay, I mean."

"She feels great. The baby is growing exactly how it's supposed to. She's due September twenty-first."

"She's excited?"

"You would think she was the first woman in history to conceive a child."

Rob shook his head and laughed. "You and Terri. Who would have imagined?"

Nick grinned. "I know, right? Best move I ever made. I guess it was just our time."

Nick looked so happy, and Terri was lucky to have someone who loved her so unconditionally, Carrie actually felt a tug of jealousy. She'd always just assumed that some day she would settle down, get married and have a family, but only because that's what people were supposed to do. Now she realized it was something she wanted. *Really* wanted.

Al, Will and Grant walked in, and Nick told them the good news. There were more handshakes, hugs and congratulations, and she couldn't help feeling a little left out. Caroselli Chocolate really was like a big family. One she wished she could be a part of.

Rob looked over at her and grinned. She tried to imagine what it would be like, her staying in Chicago and moving in with Rob. Her and Rob getting married. Making their own excited announcement that she was pregnant...

Speaking of, she thought, trying to recall the date of her last period. Shouldn't she be starting soon? She'd been so busy lately that she hadn't even thought about it.

She picked up her phone and opened her calendar. Her last period had been not too long before she and Rob began officially dating, which was...

Her heart gave a quick squeeze. *Six weeks ago.*

No, that couldn't be right. It couldn't have been that

long. Because that would mean she was two weeks late. And she was *never* late.

She looked over at Rob. He must have sensed something was wrong. He was watching her with a furrowed brow.

She closed her eyes. This was not happening. It couldn't be. She could not be pregnant. She had been working her butt off and the stress was getting to her, that was all. Didn't Terri mention that stress could throw off a woman's cycle? Even though as long as Carrie had lived it had *never* happened before.

"Carrie?"

She looked up to find Rob standing beside her chair.

He leaned down beside her and lowered his voice, so no one else would hear him. "Are you okay? You're white as a sheet."

She couldn't draw enough air into her lungs to answer him, so she shook her head instead.

"What's wrong?"

Should she find out for sure first or tell him now? She hated to freak him out until he had something to be genuinely freaked out about. But was that really fair? And did she really want to do this alone?

"We need to talk," she managed to squeak out.

"Now?"

"Yes, now."

"Let's go to my office."

She rose from her chair, her knees squishy and her head spinning, hoping she would actually make it to his office. She had never passed out in her life, but it sure felt like she might now. He must have been thinking the same thing because he took her elbow to steady her.

"Where are you two going?" Al asked.

"Carrie isn't feeling well," Rob said. "Let's postpone the meeting until later this afternoon."

"Is there anything I can do?" Al asked, and hearing the concern in her voice, everyone else turned to them.

"It's not a big deal," Carrie lied. "I skipped breakfast. My blood sugar is just a little low."

"I'll take care of her," Rob told them, walking her to the door.

She wavered a little on the way to his office, but they made it there. She must have looked way worse than she realized because when Mrs. White saw her, she rose from her chair and said, "What's wrong?"

"She's not feeling well," Rob said as they walked past her desk. "Could you hold all my calls? And get us a cold bottled water from the break room?"

"Right away," she said, scurrying out.

Rob got her seated in his chair and sat on the edge of his desk. "Are you all right?"

She nodded. The initial shock seemed to be wearing off and she didn't feel nearly so woozy. "Sorry about that."

"How late are you?" he asked.

She was so stunned by the question that for a full thirty seconds she could barely breathe much less speak. "How did you…"

"I pay attention."

"To my menstrual cycle?"

"Not specifically. But when Nick announced that Terri was pregnant, it got me to thinking—"

"Thinking what?"

"That maybe, someday, that could be us. And then for some reason it dawned on me that since we've been dating I don't recall your having had a period. Then I looked over at you and you were pale as a ghost and checking your phone. Like I said, I pay attention."

"I can't be," she said. "There's no way I'm pregnant."

"Why not?"

"Because I just…*can't be*, that's why. I'm a little late, that's all. A measly two weeks. Stress can do that."

"It can?"

"That's what Terri said. Besides, we've been super-careful, right?"

"Well…" he said, trailing off.

"Rob?"

"We did have a small breach."

Her heart slammed the wall of her chest. "A *small* breach?"

"Very small, just a little tear."

"When?"

"A month ago, give or take."

"And you didn't *tell* me?"

"It didn't seem like that big of a deal. And I was worried you might freak out. Which I should point out, you are. I figured, there was nothing we could do at that point anyway, so there was no use worrying about it until we needed to. I was so not worried that until today, I forgot all about it."

"I can't have a baby."

She heard a throat clear and they both looked up to see Mrs. White standing in the doorway with Carrie's bottled water.

"Thank you," Rob said, taking it from her.

"Is there anything else I can do?" she asked, wearing what could almost pass for a look of sympathy.

"No. But please, just…keep this to yourself."

"Carrie?" Mrs. White said. "Do you need anything?"

Feeling shell-shocked, she shook her head. "No, but thank you."

She left, closing the door behind her.

"Actually, there is something you need," Rob said. "A pregnancy test."

Fifteen

"I don't need a pregnancy test," Carrie said, opening her water and taking a swig. Some of the color had returned to her skin.

"Would you rather see a doctor instead?" Rob asked her.

"I don't need either, because I'm not pregnant."

"And you know that because?"

"Because I *can't* be. That's why. I'm not ready."

"I don't think it works that way," he said.

"Besides a missed period, what other symptoms do I have? I don't have morning sickness and I haven't been especially tired. I feel completely fine. Totally normal."

"Maybe it's too early in the pregnancy for that."

"I am *not* pregnant."

"Wouldn't you like to know for sure?"

"I do know."

Her sudden descent into total denial was a little disturbing. "Carrie…"

"Just humor me, okay? Let's give it another couple of days. If I haven't started by then, I'll take a test. I just… I'm not ready to know yet. I need a few days to process this. And if I am, well, then I am. A few more days isn't going to make any difference."

He wanted to argue, because although she may not have wanted to know, he did. But shy of forcing her to take it, there wasn't a whole lot he could do. She was obviously scared and confused and pushing her would only make it worse. And she was right. If she really was pregnant, waiting a few days wasn't going to make a big difference. And there was no reason why he couldn't start making plans now, just in case.

"We'll give it until Monday," he said. "If you haven't started by then, we'll get the test."

"Sounds fair," she said. "If you don't mind, I think I'm going to go home early today."

"Go ahead. I'll stop by after work."

"Actually, I promised Alice we would do something together tonight. Maybe you and I can do something tomorrow?"

"Sure," he said. There was hardly a night they didn't spend together. Was it just coincidence that she chose today to spend the night away from him?

She probably just needed time to think.

She pushed herself up from his chair and seemed much steadier on her feet this time.

"Would you like me to walk you to your car?"

"No, I'll be fine."

"You'll call me if anything happens?"

"You'll be the first to know."

He leaned in to kiss her, aiming for her mouth, but she turned her head at the last minute and he got her cheek instead.

"I'll see you tomorrow," she said, offering him a weak smile as she walked out the door.

When she was gone, Rob sat down at his desk, feeling uneasy. Carrie's total lack of enthusiasm at the idea of being pregnant worried him. What if she really didn't want the baby?

There was a soft knock, then Mrs. White poked her head in. "Are you okay?"

"Yeah, I think so. A little…stunned, I guess." Or something like it.

"Are you sure there isn't anything I can do for you?"

"Any words of wisdom you care to impart?"

She considered that for a minute, then said, "A baby is a blessing."

"That's it?"

She smiled. "You don't need me to tell you what to do."

No, he didn't. With her time here running short, he'd already been seriously considering asking Carrie to relocate to Chicago. No, not just considering it, but he wanted to wait until the right time. When he felt she was ready to hear it. He knew that rushing things could potentially backfire. And he was more than willing to take things slow. The way he'd figured it, she could keep renting Terri's place, and in the appropriate amount of time, when they were both ready, move into his place.

It surprised him to realize that he was in no way disturbed by the idea of moving up his timetable. His feelings for her weren't going to change. And if he was going to collect his fifteen million, marriage would have to be part of the deal, anyway. He hadn't expected it to happen quite so soon, but he was ready. But how did Carrie feel? What if she wasn't ready?

She just needed time to process it, to get used to the idea of being a mother. Right now she was just scared. They hadn't actually discussed how he felt about their having a baby. Maybe she was worried that he wouldn't step up. Although he would hope she knew him better than that by now. But wasn't she used to people letting her down? He needed to assure her that he was behind this one hundred percent. That they would make it work. And in the process, he would earn himself a hefty chunk of change. Though he couldn't deny that the idea of profiting from the situation was a little...sleazy.

There was another knock on his door, but this time it was Nick who stuck his head in. "Hey, can I come in?"

"Sure."

He stepped inside and closed the door. "Is everything okay? I saw Carrie leave. You guys have a fight or something?"

"Not exactly."

"In other words, you don't want to talk about it."

Well, if anyone could understand what he was feeling, it would be Nick.

"Why did you turn down the money?" he asked.

"The baby money?"

"Yeah. You were married and planning to have a kid, anyway. Why not wait it out in case you did have a boy? I mean, where's the harm in that?"

"Because the money didn't matter anymore."

"Didn't matter how?"

"When it happens to you, you'll know." He paused as the light bulb suddenly clicked on. "Is Carrie...?"

"Maybe. Probably. But keep that to yourself."

"You know I will."

Rob shook his head. "This is surreal."

"Are you going to marry her?"

"Of course."

"If it's a boy, will you take the money?"

He shrugged. "That's what I don't know."

"Do you love her?"

"I've sure never met anyone like her."

"But is that a good enough reason to marry her?"

"You know that *Nonno* said we have to be married."

"Oh, so you want the baby, but you're marrying her for the money?"

No, but it sort of sounded that way, didn't it? And it wasn't like that at all.

"I'm going to marry her, because I *want* to marry her."

"You think she'll ever believe that when she finds out you took the fifteen million dollars?"

"How will she find out? No one but us knows about it."

"A lie by omission is still a lie, Robby. Is that something you could live with for the rest of your life?"

"Probably." Maybe.

"Until the answer to that question is hell no, you have no business marrying her. And you sure as hell don't love her."

The words stung, but even worse, Nick was right. As many times as he'd heard her say that he deserved better than her, she sure as hell deserved better than that.

Carrie called in sick the next day—leaving a message with Mrs. White—and wouldn't answer his phone calls all morning. When he got ahold of her after lunch, she claimed that she'd shut her phone off and had been sleeping. "I must have that bug that's going around."

"Can I bring you anything?" he'd asked.

"I don't want you to catch this. Anything I need Alice can get me."

"I take it we don't know for sure yet."

"If you're asking did I start my period, no, I didn't."

"Maybe under the circumstances you should go to the doctor, if you're sick and pregnant—"

"It's a bug, Rob. I'll be fine. I just need rest."

"I'll call and check in on you later, and if you need anything, call."

"I will."

She didn't call him, and when he tried to call her later that evening to check on her, it went straight to voice mail.

The next morning she called in sick again—Mrs. White took the call—and when he tried to call her back, she didn't answer. She texted him a little while later to say that she would be fine and to text if he needed her. It didn't take a genius to figure out that she was hiding from him, and he knew the best thing to do was to give her space. Give her time to deal with the idea of being pregnant. But by Monday, when he hadn't heard a word from her, voice or text, he reached the end of his patience. He left the office at noon and drove to her condo, with a quick stop at the pharmacy in between.

She opened her front door—and thank God she did open it—wearing orange sweat pants, a stained white sweatshirt and green slippers. Her hair, which looked as if it had gone days without seeing a brush, was pulled back in a limp ponytail.

He couldn't tell if she was sick, depressed or a combination of the two.

"Come on in," she said, looking equal parts guilty and apologetic. "I'm sorry I haven't called. I know that if there actually is a baby, that it's your baby, too, and I didn't mean to shut you out. I just didn't want to be that insipid, clingy woman who couldn't deal with things on her own."

"Carrie, you are the least clingy woman I've ever met."

"I'm the opposite. When things get too hard, I bail. You might want to keep that in mind, seeing as how I'm the potential mother of your child. What if I am pregnant, and we have the baby, and I bail on you both?"

"You won't."

"How do you know that?"

"Because I do."

"How?"

"Because you're a hell of a lot stronger than you give yourself credit for." He held up the bag. "We said Monday. So let's find out."

"And if I am?"

"We'll figure it out. Together."

She took a deep breath and held out her hand. "Let's have it."

He handed her the bag.

She gestured down the hall. "You want to watch me pee on a stick?"

"Do you want me there?"

"Why not? If we're going to do this together, we should do all of it together. Even this part."

For the past five days he'd been pretty confident that Carrie was pregnant, and the test was just a formality. But as he followed her to her bathroom, a ball of nerves coiled in his gut. If she was pregnant, his entire life was going to change. It stunned him to realize that as scary as that was, he was okay with it. Maybe he really was ready. Maybe, more than being nervous, he was just…excited.

He sat on the edge of the tub while she went through the process, which was pretty simple. Pee, then wait five minutes.

It was the longest five minutes of his life.

"Ever done this before?" Carrie asked.

"Once, in college. How about you?"

"Never." She rubbed her palms together. "So I'm pretty freaked out right now."

"In this case, practice does not make perfect." He looked

at his watch and his heart started to beat faster. "It's been five minutes."

"Here we go." After a slight pause Carrie very cautiously turned the stick over and peeked at the tiny display. She put it back down and exhaled, turning to him. "Negative."

He was so prepared to hear positive that when she turned and said negative instead, he was sure he misheard her.

"Negative?" he repeated, just to be sure.

She nodded, looking relieved. "I'm not pregnant."

"Oh." He wasn't sure what to say. "I really thought you were."

"But this is good news, right? I mean, you must be just as relieved as I am."

"You would think so." So why didn't he feel relieved?

"Rob, you are relieved, right? I mean, think about it. Sleepless nights, diaper rash, spit-up. College funds."

"I thought about it. And no, I'm actually not relieved. I mean, I know the timing wasn't great, but I'm still a little disappointed."

"Oh, thank God," Carrie said, holding up the test so he could see it. "Because I lied. It's positive."

"You *lied?*" Rob said, looking at Carrie as if he wasn't sure what to believe. "Why would you do that?"

"Sorry, but I had to know."

He took the test from her and checked it, then he shook his head, like he thought she was nuts.

He was probably right.

"You needed to know what?"

"How you really felt."

"You could have just asked me?"

"No. It's that nice guy syndrome."

"Nice guy syndrome?"

"You're a nice guy…a stand-up guy. So if I told you the test was positive you would have said you were happy, even if you weren't. Right?"

He hesitated.

"The honest truth."

"Probably," he admitted.

"But if you were disappointed that it was negative, even a tiny bit, then I would know that you were okay with it."

"That was risky."

She shrugged. "It worked on *Friends*."

"Friends?" He laughed. "You stole the idea from a *sitcom?"*

"Yup."

"Out of curiosity, what if I had been relieved? What would you do then?"

Good question. "I hadn't actually thought that far ahead. But at least I would know how you *really* felt."

"Tell me what you need from me," he said.

"How about a hug?"

Rob reached for her. She walked into his arms and he held her close, and she had the feeling that everything would be okay. She wasn't nearly as freaked out as she thought she would be. Maybe she was less freaked about the actual pregnancy, and more afraid of Rob's reaction. Not that she wasn't still terrified.

"What if I'm a terrible mother?"

"Think about it. If you learned nothing else from your mom and stepdad, it was how *not* to be a bad parent."

He had a point. Whatever they had done, she could just do the opposite. "What if I get scared and I bail?"

"I won't let you get very far."

"Really? Because I can be a very difficult person."

"Really. And you won't ever have to bail if you remember to communicate. If you just talk to me, I promise I'll listen. And whatever it is, we'll fix it."

It sounded wonderful, like a dream relationship. He also made it sound awfully easy.

But what did she know? Maybe for normal people it *was* that easy. Maybe if she was lucky, some of Rob's normal would rub off on her. Or maybe it was time she grew up and found her own normal. And stopped blaming all of her shortcomings on her crappy past. At some point she had to just let it go.

She could be anything she wanted to be. "It may take some time but I'll learn. Just try to be patient with me."

"I will."

She closed her eyes, nestling up against his chest. "Five days away from you is way too long."

He squeezed her. "I was thinking the same thing."

She breathed in his aftershave. It was so familiar now. *He* was so familiar. Suddenly *wanting* him was starting to feel a lot more like *needing* him.

"So what do we do now?"

Grinning down at her, he said, "I guess we have a baby."

Sixteen

Five seconds after he learned that Carrie really was pregnant, before he'd even had time to process it, Rob finally understood what Nick had meant the other day. It was one thing to think you might have a child, but to know it? There were no words. He and Carrie had a real shot at being a family. She could be the love of his life. Would he really jeopardize that for money?

Maybe *Nonno* was trying to do more than bribe them into having families. Maybe he was trying to teach them a lesson, too. Of what was and wasn't important in life.

He and Carrie agreed not to say anything to anyone until she'd seen a doctor. And there were still all these unanswered questions. Like where would they live? And would they get married? Carrie wondered how she would work and take care of a baby. Would she have to quit, or was it socially acceptable to put kids in day care?

And shouldn't they have at least a vague idea of what

they planned to do before they started telling everyone? Before people started asking questions they didn't have the answers to? And of course after the questions would come all the unsolicited advice.

So, the day the doctor gave them final confirmation, Rob knew they had to have a plan. And first things first. As soon as they got back to his place, he dropped to one knee and asked her to marry him. It wasn't as romantic as he'd hoped, but effective, because after asking him three times if he was really sure, she said yes. They decided that until they were married they would stay in their own places, but they would start looking for a bigger place that was a bit more kid-friendly than his loft, and unlike the condo, something with a fenced backyard. There was no mention of the L-word from either of them, but that was something he was sure they would both get to later. He didn't see any hurry, as long as they were on the same page.

After all of that planning, they decided to announce their marketing plan first. So no one could accuse her of being biased.

With everyone from the first meeting there, plus the entire marketing department, the conference room table was filled to capacity. "Well, let's have it," Rob's dad said, and Al passed out the folders.

It didn't take too long for the grumbling to begin.

"I'm getting old, son, but my memory is still pretty good," his dad told him. "Which is how I know that besides a few variations, this is the same plan you proposed last year."

"It's not." He gestured to Al to pass out the second set of binders. Personally, he didn't see the need to be so dramatic, but Carrie insisted that everyone see the difference between the two proposals. "This is mine."

"The first was mine," Carrie said. "And I did it with no knowledge of the first plan."

"Which means what?" Uncle Tony asked her.

"It means that I'm not the only marketing genius in the room. And I'm sorry, gentlemen, but you've wasted your money on me. Rob doesn't need me or anyone else to tell him what's good for this business. And you would all be fools not to listen to him. I know some of the ideas are a bit radical, and it's always nice when you can stick to tradition, but to survive in business, you also have to learn to change with the times."

His dad steepled his hands, looking to his brothers, then finally to Rob. "Well, son, it would seem we owe you an apology. We should have trusted you, listened to what you had to say. But we didn't and we paid the price."

"And now?" Rob said.

"I want to see a combined report on my desk by Wednesday."

"We anticipated that as a possibility," he said. "Al, number three."

Al passed out the third round of binders.

"Here's your combined report."

"Give us a day to look these over, and we'll meet again Thursday."

As everyone was piling out of the room, Rob pulled his dad aside.

"While you're feeling so forgiving, there's something I need to tell you." Carrie cringed a little as he gestured her over. Rob slid his arm around her shoulders and pulled her close to his side. "I'm not sure if you know, but Carrie and I have been seeing each other. Socially."

"Should I act surprised?"

Meaning he—and Rob would bet a lot of other people in the family—already knew they were a couple.

"Well, Carrie is pregnant."

"Okay," his dad said. "*Now* I'm surprised." He looked back and forth between the two of them. "I don't like that I have to ask this, but can you both assure me this had nothing to do with the proposal you just presented us?"

"He didn't show me his until I showed him mine," Carrie said, then cringed when it sank in what she had just said. "That did not come out right."

"I understand what you meant," his dad said. "And don't worry, you'll fit into the family just fine. Assuming that's the plan."

"She's staying in Chicago, we're getting married, we're going to buy a kid-friendly house or condo and we are going to put the kids in day care because even though we love them to death, we both love our jobs and neither of us wants to give them up."

"When is the baby due?"

"Around Halloween," Carrie said. Which they both found a little creepy considering the basement door and cradle incidents.

Since the day they'd brought the cradle up to the living room, the door stopped opening by itself. The cradle hadn't rocked again either. At least, not as far as he, Carrie or Alice had seen. It was almost as if someone or something knew they were going to be needing it.

It was creepy, yet comforting in a strange way to know that whatever it was, it had their back.

Within twenty-four hours, everyone in the family *knew* Rob's dad was going to be a *nonno,* and then his mother made sure everyone knew it was actually Rob's baby that would give him the title, because no one was clear on that point.

Everything was falling into place, almost too smoothly,

but there was one more thing that he had to do. He called *Nonno* and told him he didn't want the money.

"I'm proud of you" was all *Nonno* said, as if that was the reaction he'd been expecting all along. And while giving up fifteen million wasn't too tough, Rob wondered if Tony would be able to resist the draw of the entire thirty million for himself.

After Mrs. White left for lunch, Nick poked his head into Rob's office. "So you're really going to do it?"

"Do what?"

Nick leaned in the doorway. "Tie the knot, have a baby. It's worth the fifteen million?"

"You're forgetting I don't get a penny if it's not a boy."

Easygoing as Nick was, it took a lot to rile him. Now he was riled. "You're seriously going to take the money?"

"What reason do I have not to?"

"Dude, *seriously?* Where should I start?"

"How about, I love her. That would be a good reason."

Nick narrowed his eyes at him. "Are you screwing with me?"

Yeah, and it was awfully fun. "I called *Nonno* and told him no deal. I'm not taking the money."

"When?"

"A little while ago. You were right. No amount of money is worth screwing this up. I can live without the money, but I can't live without her."

"What did *Nonno* say to you?"

"That he was proud of me."

"He said the same thing to me. I got the distinct feeling that he counted on us not taking the money. Like that was part of the plan."

"That might not work with Tony." While Nick and Rob both loved the satisfaction of doing their job well, Tony lived by the philosophy that he who dies with the most toys wins.

"I guess we'll just have to wait and see," Nick said. "He seems pretty smitten with Alice, and it looks as though the feeling is mutual."

Rob shrugged. "Maybe *Nonno* will actually manage to get us all married off before this year is over."

"And there's a fifty-fifty chance that one of our kids will be a boy."

So there was hope that the Caroselli name would live on for at least one more generation. Rob also didn't doubt for a second that even if there had been no baby, no accidental pregnancy, they would have eventually wound up in the same place.

A half hour or so after Nick left, Rob got a call from Alice of all people. And for some reason she was whispering.

"What the hell happened? Did you and Carrie have a fight?"

A fight? "No, why would you think that?"

"Because she's packing."

"Packing what?"

"Her *stuff*. She's shoving it all into suitcases. She's *furious*. If she knew I was talking to you right now she would kill me."

"I haven't talked to her since this morning and everything was fine then." Could it just be cold feet? "Did she say anything?"

"I tried to talk to her, but she wouldn't say what was wrong. All she said was that she was going back to L.A. *Alone*. She said I could stay at the condo until the lease ran out."

This sounded like something a bit more serious than cold feet. "Don't let her go anywhere," he told Alice. "I'll be there as fast as I can."

Seventeen

Rob made it to Carrie's condo just as she was shoving her bags into the back of her SUV. He parked in the driveway behind her, so she couldn't make a run for it.

He climbed out of his car and said, "Going somewhere?"

"Home," she said, shoving the last bag in, not even looking at him.

"You are home."

"Home to L.A."

"Can I ask why?"

"If you can't figure that out for yourself, you're an even bigger ass than I thought."

"What the hell happened?" She started to walk away and he reached for her arm.

She spun to face him, yanking it free. "Don't touch me. You don't ever get to touch me again."

She wasn't just a little upset or even scared. She was

seething mad. She stomped into the house and he followed her.

"Carrie, I honestly have no idea what's going on."

She spun around to face him. "Fifteen million dollars, Rob. Fifteen million to get married and have a male heir. Is this ringing a bell?"

Oh, crap. "You heard me and Nick talking."

"Did you knock me up on purpose, or was it just a happy coincidence? And is this the real reason why you were disappointed when I said it was negative? Why you didn't ask me to marry you until after I saw the doctor?"

"It wasn't like that. If you had heard our entire conversation you would know that."

"Did your grandfather offer you fifteen million dollars to get married and have a male heir?"

"No one is supposed to know about that, but yes, he did. What you heard was me screwing with Nick. I wasn't planning to take the money. I had already called *Nonno* and said I didn't want it. If you had stayed and listened you would have heard me say that I can live without the money, but I couldn't live without you."

"Sure you did."

"You don't trust me."

"After what you did? How could I possibly?"

"I don't mean now. You never did. If you trusted me you would have come to me first. You would have stuck to the plan. We would have talked about this, figured it out together. Like you promised. But it's so much easier to bail, isn't it?"

"That's not what I'm doing," she said, but she didn't sound quite as confident anymore.

"No, that's exactly what you're doing. It's all you know how to do. I thought that because I really love you, it would be different for us. But it's not, is it? It never will be. No matter what I do to prove how much I love you, it will never be enough. I'm going to spend the rest of my life chasing you, because running is all you know how to do."

"Haven't I told you a million times that you deserve better than me?" she said.

"You did. And shame on me for not listening. Have your lawyer call my lawyer and we'll work out some sort of custody arrangement," Rob said, then turned and walked out the door.

Carrie wasn't surprised, and still, she felt sick. Sick all the way through to her soul. He'd given her all sorts of chances, put up with more crap from her than the average guy ever would, and once again she'd gone and screwed it up. She had driven him away, when what she should have done was tell him that she loved him, too, and that she was just scared. The sad part was that she really did believe that he wasn't going to take the money, but it had been the perfect excuse to drive him away. Because he was right. That was all she knew how to do. If she had stuck to the plan and had just talked to him, they could have worked it out. Everything would be fine now. They would be making wedding plans, and looking for a place to live.

And as much as she wanted to race after him and beg him for another chance, tell him she would do anything to make this right, she didn't deserve another chance.

She'd hurt him enough.

She closed her eyes and took a deep breath, but it did nothing to quell the feeling of panic swirling inside her. The realization that she loved him. Really truly loved him. And maybe she didn't deserve another chance, but she wanted one. If she could just convince him that this time it would be different, that she would never doubt him again. If she could catch him before he drove away…

She opened her eyes and nearly jumped out of her skin when she realized that he was standing right in front of her. For a second she thought that she had conjured him up out of her imagination. Until he shook a finger at her and said, "You almost had me."

"I did?"

"I made it all the way to my car before realizing what an idiot I am. I accused you of not sticking to the plan, but I did the same damn thing."

"You did?"

"I told you that if you tried to bail on me, I wouldn't let you get far. You needed me to prove that I'll be there, that I'll fight for us. Instead, I bailed on you. So this is where I draw the line. This is as far as I let you go."

"Okay."

He blinked. "Okay?"

"Yes, because you're absolutely right. I was looking for a reason to push you away, but only because I am absolutely terrified by the idea that you might actually love me. But you know what? I love you, and being afraid and in love sure beats being all alone."

"From this day forward, for better or worse, like it or not, you are stuck with me."

Even after all that, as he held his arms out to her, it took every bit of courage she possessed to walk into them. To take that final step, that last leap of faith. But she did it, and she knew without a doubt, as they wrapped their arms around one another, neither would ever let go again.

* * * * *

 *Have Your Say*

You've just finished your book.
So what did you think?

We'd love to hear your thoughts on our
'Have your say' online panel
www.millsandboon.co.uk/haveyoursay

🌹 Easy to use
🌹 Short questionnaire
🌹 Chance to win Mills & Boon®
   goodies

Visit us
Online

Tell us what you thought of this book now at
www.millsandboon.co.uk/haveyoursay

YOUR_SAY

Mills & Boon® Online

Discover more romance at
www.millsandboon.co.uk

- **FREE** online reads
- **Books** up to one
  month before shops
- **Browse our books**
  before you buy

...and much more!

For exclusive competitions and instant updates:

 Like us on **facebook.com/millsandboon**

 Follow us on **twitter.com/millsandboon**

 Join us on **community.millsandboon.co.uk**

Visit us Online Sign up for our FREE eNewsletter at
www.millsandboon.co.uk

WEB/M&B/RTL5

The World of Mills & Boon®

There's a Mills & Boon® series that's perfect for you. We publish ten series and, with new titles every month, you never have to wait long for your favourite to come along.

Blaze.

Scorching hot, sexy reads
4 new stories every month

By Request

Relive the romance with the best of the best
9 new stories every month

Cherish

Romance to melt the heart every time
12 new stories every month

Desire

Passionate and dramatic love stories
8 new stories every month

Visit us Online

Try something new with our Book Club offer
www.millsandboon.co.uk/freebookoffer

M&B/WORLD2

What will you treat yourself to next?

Ignite your imagination,
step into the past...
6 new stories every month

INTRIGUE...
Breathtaking romantic suspense
Up to 8 new stories every month

Captivating medical drama –
with heart
6 new stories every month

MODERN™
International affairs,
seduction & passion guaranteed
9 new stories every month

n o c t u r n e™
Deliciously wicked
paranormal romance
Up to 4 new stories every month

RIVA™
Live life to the full –
give in to temptation
3 new stories every month available
exclusively via our Book Club

You can also buy Mills & Boon eBooks at
www.millsandboon.co.uk

Visit us Online

M&B/WORLD2